The Way of the Forgotten

Also by Steve Davala

Skywatch

Books are for Reading, Not Eating!

The Soulkind Series

The Soulkind Awakening

The Shadow of the Soulkind

The Soulkind Master

The Way of the Forgotten

Steve Davala

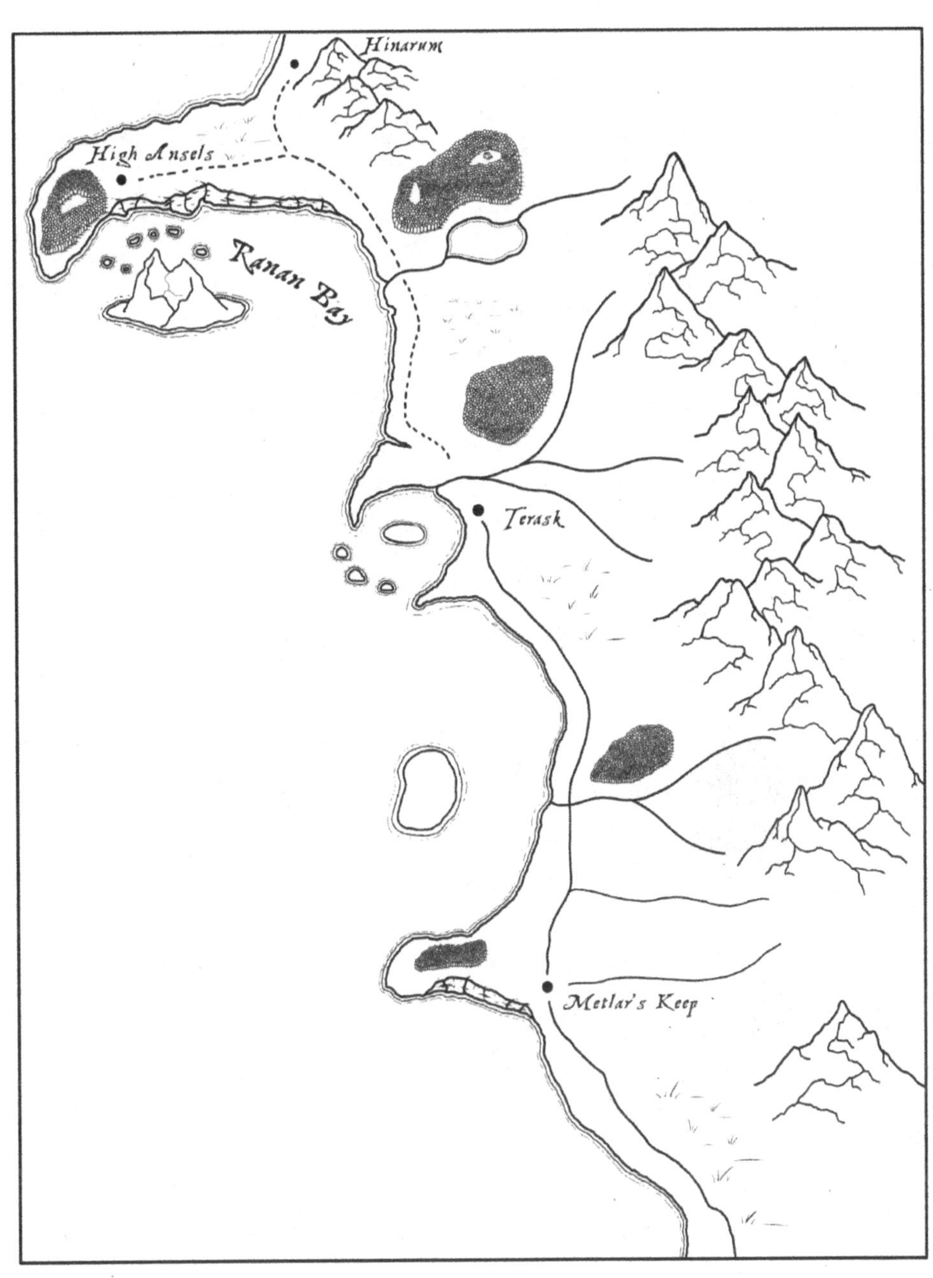

Hinarum
High Ansels
Ranan Bay
Terask
Metlar's Keep

Chapter 1

Titans rise. Titans fall. In the end, what happens must not be forgotten.

-Alterian 1294

Walk.

Hide.

Forget.

The storm raged as he climbed toward an escape. Lightning streaked across the blackest night, rain poured from the heavens, and the mountainside split asunder. His battered and weakened form shivered beneath the onslaught, and he sought a handhold on the shifting mountain. Twice he fell and felt the near calm of oblivion.

But this would not be the place of his undoing. He was still too close to the mainland. Too close to the others. If he died now, they might find him. No, there would not be a third time, not until he reached the center of the island. And then he could fall into a pit and never worry about getting back up ever again.

He fought for every step.

Cold surrounded him and penetrated his core. He was colder than he'd ever felt before, if feel was the right word for it. Nothing felt right anymore. His crumpled body shook with the stabbing pain of every step. Surely the pain itself could not be this strong? Surely not.

The lightning flashes abated, and the pounding rain beat a forgetful rhythm. The last drops of blood washed completely away from his arms and hands. He would never forget that. Or could he? He had forgotten so much already, it wasn't that hard to lose it all. Even now, the memories of the Last Days faded, just like his memories of the sun ever since crossing into this new land. Where had he been? Who had he been?

Yes. That was better. Better to be forgotten. Better for everyone.

Rocks crashed behind him on the narrow path and sealed him away. But where was he going? To the mountain at the center of the island? That seemed right to him somehow.

His eyes glanced downward, and he noticed that his arms were instinctually cradled, as if in memory of carrying something. He quickly brushed his hands at his sides and kept walking, stumbling ahead. The steep path closed behind him, debris strewn by the storm or perhaps by his own forgetful hands.

One final flash illuminated the narrow, temple-like stone structure before him. The mouth of a cave led into the depths. This had to be the place. Boulders danced across the ground, which shuddered and shambled in a tectonic upheaval. If he waited too long, he would not get inside, and perhaps someone might see him. He could not risk that. Every step slowed now to a crawl. His life force started drifting away, and he fought to keep moving, lest he fall here.

At the cave entrance, one rending crash brought a sliver of rock down onto his arm. He would have shouted if he had the energy, but the rock neatly sliced through his appendage with a shower of sparks. His limb laid there, unceremoniously covered by a pile of boulders, but he didn't stop to pick it up. What did it matter? One less thing to remember.

"The hand that sins is removed before the End."

Who said that? Where was it written? If his face could smile he would have. She would have thought it profound, would she not? He thought he heard a song on the wind as it howled across the mountaintop, but that was foolish. With his remaining hand he reached up and tapped his forehead.

The thoughts swirled and faded until he could only see the cave opening into the earth, and he knew what he had to do.

Walk.

Hide.

Forget.

The storm raged on outside and he, the last Guardian sworn to protect the Fallen Land, forgot and was forgotten.

Chapter 2

"Come on, Bel."

The springtime sun baked the back of Millar's neck, and he pulled another rock free from the pile. The scuffling sound the flat stones made as they slid past each other no longer made him smile. He didn't know why it ever did—it was such a silly little thing. The others had laughed at him when he'd tried to bring it up.

"Hey, do you like the sound of rocks hitting each other?"

It went about as well as he'd guessed it would.

That was the last time he'd spoken of it to anyone. Anyone besides Bel, of course. She laughed at him, too, but not in the way the others did. She understood what he said and laughed because it meant something to her. She understood the simplicity of such a sound, and the joy it could bring. She always would.

"Bel?"

But she was slow. Not because she moved slowly—no. She could run like anything with her little blue scarf trailing behind her. But today the little child scampered along the path fifty or so feet behind Millar, lifting rocks to see what lay underneath and taking her sweet time. She dragged one particularly large rock until it began to slide down the hill. Her face froze in an expression of wonder, and she waved at Millar, pointing repeatedly at the rock. It crashed into a boulder with a cloud of dust, and she cheered.

Millar tried to hide it, but he couldn't help smiling and cheering at that too.

Then, with a breathless stare, Bel bent over and paused to look at what was uncovered. She reached down and tugged at something just out of Millar's sight.

"Millar!" She waved him over.

Millar just shook his head and turned back up the path.

"No, Millar! Come!"

Her repeated calls fell into silence. Finally, Millar sighed. "Bel, we don't have time for this."

He turned around, knowing what to expect. And there it was. Bel lay sprawled face first in the pebbles, unmoving.

"I know what you found. And I'm not coming to see."

She mumbled something, and dirt and pebbles undoubtedly got in her mouth. How she could stand to do that he didn't know. Millar just rolled his eyes.

"I only ever want to see you find something shiny. Not something useless."

She mumbled again.

"No, I'm positive it's useless." With a sigh, Millar walked back along the path in between rocks and spur weeds until he reached his sister's inert form. He nudged her with the end of his worn sandals but she didn't react. He did it again, and still nothing.

"This better be good."

He grabbed the back of her belt looped through her oversized pants and lifted her. Dirt and pebbles fell to the ground from her pockets and her mouth.

"Seriously? You're going to break your teeth if you keep trying to eat rocks. Now what is it? What did you find?"

Still lifeless, she lifted her arm and pointed to the exposed gravel, and Millar feigned a shocked expression.

"You found that? You're the best scav ever! Better than the Great Diggoo!"

She perked up at that and looked at him, but slumped again when she saw him shaking his head. He laid her back on the ground just as the giant roly-scamp balled up and rolled down the path like a ball, bouncing and spinning out as it picked up speed.

"Bugs, lizards, and flowers. That's all you're ever good at finding, Bel."

"And parts!"

"One part doesn't count as 'parts.'" Millar walked back up the path to continue the search. He glanced above and saw with dismay that the sun was speeding its way back down to the earth.

"But it was a good part."

It was a good part—Millar couldn't disagree with that. He had never seen anything quite like it, and he'd never forget it. Mom had been so excited after she'd seen the find. They had eaten full meals for at least a week after bartering with it. But that was a long time ago and they were both hungry again.

"Am I really better than the Great Diggoo?"

Millar ruffled her curly brown hair and pulled her up to her feet.

"Keep finding more bugs like that and you will be." Millar handed her a small seeded cake, and she nearly inhaled it. "Slow down, you've got to make it last. Or maybe just find us more bugs that we can eat."

Bel paused as if considering it and then ran off to the side of the path again to look under more stones, pocketing a few pebbles she found interesting.

Millar smiled, but that faded. He drew his canteen to his parched lips and drank a few gulps. At least there was water around here.

The afternoon sun crept and began to dip near the horizon. Its light spilled over the island out in the bay, setting the clouds and fogs about it ablaze with a red glow. A gray mountain peak grew out of the fog from the very top of the island. Despite the fog almost always surrounding the island, he couldn't remember a time that the mountain wasn't showing through. He tried to imagine what it would be like to be standing out there, staring back at the hills and even farther out to sea, beyond the bay. Was there anyone looking back at him?

"I like that place, too," Bel said.

Millar fumbled for his visor and flipped it over his eyes, pretending to do a quick scan nearby.

"You're always staring at it whenever we can see out there," Bel said. "Don't worry. I don't think you're silly."

"Well, we need to be focusing on where we are." Millar scanned the hills slower this time. Pulses of energy lit the countryside without the slightest hint of a find. These hills were just so picked over by every scav for the past decade at least. Nothing worth a crug, if there ever was anything here in the first place.

Bel jumped in front of his scanner and waved her arms. A red glow surrounded her, which was the visor's way of showing there was something living there. Millar moved to the side, but she kept running to get in his sight. If she knew how much this irked him she'd never stop. So, instead, he adjusted the visor to disregard bio scans. The settings didn't take and her silhouette actually glowed a bit brighter, drowning out any indication of anything else. He sighed with a sharp exhale.

Bel giggled.

Nope, she'd never stop now.

He shook his head and turned to face the island, but the old scanner couldn't reach it, much less make it to the edge of the cliffs a couple of hundred feet away. No one had been out there to dig around, and for good reason. He never heard of anyone who could make it past those waters, much less get to the steep cliffs on the other side of them. And if no one could get there, why would there be any scrap there in the first place? He stared for a moment longer. The fog near the shore lifted and revealed an uninviting cliff that taunted him for a second, saying, 'Climb me, you can do it. And then I'll end you.' In the next moment, the fog dropped to hide its face.

Millar gave a quick tap to his visor, but nothing happened. Again, and still nothing. He tapped it repeatedly, probably a little too vigorously, but at last the visor retracted with a stuttering whir.

"Are we going to go there?" Bel asked right beside him.

He yelped. "When did you get here? I hate when you do that."

She laughed and hugged his leg for a second, and then skipped off.

"No one goes there," he said. "You know that."

Bel kept flipping rocks and humming a tune. She flipped her blue scarf over her shoulder. "Is this a lava rock?" She held up a black shiny one.

"I don't know. It looks it, but it's usually in glassy chunks."

"It's a little blob, but it looks just like the other kind. I'm keeping this!"

Millar watched her with a smile, but then he glanced around at the surrounding hill. Nothing. It was still just them. Bel didn't know about everything that could kill her out here, or if she did she paid it no mind. He'd just always have to be there to look out for her.

Bel pointed at the island. "Raly said we could borrow her skiff."

"Raly says a lot of things," Millar said. "And no, *we're* not going out there, even if she did let me borrow it. We don't need to go out there."

"But it'd be fun."

"Crashing the skiff would be fun? Paying her back for it would be fun?"

"No," she said. "The island would be fun."

"This place is fun."

Bel laughed. "You don't mean that. You always say, 'These hills are picked clean. Even when a slide exposes more rocks there ain't nothin' new.'"

"I don't say it like *that.*" Not exactly like that, anyway.

Bel rolled her eyes and gave him another hug. "Let's go home. Mom'll be wanting us."

She was right. And what he saw next made him even more sure that they should leave—down by the path, he noticed a scratch in the rocks, and it wasn't from him or Bel. Whatever scratched that was bigger and more dangerous than anything they could handle. He reached the edge of the path and glanced around the soil. His heart dropped.

There they were. Tracks. Three-toed, with a sharp spike at the end of each part. Patarks. And from what he'd heard, they usually didn't travel alone. He'd never seen one, but he'd heard the stories. They didn't move much in the day, or even an hour or two after sunset, and these signs meant they were close.

The sun dipped lower to the horizon, and by the time they got back it would be dark for sure. Even with a light, there was no way to see every hole on the path, not when the path rarely stayed a path. No sense rolling an ankle over that.

"Let's get going. I'm pretty tired, so let's hustle. Without busting an ankle, all right?" Millar gave one last glance over to the island. It'd be different over there. A chance to see some new places. And maybe some of the herbs they needed would be growing. It'd be safer too, if they could get there in one piece.

Millar cinched his lighter than normal pack up tight and made sure Bel's was too before clicking on his headlamp. The solar charge was maxed out so there'd be plenty of battery for the way home. His stomach growled. It had been way too long since breakfast.

"Think Mom'll have food for us tonight?" Bel asked.

"You heard that? Well, I wouldn't count on anything special. We'll trade up some stuff with the others when we get there."

An hour? Maybe two left before reaching home? They'd pushed themselves further up the hill out east today than they had for a long time. Even though it was downhill, they still had to take their time. As if on cue, he stepped sideways on a flat stone and nearly slipped.

"Eyes on your feet." Bel snickered, knowing what was coming next.

"Eyes are on your head, but they'd be better on your feet."

Bel full-on laughed at that. "Eyes on your feet."

Millar smiled. She was still a kid, and that was good. People grew up too quickly out here in the High Ansels, and forgot all about what it was like being a kid. He surely would have forgotten if not for Bel reminding him on a daily basis. He was glad to have made her smile, but he shouldn't have slipped in the first place. It wasn't like this was his first time out around here, and he was the one supposed to be showing her how to not fall.

It had just been such a long winter, what with the low crops and the animals dying, and the South Pass not cleared up until…

Millar laughed. He was sounding like one of the Elders or Mom, even. He wasn't even close to being that age—he was just out of his teens. But really though, could they continue to stay on these hills forever?

"Think we'll ever get off the Ansels?" Bel asked.

"You're creepy, kid. How'd you know I was thinking that?"

"When you get quiet, you're always thinking something about leaving, or getting too old, or worrying about me."

"I always worry about you."

"That's what I mean," Bel said. "You can't leave because of me. Let's just go. I can do it. I'm old enough."

"You know Mom can't leave. The camp moved here ages ago, and it doesn't look like they'll move any time soon. This is her home."

"Then we take Mom, too. I bet we could make a new home on that island."

"There's better places than that." Millar sighed. It was true. He did want to leave. To find someplace new. Someplace safer. There were safe places left in the world, right? It sure didn't feel it after being shoved from every city along the coast.

***

After an hour, the sun had almost completely set, but that was all right since the glow of the camp beckoned right beyond the trees. Other scavs' lights bobbed through the branches as they all returned home to share their findings.

"Think Trades will be back tonight?" Bel asked. "It's been a long time since they left. We've got some things to trade up, for sure. And we could use some new stuff."

"Should be," Millar said. "They've had to travel further and further out lately, not too much to deal with around here."

"But why can't we move?" Bel said. "Closer to places where we can get more things?"

Millar shrugged. "We just planted, no chance we leave now." His fingers still ached from trying to till the rocky hillsides for farmable soil just last month.

"It gets worse each year," Bel said.

"What do you know about that? You're barely old enough to remember last year. Now *you* sound like Mom."

"Do not!" Bel said with a laugh. She threw a balled up piece of dirt at Millar. Millar dusted the bits out of his hair and smiled.

He got to a tall tree, and Bel stood patiently beside it. The familiar metal contraption sat at the base of the tree, clicking and whirring. It was probably the most important part of the village, and only now did he actually feel like he could breathe.

"Seen anyone?" Millar said up into the tree.

He didn't hear anything except for the shifting of the leaves in the cool breeze blowing off the ocean, but that didn't mean no one was listening. No response meant that there wasn't anything new. No Trades, nothing trying to raid the camp, no nothing. The watch guard would've said something if anything had changed.

The machine registered him and Bel with another whir, and he knew it was okay to go past it. Again Bel was blissfully unaware of any problems, or maybe she just didn't care. To be a kid again. But he had grown up too quickly to think about that now.

"Nice talk," Millar spoke upward to the branches and walked toward the camp. He didn't know who was on duty this evening—there was no way of seeing them. But it wasn't Oen or even Raly. They would have broken silence to say something, even though that was against code. Which was probably why they weren't asked to come back often.

The evening fire was being lit in the center of the ring of huts, and the people were gathering for the evening Trades and the meal. Millar glanced to see if he could spot his mother, but she hadn't stepped out, it seemed. It had been a long day for her, and she was probably waiting for Bel and him to bring her dinner. Much like the last couple of nights.

Millar joined the Trades lines, but a quick check showed that there wasn't new stuff, and there probably wouldn't be until the old crew came back from their trips. The long faces of those in line next to him looked just how he felt. More of the same. He knew each of the faces—with the town dwindling in size to a couple hundred, he couldn't not know them all. Still, he didn't have the heart to ask them how their days were since he could already guess.

They'd all say, "No change." Just like the Trades. No new food. No new nothing. He'd still turn in his findings and scrounge for something edible. There was always something available at the stores, even if it was just food bars. They could last a few more weeks until it got really desperate. The Trades would be back in full stock by then, though. Like every year at this time.

"Get anything good?"

Millar smiled at the familiar voice behind him. "Oen!"

His friend cut in line amidst the low but not so serious grumbles of the others in front of him, and he peered into Millar's scav pack. "Not a bad day, you?"

"Oh you know, the standard stuff. Bits, bottles, and… these." Oen opened his own pack and Millar saw a prize that would trade well. Four large eggs.

Millar covered them up and continued talking in hushed tones. "You sure you want to trade those? We could eat them."

"Oh, these aren't for eating. Not yet, anyway. I've been keeping these warm. We'll be able to raise these once they hatch. Swiped them off a nest today." Oen wrapped them back in a scarf and tucked them gently under his jacket. "Then we'll get our own eggs after that. Think about it. We won't have to trade up for so much food then. Just set a pen out of your mom's house."

Millar hushed him down with a hand gesture. "Yeah, that's good, just keep it down."

Oen rolled his eyes. "Don't worry. You always worry."

"Yeah, I always worry because I'm dealing with you and your loud mouth."

"I'll go put them away now, get them set up to hatch. Shouldn't be too long now. I've been watching them nesting."

"What kind are they?" Millar asked.

"Jaylocks. Biggish birds, sharp beaks. But they lay a lot of eggs." Oen patted Millar on the shoulder. "I'll see you later. I just wanted to check in, all right?" He headed off, and a few of the townspeople eyed him as he walked past, trying to see what he was carrying under his jacket.

"Hey, Millar," the man said as Millar reached the front.

"Hey, Tobes. What can I get for this tonight?"

Tobes scratched his chin and watched Millar dump out his scav pile onto the table in front of him. He reached in, pulled out a few parts that weren't too rusty, and nodded approvingly. "If the Trades were back, this would get you some good stuff. But what can I do with this? You already know that we can't move this stuff."

"But some parts here," Millar said. "Someone in town could use them."

"I'm sure they could. But that's not what we do. If you want, you can go to them, trade with them directly."

"Come on, Tobes," Millar added in a whisper. "We need to eat."

Tobes grunted. "I know, I know. Everyone needs to eat. Bring me Toka berries next time, someone could plant those."

"I'd just eat those if I found them," Millar mumbled. He did find some earlier in the day, but they didn't last. Not with Bel around.

Tobes sighed. "All right. You can have some of the store of bars, plus this drink for your mom. Just keep your eyes open for seeds, or other things we could plant. You're good at planting, right?"

Millar shook his head and rubbed his bruised hands together. He knew he wasn't. No one here was.

Tobes handed him a few bars and held out a tall silver container. Millar drew out his flask and opened it for Tobes to fill it up. A thick dark liquid dripped in, not nearly enough to fill it, but enough for Mom tonight.

"We're getting low on this stuff," Tobes said.

"You're getting low on every stuff."

Tobes grunted. "I'm just saying, Mom won't be able to operate much without it."

"Yeah, I know. She's already cut back so much on what she needs. She's barely left the house all month."

"Trades'll be back before you know it, heading over the hills, or the winds'll blow their ships back to port. With what you find, you'll get plenty of food. Try not to worry."

Millar nodded and packed up his food. "Who'd worry about not having enough to eat?"

Tobes shrugged.

"It's been a month past when they usually come back," Millar said.

"Maybe someone needs to check the Trade Port in Terask. Sail from here to the other side of the bay. See if there's any word there. Raly said you could—"

"I'm not borrowing her boat," Millar said, and he left the line.

Why was everyone asking him to do that? And how did they know Raly had offered the boat? He walked through the ramshackle huts on his way to the edge where Mom and Bel waited for the evening meal, not meaning to ignore the faces he recognized on the way through. Today just seemed longer than most.

Chapter 3

Mom's house stood taller than the others around it. Not because she had the means to afford a bigger place, but because she had accumulated so much stuff. Antennae and solar panels covered the exterior of the cobbled-together cabin, and some lights began to twinkle from the components as the darkness grew deeper. Millar pulled a few cables from the solar array and diverted the flow to other parts. With a deep whir and a flash, the heating and lighting systems kicked on inside.

With a sigh, he noticed that Mom's charger hadn't been plugged in all day.

He stowed the cable in its place next to the door, right where Bel hung her blue scarf. He smiled. Everybody was safe at home. Light spilled out from the opened door, as did the sounds of laughing and singing, and the smell of herbs. Millar's stomach raged with the thought of food that was not in bar form. He delayed that for a moment and grabbed a tub from the water purifier as well as another cable from the panels.

"Come on in, Millar!" Mom's voice called.

She and Bel continued to both sing in a nonsensical way, but Millar could tell her voice sounded tired.

"Be right there."

He stepped inside and let out a huge sigh. He felt like he'd been holding that in all day.

Home.

Mom sat on the raised platform in the center of the hut with her metal arms attending to the various pots and pans simmering about her. Just as Millar walked in, she bumped into a pot and spilled some of the liquid onto the stovetop. She stood still for a silent moment and then mopped it up with a towel.

"You doing okay, Mom?" Millar asked. He put the water on the table Bel had set with cups and bowls. "You're not lagging too much, are you?"

She resumed the frenzy of prepping all the food. "I'm just fine. Now sit down."

"You know you can't do this all day and not take a break to plug in. Here, take this." He poured the thick black liquid into Mom's cup and then handed her a cable attached to the power terminal.

Mom nodded at him and plugged it into the socket on her side. Her internal servos settled with a whir, almost like the sigh Millar had made minutes ago. The blue sensor lights glowed brighter with the power.

"Thanks, Millar. How did you afford this? Did you find anything better today?"

"Nah, Tobes just keeps some for you, you know that. They've got plenty of stuff still in stock."

"Liar."

"What was it that gave it away this time? Temperature change? Speech variations? I've been trying to figure out how you can tell."

Mom processed for a second. "Bad breath."

Bel laughed.

"Well, that's an easy one to work on." Millar picked up some cleaner that Mom had used earlier in the day and lifted it up to his mouth.

Bel held out her hand to stop him, but then laughed again as he smiled.

"It doesn't matter how we got it. Just drink it, or it'll all be a waste."

Mom kept attending to the food with two appendages, but another unfolded from her back and reached for the cup. A strawlike finger popped open and emptied the liquid, even cleaning the sides so nothing was left behind. She never wasted any of it.

Mom's eyes brightened, and her movements, although still moving quickly and efficiently to prepare the food, exuded calmness and confidence. Both Millar and Bel sat cross legged at the table with their backs propped against cushions. Bel rocked back and forth as she waited for the food.

"You're working too hard," Millar said.

Bel stopped rocking.

Mom grabbed the two pans from the small stovetop and set them on the table with a clang. Bel looked at Millar as she slowly reached out to one of them.

"Wait until I pour it!" Mom said.

"But it smells so good!" Bel said.

Within moments, Mom poured the stew and the day was forgotten as they both drank it down.

"So, what did you find today?" Mom asked. "Anything good near the coast?"

"I found a roly-scamp!"

"How big?" Mom asked.

Bel gestured with her arms wide open.

When Mom looked at Millar, he just shrugged. "We're just going to ignore the whole 'too much work thing' then, huh? Well, not much for me. It's getting picked bare all over. And with the Trades not here yet…"

Mom rotated her head side to side to side and stood slowly. Millar reached for the empty bowls before she could and took them to the bin by the door. He'd clean up later.

"What about you, Mom?"

"You know me," she said as she settled back down at the table. "Always listening."

"And…?"

"No. No transmission on the Trades."

"But anything else?" Millar said. "You seem worried about something."

"What do you mean?"

"Come on. You're not the only one able to pick up when someone's lying or nervous."

Mom traced a circle around the table. "This vocabulator, huh? You're able to hear that?"

"It's getting tough to tell with the static. Maybe I'll find you an upgrade."

"And let you know all my secrets?" Mom said. "Not likely."

"Do you think they got lost?" Bel asked. "They're never this late."

"This settlement dug in their heels a year ago," Millar said. "Stopped wandering the High Ansels pretty much after you moved here, Bel. So they know where we are."

"They never get lost," Mom said.

Millar waited for some other explanation but she didn't continue. "What else did you hear, Mom?"

Mom cocked her head at an angle as if listening, but Millar knew she was tuned into the antennae on the roof. "It's quiet. Usually there's something, but now… nothing."

She played the feed through her speaker and they only heard a steady stream of white noise.

"Have you tried talking to them?" Bel asked. "Send out a signal?"

Mom quickly shook her head and cut the speaker. "We don't know who might be listening."

Millar laughed. "What do you mean? You said no one comes out here. Right?"

"That's right," Mom said, and she started to clean up around the large room.

Bel twiddled with a stick that she'd found in her pocket. "But what if they are lost, or in danger? Should we go look for them in the bay? Millar could get a boat and then—"

Millar gave her a look that silenced her.

"That's foolish," Mom said. "Now you all need to get some sleep. Tomorrow will be a big day. But if you're worried, you can head to the very edge of the Ansels to the north. Bring the scope and see what you can see."

Bel got up and skipped over to the expandable scope mounted on the wall. "I'll make sure it's all powered up for tomorrow!"

Millar sat and stared at Mom, but she wasn't giving any other clues about what she might suspect.

"Tell us a story." Bel plugged in the power cell and tapped it until it began to charge with a soft whirring sound.

Mom paused for a moment. "It's not time for one."

"Please Mom!" Bel said. "Something about the old bots."

Mom settled into the big chair by the heating unit, and Bel tucked in at her feet. "Oh, you know I'm a sucker for that. Which hero do you want to hear about?"

Bel shook her head. "It doesn't matter. One of the big ones."

"The size of me?" Mom asked.

Bel laughed. "Bigger!"

"As tall as this hut?"

Bel laughed. "Bigger!"

"Well that's good, because that's the only kind I know of." Mom quieted her voice, but its seriousness penetrated the room. Bel grinned. "It was an age of wisdom and power, an age of anger and evil. And there was Good. The Fallen Land was protected by it, by the Guardians."

"What could they do? The Guardians?"

Bel already knew the answer, but she always asked.

"Giant warriors that could summon power from the very core of the earth. No one could stand before them without trembling!"

Millar smiled and watched Bel listen to her stories. He used to be like that too—back then, he couldn't wait to hear more because he believed in a power that could conquer anything. But now he knew they could never come back. They could never bring back the Fallen Land. He wasn't even sure if it really existed, or if Mom had just spun tales to keep them happy and entertained, and to encourage him to keep his mouth shut about the outside world.

"I'm going out for a bit," Millar said.

Mom stopped, and she and Bel both looked at him.

"I know, I know. Don't worry, I'll be back before too long."

Mom reached over and gave his hand a squeeze. Despite the metallic grip, it always felt warm and soft. An image flashed in his mind. He remembered the very first time he'd felt that touch as she led him to the safety of the High Ansels.

"We'll be fine," she said.

Millar smiled and walked outside with the dirty dishes. Mom's voice rose again as she continued the tale. He gave the dishes a quick rinse from the hose and left them to dry on the posts. The night sky started to show its stars as the sun fully faded. The sound of leaves crackling underfoot made him start, but then he realized who it was.

"Hello Raly."

The younger girl stepped into the light spilling out from the hut. "How'd you know I was here?"

"You're always here." Millar started walking in the direction of Oen's place. She looked different somehow, but he couldn't place it.

"Did you find anything good today?" Raly sprang to catch up and tripped on a branch. "I was going to come with you two but you must've left early."

"Yeah? We must have." They definitely did.

"Did you see Oen? He had some eggs with him. He said that—"

"I already know. He told me all about it." Millar walked a bit quicker through the huts on his way to Oen's parents. Their place was just outside of town in the trees.

"Do you think that he can raise them? Make them hatch?"

Millar stopped walking, sensing that something was off. Raly, still midstream with a thought, ran into him from behind. "Oh, sorry."

Millar held up his hand for a moment, listening, and then ran ahead through the short scrubby trees to where he saw Oen. The boy was struggling to his feet and clutching his stomach.

"Hey, you okay?" Millar helped Oen to his feet.

"Yeah, yeah, I'm fine." Oen forced a laugh and dusted off his pants, but Millar noticed him wince when he did so. "I just fell, tripped on a root. You know, it's pretty dark out here."

"And your eggs?"

"They're fine. You know, I brought them home earlier. Probably going to cook them for dinner tonight. Oh, hey Raly. Did you cut your hair?"

Raly pulled her short, dark hair back behind her ear. "I did, thanks for noticing." She shot Millar a pointed look.

"Oen," Millar looked Oen in the face. "Who was it?"

Oen shrugged and smiled. "No, no. I just fell."

"Who took the eggs?" Millar had already started walking in the opposite direction before Oen could answer.

"No, Millar," Raly said. "You can't do anything. Go talk to Bruet. He'll get them back."

Millar strode off through the brush, taking a second to pick up a branch about the thickness of his fist.

"Bruet? He's not going to do anything. Whoever took it would just look at him and find some way to weasel out of it. No, that won't work."

Millar hefted the stick and swung it a few times to get a feel for it.

"Pretty sure that won't work either," Raly said.

Millar gave her a twisted smile. "It couldn't hurt."

"It might."

After a few minutes, they drew closer to the edge of the camp, far away from anyone else. A pale light grew through the trees, as did the laughs and shouting of the people who lived there. The Howden clan. Before he knew it, Millar stood in the middle of their camp, holding his stick out at the boy in the lead spot.

"Tren Howden," Millar said. He glanced around at the others. Five? Eight? There were definitely more than he thought there would be. "Give them back. Now."

Tren sat and smiled. "You seem to have gotten lost, Millar. Did your mom give you some bad directions again? She's been shorting out a lot lately."

The clan snickered at this. Millar did his best to keep his gaze on Tren, but he caught some people behind him moving about.

"The eggs."

"What eggs?" Tren licked his lips and wiped his chin with a cloth. "I don't see any eggs. Did you see any eggs?"

"I don't see no eggs," Tren's sister Perl said.

"There's no eggs here," Tren said. "So why don't you just head back to your friends and let them know." He shooed him away with one hand, and everyone laughed again.

"You're a worthless crug," Millar said. "You never do anything for us, you just leech off others around you."

"'Crug?'" Tren said. "That's not very nice. Surprised you talk like that around your girlfriend."

Millar turned around and saw that Raly was in the hands of a couple of Tren's clan. He couldn't make out who they were, not in the dim light.

"She's not my girlfriend."

Fear flickered across Raly's face as she looked back at him. When he turned to face Tren again, the taller boy was already right in front of him.

"Oh, then you won't mind if we hang out with her after you leave then." Tren stepped toward Millar.

Millar lowered the stick slightly and backed up with a slight trip.

"Millar?" Raly said in a shaky voice.

"Don't worry," Tren said. "We'll take good care of her."

Millar turned again. The boy and girl were stroking Raly's hair, gripping tightly onto her arms. Raly's chin wavered and a line of tears ran down her cheek.

Millar brought the stick up and charged at them both, swinging wildly. Reflexively, they pushed Raly toward him and started laughing. Millar caught her in his free arm and pushed her, too, this time away from the circle of people.

"Run!"

She stumbled for a few steps and then gained her footing. She stopped and stared dumbfounded at Millar.

"Run!" Millar faced the others with his stick held up defensively.

Raly hesitantly took a few steps but then sprinted away, calling for help.

"You picked the wrong night to come here," Tren said.

Millar turned around and then took a hit to the back of his head with something hard. His vision dazed and he dropped his stick.

"You just don't learn."

Another blow hit him, and another. He held his hand up weakly as the others beat him until he couldn't remember anything.

Chapter 4

Bel ran from the house where she left Millar unconscious on his bed. She had never seen him like that before. Well, when he was sleeping, of course. But not hurt so badly like this. She ran faster until she reached Bruet's hut. Most of the town was already here, but it didn't seem like she had missed too much. Just a lot of people yelling at each other. She stepped inside.

"They just stormed into our camp," Tren said. "Saying we took their eggs."

"That's because you took them," Raly shouted from the other side of the hut.

Bruet held up his hand to silence Raly, and she sat back down.

"They were trespassing, and they threatened us." Tren looked at his sister and other friends, and they all nodded together in agreement. "We didn't do anything. And they didn't leave us any choice."

"There's always a choice," Mom said. She and Bruet moved closer together and whispered so no one else could hear.

Oen and Raly exchanged silent glances.

Bel, however, couldn't keep quiet. "Millar wouldn't hurt anyone unless they deserved it."

"Hey, he came at me with a stick," Tren said.

Mom leveled her gaze at him and then at Bel. "I've taught you better than that, I hope. Deserved it, you say? What have I said about that?"

Bel crossed her arms and pouted. "'We can't judge what others do, no one has the right.' But that's what you're doing right now, isn't it?"

Bruet silenced them all again, just by raising a hand.

"The state which Millar is in right now," he said. "Will he survive?"

"He is hurt badly," Mom said. "But he will survive."

Bel scoffed. "He won't be coming out with me to scav any time soon."

Mom shot her another look.

"Then the Howdens will recompense Millar's house for the inability to go out for at least two days."

Tren and his clan all booed.

Bruet continued. "And, since this is not the first time these behaviors have happened within our whole family, the Howden's will be exiled for a week from our borders."

Not one person made a sound, not even the Howdens.

"But no one has ever been exiled before." Mom's glowing eyes brightened. "The safety of our family is from within our borders, not without."

"And yet the safety of our family appears to be threatened within it now. This is my decision. This is final. You have until sundown tomorrow to leave."

Everyone in the circle clamored at once. Tren pushed his way through the people to reach Bruet, but couldn't fight his way through the confusion. Bel looked up at his face and saw fear there. She had an idea why, although she'd never really believed all the stories. They were just stories, right?

"Mom," she said. "Why are they so afraid? They seem to be fine without us anyway. What's so bad about Bruet's choice?"

"You wouldn't know." Mom wrapped an arm around Bel's shoulder and pulled her away from the crowd. "Outside of what we've already told you."

Bel shrugged. "Other clans, and… hunters? No one's really seen them before. They'll be okay. Right?"

Mom shrugged. "Perhaps. There's worse things than other clans out there. It doesn't feel like Bruet thought this all out. You stay here, I will be right back."

The old bot limped as she walked amongst the confusion to Tren's clan. Tren spun and started yelling and pointing at Mom's face. Bel couldn't understand it above the crowd's noise, but she guessed he was blaming Mom for this. Made sense—she was a pretty big deal in this village, and this was her son they'd messed with. Of course they'd think she was behind them getting booted out. Despite the yelling, Mom didn't budge, and she nodded with Tren's anger. She was good at that, good at—what was the word? Empathy.

Mom waited until Tren was done with his outburst. He stood there with his shoulders drooping a little. He seemed to realize he wouldn't get a rise out of her, and he turned to leave. Mom called back to him, but Tren waved her off. Mom repeated herself. At this point, Perl laid a hand on her brother's arm and nodded. Tren nodded too, and then his clan left together. Mom came back to Bel as the whole group began to break up.

"What did you say to them?" Bel asked.

Mom wrapped a metal arm around Bel's shoulders and hurried her away. "That no matter what they did, they're a part of our family."

"What?" Bel said. "What do you mean? They really hurt Millar. I wouldn't do that. You wouldn't do that. They should get kicked out. Isn't that justice?"

Mom squeezed Bel's shoulder. "I know you're angry. I am too. But that isn't justice."

"But…" It didn't make sense to her.

"It isn't right," Mom said.

Her voice reached the point where Bel knew not to say anything else. She felt guilty for even thinking anything else against what Mom said, mainly because of what Mom might think of her.

As they approached their hut, Mom finally broke her silence. "I am worried they won't have enough food or supplies. Especially with the Trades not back yet."

Bel nodded. "Maybe… someone could do something about that."

Mom nodded.

Bel raced in through the door and ran to Millar's bed. His face was all puffed up and bruised, and his breathing was a little ragged, but not as much as it had been when they first brought him in.

"You okay, Millar?"

Millar groaned.

"Ooh, sorry!" Bel said. She tiptoed away from him and grabbed a towel and some water. She dipped the rolled-up towel in the liquid and blotted the wounds on his head, but this only caused him to grunt louder.

"Here, let me," Mom said, and she took the towel from Bel. She hummed a gentle tune and dabbed lightly with her thin metal arm. Millar didn't react to this, and Bel walked over to a stool, her head hung over.

"Sure," Bel said. "He knows not to make *you* upset." Despite what she said, she carefully watched Mom dress his wounds and even hummed a little, too.

Several minutes later, a quiet tapping on the front door revealed both Oen and Raly. Mom let them look in for a little, but then hustled them outside shortly after.

"He's all right, nothing major broken," Mom said.

Raly tried to peek in past Mom. "He came back for me. I was so scared."

Mom nodded and rubbed Raly's shoulder. "He often does things like that. Brave, that one."

"Even when he shouldn't be," Oen said. He stared at his feet.

"No, if you had gone, too, you'd have ended up like him. Or worse." Mom propped her hands on her hips. "Brave, but he doesn't think things through."

Bel held Raly's hand and led her outside while Oen and Mom tended to Millar. They both walked from the hut and kept walking until they were alone and away.

"Everything all right?" Raly asked.

Bel twisted her hands together. "I need a favor."

Chapter 5

Thunder crashed and shook the hut. Millar awoke with a start and a sharp pain in his head. Lightning flashed through the doorway and cast stark shadows around the room. This wasn't the first time a storm had ever hit here, but this one felt more intense than any other.

Maybe it was just the headache making it all worse.

"Hello?"

No one.

Millar called again, and when no one responded he got up. Or he tried to. The pain in his head sharpened, and he sat back down. Something was off out there. He grabbed some clothes to quickly throw on, and then he took a deep breath before getting up and heading out the door.

More thunder boomed almost instantly. Had it struck the village? Across the clearing, he caught a glimpse of people in the brief light. They scattered and strapped their belongings to the ground. The wind picked up and howled across the encampment.

"Mom?"

The storm swallowed his words before they could leave his mouth.

In the next flash of light, he saw a group working on a hut that had lost part of its roof. People ran about and gathered things that had blown out of it. He caught a metallic glint on top of the dwelling and wasn't surprised to see Mom clasping lines and strapping down roofing plates. Of course she would be up there doing something like this. Millar ran over to her and picked up a coil of rope.

"Here!"

"Millar?" Mom looked over the edge of the roof at him. "You're awake!"

"I don't think I could've slept through this one. What's going on?"

Mom gestured for Millar to hand the coil up and then she finished tying off the panels to the roof. She slid down to Millar's side. "The storm just hit. No one saw it coming. And Bel hasn't come back."

Millar stared at her blankly for a few seconds and another bolt of lightning struck nearby. "When was the last time you saw her? Is she out scavving?"

"She went out earlier today, and by the time I began to worry, the storm hit."

"With your power system, you'd shut down before you even began to look." Millar shook the dizziness out of his head. "I'm sorry I wasn't able to help."

"I still should have done something."

Millar started back to their hut. "Did she go out alone? Do you know where she went?"

Mom jumped down off the roof and overtook him in a few strides. "I don't know, she just left early today. I'll go ask Bruet and the others. We'll find her. We must."

Millar nodded. "I'll ask Oen and Raly. I'll meet you back here." He ran off through the camp and raised his hands instinctively whenever another blast of lightning struck. The rain began to fall slowly, with thick, heavy plops.

When he got to Oen's hut, the door was already closed and locked down. He rapped on the door and soon after the door popped open.

"Millar!" Oen said. "You're up! Is everything all right?"

"I'm fine." The splitting headache notwithstanding. "Have you seen Bel? Mom says she was gone all day and hasn't come back yet."

Oen shook his head. "She's out… in this?"

His father came to the door and put his arm around Oen's shoulder. "You better get home, it's getting bad out there."

Millar nodded to them and ran off. The wind blew against him so strongly he felt like if he jumped he'd be lifted away. Raly and her mom lived just down the hill, still within the circle of huts but on the border.

"Hey, hold on!" Oen called.

He ran to catch up to Millar, which didn't take too long. He hadn't eaten or drank anything for a long time now, and his body was feeling it. "You don't look so good."

"I'm fine," Millar said and tripped on the root of a tree.

Oen got to his side just in time to catch him from falling. "Obviously. Let me get you home."

"We've got to check with Raly," Millar said.

"I'm sure she's all right."

"No, no," Millar said. "She might know where Bel is."

"Ah," Oen said. "I was starting to think you were worried about Raly."

Millar grunted. "Of course you would. Come on." He got to his feet and kept walking instead of trying to run.

"Hey, I didn't get a chance to thank you yesterday," Oen said. "For standing up to Tren for me."

"Yeah, I didn't get very far with him, though."

"He and his goons got you pretty good. Bruet and the others never found any eggs there, but they still threw his whole clan out. Did you hear that?"

Millar shook his head. "Threw them out? Like, out of the village?"

Oen nodded. "They packed up and left early today. They had until night, but they just up and left."

"I bet they blame me for that."

Oen nodded again. "At the hearing last night they sure did. Mom calmed them down before anyone else got hurt, though."

"Well good. They're gone. One less thing to worry about."

When they reached Raly's house, Millar banged on the door. Her mother opened the door. Tears lined her cheeks.

"Have you seen her?" she asked. "She's been gone for hours now."

"Do you know if she was with Bel?" Millar asked. "She's gone, too."

Her mother thought for a moment. "I think so, at least she was this morning. She came back home at midday, but then left again a few hours later. Do you know where they might be?"

"Oh no," Millar said.

Raly's mother called out after them but both he and Oen were too far away. The rain began to fall even harder. Moving fast through the woods in the rainy dark was nearly impossible, but luckily Oen had brought a lamp with him. The dim light from the beam only penetrated the dark a few feet, but that was enough. Millar quickened his pace.

"She wouldn't have gone out there, do you think?" Oen asked.

Millar couldn't believe she would, but it was the only thought going through his head. He and Oen broke through the trees at the bottom of the hill and heard the pounding of the surf on the shore. Normally, this area was a relatively quiet bay, with a near glass surface at times, but the storm had driven it to a near fury. Waves slammed the shore from the intense wind, and now the rain pounded the water with leaping sprays.

Raly stood by the edge of the water staring into the darkness and chaos. She saw Millar and she fell to her knees in the sand. Her soaked hair was plastered to her face and her body shook with her sobbing.

"Bel!" she screamed.

"Where's your boat?" Millar said.

"Bel!"

"Where's the boat, Raly?"

Weakly, she lifted her arm and pointed out to the bay.

Chapter 6

The bot awoke in a great cavern covered in moss and ferns with the early morning light streaming in. The plants were arranged in neat order along the wall and floor, but still some of the thick moss grew where it chose, including on his head and body. For some reason, he remembered dreaming last night. But that was foolish. He was certain he never dreamt.

The fragments of it all still cascaded across his mind in bits and waves—lightning flashing and rain pouring into the cave. So much rain that he might have had to swim to survive. Those under his care needed to be saved from the climbing waters. Scared and fluttering. And throughout it all, a song.

The song?

He wasn't sure. It felt like it. But whatever it was, it faded quickly, and with it the dreams, too. He rose to his feet and the movement caused him to spasm suddenly, sending a family of birds fluttering from their roost atop his shoulders. They landed atop the carefully tended plants and began to chatter at him.

Whoever tended this cave must have spent many long days to get it to this state, so he did what he felt like he had to. He limped as he walked through the tunnels, admiring the plants and the birds that flitted around him. When he reached the end, some hundred or so feet from where he awoke, he bent down and, with his one good hand, picked up some rocky debris that littered the way.

And there he worked for hours, not thinking of anything else besides clearing the path and finding ways to let the sunlight through to feed the plants. Perhaps that is why he did not see the child as she approached.

"There you are!"

Her voice startled him and he turned to face her. He dropped the stone and it hit the ground, splitting into shards with a crash. This time she yelped and jumped back. She was a tiny thing. A small child perhaps of ten summers with dark curly hair which was matted down as if soaked by water. She wore a blue scarf.

"I came back, like I said I would."

He cocked his head at her.

"Last night you said it would be best for me to sleep in another—"

"What are you called?" he said in a deep voice.

The girl rolled her eyes. "Really? We're going to do this all over again? What happened to you? Did you sleep too hard? My mom says if you sleep too hard you forget everything."

"I do not remember," he said. "What are you called?"

"Bel, silly. I thought bots had perfect memory systems. Mom does. She remembers everything I've ever done. Which is a bad thing sometimes, because sometimes I get in trouble. But that's just..."

He took a step closer to her, and she didn't back away. For some reason that felt odd to him. He wasn't going to hurt her, but for some reason he felt it should scare people when he approached them. Especially particularly tiny ones such as this. He knelt and took a closer look.

"Belsilly," he said.

She laughed at this so much that she nearly fell over. "No, no! Just Bel. *You're* silly."

"Bel."

"Yes, and we already went over this. I asked you, 'What's your name?' and you just said 'I have no such designation' or whatever. I said, 'You were never given a name?' and you said—"

"Not that I recall."

"Yeah, that! Do you remember that, or is that something you always say when someone asks you that? Do a lot of people ask you that?" Bel dropped down next to a couple of plants and peered at a round rock beside them. "Anyway, I thought that was sad."

"Where do you come from?" He took one limping step and joined her. She really was a tiny being. Barely bigger than one of the birds.

"Across the water." Bel did not move when he approached. "I've been looking at your island for months now, ever since I made it through the pass last year. Millar says the water is too dangerous and that we'd just die if we came out here."

"There's more of you?" He stood up.

"Don't worry. No one's coming here. Just me. And they wouldn't do anything to you anyway, even if they could fit through that tunnel that I came through. You're too big for that. Are you sure you don't know where you came from?" Bel tried to lift one of the larger rocks nearby but she couldn't even budge it.

The large bot shook his head. He took a few seconds to sit next to her, and then he reached over to the rock and lifted it out of the ground, much like a pebble. He rolled it down the hall to where he kept the refuse pile of stones. Bel peered into the hole left behind from the removed rock with a smile and she pulled out a bug with many legs.

"Millar would like this one. He'd say I'm the Great Diggoo!"

The bot lifted another rock for her to explore, and he watched her in silence as she sifted through the dirt and pebbles.

"I found it, you know," she said.

"Found what?" his voice boomed.

Bel sighed. "This is getting old, the forgetting thing, I mean. Your hand! I asked you where it went, and you didn't know. Surprise, surprise. So I said I'd look for it, and I found it outside. At least I think I did. There was a lot of rocks and dirt, and plants and stuff. But I could see some of it still through it all. I couldn't get it, though. It's nearly as big as I am and weighed a ton. We'd bring that to the Trades and we'd be set forever. If the Trades ever showed back up."

The bot held up his right arm and inspected the shorn stump at the end covered with layers of moss. Apparently he'd had a lot of time to grow that. "Set… forever?"

"Yeah, with money," Bel said. "Anyway, what can I call you?"

He had no memory of a name, no memory of why he would need one.

"Can I call you Doran? I had a pet named Doran once. A little cat. Not that you look like a little cat, I just liked him."

He shrugged and then nodded. Doran would do for now.

"Are you just going to forget it though, Doran? I mean, do you erase yourself on purpose, or is it a problem with your system? Because we should probably write that down for you so we can at least not have this same talk tomorrow."

He did not know. Nor did he care.

"Well, what do you know?" Bel said. "Do you know what I am? Do you know where you are?"

Doran paused for a moment before answering. "You are a little girl. And I am in a cave. With birds."

Bel kept digging through the dirt. "At least you know some things, right? You could just be a huge Bruiser bot that just smashes things, huh?"

Doran balled up his left hand into a fist and threw a punch in the air. "Am I?"

"Maybe. You'd hit pretty hard, it looks like. And you're all damaged pretty badly too, like you've been in a fight. Like Millar was the other night. Your leg looks pretty bad, you got that limp from something. But Bruisers don't think and talk like you do. And none are as big as you, either. No one is. But you're…"

"I am what?"

"Well, you're scrawny for a big bot. You're just arms and legs. What were you even made for? I can't imagine. Maybe Mom would know more about you. She's a bot, too."

"Is she a Bruiser?"

Bel laughed. "Sometimes, I guess. When I come home late."

Doran paused. "Home?"

"Yeah, you know, like this place is for you. Right?"

Doran looked over at the birds resting upon the stones up above.

"See," Bel said. "You have birds to take care of, and they like you, it looks like. Who wouldn't? You're a big bot who'd keep anybody safe. That's home."

Doran reached out for the birds with his good hand but they just fluttered away. His head drooped forward and he lowered his arm with a sigh.

"Did you just sigh?" Bel asked. "Because that's weird since you don't breathe. Why would you need to sigh, unless whoever programmed you thought it would be funny?"

Doran stared at her.

"I talk too much, don't I? Millar goes on about how I won't stop jabbering. I'm sorry. I just get this way when I get excited about something."

"What are you excited about?"

"Duh." Bel pointed at Doran. "I've never seen anything like you. No one has, I think. Well, obviously someone, but no one I know. You must be really old."

Doran shrugged. "I do not remember."

"Well, I hope you remember me when I'm gone. I've got to get back to my home. All that talk about Mom, I think this time she really will be a Bruiser if I don't get back. I bet she and Millar are worried about me. There was that storm, and I had to stay here last night. I think the boat's all right. Raly will kill me if I busted it."

"You have to go?" Doran asked. "Home?"

"Come on! I'll show you." Bel ran off down the tunnel with a sweet, simple song. Doran loped after her with long strides as she scrambled away through the tunnels.

Morning sunlight streamed through and hundreds of birds flitted amongst the plants organized on precisely cut stones up above.

"What is this place?" Bel's voice echoed in the tunnel. "Is it like a temple? Are you from here? Did you make it?"

Doran didn't respond.

"I guess you don't remember that, either. But whoever made it knew to make it just your size."

Bel reached the end of the tunnel to a huge pile of stacked stones and pointed to the top. "I came in through there. It's a lot of climbing." She started to scramble up the wall by gripping onto edges with her deft little hands. "See, it's not too hard!"

Her voice cut off as her grip slipped. She gave a yelp and dropped, but she only fell a short distance. To her surprise, Doran was there with his arm raised behind her. Bel's eyes bulged and her breath quickened as she sat in his grip.

Bel took a moment to calm down. "I'm usually a good climber."

"You are a good climber." Doran shifted his hand closer to the wall until she got off and climbed up again.

"Thank you. For that, and for catching me."

"You are welcome."

Bel reached the opening and a flat space where she could sit comfortably. She looked back down at Doran. "I guess you can't really leave your home, huh? That must make it feel really safe to you. Nothing bad comes in or out."

Doran did not reply.

Bel peered out the crack into the sunlight. "But there's my home, up there! Those hills, the High Ansels, that's where I live. For now, anyway, until we move someday. Which might happen soon if we can't get more food. Come on, look before the fog comes back!"

Doran stood up on his toes but still could not see from down there. He looked around the room and settled his sight on a large, flat boulder neatly placed against the edge of the tunnel. He gripped it awkwardly with his one hand and the nub of the other and dragged it to the wall.

"Whoa, you're strong!" Bel said from above.

"Thank you," Doran said. He stood on top of the rock and then reached Bel's level until he was eye to eye with her.

"Right there." Bel pointed through the opening until they could both see the tops of the cliffs and the spot where the encampment lay. "I can barely see anything, but that's it. Do you see it?"

Doran's glowing blue eyes made a whirring sound as if adjusting to the distance, and he nodded. "I see it. Storm hit there too. Hard."

Bel scrunched her eyes to see better. "Really? I've got to go help, then."

"You all help each other?"

"We do." Bel scratched her chin. "I can come back! I can bring my family. You'll like them. And then we can all go back together, if you want!"

Doran shook his head. "I do not think—"

"It'll be all right. They're nice! Or you could just come back with me now. I bet you could take all these rocks down in no time."

Doran sat in silent thought but then shook his head.

"Okay, but I have to go. I'll be back though. But how are you going to remember me, if your brain shuts down every night? I know!" Bel dug through her backpack and mumbled until she found what she was looking for. "Here!"

Doran reached up with his left hand and precisely and delicately picked up a small black rock. He brought it close to his eyes and stared at it.

"Nodular obsidian."

"Huh?" Bel said. "That's its name? How do you remember that if you can't remember anything else?"

"I remember some things."

"Well, when you see… nodular obsidian, that means me, okay? That means 'Bel.'"

"Bel."

"Now don't lose it, I have never seen one quite like it."

Doran reached for the faded and worn pack strapped over his shoulder and placed it on the ground. "I am good at keeping things."

"How do you remember that?" Bel asked.

Doran paused for a moment. "I do not remember."

Bel laughed, and Doran's head cocked slightly to the side. "Your laugh is like…"

Bel smiled. "Like what?"

Doran stared and pulled out a small stone of his own. He held it out in front of Bel.

Her eyes grew twice as big as she gazed at the stone. "For me? Why?"

"So you remember me."

"I don't need a rock to remember you. But this is amazing!" She held out her hand and Doran placed the cobalt blue stone there. It was small for Doran, but it was nearly the size of Bel's fist. "This is the nicest rock I've ever seen. I've never seen anything like it. It looks like your eyes! Millar will go crazy. He doesn't say it, but he's really into rocks, too."

She turned it over in her hands and then placed it securely in her pack. She reached out tentatively to his big hand and held one of the massive fingers, patting it gently. "Thanks, Doran! I can't wait to see you again!"

When she let go, he pulled it back down to his side slowly.

Bel climbed through the crack in the rock wall, and Doran watched her until her head bobbed down out of sight. The fog then veiled the hillside on the other side of the bay, and all he heard was her scrambling down, and the soft sound of her humming. He stayed there for a while until her voice finally disappeared, and then he stayed there a little while longer until the sun passed through the sky, all the while humming a soft tune.

And then he reached up and tapped his forehead, and he forgot.

Chapter 7

"Bel!" Millar cupped his hands over his mouth and shouted again and again until his voice tore in his throat.

"I can think of at least one reason no one uses this boat anymore," Oen said.

Oen busily bailed water, although his pace had slowed considerably throughout the night and as the sun crept across the sky. He didn't complain, though. None of them did. Even if the boat continued to sit lower in the water. They just kept the boat as afloat as possible as they avoided sand bars, jutting rocks, and coral reefs, all threatening to sink them.

As Oen scooped, Millar and Raly fought to keep the tattered sail up in the wind, and they tacked this way and that. The island loomed out of the fog but, whether the wind or the water, their path never led to an inlet or any place to land, much less to catch any glimpse of Bel's boat. Just when they thought they were getting closer, the fog would lift and they'd see the island in the opposite direction.

"You must find her." The memory of Mom's voice echoed in Millar's head. "She's just a child."

Her sad eyes had glowed in the storm as their boat sailed off the beach. The waves pounded, the winds howled, and it was a miracle that they had made it any farther into the bay. Their weak lamps crept into the gloomy darkness, but they were barely bright enough to see anything at all. Eventually the storm abated, but it didn't do much to help them find their way.

And even when dawn came, and midday, the fogs continued to thwart them until finally, near day's end, they found a clear path in. Millar lowered the sail and dropped the oars into the water.

"How do you know she's here?" Oen asked. He had slowed down on the bailing, and now the entire bottom of the boat was filled with water.

"She told me she was going to borrow the boat," Raly said.

"But what for?"

"I don't know. She could be headed out to Terask. She thought that the Trades were somehow in trouble and she could fix it by the time you woke up."

Millar rowed one last time, and the boat grated against the stony depths next to the shore. He closed his eyes and breathed out deeply. "She'll be here. She's always talked about it."

"But why now?" Oen said.

Raly offered Millar some water. "I think she was worried Millar would be too hurt to go out with her today. Are you all right?"

Millar shrugged and drank deeply from the canteen.

Raly got out of the boat and helped the others pull it onto the rocky shore.

"I don't see her boat anywhere," Oen said. He flipped a visor over his eyes and scanned the beach in the remaining daylight.

Millar paced beside him, checking with his own scanner. "There are other beaches on the island. It all depends on the fog, right?"

"Probably," Raly said.

"Look at these rocks," Oen said. "I've never seen them fracture like this. And these columns. They look unreal, like they were made this way by a person or something."

Indeed, the beach had much less sand than the one they'd left behind on the other side of the bay, and it was more like a stone dock. Fifty-foot tall columns lined the platforms just beyond the flat area.

"Are we stuck here?" Oen said. "Look at this place."

"Let's go, we have to look for her," Millar said. He reached out for the nearest column and tried to get a grip on it, but, whether from the smooth sides or the slick fog covering, he only slid back to the ground. He rubbed his hand from where it slid over a rough edge.

"We can't even see anything," Raly said. "It's still cloudy up above, and there's fog rolling in down here."

"And our lights are drained, they'll need time to recharge." Oen knocked the side of his lamp a couple times as the light faded completely. "We should wait until tomorrow morning, or we really could get hurt trying to climb."

"I'm fine." Millar rubbed his hand.

"You're not fine," Raly said.

She checked his head and tried to dab at it with a cloth. He only swatted her away.

"What, are you my mom?"

Eventually he relented and gave in to her, and she busied away tending to the bandages on his head.

"Anyone bring any food?" Oen asked.

Millar reached for his pack, but Raly wasn't quite finished yet. She breathed out a sigh and gave up. "Go ahead."

"I think Mom put something in here, yeah, a few bars."

"Oh boy," Oen said. "Nothing we can cook?"

"Have you seen this island?" Raly said. "Unless you brought your own kindling we're not drying out tonight, much less cooking anything."

Oen eyed the dilapidated wooden boat.

"No," Millar said. "We're probably going to need that for the ride back."

"Unless we all go back with Bel." Oen tried out the railings with a few tugs.

"Not going to risk it," Millar said. "Eat this."

"And then we try to sleep until it's light out," Raly said.

Millar nodded solemnly and peeled open the wrapping on his bar. He hit it against the rock he was sitting on and it made a loud clinking sound. "How old do you think these things are?"

Oen laughed quietly, gnawing at the too-hard bars of his own. "Probably from when Mom was made."

"The rain softens them up though. I guess that's good," Raly said and held her bar up in the heavy mist. "We don't want to break our teeth."

The group ate in silence until the exhaustion of the day hit them and they all fell soundly asleep.

Chapter 8

He awoke in a great cavern covered in moss and ferns with the moonlight streaming in. Plants were arranged in neat order along the wall and floor, but still some of the thick moss grew where it chose, including on his head and body. For some reason, he remembered dreaming. But that was foolish. He was certain he never dreamt.

Fairly certain.

And why did he wake up now? Programming always ensured that he had a predetermined amount of processing. He scanned the walls where the plants sat, and he detected the birds sleeping. Not them, then. He raised his audio detectors but did not notice anything besides distant dripping within the tunnels.

Something had to have woken him up but, whatever it was, he tried to forget about it. He shut down his sensors and attempted to resume his sleep mode. Silence surrounded him, and his visual countdown bar reduced to a minimum.

Not five minutes into the shutdown cycle his eyes flashed on. This time he stood up with a jerking motion, to the dismay of the several birds who had been nesting upon him, and he walked to a tunnel off the main room. He maxed out his audio system and strained to hear anything.

A faint jingling sound came from one of the holes in the ceiling near where more of the birds slept. He focused on the sound and waited, but nothing appeared. His head didn't quite reach the top of the tunnel, so he couldn't peer outside, but he strained and swiveled his neck to try to see anything. Then the sound happened again, but from farther along the tunnel. He increased his pace and reached the place he was certain the sound came from. Something small and black darted across the opening, but it may have been only a shadow from a bird.

This time he hopped up on a flat stone at the end of the tunnel near the barricade. Had that stone fallen from somewhere? He didn't remember it being there before. The jingling was a little louder here, as if whatever was making the sound was right outside the skylight. When he peeked over the ledge he only saw the flat stone with the moonlight upon it. He reached up with his good hand and clasped onto a jagged rock, debating whether he should pull it out so he could see better. He waited a moment, straining his sensors for any sound, but he only caught the wind and the far-off waves down below.

Nothing.

He lowered his hand. After ten minutes in silence, he gave up and finally moved again to head back to his central chamber. But then it happened again. This time, the jingling was more insistent and closer, and there was a near-frantic feel to it. And now there was a low yowling sound from some small creature, like it was in danger.

That was it. He couldn't take it anymore.

He stepped back up to the platform and started pulling rocks out of the wall. Clinking and crashing filled the air and echoed throughout the tunnel system so loudly that he selected that sequence of sounds and eliminated those wavelengths from his sensor. In a few moments, he'd carved out an opening big enough to squeeze through. When the dust settled, he was able to see the jagged, gray rocks around him.

Something about this was off. While it did not feel exactly forbidden to step foot from the tunnel, something made him hesitate. The yowling and jingling, however, continued. This time he sensed them just beyond the doorway, in the rocks outside, and he knew that the creature was in serious danger. And then, perhaps for the first time, he stepped outside of the tunnel.

He waited for his programming to shut him down, to force him back inside, but nothing happened. Instead, he stood in the open and observed the landscape. Piles of stony debris littered the area, and he pushed through it as best he could and struggled to find footing with each step. To his surprise, he sensed something metallic half-buried in the ground a step or two from the entrance.

He was even more surprised when he pulled the rocks away from it and saw what it was, and who it belonged to. It was a hand. And it had to be his. So he had been outside before. He lifted the rocks away from the metal and gently pulled out a very dusty and scratched appendage. The damage to the wiring made him think it was scrap and could never be reattached, but perhaps it could be worth a lot to someone else. They'd be set forever.

He shook his head. No, that was not right. Why did he say that? He would keep it and try to repair it later. For now, he lifted it to his back and clasped it tightly upon a hook to keep it safe.

He listened for anything outside of the usual night sounds, but there was nothing. The silence made him wonder if perhaps he had crushed whatever it was, but it had probably run away when he first started removing the wall. This was it—he was already outside. There was nothing stopping him now. He took one step, then another. Nothing screamed at him. No internal alarms or sensors blaring like he had done something wrong.

It just felt wrong to leave.

Still, he adjusted his scanners for any small life forms in the vicinity, and he walked away from the entrance. The moonlight covered the mountain as he descended, making it much easier to navigate, but he still caught no sign of the creature.

Chapter 9

The fog obscured the sun's rise the next morning, and still that didn't stop Millar from dragging his friends from their sleep and getting on with the search. Despite the rocks being as slick as they were the previous night, they could at least see them and start to navigate their way.

"Any sign of the boat?" Raly said.

"Don't worry, we'll get you a new boat," Millar said.

"That's not what I meant. I don't care if it's busted. I want to see Bel as much as you do."

"Millar knew you meant that," Oen said. "He's just tired and hungry like we all are. Right? Millar?"

Millar tightened his pack down and wedged himself between some rocks to leverage himself. He grunted his agreement. "I haven't seen it yet this morning, the fog's too thick. Let's just try to get up higher and circle this island. It can't be too big around."

It might not have been too big around, but walking on it certainly wasn't easy. Steep cliffs plummeting straight into the surf, pathways that wound about for miles but then suddenly came to a dead end and they'd have to backtrack again. The hours raced past.

"I don't think we're really getting anywhere," Oen said. "Except lost, maybe."

At just past midday, the sun broke through the fog and the whole island opened before them. They found that they had progressed up the mountain several hundred feet which gave them a view of the bay facing the High Ansels.

All three of them simultaneously dropped their visors to scan the area for any sign of the boat on the island's shore. From this angle, only the water and fingers of rock jutting out of it could be seen.

"How did we make it through there?" Oen asked. "At night? In that?"

He pointed back down at the shore far below, and they could barely make out the wooden craft they called a boat.

"Just luck, I suppose," Millar said. "How Bel did it alone is another question."

Raly scanned the shore again. "It's a good boat. With an actual engine on it and its own nav system. I built it myself. I'm sure she made it here."

"And then what?" Millar said. "Did she just turn around and we passed her without knowing it? Without her knowing it?"

"It was dark," Raly said. "And maybe she didn't know how to run the nav other than to just get her through the rocks. But yeah, that could have happened."

"And she could also still be up there." Oen pointed at the peak of the mountain now visible against the blue sky.

With the fog gone, a path was visible heading up between a cliff wall and a boulder-pocked hill. The path didn't appear to be made by anyone, as did anything on the island. Some scraggly trees and thick green vegetation covered the island here, which was different from down below. Birds also circled the cliffs, flying in and out of tiny crevices and holes along the wall.

"I've never heard of anyone who came here," Raly said. "I wonder if we're the first people up here. Besides Bel, I mean."

The three of them continued up the mountain and marveled at the view.

"Doesn't look too bad from up here," Oen said. "The bay, that is."

"Right," Millar said. "We'll be able to get back home easily now."

Oen gave him a smirk and shook his head.

The crashing sound of rocks falling sounded just above, and they stopped. A cluster of birds flew from an area of the cliff, not too far away from where they now stood. The three flipped up their visors and glanced around to look for cover.

"What was that?" Oen said.

"Could have just been rocks falling," Millar said. "By some animal or something."

Oen scoffed. "That'd be a big animal."

Millar agreed. "Quick, over here!" He pointed to an overhang of rock and they hustled underneath.

Just up the path, the way opened into a clearing surrounded by tall, flowering trees. The red color was a stark contrast to the grays in the rocks and the cliffs. Nothing moved, and they were about to come back out when a tall, narrow figure lumbered into the area. It was about ten feet tall, maybe more.

"Is that a…?" Oen started but Millar cut him off with a hand gesture.

Millar squinted. It appeared human shaped, but it was way too tall and gangly. If this was a bot, it was one he'd never seen before. And it moved fluidly, too much so for a bot, even with the limp that accompanied its every step. Sure, he'd only seen a handful of scrapped bots on display in some of the cities they'd passed through, and of course there was Mom, still managing to hold on. Bots were rare to see at all, much less seen running independently. He slowly pulled down his visor and brought up the magnify mode to zoom in.

It was definitely a bot. Blue, glowing eyes, black rag-like coverings on its body, and its detached right hand clasped on its back by a few straps. It bent over as it walked, always looking at the ground. It was searching for something, going from one boulder to another.

"What kind is it?" Raly whispered. "And should we be running?"

Millar shuffled through all the bot types he'd researched. Bruisers, Lifters, Fighters, Miners.

"Maybe a Miner?" Millar said. "They used to be sent into deep mines and just dug until they broke down. It could be stuck here after getting out of the mountain?"

"Miners," Oen said. "Better hope not."

Those were the biggest ones Millar knew of that used to run back before he was alive, and none of them came close to this height. And the energy core this one had to have? The power needed to run a bot of this size would be crazy. Even Mom was a rarity, managing to squeeze energy out of the sun for a few hours a day. No, the only bot he knew to get this size was from Mom's old stories.

"A Guardian, maybe?"

"From the Fallen Land way out east?" Oen said. "That's impossible. Nothing from that age still exists, or would be found anywhere this far away. Anything that old would have been scrapped by now. Plus, look at it. It couldn't be a Guardian."

But if it was… it could change everything.

"Doran!" a voice called out.

Millar clamped his mouth shut and froze. It had just spoken. And it said something that tickled the back of his mind. Doran wasn't necessarily an uncommon name, but the fact that it had been Bel's cat's name didn't seem like it could be just a coincidence.

The big, dark bot came closer, still looking under the branches of the red-flowering trees as it did so. Millar checked the equipment at his side just in case things got to where they had to fight. His pry hammer—a two foot long tool for pounding and ripping up scrap—hung on his belt, and he thought it might be helpful for self-defense. Or it would just make the bot upset, more likely.

"Doran!" the bot called out again, this time not more than thirty feet away from their hiding spot under the rocks.

Raly and Oen both gave Millar nervous glances. There was no way this bot wouldn't look where they were. And if it spotted them there it might just be startled and kill them all. Millar hefted his pry hammer. No, there was only one way out of this.

He stepped out of the hidden space and held his hands up in a show of peace.

"What are you doing?" Raly asked.

Oen reached out to drag Millar back, but he was already back out in the clearing. "You're crazy!"

Millar waited until the bot turned and those glowing blue eyes locked onto him. If he wasn't so terrified that the thing was going to murder him, he would have been in absolute awe of seeing a bot like that on top of a hidden island. Those two emotions played in his head over and over as he stared back, waiting for its reaction.

But the bot turned away and continued its search for whoever or whatever Doran was, just like that—without a second's regard for whatever Millar was all about. Millar took that as an invitation to walk closer.

"No!" Raly said. "Time to run!"

"Yeah, for the first time, I agree with her," Oen said.

The two of them started down the path they came on, but stopped when they saw that Millar wasn't following.

"Hello!" Millar called out.

Oen ran under cover of some rocks before Raly could get there. "He wants us all to die today, doesn't he?"

The bot lumbered over to another scrubby brush tree and peered under it, ignoring Millar's question. He even started to hum an awkward tune. No, he was definitely not like the majesty of old.

"Do you need help?" Millar said.

"Definitely wants us dead," Raly whispered.

The bot didn't respond and only continued to ignore him and keep looking for something. As he got closer, Millar noticed scratches covering the bot's back. That is, whatever parts of its back were even visible between the thick mossy patches covering its body. It sure must have been hidden away for a while to gather that much moss. Had it been sitting somewhere on this island until… Millar's breath quickened as he thought about what might have awoken him.

"Have you seen a little girl?" Millar asked. "Dark hair, dark eyes. Her name is Bel."

This was the only thing that made the bot stop looking about, and he fixed his glowing blue eyes on Millar's.

Chapter 10

"Bel?" the bot said.

"Yes! Have you seen her?"

"No." The bot looked away.

"But, why did you call for 'Doran?'"

The bot didn't answer and instead turned around and searched more intently. The two other humans who had been hiding when he first came into this clearing finally came out from under the rock cover. Unlike the first, they didn't have any weapons and posed no threat to him.

"I'm looking..." he trailed off.

"We need your help!" the boy said.

"Are you crazy?" the other boy said. He was about the same age as the first.

The first one brushed him off. "Are you looking for her? The little girl?"

Initial verbal scans showed an edge of desperation in his voice.

The bot did not actually know what he was looking for. He had caught a glimpse of that small creature outside, hadn't he? But why would he care enough to leave the cave? The thing was in danger and he had to go find it, right?

"We don't need his help," the other boy said. "We need to get out of here."

The girl, the one with hair the color of autumn leaves, stepped forward now. "What are you called? Is it Doran? I'm Raly, this is Millar and Oen. Who are you? You look lost."

Lost? No. He knew right where he was.

"What are you doing?" Oen said.

"Remember Etto, my grandfather? He used to act like this when he got very old. I think he's broken. Up there." Raly pointed to her head.

"Oh great, a mentally unstable bot. What could go wrong with that?"

"Doran. That was the name of Bel's old cat," Millar said. "Did she tell you that?"

Doran. Why had he been calling that out loud? Maybe it was his name. For a reason he couldn't explain, he held out his large hand to the three children and showed them the black stone he was carrying.

"Nodular obsidian." Doran's mind reeled. Images of storms flashed in his head. Black shiny rocks. A sword. Something blue.

Millar's eyes opened wide. "Bel and I found a rock like that, did she give it to you?" His hand strayed slightly to the hammer at his side. "Where is she?"

The images faded as Doran closed his fist about the stone. "I am looking for something, or someone, and I do not know why. Maybe it is this child. Maybe I am... broken."

Raly stepped closer to him. The three humans didn't appear to be frightened of him anymore. "Maybe we should help him."

Millar shook his head. "No, we've got to find her."

"If we help him, he might lead us to her," Raly whispered.

"Uh, I think he can hear you," Oen said, still keeping his distance.

No, not all of them were unafraid. Not this skittish one.

Doran walked to the edge of the clearing and looked out at the water far below. "Whatever I am looking for, it appears it is not here anymore."

Had he really seen anything?

"You know, maybe she's already back at home," Oen said. "We probably passed her in the night without even seeing her. I still don't know how we made it past those rocks."

"Is your home up there?" Doran pointed to the rocks across the bay.

"How did you know?" Millar asked.

"You cannot have gone too far, you are not carrying much, and I see an encampment up there. With the smoke coming from it—"

"Smoke?" Millar said and dropped his visor over his eyes. "Home?"

The three villagers stared up at the hilltop, scanning the surrounding area.

"We've got to go," Millar said. "Now."

Without a word, the other two children hoisted their packs, lifted their visors, and made for the path back down to the water. Doran stood still as they stumbled over the rocks. He looked around, wondering what it was that he was seeking, and then he faced them again.

"Come with us," Millar shouted over his shoulder. "We could use your help."

They disappeared from sight around a corner and the fog came back, obscuring everything.

And then it was quiet except for the birds and the wind whistling above.

Still, in the distance, Doran thought he heard a faint sound like a song, perhaps. He tried to hum it, but it only came out in awkward phrases. Was this all a dream? Were those kids even here, or was that all in his twisted memory?

They had been loud and annoying to his sensors. He preferred the quiet of this place. He sat amongst the stones here in this clearing, hoping to catch a glimpse of whatever he was looking for, but still there was only silence and fog.

Visions of the storm shook his mind again. Raging lightning.

There was only one way he knew how to calm that storm.

He reached up to tap his forehead.

Chapter 11

No one spoke as they descended the mountain. They couldn't climb fast enough, and they were soon tripping over each other. At one point near the edge of a sharp cliff, Raly bumped into Millar and he stumbled near the ledge. She grabbed his arm and pulled him back.

"I'm sorry!"

He merely grunted his thanks before turning around to climb down. It didn't take long and soon they were back at the boat. The rising tide had brought the water up, and the boat bobbed back and forth against the rocks, straining the rope they'd used to tie it up. They didn't have time to inspect it. It was hardly seaworthy to begin with, and indeed it was the only way back, so, inspection or not, they all piled into the boat and shoved off.

"Think he'll come with us?" Raly glanced up at the foggy cliffs above them.

Millar didn't respond and instead fought to put the sail up while Oen and Raly scooped out the half-filled basin they sat in. No one cared that the cold water covered their feet—they only knew they had to get back home.

The way across the bay was easier to find during the day, but still the rocks threatened to smash the craft to pieces—or what was left of it, that is. Fog covered their way, but with the guidance of their visors they made their way slowly to the other side. A heavy mist hung heavily upon the shore, however, and they ended up farther north than they had hoped. There were several paths, and they could still make it up to the village from any number of them.

"Should we check for Bel's boat?" Oen asked. "She could have come in anywhere on the beach, maybe closer to the boat landing."

"No time," Millar said. "We can only hope she made it back and is up there."

The three looked up through a break in the fog and saw smoke curling above the hills. They were finally back on their own land, on paths they'd covered countless times. And they ran.

As they approached, the smell of burning seared their noses.

"They're all right," Millar said.

He looked back at the two behind him and saw the tears in their eyes, and not from the smoke. Oen and Raly had parents, real flesh and blood ones. Millar had Mom, but she hadn't been his birth mom, obviously. Not that that meant too much. He'd worry about her like a real mother no matter what.

When they saw the first burnt-out shell of a hut, it was too much for any of them. Oen just ran off toward his house, and Raly stumbled into the smoke. Millar called out to them but they were already gone. No cries or speaking came out of the fog, but the burning and collapsing of the huts cut his heart.

What happened? Where was everybody? The smell of death clung onto the weak breeze drifting through the village. Huts and shacks lay in shambles with their insides thrown out upon the pathways that surrounded them.

Nothing moved.

Burnt and bloodied bodies lay strewn among the wreckage. Friends he had known for years. He quickly ran and checked on them, but no one was still alive. His hands shook as he turned them over one by one. Tears streamed down his face, either from the smoke or from the shock of the whole scene. Most of them had dark marks like burns across their bodies. Who could have done this? And why? He ran to his home now and dreaded what he might find.

"Mom? Bel?"

His house, too, was falling apart, and still on fire. Black smoke coiled out of it. No one responded. Some of the wooden supports collapsed within the hut, and the roof shook. Millar moved quickly and went to the front door. If anyone was in there now, they'd be dead for sure—unless he did something. His heart beat loudly in his ears.

"Mom!"

He covered his mouth with his shirt and then he raced inside. Everything was in shambles. Pots and pans everywhere, cabinets toppled over, and the smell of fried circuitry. Movement over by a window drew him closer, and he held his breath.

"Mom!" Millar began to uncover her form carefully and threw the toppled pieces to the other side of the hut.

Bits of the roof fell onto his back in a pattering mess, and he brushed off a smoldering piece of wood. He hurried and tried to pull her metal form free from the debris, but her body didn't respond, and she just hung there limply. Her normally glowing eyes stared off blankly.

"You'll be all right," he said. "Somebody help!"

No one responded, and he pulled her harder until she sprang free from a collapsed beam. His heart jumped, and he yanked her toward the doorway. Some more roofing collapsed into the house and the flames intensified, catching the loose clothing on his arms on fire. He didn't pause this time and continued to pull her out of the door and into the clearing.

Only when she was free from the wreckage did he mash the fire out from his sleeves. He barely registered the pain that lit up his arm.

"You're not awake. Wake up."

He quickly but gently turned her over to check her power levels. Nothing registered on the panel, no charge. Nothing. He looked around for the solar power cables on the hut, but the entire roof had crumbled in a pile of smoking rubble. Millar froze. He had no idea what to do, where to go, or who to ask for help.

A cracking sound made him spin around. What he saw made him stop, as it was someone he had never seen before. It had been so long since he or his friends had seen anyone new. This person wore strange red clothing, including a short hood covering their face. They carried a wicked cudgel with metal spikes protruding from the end, and when they saw Millar, they raised it.

Millar fumbled for his pry hammer and stood in between the newcomer and Mom. He looked around to see if there were others, but there was no one.

"Who are you?" Millar said.

The other said nothing, but Millar caught a flicker of their eyes staring at Mom's fallen body. For a moment the person stood still and glanced down at Mom and then up at Millar. They were about as tall as Raly, maybe about the same age, too. Millar gripped the pry hammer tighter and stepped toward them.

That's all it took, because the outsider turned and ran. Millar guessed that whoever had raided the village had already left, and this youngster had been sent in to sweep for easy prey in case there were any survivors. He spent a second debating whether he should chase after them, but, for good or bad, he bent back down and tried to get Mom working again. More than likely, the kid would go and find someone else and come back to finish the job.

Which was… what? This was a small village in the middle of nowhere. There was nothing here.

Millar reworked some wiring on Mom's back. His heart caught in his throat as she made a small twitch. He locked the wire into place, and her systems booted with a soft whir. Something felt off though. There was a faint scratching pulse that built up and then faded. This repeated after a few seconds, like labored breathing.

"Millar?" she said. Her voice tone was off. It was much quieter and had a thin hum of static over the top of it.

"I'm here, Mom. What happened? Where is Bel?"

"They came in the night," she said. "After you left. Bel…"

Mom's eyes drifted to the still-standing door frame, and Millar noticed that there was no blue scarf wrapped there, or anywhere nearby on the ground or otherwise.

"She never came back," Millar said.

Mom shook her head with a metallic scraping. "You've got to find her."

"I know. I will. But you…" He looked around and began pulling a cable to search for the end to plug her in.

She waved him off and gripped his wrist tightly. "It's important."

"I know that," Millar said.

Mom looked flustered but after a few seconds her eyes twisted into focus right behind Millar. "You!"

Millar instinctively reached for the pry hammer and looked behind him. He nearly fell over when he saw a towering shape looming over him.

"Doran?" Millar said.

How long had he been standing there? When had he shown up? Had he followed them?

"You're here." Mom lifted a shaking arm but Doran didn't make a move to hold it. She reached feebly toward him, but he stood still. Her strength faltered and she dropped her arm to the ground. "What is wrong?"

"Mom!" Millar said. He looked up at Doran. "Can you help her?"

Doran knelt down and reached behind her neck. After a twist of his wrist, Mom seemed to relax slightly, and her eyes brightened.

"Doran," Mom said. "That's new."

Doran didn't respond.

"You've met Bel, haven't you?" Mom said. "She must have given you that name. I am glad you came, it has been so long. Even if you don't remember me."

Millar tried to get closer to her, but Doran was in the way.

"If I disconnect, she will lose functionality."

"Then don't let go," Millar said. "We'll take her with us and get someone who can fix her."

"It's okay," Mom said. Her eyes began to flicker. "I won't last much longer. And you would be the best person for that job anyway."

She reached up and put her small hand inside Doran's larger one. "I don't blame you for forgetting me. I know why. I forgive you."

"Tell me my name."

Millar watched the two of them, unable to say a word. Mom stared at him the same way she used to stare at Bel and Millar. And Doran cradled her gently.

"You don't need to know that," Mom said. "You have a new one. A better one."

Mom's eyes dimmed, and her hand drifted from Doran's grasp.

"Mom," Millar said. "Don't go."

"You will find her," Mom said in a fading voice. "Take care of him."

With that, Mom's eyes flickered once, twice, and then faded completely.

Chapter 12

It took a while before Millar could move or think about anything. Mom's empty eyes staring blankly at the sky—it was too much for him. She had always been there for him ever since she took him in as a child.

"You knew her, Doran?" Millar asked. "How is that possible?"

"They will be back soon," Doran said. "They saw her. And me."

"You can't remember her, can you? There's something seriously wrong with your system." Millar finished drying his eyes and stood up. "So you did meet Bel for sure, yeah? And you can't remember anything?"

Doran shook his head.

"And now Mom's last wish was for me to look after you. Great."

"We have to go."

"You're probably right." Millar stooped again and laid his hand on Mom's shoulder. "But I should get her memory core, she'd want me to hold onto that. Plus, we might be able to access it and figure out what happened."

Mom's head tilted softly as he turned it with care. A dark covering of black scoring laid upon her banded neck where the access panel sat, and Millar scraped at it with a small metal tool. How had she been killed? Probably the house had collapsed on her. Maybe that's why she hadn't been taken.

"That kid seemed pretty interested in her. Do you know who they were? I've never seen anyone like that. Even the Trades have never brought any clothing like that red gear."

Doran didn't say anything, again. Instead he kept scanning the hilltops.

Mom's panel snapped open, exposing a small, silvery cube about the size of a thumbnail. Millar carefully grasped it and pulled it out.

"Sorry, Mom." Millar placed the cube carefully into a small pouch at his side and sealed it tightly.

"We've got to get her out of here, they'll just scrap her if they come back." Millar tried lifting Mom up but she weighed too much for that. "Can you help?"

Doran nodded. "What can I do?"

"Bring her to—" Millar's voice was cut off by some piercing cries in the distance.

Doran snapped into a position that looked like he was ready to spring off at a dash.

"That's Raly," Millar said. "Come on!"

Millar ran in the direction of the cries, past the still-burning wreckage of the village. A red-hooded person, maybe the same one as before, grappled with Raly outside of her wrecked and smoldering home. They were locked in each other's grip, and Millar was uncertain who was in more danger—that is, until he saw Raly's face. Streaks of blood covered her cheek, but it was the anger in her eyes that made Millar stop suddenly.

The red-hooded person glanced at Millar but then stared at Doran, who had just walked up behind him. Raly took that moment of hesitation and punched the red-hooded person in the gut. The two of them dropped to the ground with Raly on top, and she kept hammering her fist into the person's face.

"Raly!" Millar called out.

Raly stopped for a moment and turned her red eyes toward him, but then she glanced at the spiked cudgel that lay on the ground beside her. Without a second thought, she bent over and picked up the weapon and held it up in the air with both hands.

"Raly, no!" Millar said.

"She killed my mother!" Raly said with a raspy voice. She gritted her teeth and with a savage scream she swung down.

With a dull clang, the weapon turned aside. Millar grabbed her arms, but Raly had already dropped the cudgel and was now staring at her shaky hands. Millar looked down at the person before them and pulled back the red hood. A metal cap covered her skull, and it seemed to have been enough to deflect the blow. Still, she wasn't moving, and a thin trickle of blood ran down her cheek. Not many things could take a blow like that to the head and come away unscathed.

Millar helped Raly to her feet, and she fell weakly into his arms. Her body shook with her sobs as she stumbled to her knees. Whether she was crying about her mom, nearly killing this person, or both things, Millar didn't know.

"Are you all right?" Millar asked.

Raly cried into her hands.

Of course she wasn't. He wasn't. What a stupid thing to ask. He looked down at the person's exposed face. The helmet had small black markings over it. On instinct, he removed it by carefully wedging it off.

It was a light helmet, made of some metal he didn't recognize. Strong, too. It hadn't dented at all from Raly's blow. The girl would be out for hours from a hit like that, though. If only she was awake, they could ask her what had happened here.

"Is this the same person we saw before?" Millar asked.

Doran took the helmet from Millar and turned it over. "Yes."

"Are you sure? Your memory hasn't been your strong point." Millar knelt and thought for a second. "What do we do about her?"

"It would be prudent to take her with us," Doran said. "Or eliminate her. That is, if she is even responsible."

At that remark, Raly's house collapsed behind them with a cloud of ash and smoke, and she cried out. Millar held her back as she tried to go headlong into the wreckage.

"We've got to get out of here," Millar said. "They'll be back here soon to finish us off. And I've got to find Bel. And get Oen."

Were Oen's parents gone, too?

"I'm not going," Raly said.

"I need your help," Millar said.

She faltered and wiped her eyes, and she finally gave up trying to enter her fallen house. Millar let go of her shoulders.

"Is that one of them?" Both Millar and Raly turned in surprise to see Oen standing there. He stood with his shoulders slumped, his face covered in ash. "Is that one of the ones who did this?"

Oen didn't even register any expression when he saw Doran.

"Oen," Millar said. "Your parents?"

"They weren't there. Ran, probably. I don't know how they got away, especially with everyone else I've seen. Or maybe they're out there somewhere." Oen gestured lifelessly to the people lying along the paths.

"We'll find them," Millar said.

Oen looked at Raly's house and then back at her.

Millar shook his head in answer to his unasked question.

"Raly, I'm sorry," Oen said.

She responded only with silent sobbing.

"Come on," Millar said. "We've got to go now."

Doran lifted Mom's body by gripping her with his left hand and supporting her with the stump of his other arm.

"Careful with her," Millar said.

Doran wasn't really handling her roughly, but it was the only thing Millar could say when looking at her in this state.

"We're not taking her, though, right?" Oen pointed to the still unmoving form of the captive girl.

How were they going to get out of there quickly with a prisoner? Doran could easily carry Mom, but someone else?

"We're leaving her," Millar said.

"But the bot said we couldn't do that," Raly said. "You heard him say—"

"I know what he said." Millar sighed. "But we're not just going to kill her."

"Why?" Raly gripped a metal spike sitting on the ground next to her. "She'd kill us given the chance. It's either that or we bring her somehow. She's got to know what happened to everyone, including Bel."

"Seriously," Oen said. "Who else knows what happened here? Look around."

Millar shook his head. "Let's go. I mean it."

"You don't make any sense," Oen said. "There's going to be more blood if she lives."

"I'm not going to do it." Millar tossed his pry hammer to Oen. "Will you?"

Oen fumbled and dropped the hammer with a clang.

Oen picked it up and considered it for a few seconds before handing the tool back. Raly picked it up and jabbed the metal spike into the ground next to the fallen girl a few times, but she had lost her anger from earlier and now her shoulders sunk.

"He could do it." Oen pointed to Doran.

Doran stood with Mom over his shoulder and glanced at the red-clad prisoner. His massive hand opened and closed. Millar looked at the tall, motionless bot and then back at the two others.

"No. We can't make him do that. We'll figure it out without her. And even if she's alive, she won't know which way we go. This is our home, we know everything about it." Millar paused. He was trying to convince himself just as much as he was trying to convince the others.

"Where to first?" Oen said. "I don't know where my parents would go."

"They're gone," Raly said. "Look around you. No one is alive."

"Shut up." Oen's voice faltered.

Millar couldn't help but agree with Raly.

A crashing sound came from the other side of the camp, followed by shouting.

"We waited too long," Millar said. "They're here."

He gripped his pry hammer tighter. Let them come. Despite what he'd said earlier, he was as angry as Raly and Oen, and he was ready to take it out on something. After all, they had Doran here. He looked up at the tall bot, but it didn't appear that he was prepared, or even capable, of doing anything against anyone, other than intimidate them.

"Can you… do anything?" Millar asked.

Doran didn't respond.

Millar arched his neck to see anything through the burned huts but only caught glimpses of some movement several hundred feet away. People, maybe. They wore the same red as the girl. When he glanced down, he noticed a quiet yet persistent sound coming from her. It was a steady beeping, accompanied by a pale flashing light around her neck.

"What is that?"

"It is a signal," Doran said. "And it seems to have caught their attention." He pointed his stump of an arm in the direction of the invaders.

Millar weighed the life of this girl once more, but he couldn't think for long. A pack of three hunting dogs sprinted into the clearing and began to bark once they caught sight of the group. They were much bigger than the ones they'd had in the village, and the look in their eyes made Millar wish they had left earlier. Now they might not have that chance.

"That's it, we've got to run now."

Millar hoisted Raly up from the ground and dragged her along, but the dogs didn't take more than a second to see them and then lunge forward. He stood in front of Raly and swung his hammer, causing one of the dogs to back up a step and growl. The two others darted at Oen and at the girl on the ground. Oen shouted and kicked out, but the dog didn't retreat from that.

With a vicious bite, it caught Oen's pants in its teeth and tore off a slice. Oen yelped and a thin trickle of blood ran down his leg. Millar swung at this one and caught it on the side of its body. That made it take a step backwards, but it didn't back down.

"Do something!" Millar shouted to the still unmoving Doran. He brandished the hammer again, and the two dogs stood at a distance growling and barking. The third dog, however, nuzzled the girl on the ground.

Doran did nothing other than walk away from the dogs, carrying Mom toward the edge of town.

"Not just run away, help us!"

The bot considered this and turned back around to face them.

The dogs halted suddenly and stopped their growling.

"What is that?" Oen said.

In the center of the village about fifty feet away, they spied a strange metal shape. It had to be a bot somehow, but it wasn't anything they had seen before. It looked vaguely like a spider with long metal bars as arms and legs. It wasn't moving—it had somehow just appeared there without them noticing.

The three dogs tucked their ears down and ran away behind the metal creature. Four of its metal extremities raised into the air and pointed at them. A whining sound—as if something were charging up—came from within the bot. Millar grabbed his two friends and turned to shield them with his body.

The whining rose to a crescendo, and Millar closed his eyes. Doran jumped in front of them and held up his arm. A sudden salvo of fire and light released from the metal bot in front of them, arcing in a jagged line of destruction toward them.

The energy slammed into Doran and caused him to stumble backward, bumping into Millar's back. The blast only lasted for a second, and then silence followed it. Millar turned around to see Doran. Despite the smoke coming from his now-scored body, he was still standing, wobbling about on his feet. The other bot, however, was motionless.

"It has run out its charge for now," Doran said. "Time for us to leave."

Millar didn't waste another second and pulled Raly and Oen along with him out through the burning village. Doran limped slowly behind, and the rain started to fall.

Chapter 13

"Did anyone see us go?" Oen asked.

Millar looked behind them, down the hill. "Doesn't look like it."

The four walked away from the village toward the hills as the sun crept across the sky. On a normal day, they would have been wandering these paths scouring for parts. Now they trudged along with frequent glances back, trying to catch glimpses of who was following them. Flashes of red shone through the branches.

"What do they want from us?" Oen said. "We don't have anything."

Millar shrugged.

"That thing would have ended us, if Doran wasn't there." Oen turned around and waved at him. "Thank you."

Doran didn't say anything. Oen frowned as he watched him struggling to keep up.

"Are you going to be all right? There's a lot more noise when you walk than when we first met."

"I am sure I will be fine. I am worried about that one, now." Doran pointed to Raly.

Raly turned away from the path and vomited behind a bush. They all paused but no one said anything. As long as Millar had known her, she hadn't been mean to anyone. If he hadn't seen her try to kill that girl, he most likely would have done the same thing, maybe even worse.

And if he had known for sure that Bel was… gone, he couldn't quite put the words into full meaning in his head, but if he knew that, there'd be no guessing what he would have ended up doing.

Raly went silent again for a minute and then mumbled, "It's true though, what Doran said. I don't even know if that girl…"

Millar huffed as he walked. "Come on, I know we're exhausted, but we've got to get moving again. We've got to hope that girl hasn't woken up yet, and that bot didn't see where we were heading. I've never seen anything like it. Then again, we've never seen anything like you, either. Doran, did you get a scan of it?"

"I did not." Doran's legs made a sound like grinding metal when he took another step.

"What, in between jumping in front of us and taking that blast, you didn't scan it?" Oen said.

"All right, all right," Millar said. "If I didn't say thank you enough for saving us, I'll say it again, for Oen's sake this time—thank you."

Doran watched the two joking back and forth in silence. He turned something over in his hand, too.

"What's that?" Raly asked.

Doran held the metal helmet they took off the girl. "This is familiar. This material. And that bot had the same type of plating on its chest."

"Can I see that?" Millar said.

Doran handed him the silvery helmet. Raly's blow neither scratched nor made any mark at all.

"Look, these symbols." Millar pointed to a bit of paint on the side. "Is that a rank or something?"

Oen and Raly shrugged. Doran said nothing.

"Whatever this alloy is, it's amazing." He handed it back to Doran, who continued to stare at it as he limped along. "One of us should be wearing it."

No one made a move to call for it, however.

After thirty minutes they took a rest at the side of the path on some rocks.

"Millar?" a voice called out from inside the woods. "What are you doing here?"

"Who is that?" Too tired to do anything, Millar waited on the rock he was sitting on for whoever spoke. The voice was rough and sounded scared. It had to be someone from town, someone who'd survived. When he stepped out from the trees, Millar nearly laughed.

"Tren?"

"Yeah, it's me," the older boy answered. He sounded about as pleased as Millar felt.

"What happened down there?" Millar asked. "What happened to everyone?"

"I thought you could tell me, since you still live there. Or used to live there, it seems. Judging by the amount of smoke."

"We caught the end of it," Millar said. "There's a group of raiders we've never heard of. They didn't seem in need of supplies, but they destroyed a lot of homes, and our people."

"We think they did," Oen said. "But it could have been that bot, too. Did you see, though? It didn't seem to care that it could have hit that girl."

Perl walked out and stood beside her brother. Her eyes had dark rings beneath them. "Sorry, crugs, there's no more room in—" She stopped short when Doran, still limping, came up the trail behind the others. "What is that?"

Doran stopped walking and towered over the two. Tren scrambled and pulled his sister away.

"Relax, that's not the same bot that was shooting everyone," Owen said. "He's with us."

The two gaped up at the bot, and at Mom slung over his shoulder.

"So you don't know anything about what happened down there?" Millar asked.

Tren was the first to break away his staring. "It happened the night of the big storm. After we were kicked out." He seemed to be dazed, thinking about what had happened since then. "I guess we should thank you."

Millar shrugged. "What do you mean?"

"We'd be dead too, I mean." Tren slapped Millar on the back. "So it's a good thing we took those eggs, huh? No hard feelings Oen, huh?"

Oen muttered something no one heard, and Millar tightened his grip on the pry hammer.

"Did you see who did it?" Millar said. "How many were there? And did anyone escape?"

"Do you have any food?" Perl said.

"What?"

"You heard me," she said. "We didn't get much after getting kicked out. If you give us some, we'll help you out."

"We don't need your help," Raly said. "We just want to find out what happened."

Perl stood with her arms crossed, tapping her fingers in an annoyingly impatient way.

"Come on, let's go," Millar said. "They're not going to tell us anything."

The three of them started walking away, followed by Doran.

Tren and Perl stood close to each other and whispered something back and forth.

"Wait," Tren called. "That's your mom, isn't it?"

Millar nodded.

"I'm sorry."

Millar stared at him and narrowed his eyes.

"She was nice to us, even after Bruet kicked us out. Said something about family, and that we should stick together."

Millar would never have said anything like that—no one here would have—but it sounded just like Mom. He sighed.

"How many of you are there?" Millar asked.

Oen and Raly shot Millar confused and angry looks.

"There's just me and Perl now. The others got separated after the attack. We haven't seen them since. We haven't seen anybody."

Oen pulled Millar to the side of the path. "You're not seriously thinking of bringing them with us?"

"You heard what they said about Mom. They probably know more about what happened and just don't trust us enough to say anything right now. They might even know where your parents are."

Oen nodded reluctantly.

"Plus, we've got a killer bot that will protect us, right?"

"Killer?" Oen asked. "More like forgetful and crippled."

"Yeah, but *they* don't know that." Millar smiled.

Perl and Tren kept their distance from the bot, but they couldn't hide their wide-eyed stares.

"What do you think, Raly?" Millar said.

She shrugged. "I don't know. He creeps me out. And she's a stinkin' crug."

She said it just loud enough for them to both hear. Millar's eyes widened at this, but even though Perl and Tren may have heard, they didn't seem to care, or at least they pretended not to.

"So, do you two want to come along with us?" Millar asked.

They both walked toward the treeline without answering, talking to each other quietly so no one else could hear them. They were clearly arguing about something, though. In a second they went into the woods and disappeared from sight.

"Good riddance," Oen said. "I'd always be worried that they'd—"

"Did you hear anything they said?" Millar asked Doran.

The bot hesitated.

"I heard them discussing the matter. But they were speaking in a language I could not understand. It appears they have made this up."

"You remember some things, that's good," Raly said.

"But I do not know if I trust them." Doran would say no more on what he thought them capable of.

"Me neither," Millar said.

"Oh, I can trust them to betray us," Oen said.

In a minute, the two returned fully loaded with their packs and other gear.

"Sounds like you all take after your mother," Tren said. "We'll come with you."

"For now." Perl's sour expression made it clear she wasn't enthused about the decision. The group then walked in silence up the hill away from the village.

Chapter 14

"This is the first place Mom showed me when I got to the High Ansels." Millar stared out across the bay. "We saw the sun setting right over that island."

He heaved a sigh and placed the final stone on top of Mom's grave. Doran had offered to help throughout the whole ordeal, but Millar wanted to make sure he did the work himself.

The big bot stared out at the grave, nearly silent except for an irregular humming. Millar couldn't tell if it was a song or just some fragments of words or whatever. When the humming fell silent, Millar spoke.

"Mom brought me away from my first home after the fires and the raids had killed my parents. She'd heard tales of a traveling group on the High Ansels somewhere and knew we'd find a home there, too."

Millar looked down the hill to the smokes still rising from their village, and his eyes burned.

"Mom saved me. And then she saved the village here. She created the barrier that protected us, made us all safe." Millar slammed his hand onto the ground. "Maybe if we hadn't gone after Bel we'd have been able to save the town. But now it's over. Nothing is left of it all."

"We've got to hope that Bel is alive." Oen's voice cracked.

"I will find her, Mom," Millar said.

"Prism."

Millar turned around. "What?"

"Prism," Doran repeated. "That was her name."

"What do you mean? Do you remember her?"

Doran slowly shook his head. "It is a beautiful name. I don't know how I know. The word is just there, and nothing else. And I know it is her name."

Millar smiled. It was a pretty name. But it also saddened him to think he never knew it while she was alive.

"This is all great," Tren said. "But can we get going now? Those raiders'll be searching for us up these hills."

"That's the only thing you have to say right now?" Oen said. "Crug."

"Just being practical," Tren said. "We don't have time to waste worrying about who's still alive. If we hurry, we can get to that trail that leads to the other towns."

Oen started at this and clenched his fists, but Millar put a hand on his arm. "Don't listen to him. We'll find your folks."

Millar looked up at Doran. "Do you think we could stop that bot?"

Tren sputtered. "Are you crazy? We should be moving away from that thing, not closer. We all barely escaped with our lives."

"You hid up in the hills while everyone in the village was attacked," Raly said. "I wouldn't call that barely escaping."

"Hey," Perl said. "We weren't hiding. We were kicked out, remember?"

She approached Raly, but Doran, who had barely moved since the burial, stepped between them. Perl stopped suddenly and held up her hands, backing away slowly. Doran stared at the older girl.

"Well, if you didn't see what happened, we're going to have to go back," Millar said. "Bel might be down there. Oen's parents too."

Tren and Perl looked at each other. "Not a good idea," Tren said. "They've got about fifty raiders with them, and that bot."

Perl glared at him.

"I thought you didn't know anything?" Millar said.

Tren shook his head. "We saw some of it, all right? They captured some of the people there. Not sure what they're going to do with them, but they have them caged and chained up just outside of the village."

"Who did they capture?" Oen said. "Did you see my parents?"

Tren shook his head. "Didn't get that close a look."

"We didn't see any cages," Millar said.

"They're there. They shoved whoever they could in there, those they didn't kill anyway. And then took everything they could find in the huts."

Oen put his arm around Raly's shoulder.

"They only captured everyone because of that bot they have," Tren said. "Those people followed it and it did all the work. Killing, that is. First it took out the barriers, then it moved in. That was the hardest hit."

"They got through that?" Oen said. "How'd they even get close to it? That should have stopped them, right?"

Tren shrugged. "The raiders streamed in after that and just grabbed the people out of their homes. Those that didn't fight back, that is."

Millar tossed a pebble and it bounced off the bigger rocks. "Then we've got to free our people."

Oen nodded without a word.

"What good are you going to be against everything they've got down there?" Perl said. "It's not like your bot here could lend any help. Have you looked at him lately?"

Doran took his right hand—which was strapped to his back—and twisted it onto the stump of his arm. It made an unpleasant grating as he jammed it on, like it was being forced in against its will. The hand made several spasms before completely sputtering and going still.

"I will help you, as much as I can," Doran said.

"Oh wow," Perl said. "We're saved. Cripple Bot with his gimpy fist. Our enemies will cower before him."

"Do you have any better ideas?" Millar said.

"Yeah, we already said—run away."

"Shut up, Perl," Tren said. "Everyone else could be down there."

Millar and Oen caught each other's eyes at this.

"She's right," Millar said to the bot. "You don't have to help us. It's not your town."

"Your chances of surviving with me are slightly better than not," Doran said. "And Prism told me to protect you."

"But…" Millar said. He had thought it was the other way around.

"The bot must take time to recharge after it releases a blast of that magnitude," Doran said. "Tell me what you remember from the attacks."

Tren gulped and sat in silence for a few moments.

"You can think on our way back," Doran said. "Anything you remember will increase our odds considerably."

Oen pulled Millar aside and whispered to him. "Tren said there were about fifty raiders with them. There's no way we can do anything about that, and you know it."

"No, but if we can take out that bot, that'd really shut them down. Plus, since when can Tren count?"

Oen laughed.

"And I bet if the raiders see Doran wreck their weapon they'll run away themselves."

"Maybe," Oen said as they watched Doran limp slowly back down the path. "Most I've seen him do is wave that one hand."

"Come on," Millar said. "He took that blast for us, saved our lives."

"And he's barely able to move after it. What's the next blast going to do?"

Millar didn't say anything. "Maybe nothing. But now he's got two hands."

Doran, as if on cue, turned around and waved with his right hand. The digits didn't bend at all, but the whole thing spasmed as it moved.

Millar smiled and pointed at it.

Oen shrugged. "I still say one."

Millar waved back at the bot and watched him with Tren, who cowered beside him as they walked away. Doran was still covered in that sooty blast scoring and now wobbled slightly with a limp down the path. Despite how foolish it sounded for Millar to protect the bot, he did feel a responsibility for him. Mom's last words repeated in his head as they headed back home.

Chapter 15

"I think you should wear it," Millar said.

Raly shook her head. "It feels weird." She turned the lightweight helmet over in her hands.

"There's a good chance we're going to get hurt, or worse," Millar said. "Just put it on."

Raly nodded finally and slipped the silvery helmet onto her head. She pulled her dark hair to the back so it didn't mat down in front of her eyes.

"See?" Millar bonked her on the head a couple times with his knuckles. "Can't feel a thing. Unless I hit it as hard as you did with that cudgel."

Raly smiled a little. "Don't joke. I was really mad."

"No one would have blamed you if she died," Millar said.

"I would have."

Doran strode over to her with a grinding sound and placed his hand on her head. "The path that girl chose crossed with yours. She is still alive, as are you."

"But my mother," Raly said. "She's gone. And I…"

"You have your friends." Doran pointed to Millar and Oen. "And they have you."

"Wow," Tren said. "Sounds just like your mom, doesn't he, Millar? Spouting off some spiritual nonsense."

"Really?" Millar said.

Tren shrugged.

"We've got other things to worry about besides this crug," Oen said. "Like how we're going to kill fifty raiders and eliminate a death bot."

Millar stared down the hill in the fading sunlight. "You're right. Let's look at what we know."

"Not much," Perl said.

"Not helpful," Millar said. "Seriously, let's think. We know the one thing that could have stopped everyone was wrecked, right?"

"The barrier," Oen said.

Tren nodded. "I mean, I think it was destroyed. I haven't really seen it." He and Perl exchanged glances. "I just know that it was working, and then it stopped, and that's how they got in."

"You're saying someone might have shut it down?"

Tren shrugged again.

"So maybe it's not wrecked. That's good. If we could get that up and running that'd be one thing." Millar's mind raced. "We'd need to get that checked out. Oen? You're good with that, right?"

Oen nodded. "Yeah, I know how they work. Four barrier points, interconnected, interlaced and ready to shock—when there's power, that is. In the center of the village, there's the power vault buried there. I'd need to check that out, too. I helped Bruet run it, along with some others, but I can figure things out. Or not. It could be trashed, for all we know."

"So we get that working," Raly said. "Then what? They're already in there, or at least most of them are. What good's the barrier going to do against that?"

"We'd have to get them outside of it—a distraction somehow." Millar started pacing. "And we'd need them out of the village limits for Oen to get inside. Are you feeling particularly sneaky, Oen?"

"It's night, so we have that going for us, I guess. The fires are down. Yeah, I could check them out before we make a move. And be sneaky."

"What kind of distraction would get them out of the village?" Millar asked.

Tren pointed at Doran. "That's a distraction."

Millar nodded. "Yeah, he is. But that also makes him a target."

"Affirmative," Doran said. "Do not worry, I did not expect any of you to do it, as I am the only one properly suited for the task. I analyzed its attack pattern, however briefly. And this 'crug,' as Miss Raly and Oen put it, has shared some helpful things."

Tren opened his mouth to say something but clamped it back shut.

"As soon as Oen is done with the barrier system," Doran said, "I will lure it out of the village."

"That's an awful lot of pressure," Oen said. "What if I can't even do that?"

"Don't worry," Millar said. "I'll come with you."

"Me too," Raly said. "We could both see you do your work, and then we could check out the others, too. Do it faster."

Oen shook his head. "Have you ever worked on these before? I couldn't expect you to know what to do after one check. We don't even know what's wrong with them. Three people are easier to spot, too."

"Well, at least take one of us," Millar said. "I'll go, and watch your back. Make sure none of those raiders gets the drop on you. Raly, can you stay with…" He paused.

"Don't worry," Tren said. "We'll keep an eye on her."

Millar's stomach twisted. He didn't trust them at all. What if they ran, and left her alone?

"I will stay behind with them," Doran said.

Raly smiled. "Thank you. I'll also go check on the prisoners. We're going to have to spring them from that place too."

"You're right," Millar said. "Before we trigger the barrier, we're going to have to get our people in, and theirs out."

"This is getting crazy," Oen said. "How are we going to tell each other what's going on? What if something goes wrong?"

"We can do this," Millar said. "We have to. For those who are still alive, and those who are in the next town. Oen and I are going to go in and do our part. Raly, you head to the prisoners."

"I'll go with her," Tren said. "I've seen them in their cages—a little bit, anyway."

Perl punched her brother's arm. "No way, we're not getting more involved with this. Plus, they kicked *us* out, remember? What do we owe them?"

Tren pulled her aside and whispered something to her Millar couldn't understand.

Millar walked closer. "Hey, if we're going to do this, we need to all be talking the same language, yeah?"

Tren raised his hands up in an apologetic fashion. "Sorry. Habit. I was just telling her that I had to do this. Okay?"

"This could get messy." Millar dusted off his shirt with shaky hands. "Well, we all know what we're doing, right? Give me and Oen ten minutes or so, and then Raly and Tren head to the cages. See what you can find from them. Don't bust anyone out yet, just check it out. And Doran, find out where that bot is, but don't fight it. We'll meet here in an hour, all right?"

Everyone murmured in agreement and double-checked their packs for tools and whatever they needed. Doran walked beside Millar and spoke to him in hushed tones.

"That wasn't what those two were speaking about." Doran gestured to Tren and Perl.

"I figured," Millar said. "Can you tell what they said?"

Doran shook his head. "Not exactly."

"Well, they're what we have right now, and we need to trust them to do the right thing."

He hadn't spoke about what had kept burning his mind, though. What were these raiders waiting for? After capturing the people, taking their belongings and scrap, why didn't they just leave? He watched Doran stand in silence, and then he and Oen headed to the village.

Chapter 16

From the hill, they could see down below into the village remains. A fiery glow lit the middle of it all, and through his visor Millar saw several shapes walking around. Night had settled fully, but silhouettes of the raiders appeared in front of the fire.

"What are they doing?" Oen asked.

Millar shrugged. "Trying to find more scrap? There's not much there, anyway. Minimal food, and all of our good stuff has been sent to the Trades."

They both viewed the town through their bio scans, as it was difficult to see much with the limited light. Raiders showed up on the visor from the center of town, but Millar counted at most only twenty.

"The rest are probably with the prisoners?" Millar said. He hoped they hadn't tried to move them out at night. They'd wait for the next morning, right?

"The first barrier station up ahead is the farthest away from all the raiders," Oen said. "Come on, we're almost there."

"Any sign of their bot?" Millar scanned back and forth but still couldn't spot it.

"Not yet, which is good for us."

"Not so much for Raly. But I guess that's why Doran is there. We need to trust that if it comes down to it, he'll try to stop that thing, somehow."

"He's got a better chance than we do," Oen said. "But he doesn't look like he can take too much more."

Millar shook his head. "He's stronger than he looks. He can hold his own."

Millar motioned to Oen to stop talking as they followed a well-worn path to one of the spots where they used to enter the village. They were close now, and stopped frequently to listen and scan for any raiders at the first barrier.

Oen got to the metallic contraption first and knelt over the components as Millar kept watch. He pulled out his tools from his satchel and began testing the barrier. He didn't say anything, and Millar began to worry.

"They've got no power," Oen whispered. "Which is what we figured. Doesn't look like it was heavily fried, though. It looks like this one was just switched off. I'll have to do an internal diagnostic though, to be sure. Then I'll see what I can do to make sure it's still running a charge."

Millar nodded and listened carefully for any sound. He knew a thing or two about the bigger component pieces of equipment, but not necessarily the inner guts of the security system. Sure, he could still figure out wiring components from a schematic, but not like Oen could. He gripped his pry hammer tightly. At least he'd be able to bash anybody if they got close to them. He was pretty okay with that skill set.

"Yeah, okay," Oen said.

"Okay what?"

"I mean it's good! Nothing damaged. We've just got to make sure the power can get here, and we're not going to know that until we try. No way we can dig up the cables and see that way. But since the ground isn't dug up already, we can hopefully assume they're intact."

"All right then," Millar said. "That worked."

"You sound surprised."

Millar shrugged. "The way this day's going... Center of town next?"

"We should get the outer ones cleared, then we can fire it all up at once from the middle."

"If it works."

"It'll work."

"Should I go...?" Millar pointed vaguely in the direction of another barrier.

"Really?" Oen said. "You caught enough of what I just did that you'd feel confident in your assessment?"

Millar shook his head. "I just wanted to feel like I was doing something."

"I'm still alive, that's something." Oen hefted his pouch over his shoulder. "Plus, you don't have any tools. Nah, we're much better off this way. Stick to the plan."

They headed east next and crept from one tree to another. They knew the area well, which was good, because there was no way they were going to be able to have any lights on.

This next barrier station wasn't as quiet as the first. Two raiders walked up ahead in the trees carrying a torch. Millar hadn't seen any of the raiders yet—besides the girl Raly had dropped—so seeing two at once gave him a start.

It appeared they were on watch and doing rounds by the outer limits of the village. Millar's heart raced, and he gripped his pry hammer tighter. The two men kept walking past the barrier console and into the treeline. Millar and Oen let out a collective breath, and then scurried over to do another check.

"Hurry," Millar said. "They might come back, or there might be more behind us."

Oen nodded and knelt over the metallic console. He opened the port to this one, hooked up the wire to it, and began his scan.

"These definitely weren't smashed or shorted out, but I'll have to check internally to be sure."

Millar peered into the woods all around. "Did they know how to do this? Did they get lucky?"

Oen didn't answer. He hooked up the small power meter. "This one's dead, too. Give me a minute."

Millar's heart pounded in his neck, so hard he thought he was going to explode. "Do you think the others are okay?"

"I don't hear anything, do you?" Oen said.

"Quiet is good," Millar said.

"Scan complete," Oen said. "It's the same as the last one—like someone just disconnected the power, but nothing's damaged internally. It's weird."

"So what's going to prevent them from just turning them back off again if we do this?" Millar asked.

Oen unplugged his cords from the console. "We'd have to get people on each spot, to prevent that specifically. Now that we know what they're doing, we'd be able to stop them."

"Maybe," Millar said. "How did they get close enough to do it the first time, though? Don't these give a strong shock to anything around them, regardless of who they are?"

"They should have. And maybe they did. Here, let me get this ready for a reboot." Oen tinkered with some wires internally and closed it back up after a minute. Oen signaled to Millar, and they moved on.

They moved centrally across the village now instead of heading to the closest barrier system. That would lead them too near to the prisoners, and they didn't want to draw unwanted attention that way, although going through the center wasn't ideal.

Millar tried to keep his eyes up, to be aware of anyone who might be wandering around, but he kept looking at the ground—all the wreckage and the bodies were still there. He wanted to say something to Oen but didn't want to risk alerting anyone, either.

Oen tapped Millar on the shoulder and signaled by pointing ahead. Millar nodded. The central hut that housed the controls for the barrier was about a hundred feet from them, and now they could see that there were many people walking in and out of it. The two crouched and darted from hut to hut and tried to keep out of sight of the raiders.

"That's going to be difficult to check out," Oen whispered. "How are we going to know if it's still got a charge?"

Millar nodded. The system needed to charge all day long, just like Mom used to, and then at night it would be ready to go. Had it been doing that?

"That's something we just have to hope for." There would be no other way to stop all these people, at least none that he could see. Despite what he'd just said, his mind scrambled for something else, another way to stop this. But, mostly, he thought of Bel.

Was she in one of the cages? Somewhere else beyond the village? Perhaps just waiting and watching? It sickened him to think there was nothing he could do for her, but perhaps it was the hope he had, the belief that she was all right, that kept him from going insane. He pulled his visor down and flipped on the bioscan, peering at the northern end where Tren said the cages were.

"We've got to save our power," Oen said. "Do you see something?"

Millar shook his head and turned off the scan. "Only a mass of people there—I didn't get a count. But you're right. I'm worried about what we'll see at the end of this."

DAVALA

Two more barrier stations to clear, and then he could see for himself whether Bel was being kept a prisoner in her own home.

Chapter 17

Raly searched through the trees where Oen and Millar had crept through earlier. Every few seconds she thought a red-hooded raider would pop up in front of her. It had been about ten minutes, and she still couldn't quite get herself to go despite knowing her friends might be trapped there.

"It is time," Doran said.

Raly let out a sigh and nodded.

"We get close enough to count everyone we see, then we get back here. Right?"

Tren looked back and forth between Raly and his sister and then nodded and shrugged at the same time.

"You're not instilling me with confidence," Raly said.

Tren looked up at Doran, whose head brushed against some high branches of the trees. "You know, he wasn't made to be stealthy."

Raly shrugged. "I'd rather he was with us if a raider shows up."

"Sounds like fun, but I think I'll wait here," Perl said.

Tren gave her a hard look. "You should come with us. Better to stick together."

Perl shook her head.

Tren sighed. "Be safe, then, and run if you get spotted. I'll find our brothers."

They huddled close and spoke a few words from their language. Then Tren joined with Raly and Doran and they all made their way into the trees.

"Can you still see them?" Raly asked.

Doran nodded. "I catch glimpses of them. The last I saw they had checked on one of the barriers you use to protect your village."

Raly nodded. So far everything was going to plan, but, then again, she hadn't really done anything yet. A deep panic filled her, and she was suddenly glad that Doran was there. Despite him being a gangly thing, she still felt safer. A lot safer than she would have if it were just her and Tren. She remembered quite vividly the night Millar got beat up, and how Tren had threatened her.

She took a deep breath and let it out slowly. Time to do this.

Raly led the way. Tren, for some reason, hung back and allowed her to lead without question. And then Doran followed him, presumably to make sure he didn't do anything stupid.

"You seem to know this way pretty good," Tren said. "I've tripped over roots and rocks nearly every step of the way and you're not breaking your stride."

"I should know it," Raly said. "I come this way every day from the beach right about this time."

"You like the water?"

"My skiff," Raly said. "Now keep it down, we're getting closer."

The going was quiet. They soon passed one of the barriers, and despite knowing that the power was off—and that maybe it would never work again—Raly's heart thumped in her head with fear. She'd always avoided passing by the barrier at night. There was always a guard in the tree platform, watching out for whatever was on the other side after they all went to sleep. Now she was on the other side with whatever prowled these woods and hills. But which was worse? The threat of the patarks hunting, or these raiders?

Those creatures had always been one of Raly's worst fears, but now she was starting to rethink that—how could another human do something like this? What had to happen to them to make them want to hunt and kill other people?

Raly noticed a pale light off to the right—it came from the center of the village. Occasionally a torch carrying raider would pass by, too. They didn't appear to be doing any more here, so why didn't they leave?

Maybe they were waiting for stragglers to come back to town. They were rounding everyone up, so maybe they were slavers? But then why did they kill Raly's mom? A sudden wave of sadness and anger hit her. Finding her house smoldering, and seeing her mom on the floor—she found herself thinking of when she was standing over that raider, pounding her in the face, reaching for the cudgel and...

"Hey," Tren whispered. "What are you doing? Slow down!"

Raly snapped out of her mind to see they were already in sight of the prisoner encampment, and she was in danger of walking right out in front of them. Doran's large but gentle hand on her shoulder pulled her back to some cover behind a scrubby tree. She looked up into his soft and somehow understanding blue eyes and held her hands up, trying not to exclaim aloud after being abruptly brought back from her thoughts. It was all right, no one had seen them.

There were about twenty raiders camped out here in front of a fire, and then there were the cages filled with her friends and other townsfolk. She couldn't see them to identify them, but she could hear them, especially the children, crying and wailing. The raiders just ignored them.

"How many are there?" Raly asked Doran.

"I will continue to scan them," Doran replied in a low voice. "For now I see twenty-three raiders, but perhaps more will arrive. It appears there are more in the village center, and I will do my best to categorize them."

"Good," Raly said. Categorize? She supposed that was how she determined differences in people too. Still, the word felt odd.

"Millar just wants us to count them and head back, right?" Tren said.

Raly shrugged. "I guess. Doran, do you see their bot?"

Doran scanned a full circle around him. "Negative, but I do detect a power surge at the center of town. There is a high probability it is there."

"That'll give us more time, but we still have to worry about the raiders." Raly squinted in the darkness. "There's a few cages set up, but they don't look super strong. I guess they can't be that heavy since they would have had to have brought them from a long distance. And they don't have any pack animals, at least none that we can see. I think I should get closer, you know, to hear them, maybe get some clues as to what they're doing here. And see if we can break those cages."

"That's not what he said for us to do," Tren said.

"And since when do you ever listen to Millar?"

"When I'm worried about my own skin, yeah?" He crept away from the cages. "Come on."

"Crug." Raly shook her head but then stopped. "Wait, look!"

A few raiders unlatched one of the cage doors, holding their weapons at the ready and yelling something unintelligible at the people. They backed away, but their cries got louder. After some urging, the villagers were led out of their cage one at a time, sometimes with a rough shove from a hand or one of their cudgels.

"Where are they taking them?" Raly asked.

"We need to go. Now!" Tren grabbed onto Raly's arm and pulled her, but she yanked herself free.

She flipped down her visor. "Wait, those are Trades, what are they doing here?"

"I don't know, but things just got worse and we need to regroup." Tren gave up pulling her and took a few steps away. "Now come on, or I'm just going to leave."

"Go then." Raly scurried closer. She was determined to get a better look at what was going on, especially with the Trades.

"It is not safe," Doran said. "I insist you follow Tren back to our rendezvous spot."

Raly didn't move. "Tren, look!" She pointed at the person being dragged out of the woods.

"Perl?" Tren stood with a disbelieving expression and started walking toward the raiders.

"Get down!" Raly said.

"She… she said she was going to talk to them, to get our brothers out, but…" Tren stumbled, but Raly yanked him down before they spotted him.

He pulled a knife on her and a fire lit in his eyes, not unlike when he was with Millar the other night.

"Put it down." Raly backed away. "What is your sister doing?"

Tren started toward the raiders and then stopped himself. He did this a couple of times as the color drained from his face. "Our family was taken. She's trying to get them out."

"Now?" Raly said. "She's going to ruin everything."

Tren lowered his knife slightly. "I didn't think she would do it. I told her not to. She might not, maybe they'll just…"

One of the raiders drove a club into Perl's stomach. She dropped to her knees. They yelled something at her but she didn't respond. The raider raised the club again. Perl held her hand up to stop it and then pointed wildly in Raly's general direction. Several raiders drew their weapons and started into the woods, and then they hit Perl again.

"No!" Tren yelled.

Before he got to his feet, a blur flew past him in Perl's direction. Doran crashed through the trees, still limping and stumbling, but nothing slowed him. The raiders all looked up and stopped for a second as the bot came barreling at them. They didn't seem surprised, as if they might have actually expected this. Two of the raiders raised horns to their lips, and a wailing sound pierced the dark sky.

A shower of arrows flew into the air, but they ricocheted with sharp twangs when they hit him. Raly ducked behind a tree just as an arrow stuck into the ground where she had been standing. Doran reached the first cage, but the raiders hadn't been idle. They dragged Perl into the trees and held their ground by raising spears that had been lying in the grass. Three raiders stood with their legs locked, their spears firmly planted in the ground.

These didn't slow the bot down—not until the raiders flipped a switch on their weapons which made small sparks cascade from their tips. Doran rammed into the first line of raiders and lightning ripped into him as it leapt from one spear to another. The line didn't last long—there were only three of them, and Doran backhanded two of the raiders in one sweep. Their bodies flew into the cage and their spears splintered. For a moment, residual energy charged through Doran, causing his hands to spasm even more than before.

The prisoners inside the cage rushed to the back as Doran swung his arms again. Another crack and a spray of sparks, and this time when the raider hit the cage the gate collapsed.

"Come on!" Raly shouted, both to Tren and to the others inside the cage.

If they were to run, they needed to go to the center of the village so Millar and Oen could finish their job and protect them. But in this madness they might just scatter or not even leave the cage. Raly sprinted to them and ducked to avoid Doran's wild attacks.

There were about twenty people in the cage, all backed into the corner. Parents clutched their kids close to them as they watched the mayhem outside.

"Raly?" It was Bruet, the leader of the town.

"We've got to get everyone out and into the center of the village," Raly said. "Millar's got a plan."

The cage shook with another blow from Doran.

"But the barrier," Bruet said. "And that bot? They've got another one?"

"He's one of us."

"One of us?" Bruet said.

Raly smiled. "That's right. And Millar and Oen are working on the barrier."

One of the people she didn't recognize, an older Trades man, stepped forward. "That's not going to work."

"What do you mean, not going to work?"

"They know how to run the system now, even if your friends start it up again."

"How do you know?" Raly asked.

"They stole the schematics from us and can power it up or down by themselves with that bot of theirs."

And then the whole attack became clear to her. The Trades had been missing for weeks now, but they weren't just lost or waylaid by a storm. These raiders had captured them and tracked down the village. They'd brought their bot, shut down the barrier system, and could use the very system that protected the town against them. Raly cursed.

She looked outside to see Tren running headlong toward his sister. He struck the first raider next to her with a metal rod he'd picked up, and the raider dropped to the ground. Tren wildly swung it at the next one, but they had time to react and had him surrounded and disarmed in a second. That didn't stop him, either, and he swung his fists and tackled one of the raiders.

Perl, injured but not helpless, kicked the raider nearest her and soon there was a brawl going on with her and Tren at the center of it.

Raly's mind scrambled. Millar and Oen were still working, but maybe this whole thing could still be salvaged.

"Just get to the center of the village," Raly said. "I'm going to open the other cages. Can anyone help?"

A few others stepped forward and offered to help her out while the rest of the people clung together and shuffled out. She ran out and headed to the next one. The raiders were distracted by Doran, so she used that as cover.

"Just stay together, we'll be right—"

She was cut off as a new sound broke over the clashing of the spears. A high-pitched whine pierced her ears, and the air vibrated. Raly thought it sounded like something charging up. Doran sensed it as well, and turned to face it. The trees toward the center of the village cracked and crashed.

"Something big is coming," Raly said.

She ran to the next cage, and the raiders didn't even give her a second glance. Even the ones fighting with Perl and Tren left to pick up more spears stashed on the ground. Perl stumbled into a tree and clutched her stomach. Finally, she fell to the ground, and Tren knelt and shook her insistently and turned her over. A pool of blood trickled through her unmoving fingers.

Raly grabbed a discarded club from the ground and smashed the handle of the next cage. The lock broke easily and clattered to the ground. Those inside didn't move, and couldn't stop staring at the massive bot fighting the raiders or the other one decimating the trees in its path.

"Get moving! Follow the others!" Raly hustled the prisoners out of their cage. She made eye contact with Oen's parents, who were soot covered, their eyes filled with terror and wonder. "Your son is waiting for you, get going to the center of town!"

It took them a second but a look of relief spread across their faces. Then they finally listened to her and began to corral everyone out.

"Thank you, Raly." Oen's mother touched her face as she stumbled past her.

"Have you seen Bel?" Raly scanned everyone in the cage as they ran out, but she didn't spot the little girl. "Anyone?"

No one answered, and soon the cage was empty. When Raly left, she saw that the raiders were finally beginning to take notice of the villagers, although they didn't do anything about it. They focused on Doran and the approaching bot more than anything else, but the ones without weapons made sure the townsfolk kept moving to the center of the village—almost like they wanted them there in the first place.

Raly started running.

Chapter 18

A piercing horn sounded through the cold night air. Millar looked up from the third barrier console. "What was that?" It definitely sounded like an alert. "Are you almost done?"

Another horn cry blasted, and Oen dropped his scanning tool. "Yeah, almost. But that came from the cages."

"You keep working on this. I'm going to go to the next one, all right?" Millar felt uneasy about leaving Oen here, but their plan was definitely being accelerated.

Oen mumbled something as he rushed to finish up.

"I'll meet you there." Millar ran off toward the station. "Hurry!"

Something started to vibrate inside his head and tickle his ears. The resonance grew, and soon his whole head shook with it, and his teeth seemed to rattle in their sockets. A bright light shone through the branches coming from the center of the village. The burnt and smoldering huts shone briefly in the light, and so did something else—the other bot emerging from the main encampment.

And behind it, the red-hooded raiders formed a line stretching across the center of town. They each carried a tall spear and pointed them all in the same direction. It was like they were trying to herd something. But what? They already had the prisoners in cages. Unless…

Millar ran faster now and headed to the last barrier control center, trying his best to keep out of view of the raiders. If what he thought was happening was true, this last station would be just like the others.

The spider-armed bot crept toward the cages on stout, short legs, and swung its blades at the trees that stood in its way and crushed any huts in its path. Following closely behind it, but hopefully out of eyeshot, Millar stayed in its wake of destruction. He tried not to trip over his own feet or anything else in the darkness, which was difficult with his headlamp off.

What kind of bot was this? It was heavily modded, with extra arms and that strange metal plating covering its body. It didn't quite fit it right, like whoever put it on couldn't adjust it enough. The bot was shorter than Doran, probably some modded loader with a pretty rare weapon and armor system. How did it have enough power to charge up that cannon? Doran was lucky it hadn't gotten another shot off before they escaped last time.

The last barrier station appeared through the trees. The bot's path had diverted around it to get to the prisoners. They wanted these stations operational, but Millar couldn't think as to why yet. Did they want to live here? Continue to let the villagers work and then just take their resources? The village was barely scraping a life out of this as it was.

Just as he expected, the barrier console was intact but powerless. He popped open its hatch, but he was useless with this stuff. He had never taken the time to learn the circuits like Oen had, at least not in this system. How different could it be from Mom's? He had helped her plenty of times when she needed a small bug checked out.

Millar scanned the panel. Apparently it could be a lot different.

"Move over." Oen was out of breath, but he pushed Millar aside. After ten seconds of scanning, he looked up. "They're all the same. Just shut off. What is going on?"

"I don't know, but I think we're going to have company real soon."

Millar searched for the raiders he had just seen at the village center, and soon they appeared through the trees, waving their spears as they came. They were a couple hundred feet away and slowly advancing. They each stood the same distance apart, maybe a few feet. The spears all had sparks coming out of them now, and occasionally an arc of energy leapt through the entire chain.

"Looks like they're trying to trap something," Oen said. "Maybe someone let the prisoners out and they're rounding them back up? That's what that horn was for?"

"Maybe," Millar said. "We need to stop them."

"All of them? You're crazy. They're coming this way, we've got to run."

"Can you overload this barrier?" Millar asked.

"Not from here, there's no power."

"What if you got back to the center?" Millar pointed at the hut directly behind the approaching raiders.

Oen paused in thought. "Yeah, I could. Depending on what condition it's in. Considering all the points are clear, I'm guessing they want the center in working condition to get them going again. But they might have people guarding it."

Millar looked back at the cages and flipped his visor down with the bioscan active. "Looks like Raly got the people out, and they're on their way here."

"If they get around the bot, they'll be walking right at these raiders." Oen gulped. "You go warn them, I can get into the control room."

Millar weighed the two options and handed his pry hammer to Oen. "You might need this."

"And you won't?"

"You'll need it more than I will. I'll figure something out. Just overload this point and wait for me to bring the others further in. Shut the barrier when we're all safe, got it?"

Oen hefted the weapon. It looked huge in his grasp. "Yeah, I got it."

"And stay out of sight." Millar clapped Oen on the shoulder and headed to the sounds of the bot crashing through the trees.

Chapter 19

"Move!" Raly yelled.

Tren didn't get up—instead he held onto his sister's lifeless shoulders and shook them insistently. "What did you do, what did you do?"

"Help me get the others." Raly smashed the lock on the last cage, but it took a couple of hits to get it open. "Keep everyone together, we don't want anyone running off into the woods."

Raly yanked the door open and began pulling people out, although by now everyone knew they had to follow the others. There was still no sign of Bel. Where could she be? Raly's heart sank, wondering if she was in one of the piles of burnt huts. But she didn't have time for that now.

The long-armed bot finally arrived and slashed and ripped through the trees around it. A renewed force of ten more raiders stood at Doran's back, pushing him up against the approaching bot.

Doran and the other bot smashed into each other, toppling into one of the empty cages, and fragments of wood splintered into the air. A few pieces hit Raly in the head, but they bounced harmlessly off her armored helmet.

The bot's metal arms swung, and Doran grabbed the ones he could while the other bladed ones slashed at his sides. Most of the hits glanced off, but a few connected with Doran's body and tore at the coverings there, leaving gouges that exposed some inner parts.

"Tren!" a boy called out. It was one of his clan, a brother or cousin, Raly couldn't tell. He ran over to Tren and pulled him up to his feet. "Let's go!"

Tren stumbled back and stared down at Perl dazedly. He nodded slowly and followed the others while wiping the blood from his hands onto his shirt.

Three raiders ran at the escaping villagers. Doran saw this and brought his right fist down onto the other bot's armored head with such force Raly felt it in her back teeth. The bot slowed a second which allowed Doran time to swing his arms at the approaching raiders. They crumpled under his fist and flew back into the trees.

The line of other raiders advanced a few steps toward Doran, and energy crackled and surged from their raised spears. An arc of blue light leapt to Doran's arm and sizzled through his body to the ground. The other bot assaulted Doran again with a flurry of hits and knocked him back into the line of raiders. He fell to his knees for a moment, and they prodded him again with their shockers.

Doran leapt forward into the armed bot with a shout. His left hand grabbed onto two of the other bot's arms and gave a furious yank. A shower of sparks sprayed outward as he wrenched the limbs free and continued the arc toward the raiders. He flung the arms and they crushed two raiders into the ground.

More raiders took their places and kept advancing.

Raly hustled the last people out of the cage and followed them to the village center.

"Get safe, Raly," Doran said.

"You too!" she shouted.

One of the blades of the armed bot sliced into Doran's hand and hacked into his palm. Raly took a few steps closer to him.

"Go!"

Her eyes widened as she thought about what she had been doing. Thinking of helping him fight that spider-armed thing? What could she have done?

As she hustled her friends through the woods, she wondered how it had all gone to hell in such a short time. She couldn't be mad at Perl, even though she'd probably alerted the raiders. The girl just wanted to help her family. Raly would probably have done the same thing.

Only a couple more hundred feet and they'd all be in the village perimeter.

"Raly!"

It was Millar, running from the center of the village.

"I've got them all," Raly said. All that she could anyway.

"What about Doran? What happened?"

"Doran's fighting that other bot. And there's a bunch of raiders with spears, pushing him this way." Raly could barely breathe from speaking so quickly, and running, and smashing locks.

"Hey!" Millar grabbed her arm and pulled her along. "You're all right. There's more of those raiders coming this way, with those spears, too."

"What are they doing? They don't care about us anymore."

Millar raced to reach the front of the group of villagers with Raly close behind. "I don't think they ever really did."

"What?"

Millar didn't answer her, but instead directed the group further into the village away from where Oen was going. "Bruet!"

The old man, out of breath now and limping heavily, stopped and looked back at Millar.

"Raly is going to help you all, just stay within the bounds of the village. In the eastern quadrant. That's important."

"Where are you going?" Raly asked.

"Oen is going to need me. I'll be back as soon as I can, but if we do this right we'll be safe."

"They know how to use the barrier," Raly said. "One of the Trades told me. You turn it on, they're going to be able to turn it right back off again."

"How?"

Raly shrugged. "With their bot, I think."

"Oen could be hurt. I've got to go. We'll figure that out later."

Raly nodded and then helped Bruet walk by putting an arm around his shoulder. "Follow me!"

No sooner had she said that than howling arose from the distance where the central raiders were.

"Their dogs are coming! Get something you can use to fight." Raly picked up a metal strut that looked like it had once been part of someone's hut. "Tren, help the children! Keep them all together and safe!"

Tren stared around blankly at the chaos of the remainder of the village. Two of his brothers gripped his arms and pulled him along.

Millar yanked a wooden pole out of the ground and stood at the rear of the escaping group.

"We're all good," Raly said. "Go help Oen!"

He didn't wait another second and sprinted to the village center.

Chapter 20

Millar looked off to his left as he ran and saw the line of raiders slowly forming into a wide semi-circle. Electricity arced from one spear to another. They were inside the barrier limits, just waiting now—waiting to trap Doran. Millar didn't have time to think about how this all had happened. He only knew that he had to stop them.

How did these spears have enough energy? They didn't appear to have charge cells on them, at least not the size needed to keep that going. Something else must be giving them power.

Millar approached Bruet's central hut slowly now. This hut was bigger than the others since it housed the power supply and control center for the barrier. Millar hid behind piles of fallen huts as he made his way closer. Two raiders stood on either side of the main entryway, and luckily they were too distracted to notice him sneaking up. The fact that these guards were here didn't give him much hope that Oen had made it inside yet.

He skirted around to the back side and kept an eye on the guards. With his eyes up, he didn't notice the body at his feet until he tripped over it. Darkness veiled the figure, and fear rose in his chest as he turned the unmoving body over.

It wasn't Oen, or anyone else from the village. He didn't recognize this man. But why would one of these raiders not be wearing a hood?

Millar felt something metal touch his back, and he froze.

"Hey, it's me!" It was Oen.

"You scared me." Millar turned around and hugged his friend. "You're wearing their stuff, good idea."

Oen pulled the red cloth down from his face. "It took me a minute to get it. Here, you can have this back."

Oen handed the pry hammer back to Millar. He noticed a shimmer of red glistening from the end of it as he turned it over. Oen didn't look too pleased about it.

"I know how Raly feels now, but worse. I think." Oen stared at the body on the ground. His hands shook.

"It's all right, we've got to stop them. It was either you or him. But we've got to hurry. The rest of town is safe over there." Millar gestured in their direction with the hammer. Then he looked at the body closer. "And he's still breathing, so don't worry. But he'll be out for hours it looks like."

Oen paused and let out a breath. With his head cleared, he began to calculate something quietly. "I can divert some of the barrier points and put the field around them."

"Raly said they know how to control the whole system from the Trades. Apparently they're here now as prisoners."

"That changes things then," Oen said. "Maybe."

"Well, they're all coming here right now, leading Doran into a trap." Millar gestured to the spear-carrying raiders.

In the distance, he caught glimpses of Doran fighting with the other bot. The clanging of their attacks resonated throughout the air. The other raiders from behind now formed a circle around the two, and the electricity that had been sparking from one spear to another reached its full charge. The sizzling sound of its energy pulsed as massive blue beams circled them.

Doran reeled from a blow and stumbled to the edge of the encircling raiders. The spear tip touched his back and all the energy converged on him, sending shocks through his entire body. He reeled from the blast and stumbled forward. One of the enemy bot's arms caught him in the face, and Doran spun to the ground.

Millar wanted to shout out.

"He's down," one of the guards at the door shouted. "Turn it on!"

A humming sound emanated from the hut, and the barrier system engaged. The electricity around the spears intensified.

"They're right on the console over there," Oen said. "They connected to it. They must have."

"Well then, kill the power. They're going to take Doran down if we don't hurry up."

"Or we stick with the original plan," Oen said. "Come on, help me with this."

Oen started to lift the vent at the back of the hut and struggled until Millar grabbed the other side. Together they lifted it as quietly as they could to avoid alerting the guards. Oen jammed a stick under the heavy cover to prevent it from falling back on them so they could get inside.

They both crawled inside slowly, watching carefully for any guards. Millar did a quick check but saw no one except the raiders right outside. All of Bruet's things had been removed, and the only thing remaining was the barrier control system and a large cable snaking out of it. Large tracks led from the console to the door. The bot's, presumably.

Oen crept to the control panel in the center of the room and flipped open the screen. Soft beeping accompanied the powering up, and the two of them looked up at the doorway. The guards there hadn't moved, so they probably thought it was just normal sounds from the machine.

"Is this thing going to get any louder?" Millar whispered.

Oen held up his finger to his lips and shrugged his shoulders.

Millar clutched his pry hammer and ducked behind the metal console to keep an eye on any movement out front. The sounds of the fighting outside still rang in the air. At least that should cover up anything in here. The two raiders didn't budge from their post, though, despite a battle between two massive bots that Millar couldn't imagine anyone would want to miss.

"Power supply is really low." Oen pointed to the screen.

"Can you overload it at Doran's position?"

"I could, but then we wouldn't have enough to power up the barrier to protect everyone else."

Millar froze. "Are you sure?"

Oen nodded. "That thing must have drained it. And they're hooked up to it now—there's a steady draw from those spears. Problem is, it won't recharge until daytime, and that's if the solar array hasn't been damaged."

Millar saw the arcing of the electricity beyond the open doors and heard a yell.

"That sounded like Doran."

"I can cut off their power," Oen said. "Give him a better chance without those spears. And then set up the other remaining stations to protect our people."

The sound of barking in the distance cut into Millar's head. Those attack dogs were probably already on the townsfolk, and possibly more raiders were on the way. Oen was right. They had to save their people first.

"He's down," one of the raiders said and clapped the other on the back. "Now we can get out of this forsaken place."

"Let's go watch," the other said with a laugh. "Looks like he wasn't as tough as they thought."

Something inside of Millar snapped. "Do it. Overload that station. Now!"

Oen didn't argue and instead typed onto the control panel. "Give me a minute."

The system emitted several beeps, louder than before. One of the guards finally turned around and his eyes widened.

"We don't have a minute!" Millar stood and charged at the raider.

He swung his pry hammer as he ran and caught the raider off guard. With a solid swing he connected with his helmet. Millar felt like he was ringing a bell. The raider dropped to his knees dazedly and then fell over. The other raider, having time to think, stood at the ready with his cudgel and easily blocked Millar's next blow.

The raider stood a head taller than Millar and twice as wide, and he grinned at him. "Nice try, grunt."

Millar swung again, but the raider turned aside so that Millar crashed into the doorframe. The raider laughed and swung his cudgel down. Millar, still filled with adrenaline, rolled out of the way to avoid the blow and stood back up, this time outside the doorway.

There was no way he could beat him, so he tried to lead him out of the hut to let Oen do his work. The guard, not as stupid as he looked, didn't chase Millar immediately and glanced back at Oen on the device.

"Come on, crug!" Millar yelled.

The raider slowly backed his way into the hut. Millar knew Oen didn't stand a chance against him, and so he charged again. He swung his pry hammer hard but the raider was expecting it and easily blocked it. His own cudgel drove into Millar's gut and he felt the air forced out of him. He fell backward and dropped his hammer.

"Oen?"

"Now!"

There was a loud sound that vibrated the ground. The raider looked up and Millar saw the bright lights reflected in his eyes as he stood there, dazed. Millar stumbled to his feet, grabbed the hammer, and brought it down into the raider's foot. The bones crunched and the man screamed. With another swing, Millar connected with the side of his head and he dropped like a bag of stones.

Millar turned around to see Oen's work paying off. A blaze of electrical light erupted around the ring of raiders. In the center, Doran took a stance amidst the glow and Millar's jaw dropped. This once awkward and crippled bot now stood with an internal power. Perhaps it was just the electricity, but Millar thought that there was new strength emanating from within him, or perhaps it had been merely masked.

The spears exploded in a shower of sparks and the raiders dropped them if they could. Those that still held on shook with the energy coursing through their bodies until they fell in smoking piles.

The others, stunned, tried to gather themselves to keep the bots surrounded. The spider-armed bot didn't relent, and swung with its remaining limbs. Doran effortlessly deflected each blow. Millar didn't know if a bot like that could be confused, but it sure looked like it as it stood motionless after Doran easily countered its attack. It took a step backwards.

Doran leapt and drove it to the ground. He stood over its body, ripping its arms off one by one until it was only a quivering chunk of metal with sparks flying. In one last-ditch effort, a panel opened on the bot's torso revealing its cannon. Doran drove his fist straight through an exposed section directly above its armored chest and grabbed onto its spinal shaft.

He picked up the entire bot and spun it around so the cannon faced away from him, snapping its neck so that its crack could be heard all the way back to Millar. The cannon charged up with a whine and Doran spun the bot around just as the beam of energy blasted out of it. The raiders screamed but were cut short as they disintegrated after the beam hit them. The blast stopped, and Doran stood there in silence.

Millar finally let out his breath. He made eye contact with Doran and shrunk back a bit. Doran seemed surprised by his actions and dropped the unmoving bot with a clang.

Other raiders in the distance stumbled after the attack and dropped their weapons. They ran away from the newly leveled clearing where Doran stood.

Only the baying and growling of the dogs could have broken Millar away from the scene. His friends were still in danger. He ran into the hut and tried to catch his breath after that last blow from the raider.

"Can you activate the barrier?"

Oen shook his head. "That drained it."

Behind him, Doran approached while dragging the armless bot's shell behind him. He stood at the doorway.

Millar didn't know what to say. In fact, he was a bit terrified of the bot in front of him now. But the power that was in him earlier seemed to have faded already, and the destructive form he had taken on—for only a few seconds perhaps—had already changed back to the bot he knew. And now he was crippled, limping, and scored with so many cuts that he didn't look like he could still be walking around.

"Use this." Doran dropped the bot's body into the center of the room. "There is minimal power left, but perhaps enough."

Oen, speechless, grabbed the cable connected to the barrier console and looked for a way to couple it to the bot.

"I've got to help the others," Millar said. He left the hut and headed to where Raly and the villagers had made their way. "Get that thing fired up, they might come back!"

"On it."

Millar followed the barking sounds to where the villagers were. They stood back to back with the dogs all around them and swung makeshift weapons and torches at them. Raly stood out in front with blood dripping from her forearm. Some people were on the ground but had been pulled into the center of the circle. Millar hefted his pry hammer and ran at them.

Suddenly a high-pitched whine called out, and all the dogs stopped growling and barking at once. It was like earlier when the bot's sounds had called the dogs away. Did that mean it was still operational?

Doran stepped behind Millar and approached the dogs—the whining had been coming from *him*. The dogs pulled their ears back and ran away into the surrounding woods.

The villagers cheered. Millar ran to Raly and checked on her. It appeared she hadn't been scratched or bitten too badly, and she was now tightening some cloths around her wounds.

A series of clicks and whirs reverberated in the ground, and the barrier system kicked in.

"You did it!" Millar said. "Everyone's here. It worked!"

Raly nodded and ran over to some of the fallen villagers. "Tren?"

She knelt by him and examined his wounds. Blood spilled from his stomach and the color faded from his face. Three or four children sat around him with tears running down their sooty cheeks.

"You saved them," Raly said. "From those dogs."

"Some good it did me," Tren said through heavy breathing and coughing. "Remind me not to do that again."

He held his hands over his stomach and groaned.

"I'm sorry," Raly said and clutched his hand tightly. "You did good. You're no crug."

"Yes I am." Tren smiled grimly and then his body seized. Raly watched the life fade from his eyes.

Tren's brothers knelt by his side. They sat silently and patted Raly on her shoulders.

The fires crackled and finally smoldered into nothing. The night passed slowly, but the raiders were gone.

Chapter 21

"Oen!"

Oen's parents called out to him as he approached from Bruet's hut. They hugged him tightly, and he practically fell into their arms from exhaustion. Now that he had found his parents alive, he could finally rest. So could everybody.

Well, almost everybody.

After almost everyone had fallen asleep, Millar and Raly sat away from the others, close to Doran, and they kept watch on the encampment. The light of their campfire flickered on the remains of their home. Not that it really felt like their home anymore, with the pitted huts, burnt down trees, and the smell of death in the air. It would take some time for this place to go back to the way that it was before, that is, if they were even going to stay there anymore.

Millar stared at a tied-up raider, unconscious and tied up beside the campfire. It was the same one that Oen had knocked out with the pry bar.

"Is he up yet?" Oen prodded him with a stick. "We've got to find out if this is all of them. Or if others are coming."

Millar shook his head. "All the other raiders fled and only left this one behind. No one saw Bel, did they?"

Raly shook her head. "Not since a few days ago, since she left with the skiff."

"I miss her voice," Doran said.

"What do you mean?" Millar said. "Are you starting to remember her?"

Doran's shoulders creaked as he shrugged. "I think I miss her voice. It is hard to tell anymore." He stared at the black stone in the center of his palm.

Raly started sobbing again, and Millar knew it wasn't because she was thinking about Bel. She looked over in the direction of her former home and wept. Millar reached out his hand, yet hesitated and withdrew it again.

It was Doran who comforted her then. His massive hand gently covered her back, and he hummed that same off-key melody that Millar thought he'd recognized somehow. Raly didn't stop crying, but she did reach up to touch Doran's hand.

"This hurts," she said. "I feel so angry. And empty."

Millar nodded. He felt the same way, but he couldn't speak about Mom yet. And with Bel out there somewhere, he felt torn apart.

"Time," Doran said. "Time will erase everything."

"I don't want to erase her," Raly said. "I just want to see her."

The campfire crackled as the wind gusted. The cold night air chilled their bones, but they didn't care. They couldn't feel it. They couldn't feel anything.

"Tell me again what happened," Raly said.

"He fought like… the Cora'chan," Millar said.

"The Cora'chan?"

"Just when it looked like it was all over, he…" Millar struggled for the words. "He summoned something. Just like Mom's old stories. Remember?"

"Of course I remember," Raly said. "I just didn't think he was, you know, capable of that. You're sure he's one of them?"

"Are you?" Millar said to the bot.

Doran turned his hands over and back again. "I do not remember."

"Well you remembered *something*," Millar said. "I saw it. And nothing stopped you."

Doran stared quietly out into the darkness. His twitching hand drew closer to his head, but then he lowered it again. "If not for your help, I am not sure how that would have ended."

Millar shrugged. "Thank Oen. He did all that. But I think you probably would have been just fine without it. The help that is."

"Perhaps."

"What is a Cora'chan doing out in the middle of nowhere?" Millar said. "And you certainly don't look like how Mo… I mean, how Prism described them. What happened?"

Doran didn't respond.

The prisoner started to shift around and then finally sat up. His hands and feet were tied up, and he was bound to a large stake in the ground. His metal helmet lay at his feet.

"Finally." Millar stood and held his pry hammer at the ready.

"What happened?" the raider said. "Where are the others?"

He glanced around and his eyes landed on Doran.

"You lost," Millar said. He watched the anger grow in Raly's eyes and felt his own fists clenching around the hammer. "That's what happened."

"But, you have him," the raider said. "How?"

"What do you mean?" Millar asked. "Why did you do this? We have nothing of value, and you've destroyed what little we had. And where is Bel?"

The man seemed to think about what he was saying and looked away. Millar prodded him.

"What did you do with my sister?"

He was silent.

"They have her," Millar said. "I know it. And we've got to follow them."

"Do you know who they are?" Raly said. "I've never heard of them before. But then, I don't know much about the outside."

Millar nodded. "Me neither. Just a little. I suppose you don't know anything about these people?"

Doran shook his head. Millar sighed.

"I bet the Trades would be able to help. We can ask them in the morning. But I can't sleep yet. Want to go check out that other bot? Maybe it can tell us something."

Raly yawned but nodded. Doran rose to his feet as well.

"You're just going to leave me here?" the raider said. He yanked on the cords and eyed the darkness beyond the firelight.

"Go ahead, try to escape. Start running. See how far you get."

The man looked confused until a shrieking noise broke through the trees and he grew still again. "What was that?"

"I've heard they're native to these hills," Millar said. "They only hunt at night, too. Which is why it's a good thing we got this barrier running again. But if you want to try your luck…"

The man scowled at him and looked back at his helmet on the ground. It emanated a short beep and then silence. Raly picked up the one she had acquired from the girl raider and checked out the inside of it.

"I heard it do that before, but I wasn't sure what it meant. What does it do?"

Millar picked up the raider's helmet and inspected it. It had very simple wiring and a small component box near the base of it.

"Not sure. Doran? Care to take a look?"

He tossed it to the bot and his eyes scanned it with a blue bar of light.

"It is a very rudimentary communication system. It seems to be connected to the others, but it is very weak now. Perhaps it is because of the distance. I believe we can use this to track them down, if we don't get too far away, that is."

"That's good!" Millar said. "Can you see if you can figure out any more of it?"

Doran nodded and kept scanning it.

"Then let's go look at that other bot, and our guest here can decide if he wants to spend the night here or outside the barrier."

Millar stepped through the hut's entrance and saw the bot strewn upon the floor with a black cable hooked up to its neck. Oen had managed to pipe into its energy system and use it to power the main system.

"Oen said there isn't much left in it, not after that blast," Millar said.

It looked like the shell of some curled-up and dead insect. The broken stubs of limbs made it look even more like someone had plucked the legs off a spider. The main body armor really didn't look like it fit right, either.

"That kind of looks like it would fit you," Millar said.

Doran stood in thought for a moment and then reached down to grasp the sides of the armor. He stepped on its legs and yanked with such force that the front plate popped off immediately and spat connecting rivets into the air. Raly and Millar ducked as the pieces flew over their heads and around the room.

A mass of parts like spilled guts lay on the ground in front of the de-shelled bot. Millar's instinct to scrap things took over, and he bent down to see what was useful. After a second, he held up one larger curved part.

"I know this thing. I've seen it before." Millar turned it over and hefted it. "Yeah, it has to be the same one. Bel found this part, or another identical one to it, right here in the High Ansels. I swear though, it has to be the same one. I've never seen anything like it before. A true custom part."

Doran picked it out of his hands and linked it to the armor, and it snapped into place. He rooted around the wreckage and found a few other parts that also fit right together, and then he placed it over his chest. Some internal sounds whirred, the sound of bolts turning, and the chest piece cinched closer to Doran's body until it clicked in place. It was seamless.

Millar stared. "It didn't look right on that other bot. But it fits you like it was built for you."

"That's more like it," Raly said. "That's how I pictured a Cora'chan."

Millar agreed. It added an air of strength to him somehow. It covered all the gouges from the battle, too, which left him appearing new and powerful.

"This is mine." Doran removed the other armor piece from the bot and began to attach it to his back side.

"Do you remember?" Millar asked.

"I know. For good or ill, I just know."

"What about its cannon?" Oen asked. "Can you use that, too?"

Doran tilted his head and looked at the remains hooked up to the system. "It appears pulverized beyond function."

"Pity," Oen said. "Although you didn't look like you needed one just then."

So many questions ran through Millar's mind. Where had Doran lost the armor, if it was his? And why had he removed it? Or had someone else done that?

And then suddenly it all made sense.

"That part—Bel and I gave it to the Trades almost a year ago. They had never seen anything like it. No one had. Although now that I think about it, I wonder if Mom had? Anyway, the Trades must have sent it back to where they do their bartering. And someone noticed it and recognized it. And then they must have tracked the part back here though the Trades. Capturing them, questioning them. We can ask them when we see them in the daylight, but I bet I'm right."

Raly nodded. "Makes sense. But why try to come out here and destroy him?"

"I don't think they were. They had those spears and it looked like they were trying to capture him. Although, I don't think he would have ever gone quietly."

"Unless they could shut me down. And they almost did." The bolts whirred in place on Doran's back and the full suit of armor molded completely around him.

"Cora'chan," Millar said. "Will you help me find Bel?"

Doran nodded. "I was always going to."

Millar smiled and felt hope rise. They would find her and bring her home. Nothing could get in their way. Not now.

Chapter 22

The sun broke through the trees, and Doran's processors kicked in. He awoke to find himself standing upon one foot, his arms held out in front of him. Villagers had arisen and were gathering in groups upon the burnt waste of the town, preparing food. Those that noticed him stared.

He quickly dropped his leg and brought his arms to his side. Flashes of images burst into his head. Storms. Clashing arms with that other bot. Fire raging. But there was something else, too. Something beyond what happened yesterday. This was somehow more intense. An entire city in flames. Screams that tore into his wiring. He reached up to his head to stop the pain, to forget.

And then he saw what was in his hand. It was the small black stone, the nodular obsidian, that Bel had given him. Or so Millar had told him. He must have erased his memory after she gave it to him, but he couldn't do that now, no matter what his programming was insisting.

"What was that?"

Doran started and dropped the stone. He looked down. It was Raly.

"What was what?" He bent over to pick the stone back up.

"What you were doing just then. With your legs, and arms?" Raly tried to stand like he had been but she could barely hold the balanced position for a few seconds.

"I… I do not know."

"You looked at peace," Raly said.

Doran detected a sense of sadness in her words. Sadness? No, that wasn't it, not entirely. He couldn't quite decipher what she was feeling.

"How are the power levels in your barrier?"

Raly stared at him for a moment before answering.

"That bot still has some energy left for one more night, and Oen is checking the solar array right now to make sure it will still be working when it dies. The raiders took whatever they were using to charge it with when they left."

"I do not think their bot will work anymore."

"Yeah, you pretty much ended it last night. Millar says there's no memory core to scan. All those components are glassed from when you fried it. He's trying to figure out where Bel is, or at least where the raiders came from. And that prisoner isn't talking."

"I will take another look at the bot to see what I can determine. Maybe there is something about where it came from."

Raly laughed. "Maybe your memory is better than you think?"

Doran reached down to pick up the black stone. "There are small things I know, and cannot forget."

Raly stood there for a minute in silence, fighting with something to say.

"Is there something you want?" Doran asked.

"Can you help me with something important?"

Doran nodded.

The two of them walked in silence across the village until they came to one of the burnt huts.

"She's still in there." Raly pointed into the charred remains. "I can't get her. I just can't do it."

"Of course. I will help."

Doran brought a blanket with him into the hut. There were burnt wooden beams, and piles of metal bits and boxes all around. Underneath some of the roofing he found her. He wrapped her gently in the blanket and stepped outside to where Raly was waiting, crying.

"Where do you want her?"

Raly beckoned Doran, as she was unable to speak yet. The three of them left the village. It didn't take long and they soon climbed a path to where a gnarled tree overlooked the foggy bay.

"She said this was her favorite place. I asked her why—it was such a simple spot, after all. But she never told me. We'd just go up here whenever I felt sad, or when she needed to talk about something, or just to pick flowers in silence." Raly picked a small purple flower and tossed it over the edge of the hill.

"I think those are very good reasons."

Raly smiled up at Doran. "You're right."

Doran placed Raly's mother on the ground, and together they dug her a grave and laid her to rest.

***

For the first few hours of the morning, that's all the villagers did. They cleared the streets of their fallen family members, burying them in a quiet spot right outside of the circle of huts. Tren's clan was about to bring Tren and Perl to rest outside of the village away from the others, but Bruet insisted that they belonged with the rest of the fallen townsfolk.

Doran helped all he could. At first the villagers were hesitant to have such a large bot around, but it didn't take long for them to accept him. The younger ones even began to play around his legs as he loped past them. They rolled balls back and forth between his strides. When one shot through to the other side, they cheered.

Doran walked into the center of the village, right outside of Bruet's hut, and he heard people already in conversation about what to do next.

"It'll be hard to salvage the solar array," Oen said. "Part of it's been wrecked, and the rest is in real bad shape."

"Then we will have to abandon our home, for now," Bruet said. "Without a way to protect us, and since those raiders know exactly where we live, they'd come back and finish the job. Even if they do not, the patarks are still out there."

"But this is our best chance," Oen said. "We have enough power for a day or two as it is, and then we have the Trades here to help."

One of the members of the Trades, an older woman of perhaps forty years named Kech, rose to speak. She wore a strange-looking oversized belt that seemed like it should be awkward, but its perfectly balanced straps made it easy for her to carry.

"Oen is right," Kech said. "We should stay here. It is not as safe out there. We were kidnapped two months ago by these raiders. They are from the mainland beyond the sea here, although we don't know from where exactly. Our people tend to believe they found something worth salvaging from our supply and tracked us down back to the High Ansels."

"They found pieces of him." Millar pointed to Doran. "I think they were after him."

"That is true," Kech said. "They asked us who found the parts, where they found them."

"He is indeed rare and powerful," Bruet said. "But why so much pain and suffering over one bot?"

"That is uncertain," Kech said. "Their numbers have grown recently, perhaps they are attempting to grow their army. Their bot, however basic it was in its functions, did have that armor, but it was not its own. This bot, Doran, looks to be the true owner, yes?"

Everyone looked at Doran's armor and agreed.

"We overheard some of them speaking of how they found it hidden in a mountain somewhere. I believe they will keep looking for him."

"Then perhaps he needs to leave," Bruet said. "And the captured raider needs to know that, too, so he can tell his people he has left."

"That's great," Millar said. "Doran saves the entire village, and now you want to kick him out for it?"

"Would they have come if he wasn't here?" Bruet said.

"But…" Millar got up and balled his fists up. "But I was the one who found the part in the first place. Or Bel did, anyway. I'm the one who gave it to the Trades."

Doran put his hand on Millar's shoulder. "Prudence implies he is correct, and I should leave."

"It's not fair though," Millar said.

"I apologize for all that has happened, if it was because of me," Doran said to Bruet and the others in the circle. "I will leave immediately."

"Me too," Millar said. "It's my fault you're here. And Bel being gone. I will go look for her."

Bruet sighed. "It is unfortunate. You were of great help to us, Doran, and we thank you."

Doran bowed to him.

Kech stood. "I need to see if the path is clear for the rest of the Trades. I will go with you too."

"That is good," Doran said. "You can help us to track down the raiders."

Kech smiled. "I will do my best."

"Oen?" Millar said. "What about you? Are you coming?"

His friend froze up for a moment. "But, my parents, and the village. I should help where I can, right? They need to get this system up and running again. Without it, we've got no protection."

"That makes sense," Millar said. His voice sounded dejected. "What about you, Raly?"

Raly lit up. "Yeah, of course I'll go."

Millar stood up. "Then let's get moving, Bel is out there somewhere."

Chapter 23

"How long do you think we'll be gone?" Raly said.

"Days, weeks, who knows," Kech said. "I need to travel to the nearest settlement east. Terask, just past Ranan Bay. That's a few days of travel at least. Better take along as much gear as you can carry."

Millar hadn't thought of that. He could only think of Bel being right around the corner. The furthest he had ever traveled was when Mom brought him here from his old home, and back then he didn't have to worry about packing.

The Trades helped them with food, water, and some other items they thought they might need. Millar strapped the pry hammer onto his back like he would have done for any scav trip.

"Where did you get that thing?" Kech asked. "I've always meant to ask you that. It's a real piece of work. A solid tool, and a weapon in a pinch, too. I might have to submit a request for a weapon like that to become standard equipment for the Trades guild."

"I got it from my home," Millar said. "My other home, I mean. It's the only thing I took. I guess Mom took it, though. I was too little to carry it but I wouldn't let her leave it behind."

"Was it someone else's?" Raly asked.

"It was from my parents. My real parents." Millar stuffed the last few items into his pack. "All right, I think I'm ready. Am I all good, Kech?"

She checked his pack and slapped it. "I think you're as good as any Trades on their way through a route. I think you'll be all right."

"Just all right?" Millar asked. "Not what I wanted to hear."

"Well, I've been doing this work for twenty years now. I've been through some real stuff, and we've come to expect something new every trip. But this is the first time I've seen anything like that." Kech pointed to Doran.

"His name is Doran, by the way," Raly said.

"Nice to meet you, Doran." Kech walked over to him and reached up her hand.

Doran bent over and held her hand and shook it. "The pleasure is mine, Tradesperson Kech."

Kech smiled over to Raly. "Did you hear that? He's heard of me."

They all laughed. Millar thought it good to start off the search mission this way. He hefted his pack and looked over at the villagers seeing them off. Oen stood to the side, looking anxious and a little upset over the decision to stay behind. Whether it was fully his decision or the will of his parents, it was hard to tell.

"We're going to miss you," Millar said. "You sure you can't come? If your parents are worried about the danger, we've got a heavily armed Trades and a huge bot with us. And there's Raly too, she's pretty fierce."

Raly laughed.

"Yeah," Oen said. "I want to go, but they need me. My parents, and the village."

"They've got a half-dozen more Trades there with working knowledge of the barrier system to get it all set up. They helped Mom develop its schematics, including getting some hard to find parts for it and all. Don't you think they should be here instead of you?"

Oen shrugged. "I've been around since it started needing repairs and updates."

"Well, you take care of yourself." Millar started to walk away but then turned back around. "Your parents are lucky to have you. Really, I'm going to miss you."

Oen looked away.

"Come on," Kech said. "We're losing daylight, and we want to be at the South Pass by sundown. And kid?"

Oen turned around.

"If you want, you can travel with the other Trades and cut across the bay if you change your mind. They will wait here until the village is safe and then some will move on there. You'll save time to meet us in Terask by going that way. We should be there in four days."

Oen nodded.

Millar slowly walked away from the village and waved to them all. Bruet held up his hand.

"We are going to give you three days head start before releasing the prisoner," Bruet said. "That should give you a big enough lead on him so he can't directly tell his people where you are going, only that you are all leaving. Farewell, friends."

The four of them left the village just as the sun rose to its highest point in the sky. The path to the pass would take a few hours, and despite the excitement of the adventure and the prospect of finding Bel, Millar felt strangely reluctant to leave. Perhaps it was the unknown. Perhaps it was saying goodbye to home and friends.

As if reading his mind, Kech held up the prisoner's helmet. "We'll use this to try to track down the others, see if we can get a location on them. Doran, think we can take a look at the tracking system that is embedded here?"

Kech seemed excited to be out here again, in her natural element, and even Raly seemed freer now, having left the confines of the village. Millar felt jealous of them both for that.

"Anyone hungry?" Kech asked.

"We just left," Millar said. Despite that, he felt the need to grab something from his pack.

"Huh," Kech said. "I never thought about it, but what about you, Doran? I haven't seen you need to recharge. What kind of power source are you running?"

Doran walked a few more strides before answering. "As far as I know, I have woken every day and not needed an energy charge."

"What, is it an ultra solar, maybe? Some sort of fusion reactor?" Kech peeked up at his access panels. "You're pretty old and dinged up. Whatever you've got in there is a solid system."

"I will run a diagnostic," Doran said. He sounded like he had never had to run one of those before.

"Hmm," Kech said. "All right, but I'd love to take a look under the panels sometime, maybe on our next break?"

"Is that why you wanted food so soon?" Millar said. "An excuse to check him out?"

Kech laughed. "I meant it when I said I haven't seen anything quite like him before. I guess it is just my curious nature. To tell you the truth, one of the reasons we decided to help you was to find out more about him. But yes, that would have made a fine excuse to examine him."

"What do you know of the Cora'chan?" Raly asked.

That broke Kech's stride. "The Cora'chan. Is that what you think he is?"

"So not much, then?"

"That's hard to say," Kech said. "No one alive has ever seen one of them. So anything you have heard is perhaps only a tale about a story about a legend about a kernel of truth. I am sure you and I have heard, and probably told, our share of these tales, yes? It is one of the Trades' greatest dreams to find a Cora'chan. In fact, it is one of our five Life Quests."

Raly and Millar smiled at each other.

"Life Quest? Really?" Millar said. "That sounds so epic. I thought you just, well, traded things for us."

Kech smiled. "That is a small portion of what we do. As a rule, we don't share much of that with outsiders."

"But, you're a part of our village!" Raly said.

Kech bowed. "I thank you for thinking that. I suppose we have been doing what we do for years with you, for you to think of us as one of your own. Most villages, however, don't feel that way. In fact, most don't even know our names."

Millar blushed.

"Ah, it's all right," Kech said. "I don't know if we've ever spoken before for you to know mine. I only know who you are because of Tobes."

"Huh?"

"Tobes speaks highly of you and your friends. You always find the most choice parts. You're one of the main reasons why the Trades keep such strong routes with the High Ansels."

Raly smiled. "We're famous, Millar."

"Don't be silly," Millar said. Although he couldn't quite wipe that grin off his face, either.

"I'm just saying, you two are fine scavs. Keep up the good work. As for the Trades, my paths have led me to study at the back end of the country here. The bay and the High Ansels are all that's left to the west. Few have gone over the seas that way." Kech waved away beyond the hill.

"And don't forget that island." Millar pointed down the hill into the middle of the bay. "You must know all about that?"

"Too dangerous," Kech said. "The waters can be very rough and combined with the razor sharp rocks, they'll chew up your boat. And the cliffs? We've only seen them from afar. No one has been there, or at least no one has recorded it."

"We made it," Raly said. "And that's where we found Doran."

Kech stared. "That's impossible."

Millar shook his head. "We chased Bel there, the other night. She came there on her own. She was in a really good boat, though."

Raly smiled.

"Then your path was blessed," Kech said. "For we have ever failed in our attempt to get there. And that was even during the day."

From the oversized belt, Kech removed a strange-looking book that was bound in metal plates, and she flipped out a stand from the front of her jacket. She propped the book in front of her. There was a large number fifteen engraved on the cover of the book. She flipped the book to a fresh page of gray paper and drew a pen from her pocket.

"That is really something," Millar said to Raly. She nodded in agreement.

"Thanks, it makes it a lot easier to walk and write or read at the same time."

"You have to do that a lot?" Millar said.

"It saves time. Now, tell me all about what you found there."

"If you want to know about the island, you should ask him," Millar said. "He'd be happy to talk about it, right Doran? That was your home, right? Although, his memory is a bit spotty about lots of things."

Kech smiled. "This day is just getting better and better. Why doesn't everyone just tell me what you found, and I will be happy to record it all here. One at a time."

***

By the time they reached the South Pass at sundown, Kech had filled several pages with her neat script. Millar and Raly had to often go back on their descriptions to make sure they were exact before she would write anything, and when she found out that Oen had gone with them, too, she almost just scrapped the whole idea of recording everything. But, in the end, she recorded what they said, leaving a note that Oen's recounting of the trip would need to be added at a later time.

Doran, unfortunately for Kech, didn't have much to add. She still wrote what he had to say, with interest, but she included that his memory was not one hundred percent reliable and that he'd probably left out some things of importance.

"Hey, you're not really limping anymore," Raly said. "Did you fix yourself up?"

Doran shook his head. "Not directly. The subsystems rewired themselves."

"Like, they healed up?" Raly asked.

"I suppose they act like your own subsystem in that regard."

"And you, Millar," Kech said. "You haven't spoken to anyone in quite some time. What's on your mind?"

Millar flipped his visor down and scanned the hills. "No one seems to know where the raiders came from, and they sure left in a hurry without much of a trace. It's Bel. I'm worried about her, obviously."

Doran handed the raider's helmet to Millar. "I have been working on this to see what it does. It is a crude system of tracking, and I may be able to get it to register something if we can boost its signal."

"Really?" Millar breathed out a sigh. "Because I've been kind of lost on how to find her. How does it work?"

"Try it on."

The helmet was a snug fit, but it felt solid. A warbled signal resonated from the back and changed frequency as he turned his head.

"I don't get it."

"It is a very subtle mechanism. I believe they would say there is a certain art to using it. If I keep studying it and upload it to my own processor, I will decipher it."

"Is this what you get from yours?" Millar said to Raly. "A bunch of static?"

"I guess I've tuned it out." Raly tapped the side of her helmet. "Is there a danger of it sending a signal to them, as well?"

Doran paused. "I will check on it, and update that if needed. Block outgoing signals. Good idea."

They both handed their helmets to Doran and he busily got to work on them as they walked into the South Pass camp. The area was situated between the way back to the Anselian Peninsula and a crossroads heading south to the town of Terask and the other way north to the Coastal Cliffs. From here, they could look back at their home far away beyond Doran's island in the bay. Of course, from this distance they couldn't pick out anything beyond grays and greens, but they knew it was there.

Other travelers, probably the Trades, had left split and dried wood covered just beyond the campsite. Kech took off her pack and went to gather the firewood there.

"It's going to be dark soon, and despite being off the hills, there's a chance we might see patarks out here."

"Need help?" Millar offered.

"No thank you, there's a spring you can help refill our skins with, though. You must be tired though, yes?"

Millar shook his head, as did Raly.

"That's good, because today was an easy day." Kech smiled and left the site.

Raly waited until she was out of earshot. "An *easy* day? I thought we were in shape."

Millar stretched his back and neck. "Me too."

Doran sat down on a flat slab of granite. "Me too."

Millar gathered the water skins and brought them to a clear flowing spring near the fire stones to start filling them.

"Have you ever seen a patark?" Raly said.

Millar shook his head. "I thought maybe I did once. I guess I'm glad I haven't. They say if you see one, they've already seen you. I've sure heard them, though."

Raly shivered. "That was them, back before we left, right? I don't want to think about being caught out there without a camp, or whatever. We won't have to worry about them here, right? Kech didn't sound too worried."

"I don't think so. I'm just wondering where the raiders went off to, and if they took Bel with them."

"Don't worry," Raly said. "We'll find her."

Kech returned with an armload of logs and threw them near the pit. "Can you get this going? I'm going to check the area for tracks, to see if any raiders or anything else has been here.'"

"Of course," Millar said.

"Are you sure you don't want any help?" Raly asked.

"What you're doing is enough, and needed. I'll be right back."

Kech walked away, and Raly slumped onto a stone near the fire pit. "She's in charge of everything, apparently."

"She has good reason," Millar said. "Have you ever been out of the village like this before?"

Raly shook her head.

"Me neither, not really. Not in a while. Not since I was little, and even then I was with Mom."

He found some tinder and began a small fire. Its crackling was the only sound as they both thought in silence.

"You came this way, right?" Raly asked a minute later.

Millar nodded. "I barely remember the trip here, but yeah, we climbed in, not by boat. I was no more than five, I think, so I don't remember much. Fires, screams. And Mom. I barely remember my real parents now. You know, just images of them. What about you?"

"I don't remember coming to the High Ansels. My mother said I was two when we came, so I have no idea. I've only known our home up there. And now, it's gone."

"It's not gone," Millar said.

"I know it feels gone," Doran said.

Millar and Raly started, they had almost forgotten he was sitting behind them.

"Your biggest memories have been taken away from you, and it feels like there is nothing left. And that your world will collapse. But they will always be there for you."

Millar took out Mom's memory cube and stared at it. "I guess I still have this."

"Do you think there's something on there that can help us find Bel?" Raly asked.

"Maybe," Millar said. "But we've still got to find a place to view it."

"A memory cube?" Kech said as she returned. "Not many places that still have equipment to operate something like that. If you're serious about it, though, we could get to Terask and see."

"That's still days out though, right?" Millar said. "If there's something on there that might help it'd be better to check it out sooner than later."

Kech pondered this as she threw a bigger log onto the small fire. "We can't see it now, but up there to the north is the village of Hinarum. Up in the Coastal Cliffs. They horde old tech and they've got it for show, like a museum. A little bit of a hike, but they might have what you're looking for to access that cube."

"You okay if we go there?" Millar asked.

"I can lead you there safely, so it's no problem for me," Kech said.

Raly yawned. "As long as I get some sleep tonight I'll be up for anything."

Millar smiled. "Thanks, I just want to be sure of every possibility."

"Well, if that's settled, let's eat!"

Kech surprised them all with a food stash that had been left behind the encampment, care of the Trades. It contained dried meats and fruits.

"Real food?" Millar said. "We've had nothing but bars and some berries as of late."

"You ate those berries?" Raly said. "They couldn't have been ripe yet."

"What about you, Doran?" Kech said. "We don't have anything to offer you. When was the last time you consumed anything?"

Doran looked up from the helmets he had been tinkering with. "I do not know."

Millar pointed to his head.

"Is it a faulty wiring system?" Kech asked. "I can take a ..."

"No," Doran said, startling them all. "No thank you," he followed up with a quieter tone and then stood up. "I will take the watch tonight."

"Thank you," Millar said. "And you're okay with going to Hinarum tomorrow?"

"There is nothing in my data files regarding it. I only wish to help you find your sister. And I am sorry for my behavior at times. I am learning again. Or perhaps for the first time."

Raly laughed. "I'm sure you learned before. You knew Prism. She would have taught you a few things."

Millar laughed. "Yeah, she would have."

"We just want to make sure you're not going to lose your memory," Raly said. "That's why Kech wanted to look."

"I do not think it is a hardware issue."

"What do you mean?" Millar said.

"I believe it is me."

"You?"

"Ever since meeting you, I have kept my memory. But there are times when I feel myself starting to try to reset my memory system. I may have erased everything I have ever known." Doran pointed to his head.

"But why?" Millar and Raly said, almost at the same time.

Doran was silent.

"Have you ever wished you could forget something?" Kech said. "Something that happened to you, or someone else?"

Raly nodded.

"Then is it so hard to believe a bot would do that too?"

"I guess not," Millar said. "But what would a bot need to forget?"

Doran walked over to the edge of the campfire light and began his watch while humming a soft and gentle tune.

Chapter 24

"Hey, are you awake?"

Doran started and shook his head. Where was he? What was he doing? He looked down at the person standing next to him.

"You just froze. Is everything all right?"

It was Raly, standing in a peculiar but familiar way. She was trying to balance on one foot and her arms were out in front of her. It was not so peculiar, however, as he noted that he was standing in the exact same stance, albeit with less swaying. She waved her hands in front of his face.

"You said you would show me this some morning," she said. "I woke early and you were already out here. I asked if I could stay and you said I could."

"I do not remember coming out here… Wait, I talked to you?" Doran ran through his memory history for the last hour.

Raly relaxed her posture and walked to his side. "Maybe you were dreaming, and sleepwalking. Is that a thing bots can do?"

Doran finished his scan and came up with nothing.

"I have no record of any of that."

"That's all right," Raly said. "Sometimes I know I had a dream, but then when I wake up, it's gone. It's like my mind wipes it all away. Maybe that happened to you?"

"Maybe," Doran said. "But, I am…"

"A bot? You still have a brain though, right?"

"Of sorts." This was confusing, and he did not like confusion. It was almost like that cat he thought he'd chased out of his home. Was he glitching?

His arm moved again toward his head, but he caught himself. That was a subconscious action he really wished he did not have to deal with every time something concerning arose, making it so he felt like he had to erase his memory.

They stood there in silence for a moment, staring at the sun rising in the eastern sky over the top of the island that had been his home. How long had he been out there? Long enough for no one to have any memory of him. It was like the land had wiped its memory of him.

He laughed.

Prism would have thought that was funny, too.

"Shall we continue?" Raly struck the awkward pose she had been in earlier. She couldn't hold it for very long, and she fell off balance back onto two feet. "I'm not very good."

"You just started," Doran said. "It will take some time to practice."

How long, he did not know. He, too, stood on one leg and greeted the sun, only briefly noting that he had just thought something that Prism, a bot that he had no memory of, would think funny.

***

"Those are the cliffs?" Millar asked.

Kech pulled up her visor first. "That's them. They may look like they're way up there, but there's a road that will do the trick. The Trades use it all the time to get up there."

"Still looks like a rough road."

"I never said it wasn't." Kech strapped her pack onto her back and inspected the campsite. "Is it worth it to you to still head up there?"

Millar turned Mom's memory cube in his hand. "For now, yes. Although if we don't find anything out through this I guess we're still learning something. Let's go."

The four of them turned to the north and began the switchback road that led to Hinarum. It didn't take long for them to be huffing along the trail as it grew steeper.

"They don't expect a lot of traffic up here, do they?" Raly said.

"Mainly the Trades," Kech said. "Although there are pilgrimages from the local tribes along the south to Terask and beyond."

"What, like a religious thing?" Millar asked.

"In a way. Like I said, they have more of a museum than a shrine or temple. You will see what I'm talking about when we get there."

"If we get there," Millar said.

After another half hour, they barely had enough breath to say more than a few words. Kech fared better than the other two, but still she was offering breaks more readily now. Doran had no issues navigating the landscape.

"Shall I carry you?" he offered to Millar and Raly.

"No!" they both said.

"And why didn't you ask Kech?" Millar said. "She looks tired, too."

"Comparative analysis. I have monitored your heart rates and collectively, you two—"

"That's all right. I don't need to have an examination done. I guess I need more work in this area." Millar let out a deep breath and carried on.

Thick mosses and ferns peppered the hillside, and through the trees and cliff tops they began to spy towers jutting into the sky. Their pace picked up when they noticed they were getting closer, and perhaps because the intense climb began to level out a bit.

"How many people live there?" Raly asked.

"Two hundred, perhaps," Kech said. "Not much bigger than your village. People do not move there intentionally, I believe. The young ones often move out to bigger towns, as most are not as interested in the elders' study of lore. For me, I rather enjoy the idiosyncrasies of the town, as I often get to research when I am there."

"What is it that you do?" Doran said. "From what I initially gathered, I thought the Trades were mainly a way for the people of the High Ansels to get food."

Kech smiled. "That is part of it, that's true. But our main passion and training lies elsewhere. We are historians. But unlike the people in Hinarum, who dig up artifacts on their cliff and revere them, we travel and explore. And then we gather our work, write books, and share that knowledge."

"So, you should know about these raiders, then?" Millar said.

"We should." Kech frowned. "We know much, but not everything. These people just appeared. Along with that many-armed bot, that you destroyed."

Doran bowed.

"I don't think she was thanking you for that," Millar said. "It sounds like she wanted it to be functional."

"A necessary evil, I suppose," Kech said. "We did not have a chance to study it, where it came from, why it arose. I should say that although I did not have a chance, I am sure the others are examining what remains now."

"I will try not to do that if I am in that situation again," Doran said.

Kech started to laugh. "A sense of humor in a bot? That's new for me."

"Have you seen many of them?" Millar said. "Bots that is."

"Mainly in pieces. Your Mom, Prism? She was an anomaly. And there are fewer than ten fully functional ones I have seen in my lifetime. Trades records indicate more, but I haven't seen them. I believe that whoever still possesses such things keeps them functional only for show. The nearest in Terask needs to be cabled up to a power source and even then their primary cores don't allow for independent use."

Raly raised her eyebrows.

"That was a lot of words," Kech said. "I am sorry, I am used to just going on like that. The one in Terask is remote controlled."

"Got it," Raly said.

"So, needless to say, Doran here is pretty special among bots." Kech looked up at him and then at the cliffs. "Ah! We're here!"

The path reached a couple of rock towers at the top and then turned down into a large, bowl-shaped area filled with yurts and huts, like those found in the High Ansels. The cliff wall formed a circular barrier around the village. They walked into the center of it all and stared around. What struck them the most was the beautiful building set apart from the huts. Gilded with gold and two-storied.

Doran paused and reached for his head.

"What is it?" Millar said.

"When we entered this place, there was an influx of energy." Doran wobbled slightly. Images flashed into his mind, this time of wind through the cliff tops.

"Where is everybody?" Millar asked.

Kech put her hand on the spiked mallet by her side. "They're usually out here, greeting us."

"Did the raiders hit them, too?" Raly said.

Doran scanned the village. "There is no major damage, but that does not mean they did not pass through here. Perhaps they kidnapped them all."

"That's awful," Millar said.

A sudden deep and rhythmic drumming reverberated out from the cliff walls. They all froze and stood back to back to scan the buildings for movement and wondered who or what was being announced.

No one.

Boom, boom, the drums continued.

"Raiders?" Millar said. "Did they lay a trap for us? Did they track us on these helmets?" He drew out his pry hammer.

Doran tried to shepherd the others behind him, but it wasn't clear which way was the front as the sound came from all around. Behind them, there was a huge crash like something falling and hitting the ground. They turned around and saw a strange sight. It was a bot, but it was on its side struggling to right itself after jumping from the ledge. It rolled back and forth several times before getting to its feet again.

It was a stout thing, wider than tall, and little more than half of Doran's height. It had a strange head built right into the front of its wide body. Three eyes stared out at them, blinking blue and red lights. It stood there, assuming an offensive position. Doran relaxed a little, after assessing the potential threat. Millar, Raly, and Kech all lowered their guard as well, and Kech even chuckled a bit.

The new bot gave them a short salute with a flick of its metal fingers.

A sudden sound of strings snapping made them all duck. A volley of arrows whipped past them and a few plinked into Doran's armor and bounced off. They spun around to see who shot at them, but there was no one there, just the towers surrounding them.

In that split second of confusion, the other bot ran up right behind Doran. No one noticed it until it swung a massive arm around like a wrecking ball right into Doran's back. It struck with a clang and Doran flew face first into the dirt and skidded leaving a large track behind him.

"Get to cover," Doran said through the dust in his mouth.

Millar looked around, and there was nowhere to hide besides a few huts. They'd have to do.

"This way!" Millar pulled Kech and Raly over to a larger one and opened the door.

Three villagers dressed in leather aprons waited for them with bows drawn and the arrows pointed right at them.

Another volley of arrows shot at Doran, this time including something larger than before. When this one struck near him as he tried to stand up, it shook the ground with a small explosion. He rocked, unbalanced, on his feet once again. The other bot railed into him with his two arms clasped together this time and swung a massive uppercut into his chin.

Doran was knocked back into the air and landed with a thud and a splat into mud. It was a harder struggle to get to his feet but this time Doran was angry. The awkward little stout bot was more nimble than they suspected, or perhaps that had been a show all along. Doran spun in the mud to try to get his footing but slipped and fell.

Millar backed away from the leather-clad villagers, confused. "We're not trying to hurt you, what are you doing?"

They looked at each other, confused. "You're one of *them*."

Doran got to his feet, but now another projectile launched high into the air and exploded above him. A shower of bolts rained down, and at the same time a net unraveled and flung onto Doran, catching him unbalanced again. He wavered on his feet, and this time he saw the smaller bot make a dash for him, his fists reared back for another blow.

Before he could make contact, Doran sidestepped the attack and reached down for the bot's arms. He grabbed onto them through the net and twisted and stepped through the attack. Doran used the bot's forward momentum against it to keep it barreling forward and it careened into a hut, smashing it into pieces immediately.

"I'm sorry!" The bot picked up some of the pieces of the hut and carefully looked underneath. It appeared relieved when it didn't find anyone inside.

Doran grabbed at the netting and fought to pull it off of him. It tangled onto his limbs, though, and he struggled.

Raly removed her helmet. "We're not them, we're looking for them after they attacked *our* home."

Kech pushed herself in front. "I am from the Trades, you know me. Call off your bot!"

But the stout bot had spun around and launched at Doran one more time. Doran stripped off the remainder of the netting and stood now at the ready, balanced upon one leg, his arms out in front of him. The bot pulled out of his frantic run and swung his arms, but Doran was ready. He slipped by the attack and spun around and drove his foot into a sweeping kick right into the bot's upper body.

The bot's whole top half cracked into a sharp angle and it staggered around like a drunk. Millar cringed, wondering how it still stayed on its feet. Doran closed in and pulled back his fists to finish it.

"Two, stop!" a voice cried out, and a whistle sounded.

The drums ceased. The other bot wobbled awkwardly from one foot to the other until it sank onto the ground with a thud. Doran stalked up to it, staring at its head.

"That is mine." Doran pointed to the bot's face plate and then balled up his fists. "I will take it back."

Millar ran up just as Doran reached out and grabbed both sides of the bot's wide body.

"Wait, stop!" Millar said. "It's not our enemy."

Doran tightened his grip on him and began to squeeze. Gears seized up and it started to grind as he crushed his fists in anger. The bot's big eyes flashed red and blue in a thoughtful, almost sad way.

"Doran," Raly said, now behind him as well.

Doran turned around and saw his friends and also others. They were the people of Hinarum, all out from the hidden places in their huts and climbing down from the cliff walls. None of them held weapons, but many held their arms out to him in reverence.

"It is you!" some cried.

"He is here!"

"The Cora'chan!"

Chapter 25

"Please let go of my head now."

Doran turned to face the round, shorter bot pinned beneath him. He removed his hands in a start, as if suddenly realizing what he had been doing.

The other bot's body twitched violently for a second, but then it reached up with one arm and smacked the side of its head several times. The twitching stopped.

"I got that installed the other week and it was working just fine, too. And you had to go and twist it all off kilter again. Thanks a lot."

Doran stood up. "I am… sorry?"

"It's fine, it's fine. These people gather these pieces from all over the place, flip me on, and there we go. Back in the scrap pile. Can you give me a hand here please, uh…?" It reached out its arm.

"Doran." Doran gripped its massive fist and pulled it up to its feet. "And your designation is…?"

"Two."

"Two what?"

"Just Two. I know, I know. I don't think these people had a chance to come up with anything better, and my systems are still booting up since gaining awareness, so I can't think of a better name. But I guess anything would be a better name, no? I could pick one now. Dirt. Grass. What do you think? Better than 'Two?'"

Doran looked around at the people surrounding them now.

"Can someone tell me what is going on here?" Millar said. "Who are you? Why did you call him the 'Cora'chan?'"

The rest of the townsfolk came out of their houses now and streamed toward Doran. An old woman carrying a walking stick stepped out of the group and held out a wavering hand.

"That is their leader, Intari," Kech said.

"We are sorry," she said. "First we saw your helmets, and then we mistook you for that other bot from a distance. Once we saw that armor we called on Two to lead an attack."

Doran nodded. "No harm done."

"Really?" Two adjusted his wide upper body with a crack. "Because I'm not sure if this will ever be the same. And what did you mean by 'that's mine?' earlier, followed by trying to rip my head apart? I'm not going to lie, that was a little terrifying."

Doran reached out and pointed to Two's head, and the other bot flinched. "I can sense a part of you that belongs to me. I think I am going to need it back."

"Whoa, not so fast. In my head? You're just going to have to trust me that by removing this, you're going to kill me, or at least lobotomize me, which is essentially killing me. Back me up on this, people." Two turned to the villagers and waved his arms to drum up a response.

The old woman walked around Doran, inspecting him.

"You are not complete," she said. "You are only the core of what you were. But you are building yourself up again."

Doran self-consciously touched the new armor he wore.

"You know him?" Millar asked.

"No, but we know of him. We have studied, we have read, we have learned much. But we have never seen. The Cora'chan will walk the path once more, it is said."

"Come on," Two said. "For the past month you've been praising me. Now you're thinking of ripping my head apart and giving this guy his nav system back?"

"My nav system?" Doran asked.

A flash, a part of a vision, flitted in front of Doran's eyes as he drew closer to Two. He saw more lightning storms and pouring rain, but the images only lasted for a fraction of a second.

"Where did you get that?"

"They built me," Two said. "Put me together from parts they found."

"But where did this part specifically come from?"

Two shrugged with a metal creak.

Kech stepped forward and addressed the villagers. "You know me, I have been to your village before. Perhaps we should head into the museum and discuss this?"

Intari smiled and pointed to the gilded building. "The temple? Yes, let us go together. Come. See what was left behind."

She reached out to Doran's hand lightly and led him across the village to the temple. Two lumbered behind them and tried to peek around to see what they were doing.

Kech walked back with Millar and Raly, both dumbfounded from what was happening.

"I have seen Two before, but they were constructing him. The people here have been collecting parts from us for years but he was never working until recently. Look, he is not all the same. He is a collection of pieces from different bots."

Doran overheard this and looked closely at the other bot. He did have different types of metals on his body, and he even walked with a slight limp, not from an injury, but because one leg looked taller than the other.

They reached the temple, and the mass of villagers behind all dropped to their knees as the great door opened. The leader walked inside with Doran holding her hand. Two lumbered in behind and followed them onto a great dais at the center of the room. He eased himself down onto it like settling upon a well-used chair.

"Intari," Kech said. "Tell us what you know of the raiders."

The old woman settled onto a stone bench surrounding the dais and motioned the others to do so as well. Doran looked around the room and noticed display stands everywhere. They all held different objects, some hand-written scrolls, others containing a variety of different sized metal pieces.

"A few days ago, a large group of warriors arrived. They came in from the south hills, as you did, so we were able to watch them before they got here. In that short time, we could not prepare ourselves for an attack, especially not against their arsenal, and what they brought with them."

"I scanned them." Two tapped his head. "With this. Made a quick decision to hide our children and took them into our cliffs. I realized I would not be able to defeat their bot. But it looks like you did."

Doran nodded.

"They wanted our food," Intari said. "And information."

"Information?" Kech said.

"About the High Ansels."

"A group of them must have broken off from where we were being held," Kech said. "They got the information about the security system from us, mostly."

"They asked about their other defenses, and since we didn't know, they left us alone. I was afraid of them finding Two."

"See, just hearing it sounds wrong," Two said. "You've got a good name, Intari. You couldn't have thought of a better one for me?"

Intari smiled at this.

"And that's it?" Millar said. "They just left after that? Because they destroyed our village out on the High Ansels."

"They said they would be back," Intari said. "Which is why we were prepared for a fight. What would they have done this time? Destroyed our people? Kidnapped them? In our fear, we thought their bot was leading the attack. Two was brave enough to lead the defense."

"Do you know where they came from?" Kech asked. "They took someone from the village, we think."

"We only know they came from the south."

"Terask," Kech said. "We were going there next, someone there will have to know something."

Millar stood up. "You've got a lot of old tech around here, do you have something that could read this?" He held out Prism's memory cube.

Intari reached for it and turned it over in her wrinkled hand. "Yes, yes. Model A12 from the Spark series."

She bowed her head in reverence as she spoke.

"The Spark Series," her people repeated behind her, almost as a chant.

Intari raised her hand in summons, and a white-vested child with a shaved head ran over to her. Millar looked at Raly but neither said a word.

Intari whispered something to the acolyte who then turned and ran to a glass box at the far wall. The child drew out a chain with a key attached to it from around his neck. After several neat motions, he opened the glass and pulled out the metal box inside. It was no bigger than his hand. He brought it over to Intari, head bowed and hands holding the box in front of him.

Intari took it and showed it to Millar. "By itself it will not work. We can install this in a bot, such as Two, and he can read it for you."

Two banged onto his chest plate below his face and a hollow sound rang. "That's me, a bunch of old parts slapped together, with plenty of room for more components. Here, I can install this, but it will take some time to boot up and interface with my system. May I?"

Intari smiled and offered up the part. "For this sacred quest, you will take this and join them."

"Join us?" Millar said.

"Join them?" Two said.

"For the Cora'chan, the mission must be of the utmost importance."

"Are you sure you have the right bot?" Doran asked. "I have no memory of being the Cora'chan."

Intari pointed to a simple painting hanging upon a wall. There was a simple image of a large bot holding a sword aloft, drawn with black paint in quick, sweeping strokes.

"Is that one of them?" Doran asked.

"If it is, it doesn't really look like him," Millar said.

"It is," Intari said. "This metal that you wear, it is yours?"

"I believe so," Doran said. "I took it off of another bot that attacked their village."

"It clearly fits you. It is made of material found far to the south, as are these helmets." Intari pointed to Millar and Raly. "Perhaps you should look there.

Perhaps even to Metlar, to the Keep there. Surely they would have information about the armor."

Kech shook her head but said nothing.

"I just wish I remembered something," Doran said.

Intari smiled. "Your memories are gone, like the wind. But that doesn't make you any less powerful. Your armor has been returned. Other pieces will return in time. And perhaps your thoughts."

"Sorry," Two said. "Must be rough to lose your memory like that. But, like I said, I don't think it's a good idea for him to take this back. I will come with you and help you. This thing of yours has got some pretty high-tech tracking and analysis systems."

"Do not worry," Doran said. "I have no intention of taking it back now. But where did you find it, Intari? This piece?"

"His parts have come from all over." Intari walked next to Two and pointed out different pieces as she spoke. "This leg from the shores of Gern. His shell from the mountains of Ja-wye. But the system that was yours came from right here in Hinarum."

She pounded the ground with her staff. "On this very platform. Years ago we came here and excavated this site and unearthed the relic from beneath the cliffs. The piece was most cleverly hidden and it was but a chance find. Thus our village was founded. We then tried to recreate the Cora'chan with what parts we could find or collect through the Trades. Little did we ever guess that he would come to us."

"And they got me instead." Two sighed. "I can maybe guess where my name came from, after all."

There was a moment of silence in which Two tapped his hands against the platform.

"We would be honored if you joined us," Raly said. "Right guys?"

Both Millar and Kech nodded enthusiastically. Doran reached out his hand, the right one that still twitched ever so slightly. Two sat there silently, toying with the metal box. After a minute, he gave an affirmative grunt and grabbed Doran's extended hand to hoist himself up.

"Well, I haven't known these folks for long, but I can already tell they're going to drive me nuts. You four look like an interesting lot. A change of scenery would be nice."

A panel in Two's chest opened and Millar gaped as he looked inside.

"That's some pretty complex work," he said.

"I don't feel comfortable with people staring into my chest after I first meet them."

Millar blushed a bit and stepped back.

"Nah, I'm just kidding. Take a look!"

Millar peeked inside again with a smile. "There's a gold component in there, with a white crystal in the middle. What is that? I've never seen anything like it."

"That's *his* piece. Or *mine* as I like to think of it now. You promise not to take it back, right?"

Doran held up his hands.

"Thank you. Now, let's get this on board."

Two inserted the metal box into an opening in his chest and a panel sealed shut. "It will take some time to install, give me a minute."

He and Intari walked away from the group for a short time, heads close together in quiet discussion. Intari reached up with her hand and touched his.

"Come on," Raly said. "Let's give them some space. I think they're having a moment."

The four of them walked to the main door of the temple and waited for Two and Intari to finish speaking. After a few minutes, Two joined them at the door.

"Are you all ready to go? I'm ready." Two quickly walked away from the temple museum. His voice was a little higher pitched, and he spoke quickly.

Doran looked back inside and saw Intari standing upon the platform with her hand raised in farewell.

"Take care of them," she said.

Doran knew she'd whispered, but his sensors still picked it up. It was funny, he realized as he joined the others—those were practically what Prism's last words were, and he still didn't know who she was talking to, either.

Chapter 26

The two smaller humans talked closely as Doran walked out of the village and down the slopes of the Coastal Cliffs. Doran could have sworn he saw a flicker of something black scoot past in the underbrush, but it only reminded him that he had not seen that cat for days now. It did not appear that anyone else saw it though, and despite worrying about the little thing, something held him back from talking about it. He felt Millar's questioning gaze on him, so he walked a little faster to get ahead.

Two lumbered by his side and was strangely quiet. They had just met him hours earlier, but still this silence seemed unlike him.

"They appeared to be nice people," Doran said.

"They were the only ones I knew." Two glanced back over his shoulder to the cliff walls above but then quickly returned his gaze forward. "Hey, if anyone wants an update on the memory system I installed, it's just about ready to run."

"Do you know how to operate it?" Millar said.

Two cocked his head at an angle for a second and he outputted a soft whirring. "Yup. They uploaded the schematics to my data system when they initialized me. Depending on the size of the memory content and the specifics you want me to search for, I am not quite sure how much time it will take."

"Thank you, Two," Millar said.

Doran eyed Two's head as he walked.

"That's starting to worry me," Two said. "I know you're trying to be nonchalant about it all, but am I going to have to activate my security settings when we shut down for the night?"

"You should be all right," Doran said.

"That's encouraging," Two said.

Doran patted him on the shoulder. "I have too many questions is all. If that is my part, then how did it end up buried in your town? And why did I end up inside an isolated mountain top, still operational?"

Two shrugged. "There's nothing in here besides the operating system."

"Does it give you… flashes of anything, from time to time?"

Two looked at him sideways. "I don't think so. Intari told me of dreams, however. Of how her central processing unit needs to refresh by clearing out old data. Or something like that. I believe I dream of things in that sense. The strange thing is I don't remember always having those thoughts to process to begin with."

"Dreams don't make sense most times," Raly said.

"Maybe," Two said. "I do remember storms from my dreams, however. Vivid ones. Does that mean anything to you?"

Doran nodded. "That is the main thing I remember. And the storms have gotten stronger and more lucid lately. Especially since entering your village, and also when I put on this armor. There are phantoms inside. Memories. Possibly my own that I have forgotten."

"I will set up a scan, then, to monitor and record anything like that." Two turned around one last time as the cliff tops passed from sight. He raised a hand and waved weakly at the stony outcrops before continuing on in silence.

***

"Why did you react the way you did?" Millar said. "When Intari mentioned Metlar?"

"It is not safe," Kech said. "We have avoided that run, even taken drastic measures to pass around that area, despite its key trade route position. How many items have we missed? Possible tech that would give us direction, maybe even help to lead us on our Quests? Like Intari and her people have done in the past. Even with our peaceful and neutral standing, some people will surely still attack us. But perhaps now that we have Doran and Two we will be able to face the dangers there. That is, if you still want to go, for I can lead us there."

Millar glanced around at his companions. "I'll do what I must to find Bel."

"And I'll go where you go," Raly said. "No matter what."

Millar looked at her and smiled.

"You think you're up for it?" Two thumped Doran on the chest like knocking on a door.

Doran paused and looked down at his chest without saying a word.

"Come on," Two said. "You know how to joke around, right? Even I can laugh with folks back home. They're not all as serious as Intari came across."

He bent over and walked with a pronounced hobble. Kech laughed, and Millar and Raly snickered.

"I am afraid I do not know how," Doran said. He hoped that Two did not think he was too much like Intari, and so he focused on downplaying his own limp.

171

Two laughed loudly. "Maybe you did hit your head a little too hard or pressed that button one too many times, yeah? That's a hell of a nervous tick, to reset your memory every night. And you don't know why? Could it be part of your programming?"

Doran shook his head.

"Are you sure you want your memories back?" Kech asked.

"It would appear that I do not," Doran said. "But it is not as if I left myself a message about this. No reasoning. I can only assume that I should not be seeking them out. And by default, I should not be seeking out any parts."

"Phew!" Two wiped a hand across his brow. "I get to keep my head after all!"

The rest of the day was quiet as they traveled down the coast. The high cliffs of Hinarum settled, and the going was easier. They headed mainly downhill, to sandy coastlines and scrubbier trees. The wind had not lessened nor had the temperature warmed up, and the humans bundled up in what clothes they had. The darkening skies as evening approached did not help, either.

Doran scanned the ground to see if there were any possible tracks he could identify, but there were so many on this main road that it was difficult to tell who or what had come by, and when. It was possible, he figured, that the raiders had escaped this way, but there were no clear signs yet. Mixed among the boot prints were other animals that either used the trail or perhaps were led by humans.

"Are you any closer to decoding the memory cube?" Millar asked for the fifth time in the last hour. "The further away we get from any possible clue Mom might have left could really affect what we're doing. Or which way we should be heading."

Two paused, and Doran could sense him adjusting the coding in the reader. "Nearly there. I do have a framework of the whole system, and it does contain a lot of stuff. Some of it encrypted, though. I guess she didn't want *everything* getting out. I'm assuming I should sort by the last few hours, yes?"

Millar nodded quickly. "Yes, yes."

Doran wondered how far back the memory cube actually went. Would there be memories of when she apparently knew him? If he was avoiding his own memories, should he avoid their shared ones, too? Luckily those would probably be from a long time ago. It felt weird to spy on her like that, though. He would not ask about that.

The wind shifted, and Doran detected something in the air. Some particulate contaminants containing carbon and sulfur had steadily begun to increase as they walked downhill.

"Do you smell smoke?" Millar asked.

"Yes," Doran said. "The chemical concentration is increasing in this direction."

"Look!" Raly pointed ahead to a thin trail of smoke flitting over the horizon, just barely visible in the remaining daylight.

She and Millar flipped down their visors and scanned, but Doran was already ahead of them. Multiple readings revealed the temperature, range, chemical content. He was about to share that information with them, but when he looked down the two of them had already run off in the direction of the smoke trail. Two glanced up at him and back at Millar and Raly running, now gone from sight beyond the tall brush and trees.

"I think we should follow them."

Doran did not reply and instead ran after them on the road, not even limping anymore. Intari and Prism shouted in his head, repeating, "Look after them."

In twenty seconds he overtook them, with Two and Kech not too far behind.

"Stop," he said. "We cannot run into this—we do not know what is out there."

"But someone might be in danger," Raly said.

"Which is why we need to be careful." Doran held his hands out.

"What are you talking about?" Millar said. "We've got you, there isn't anything you can't handle, right?"

Two clambered next to them. He somehow sounded winded when he spoke. "They're right, and you meant the both of us, right? Not just him that could handle things?"

Millar smiled. "Yeah, of course. So let's just go."

"I will go first," Doran said. "With Two, yes?"

"Thanks for the condescension." Two balled his fists and smashed them together.

When Doran got closer, sounds of shouting and screaming drifted through the trees. He caught Millar's eye, and they both knew that meant that it was time to take action. Broken and smashed sentry equipment lay about them on the ground. It looked like someone had busted through a security post here.

"Could be a Trades camp," Kech said. "But I can't tell until we get closer. It's a mobile encampment for sure, from the look of things."

Doran scanned the area and noticed the trail wasn't as solid as the main road out of the High Ansels. Not a lot of tracks led in or out of the area, but there were enough. And some similar to what he saw on the main road. He caught Two's eyes.

"Don't look at me!" he said. "This is my first time out into the world, so I'm assimilating all the data out here."

"I just assumed my—I mean *your*—nav system would have information on something like this."

"Not today," Two said.

"Whoever it is needs our help, by the sound of it," Millar said. He hefted his pry hammer.

Doran did not wait any longer and shot ahead through the woods before the others could go. When he broke into a clearing, things were more chaotic than he could have imagined. There were several groups of humans of different ages, possibly families. Adults carried lit torches and swung them around, keeping children in between them.

"What is going on?" Raly said. "What are they fighting?"

Initially, Doran could not see what they were doing either, so he switched his scan mode to other settings until he saw them—they were a strange type of bird-like creature he had never seen before, about three feet high and swarming the people.

"Help!" a woman yelled. She locked desperate eyes with Doran and clutched a child close to her.

"What is it?" Millar said. "I can't see anything!"

"Infrared mode," Two said. "Switch to it if you can."

Millar adjusted his visor and after a second gave a gasp. "Patarks!"

Patarks? Doran tried to access anything he knew about them, but his memory system drew up a blank. He silently cursed himself for erasing that part, and actually any part that might be helpful right now. Two, meanwhile, barreled forward into the camp and swung his long arms side to side at anything moving.

Three of the creatures clambered up onto his back and gripped onto his metal casing with their three-toed grips. They began tearing at him and scratching into the metal around his neck.

"Get them off me!" Two spun around and tried to reach backward when another patark gripped onto his front side.

Doran dashed ahead and grabbed the one on Two's chest by the neck. It screeched and wriggled so fiercely that he almost let it go. Instead, he readjusted his grip and hammered it again and again, face first into the ground.

Two spun around with his backside facing Doran so that he could swat them off with his flailing fists. Something drew the creatures off Two, and they shifted away together as birds do in flight. But these creatures did not fly. They seemed more comfortable—and dangerous—on the ground. Millar, Kech, and Raly stood back-to-back with their weapons raised.

"That's not going to do much," Two said. "They're too fast, and there's too many of them. Give me a second."

Two scooped all three of them up in his arms just as a group of patarks swarmed them. If not for the visor scanners, no one could have seen the creatures.

"Everybody," Two said. "Get in one circle. Move over there."

Two pointed to a large boulder that stood about twenty feet tall. The people in the encampment drew together and backed up to the rock, keeping the children in the center. Two deposited those he carried and joined Doran again, standing in front of the group.

"Help her!" a man called out.

Doran saw a little girl that had climbed up into a tree. It wasn't a very tall tree, only about fifteen feet off the ground, and several patarks had clustered around its base. They began to peck at the trunk of the tree and easily cut through the bark. Chips of wood splintered and flew off.

The child cried and yelled for help.

Without hesitating, Doran ran at the tree, kicked the first patark in the side, and knocked it into the air. It opened its skin-like wings and glided away until it touched the ground, and then it sprinted away into the trees. The remaining creatures hissed at Doran, but he didn't wait to see what they would do. He punched them in quick succession with such precision that each one crumpled under his blows and sank, dazed, to the ground.

The tree started to fall, and the child screamed again but still clutched onto the main trunk. Doran planted his legs and grabbed onto the trunk, causing it to stop suddenly. The child still hung on, but was dismayed about the surrounding patarks and the strange bot in front of her. Doran urged the child to climb onto him when another two patarks clambered onto his back to reach the tree. They hopped forward and were about to slash out at the child when Two swung a large log and smashed them to the ground.

That was too much for them. The patarks that could still move swarmed together and disappeared from the clearing. Two pummeled the fallen ones until they no longer moved.

Doran strained under the falling tree and urged the child to climb onto him.

"It's all right!" Millar said. "He's not going to hurt you."

The tiny child deftly scaled Doran's arm and clung onto the back of his neck. Doran shifted the tree so that it fell with a crash to the side. He walked over to the stunned travelers and reached back to pluck the child off his shoulders and place her safely at their feet. A woman, presumably the girl's mother, cried with relief and threw her arms around her.

Doran and Two made sure the area was clear, and then all the travelers began to speak at once.

Chapter 27

The little girl, who was named Clar, never wandered out of sight of Doran. Her eyes were stuck on him and she barely spoke, except to say something bot related. The rest of the group of travelers offered them what meager things they had, and showered them with thanks and praise.

Doran counted forty of them, mainly families with small children. "Where did you come from?" Doran said.

Clar's mother, Elin, spoke up. "We come from the south, past Terask, near the Metlar region. We fled the area because of the threat of fighting. We are mostly farmers, and our lands were in danger of invasion. For many generations our families worked those fields and now we have no homes. But if we stay there we'll die."

"We didn't know things had grown so bad there," Kech said. "We never used to travel there in the first place, but we should have heard warnings out of the south."

"It all happened so quickly," Elin said. "A nameless enemy entered the keep, it is said. Bearing a red crest upon their backs. And armor like theirs."

Millar removed his helmet. "We took these off the ones that attacked our home on the High Ansels to the west. They must have been the same raiders that attacked your land."

Elin nodded. "They drove us north with machines like we have never seen before. Burning and killing. And now it appears the land is awakening. Who are these two? And where do they come from?"

Doran and Two both introduced themselves, and there was much whispering and repeating of their names among the people from the south.

"We are lucky you came upon us," Elin said.

"I know," Millar said. "These hills are home to those creatures, called patarks. Even out where we're from. But it looks like they destroyed your sentry systems. I've never seen them do that before."

"They didn't," Elin said. "Earlier today those raiders found us. They wrecked what we had when we would not give them our food, for we have little. Still they took almost all of it anyway, and now we don't know where to go, or how to survive. We cannot go back home, for that is the way the raiders went. And we won't be able to spend another night here now. That was the only thing protecting us."

"We could take a look at it," Millar said. "Although the best person for it is back home. You should all go there, back to our home. I am sure they would welcome you in."

Raly nodded and smiled. "It sounds very different from the plains and fields of Metlar, but you could find a home there. I did."

"I don't know," Elin said.

Doran detected some excitement about a new home, but also fear of something else. The dangers of the hills, the attack from the raiders. It was all new to him, this land of problems. He longed for the restful peace of his mountaintop on the island, his home, where he could forget in solitude. His hand reached subconsciously for his head but he stopped.

The children that were still awake listened carefully to what Doran and the others were saying. They also longed for safety.

"These machines the raiders had, you said they had more of them?" Doran said.

"From what we have heard," Elin said. "We have seen some, but not as big as you or Two. And we don't know their exact number. They did not go very far from the keep. Rumors are the raiders have found a few that are bigger and reassembled them, but they cannot power them for long."

"They sent one here," Millar said. "It helped them to nearly wipe out my people. And Two's."

"You are in for a challenge, then, if you go there," Elin said. "They will want your tech. They are searching for anything like you. Any system they can scav to grow their army. Look at what they did to our system. They destroyed it, yes, but they also took pieces they could use."

"They might have someone—my sister." Millar's voice caught as he talked. "Did you see anyone they might have as a prisoner?"

Elin looked around at the others but no one said anything. "I did not see anyone like that. But then again they might not have brought everyone within sight of us. They did head south though, after they attacked us. Why couldn't they just leave us alone?"

Raly began to softly cry, and Millar put his arm around her.

"They took our lives from us, too," Millar said. "But you can find a new home among our people, I promise. They are broken, but they are always open to bringing in others. My mom would have welcomed you in."

"I am sorry for your loss," Elin said.

Raly sniffed. "You are farmers. That is something we don't have much of up there. We just live off Trades and what we can scrounge from the hills."

Elin smiled. "Then I think we shall go. Come, eat what food we have left. For we will find a new home tomorrow, and begin a new life there."

After the meager meal, Kech gathered the others around the broken sentry system. Two did his best to fix the circuits, but he threw it back on the ground almost immediately.

"They knew what they were doing," he said. "They gutted these things for the power cells. I can have them run off my backup system for the night, but they won't have a way to charge them during the day."

"We just need to make it through the night, and I think those patarks won't be coming back soon." Millar paced back and forth along the border of the encampment.

"Elin was saying we will be outmatched if we continue south after the raiders," Kech said.

"We just need to find Bel and bring her back home," Millar said. "We don't need to fight the whole raider army."

"But if Doran found more of his lost pieces, we certainly could." Kech consulted a book from her pack.

"Where would they be?" Millar said. "Just because he found two of his parts already doesn't mean anything. They could be anywhere. If people found them, that is. Look at what the raiders have already done. And Two."

Two put one hand on his hip and scratched his head with the other. "I have been thinking about that, actually. We at least have a direction of how he got to his island."

"Can bots have itches?" Raly said under her breath to Millar.

"I think he's thinking like a person might," Millar said.

"Do you mind?" Two banged on his chest and a screen opened up. A digitized map of the region appeared, crude and out of focus in places, but still visible.

"Based on the limited data so far, he came from the south or east. There was a half day's journey to my home of Hinarum. Possibly two days from Metlar's Keep, where the armor was probably found. There is a high likelihood of another part in between here and there."

"That map looks nice, Two," Raly said. "Good work."

"I…" If Two could blush, he most certainly would have. As it was, he squirmed uncomfortably. "Thanks."

"What do you say, Doran?" Millar said. "Are you up for upgrading?"

Doran stared off into the night. "I am not certain. I feel I got rid of my parts for a reason. But if it means getting Bel back, I will do what it takes."

"What kind of parts are we talking about?" Raly said. "He's pretty powerful as it is. Does anyone know? Kech?"

"According to our tomes, ancient tech for a Cora'chan was varied. They were fitted for wars, so he probably had some weapons. Possibly some mobility enhancements. I take it you do not remember?"

Doran shook his head. "None of this will matter if we do not know where Bel is. Are you any further in your analysis?"

Two nodded. "It's not like Prism categorized her memories in a functional way. She'd been around for a long time, and her thought patterns were more like a web than anything else I've seen. Granted, I've been alive for a short time. I've been trying to rewind as best as I could, but the longer I try to maintain a grip on her memories, files get corrupted, and just lost. That being said, I did isolate an area around the most recent time before she passed, to see if there is anything. We can take a look there. I tracked it back a few minutes."

Two sat on the ground with his legs crossed and faced a flat rock. The panel where he inserted the memory playing device opened, and two lenses began to glow and project a lit image in front of him. He adjusted a dial on the panel and the image cleared up, showing the inside of someone's living quarters.

"This is from thirty minutes prior to system shutdown."

"That's our home," Millar said in a low voice.

Some sounds, more like crackly static, accompanied the video, but they could also hear someone moving around the room. Prism did not talk, and it seemed like they were only watching an empty room. She busied herself around by straightening things, arranging and then rearranging items on a table. But she was clearly nervous about something.

"We were all gone," Millar said. "She didn't know, but this is when we were coming back from the island."

"What's that?" Raly asked.

Millar looked closer, but the image shifted, and now Prism faced the open door. "Go back a second, and hold it on the table."

Two immediately rewound the scene until the table was centered again, and then he froze it. The image was grainy but they could see a black box there. "Does that mean something to you?"

"I am checking my memory now," Doran said. "Give me a moment."

"That hasn't been your strong suit, I've heard," Two said under his breath.

Doran paused and then after a minute he spoke. "There, I can see it from when we removed Prism. It was damaged. Smashed open by a wooden beam."

"But what is it?" Millar paused and squinted his eyes. "Is that the best you can do on that box?"

Two silently adjusted the image until it became as clear as he could make it.

"Thanks," Millar said. He spent a minute staring at it, having Two move the image back and forth until he just shrugged his shoulders.

"I've never seen it before," Millar said. "And our home wasn't very big. Whatever it is, she's spending a lot of time looking at it. Can you… go to the end of the memory? To see if we can tell anything about it?" He was reluctant to ask this, and the words came out choppy.

The scene advanced, but Prism only ever glanced at the box. Each time, Two froze it but the clarity never increased. Finally, Prism stood at the door looking out, and chaos ensued. Before she could even react and help others outside, a bright beam of light arced through the distance, swept across the village, and then ended with it lashing through their house. The memory stopped suddenly.

Millar sat silently, and Raly rested her hand on his arm. So that was how her life ended. Maybe both of their mothers.

"Being connected to this security system, and operating this memory viewing device is really running my system down." Two's head drooped and his glowing eyes faded a bit. "I'm not built to last like Doran here."

In response, Doran gripped onto Two's upper torso and gave a slight twist and a click. Within seconds, Two's eyes flared up with the rush of power flowing through him.

"Whoa, there," he said. "That's crazy. I knew you were built differently, but wow. How do you have all that power at the end of a long day? What did you eat?"

Doran chuckled. "Perhaps I can show you a few things later."

"Yeah, all right, I'd like that. I feel like I'm good for the next week. Anyone else need me to run any of their subsystems around here? But seriously Millar. What next?"

Millar had a chance to gather himself and was able to talk again. "Go back further, maybe when she gets the box out?"

Two responded in an instant by spinning the reel backwards. His reflexes were faster with more energy in him, but that didn't clarify the image at all. He spun back again.

"Stop!" Doran said.

Two halted immediately. There was Bel, and for some reason Doran's own processing system seemed to speed up. It was at the end of their interactions, so all they saw was Prism hugging Bel and then urging her out the door. Prism watched her leave reluctantly. Bel kept glancing back, but Prism shooed her on.

"Why would she do that?" Millar asked.

They kept watching the scene in silence. No one knew why she would send her away like that. Prism set the black box on the table and watched a light flick on and off. With a nod and a sigh, she ran out of the house toward the center of the village, to Bruet's hut.

"We're in danger," she shouted as she ran. She did not move very quickly for her age. "Everybody, back to your houses and stay there."

The cries of the villagers grew as she ran past, but they listened to her. They pulled their families into the huts and shut the doors. There was no safer place to go than right here in the village. But then why would Prism send Bel away like that? Why couldn't she protect her child better here than away? It did not make sense.

Unless she knew that the danger would be too great, even for her. But why not leave with her and protect her? Doran watched Prism's slower movements and perhaps thought he might guess why she would not be capable of that anymore. That did make sense to him.

She walked into the hut where Bruet awaited, and she checked the security systems. Only after a thorough inspection did she begin to speak.

"They are coming," Prism said. "I feel like our fears are finally awakening."

"How do you know?" Bruet said.

"I just know. It has been quiet for days now on the radio. No contact with anyone."

"But we've been out of touch with the Trades for months. Why now?"

Prism did not respond. "I had to send her away, for her own protection. My power cells won't hold much longer to watch over her. If only Millar were back. He could take her to safety."

"Are you sure the system won't hold?" Bruet said.

"Perhaps," Prism said and then left.

She went back to her home, and then the recording caught up to where they had seen it before.

Millar pounded his fist on his thigh. "But where did you send her? Two, rewind it until Bel shows up, all right?"

"On it."

The memory spun for a few seconds until Bel opened the door.

"Mom! You wouldn't guess what I've seen!"

"There's no time, Bel, my love. We're in trouble."

Then a strange thing happened. The video seemed to glitch for a beat and paused. The sound cut out and when it came back on the memory had advanced a few seconds. Prism hugged Bel and then ushered her to the door as they had seen before.

"What is that?" Millar asked.

Two shrugged and rewound it. Again, the frames flickered.

"Looks like she did that on purpose, somehow," Doran said. "Like she did not want anyone to see that."

"Huh," Two said. "Maybe she didn't want someone tampering with her memories later on."

"That would make sense," Millar said. "But only if she knew things were going to get worse. Keep going, I want to see that box again."

The memory advanced after Bel left, and Prism turned to the box, and that singular light flickered on it.

"Is that a tracker somehow?" Millar asked. "Did she put a tracking signal on Bel just then and she was going to find her?"

"It would appear so," Two said. "And you're sure the box was destroyed?"

Doran nodded. "I saw it smashed. I first thought by a beam, but perhaps something else did it. But I think there may be a way to find her. Let me see those helmets again."

Chapter 28

By the time the sun rose early the next morning, Millar was up staring at some of the food the farmers had given them. It was a rough mash of grains with some dried fruits. Having been used to processed bars and dried meats, preparing the mash was quite different. He could boil water easily enough, but he ended up burning some of the food when he didn't stir it enough. He didn't like this.

"Wow," Raly said. "Smells delicious. Save some for me."

"If you don't like the smell, you don't have to eat it." Millar flicked a spoon of the grains in her direction with a small grin.

"If that's a promise, our day is looking good," Kech said with a yawn.

Millar sighed. "I don't have enough here to throw at everyone, so please keep your comments to yourselves."

Millar scooped the food into wooden bowls and added the fruits to them. He glanced over the camp at the farmers all enjoying their food.

"I should have taken her up on her offer," Millar said. "Elin said she'd cook us breakfast."

"Yeah, but that's not your style." Raly grabbed a bowl and tentatively brought the spoon to her lips. "Hey, it's not too bad."

"Not *too* bad," Millar said under his breath.

Raly just laughed, and she and Kech both ate the food without further complaint.

When everyone had finished, Raly took all the bowls and went to wash them up in the stream near the camp.

"Have the bots been up all night?" Kech asked.

Millar stretched his arms and back. "I think so. Two is still fired up from whatever Doran did for him, and the two of them have been looking over the helmets since I got up. The security system seemed to work just fine, too."

When Raly came back, the three of them walked over to the bots to see what they had been doing.

"But why?" Two was saying. "I don't even know her and I'm pretty sure she was crazy. Oh, good morning everyone."

"Two. Doran," Millar said. "Thanks for keeping watch last night. Doesn't seem like any patarks got even close to the camp."

"Either from the system, or from my fighting prowess, the camp is safe." Two flexed his arms and bowed.

Raly walked over to Doran and patted his arm. "Yeah, thank you both."

Doran awkwardly patted her hand back before speaking. "We scoured the memory recording many times for a clue to what Prism had been doing. As far as we can tell, she sent Bel away before the attack came."

"And that's what is crazy," Two said. "How would she know there was an attack coming? And how could she convince the girl to leave by herself, especially in such a short time? To leave the only place she'd ever considered home? And then send her by sea, even."

"By sea?" Millar said. "You know where she is?"

Doran nodded. "We finally configured the matrix for her tracking beacon after revisiting the images multiple times—"

"Multiple multiple times," Two added.

"Yes," Doran said. "And we entered that information into the helmet's guidance system. We have determined she is south of us right now by about ten miles. Or at least the beacon Prism attached to her is there."

"That's close," Millar said. He almost tripped over himself getting to his gear. "Isn't that about where Terask is?"

Kech nodded. "Yes, approximately."

"Can you tell me any more about her? Is she safe?" Millar shoved everything in his pack and his hands shook.

"I am afraid that the beacon is only that. It will only alert us to where she is."

"That's good, that's good." Millar threw his pack on and paced back and forth. He peered into the mists along the southern coast. "You both did good."

"Here," Doran said. "You take the helmets back. We're not out of danger, and these will protect you."

"Won't you need them, you know, to help track her down?"

"We have cloned the process in our systems for redundancy," Doran said. "We can all track her now."

Millar put on his helmet. "Then let's go, yeah?"

"Are you both set?" Raly said. "You've been sitting here all night, awake. There's no way you can be rested and charged up for the day."

"I will make sure we are both ready," Doran said.

The farmers stood in awe as the two bots walked between them, and so did the children, who had been playing a game in which they held sticks and pretended to duel with one another—Millar supposed they were pretending to be the savior bots.

Elin approached the central security system and inspected it. "Looks like they fixed it. And charged it. I can't believe we're all still alive."

She directed a few others to dismantle the station, and they got to work on it immediately. Apparently, they didn't want to be stuck out there for another night, even with a working security system. Millar wondered how differently he would feel if he didn't have the two bots to protect them.

"You are blessed," Elin said, "to have the Cora'chan with you. And we will have a home again."

She bowed her head repeatedly and handed Millar a parcel, which he figured was more food.

"We are grateful for your gifts," Millar said.

"And we are forever indebted to yours." Elin bowed one last time and joined the others.

Millar looked out upon the great ocean, past the cliffs, to where Bel awaited. He squinted and tried to see a boat, something upon the waves. Could they even see it from there? They weren't very high up in elevation, so they couldn't see out much. Even with the visor down he couldn't see that far, and the morning fog blocked his sight, too. Still, he felt better, even excited now, to get moving.

Slightly impatient, he glanced around at the others. Kech was helping Raly pack and talking softly to her about something. Two and Doran, a short distance away but still visible because of their height, were also engaged in conversation. Doran moved his arms in a flowing fashion. Two copied this as best as he could, always nodding his head vigorously when Doran showed him something new.

Millar couldn't wait any longer and began walking along the path south. He didn't get too far ahead before the others noticed and raced to join him. No one said a word. They had a clear direction, and they would find Bel soon.

Chapter 29

The next day was spent mainly walking in silence, except for during the small breaks they took from time to time. The sun shone brightly on the ocean to their right and reflected like glittering stones. Millar spent most of the time squinting to try to spot any sign of Bel, but by midday, no one had seen anything besides an occasional shore bird or some other creature upon the waves.

"Who knows about Terask?" Millar said.

Perhaps Doran did at one time, it was clear from the trail of parts that he left that he probably had been there. But he did not remember now. Two was too young, Raly knew nothing else except the High Ansels. Kech, having been from the Trades, knew it well.

"It's a small town, located on the edge of a river and the shore. They mainly fish and trade. Being on the main road, it is a trading hub, but it is difficult for large boats to enter their bay, so that prevents some major passage. They fish those shoals, however, and that's how they make their living. They do a lot of trading with Metlar to the south."

"I didn't know that's something the Trades would deal in," Millar said. "Raw fish."

Kech smiled. "It's more than that. They've actually made some things with fish you might not think of. Medicines, fuels for lamps. The oils are much sought after for lots of things. One thing is for sure, we'll smell the town long before we see it."

"Yay," Raly said.

"But our main reason for going to that region is for their temple."

Millar's eyes widened. "Their water temple? What do you know about it?"

"It's very old," Kech said. "From a past age. And they're very secretive about it. They don't allow most people to go out there—they say it's haunted now, and the temple itself is derelict. It used to be a place where people would travel from all over to worship. That was long ago, way before I was around. Now we're sworn to secrecy about any of the things we see. In fact, they do not let us take any of it."

"Then, what's the point?" Millar said. "If you can't take it and trade?"

"They study it," Raly said.

"That's right," Kech said. "Most people think we only take things to earn our way. But some things out there are worth studying."

"Is that what all your books are for?" Raly asked.

"Indeed. Some are dedicated to the study of this region, specifically the temple at Terask."

"I've analyzed the maps of this region," Two said. "I find the landscape interesting, and hearing about this temple makes it even more so. I would love to read your texts."

"Of course."

Kech handed him one of her books, and he took a moment to orient it in his hands. He flipped the pages quickly, but also so carefully that Millar started laughing. In ten seconds it was closed and Two's processor parsed the information.

"Next."

Kech removed the large pack wrapped around her and unfolded the casing to show the volumes of books stored inside.

"That seems really heavy," Raly said.

"You get used to it," Kech said. She stretched her arms in wide circles and arched her back. "The belt helps, also. Have at it, Two. Just be careful."

"I will."

Doran thought that Millar seemed worried—perhaps he was worried that ingesting all that information would take too long. But Two went through the entire set in a short time. Afterwards, Two leaned back and patted his stomach, much like he had just finished a large meal.

"Intari let me read things back home. That's how I learn best."

"Now you know what we know," Kech said. "Perhaps you'd like to be a part of the Trades?"

Two thought it over for a moment. "Perhaps. When this is over."

Raly looked like she was about to say something when Millar stood up from their break. "We should get moving."

Raly nodded and then helped Kech pack her mobile journal belt and fasten it around her waist. "Any change in her position?" Raly asked. "I can't quite get a good read on this helmet. Or maybe I don't know how to use it yet."

Doran checked. "She is closer. And still south of us."

Doran did not speak of the flashes of memories that seemed to be increasing in intensity. Ever since meeting Two, he had picked up some more frequencies that struck images into his mind. Now they were becoming more frequent. And they weren't just about the storms anymore. These were different. With each step south, he felt more.

Flashes of... pain. His own? Others? He could not quite tell. But it came from Bel's direction.

Was this somehow tuned to his search for her? Or something else? Two looked at him with a question in his eyes, but Doran waved him off. Just a glitch from not having erased his memories in a while. If the pain of the memories increased, he could possibly understand why he might have erased them.

The road led south in general, but it was not an easy path to follow. Elevation changed rapidly, cliffs opened to their sides, both left and right, and slippery mud covered the paths. It was no wonder that the High Ansels were not traveled very often—that was what made it the perfect haven for anyone trying to hide.

Perhaps that was why Doran chose it in the first place to abandon his life wherever it may have lain before.

"I can see why you said the best way to Terask was by water." Millar slipped on some rocks but caught himself before falling. "It couldn't be any worse than this."

"Yeah, but then you would never have met me," Two said.

"And we would never have learned how to track Bel," Raly said. "And we helped those farmers."

"I didn't say I wasn't glad we came this way," Millar said. "I just nearly stepped off the cliff there. Give me a moment to breathe."

"I had you." Doran reached down and patted Millar's shoulder causing him to nearly trip again.

"Thanks."

"Is that Terask?" Raly said.

Doran looked up as they headed down through the trees. The fog lifted and a fishing village appeared in the distance. Docks jutted out into the bay and fishing boats peppered the water's surface. He caught a flash then, almost like he had back in Hinarum when he felt the energy pulse. They were farther away, and maybe this was just his own memory starting to engage, but it could possibly mean there was another part here, just as Two had predicted.

"That's it," Kech said.

"I hadn't really thought of this before," Millar said. "But should we be bringing two bots into a town like this? Bots like these? No one has ever seen anything like them. Are the people going to be all right with this? And what about the raiders? If they're here won't that tip them off and they'll all just attack us?"

"Are you saying we need to just go in by ourselves?" Kech said. "I suppose that actually makes sense. We'd go in and scout around first, and make sure there's no raiders about."

"I don't like it," Raly said. "I feel safer with them around, you know?"

"If we're worried about raiders, then we'd also need to ditch these helmets." Millar lifted his helmet off and handed it to Doran. "There's no reason for them to attack us if they are there, right? They don't know us, they don't know where we came from."

Raly shrugged. "I still don't like it."

"We'll stay close enough to monitor you, far enough to stay out of sight, right D?" Two clapped Doran on the back.

"Yes... T," Doran said.

Millar grinned at this interchange. "And when we find Bel, we'll just get straight out of there. Is she close? I never really figured out how to work that thing. To be confident with it, anyway."

Two paused. "I am pretty certain we went over the tracking protocol with you already. A few times. Is everything all right with your brain?"

Millar laughed. "I think so. I just wanted to make sure she's still close."

"Less than a mile now," Two said. "That direction."

"There?" Millar double checked.

"Your confidence protocol is lacking," Two said. "But yes. *There*. We'll be just in these hills, less than a quarter of a mile away. Don't worry. If we smell any hint of trouble we'll be right there."

Doran stood silently. He had not been away from this group since he met them, practically. Prism had nearly spelled out that he needed to look out for them. He would only feel comfortable about this if he did not stray too far.

"Use this, if you need," Two said. He handed Kech a small package wrapped up and attached to a small stick.

"What is it?" Millar said.

"Intari and the others have found a way to create light and smoke from the earth. Light this with a torch and stick it in the ground. We'll see the signal it will make."

"Where were you keeping that?" Millar asked.

Two shrugged. "I have my secrets."

"Be careful," Doran said.

Millar waved and walked away with Kech and Raly toward the town.

Chapter 30

"I know what you mean about the bots," Millar said. "I feel exposed now."

They were about a quarter of a mile away from where they'd left Doran and Two. Millar never used to feel like this—he used to walk along the High Ansels without a care. With Bel close by however, he was feeling the pressure of it all. Was she hurt? Was she just hanging around in the city, ready to just jump out at him and laugh?

So many questions. It was time to find her. Without the bots.

"Like they said, they're close by. I bet they could really move if they had to." Millar looked back but couldn't see them anymore behind the treeline.

A jetty nearly encircled the bay, broken apart at the seaside by rocky islands and a wide circular opening Millar could only guess was the entrance to the water temple below the surface. He'd grown up hearing tales of it, mostly from Mom, and they were enough to ignite some childhood dreams. Somehow the temple was built directly into the water, but it was never in danger from collapsing in on itself, or filling with water. It was a brilliant piece of architecture he could only imagine was constructed with magic, if there were magic in this world. Such was his childhood imagination. He used to make up the most unbelievable stories—most of them featuring a massive bot that fought at his side. Kind of like now, he realized.

The jetty, both the northern and southern sections, slowed the waters as they entered the bay, but that didn't mean waves didn't find their way in. A huge wave crashed and broke upon the temple barrier, sending glittering spray into the air and forming a rainbow in its wake. Seeing it now, and even though he was a little older, Millar could only really think magic had to have been used. He glanced over at Raly and saw her with her jaw agape as well.

"Think we'll be able to get a close-up look?" Millar said.

Kech shook her head. "Not likely. We might get out to those docks though."

She pointed at a town of docks between the temple and the shore. Small fishing boats moored up to the docks and began to unload their fish, and others finished and went back into the bay to continue. It was a busy place.

"Hold up," Millar said. He flipped his visor down to get a better view of the docks.

"Do you see her?" Raly said.

Millar scanned for a minute. "Too hard to tell with all the boat traffic. It could be tucked in there anywhere. Wait—were you referring to Bel or your boat?"

Raly smiled. "Your sister, of course."

The pathway they followed from the cliff eventually turned into a road paved with cut stones, and it led to the docks along the shore, and to the jetty. In the midday sun, not many carts were on the way, possibly because fishers would be out on the water for most of the day. But still, some craft rowed or sailed back to the docks, ready to be unloaded to go back to town.

The people they came upon paid them no notice. Workers loaded fish and hauled the carts drawn by horses back to town along the roads. One cart drove close by, and Millar shouted at the driver.

"Have you seen any travelers come through here in the last few days?"

The cart rolled by, and the old man driving it paid them no heed. The cart lumbered past, smelling strongly of raw fish, and Millar caught his friends' attention.

"Are they usually this friendly to newcomers?"

Kech nodded. "This is about the extent of it. At least out here among the fishers. They'll be more eager to talk to us in the village center."

"You mean sell us fish?" Millar said.

Kech laughed. "Probably. But they'll talk to us about other things, too. Come. Let's head there first. They'll know more about anyone passing through."

"You think they'd be more excited about a passing band of raiders and a kidnapped kid," Millar said.

"Well we don't know if the raiders came here," Raly said. "It could be just Bel, right?"

"It's at least just Bel, and that's all that matters."

Millar quickened his pace along the road, always ready to veer off to the side to avoid another cart driver who didn't even make eye contact. Coming from a town where everyone knew everyone else and always greeted each other, this was pretty shocking.

Up ahead, the wooden buildings of Terask came into view. This was also a shock to Millar and Raly. They were used to yurts and small huts, able to be broken down and moved quickly. These were permanent structures that rose to two or three stories in some places. They seemed solid, despite the weathering each structure had taken from the harsh coastal winds, rains, and sand all about.

With Bel close now, Millar could barely keep from yelling out her name along the streets. His temperature rose, his breathing quickened, his chest tightened. Raly noticed and put a calming hand on his arm. He took a deep breath, held it for a second, and let it out.

"We'll find her," Raly said.

"I know."

They walked for several more minutes until they reached the town center. A wooden pathway encircled the area and branched in and out of the main areas. The carts all veered to the eastern side of town, away from the footpaths where villagers met and sold their wares in a marketplace.

"Don't they all have fish?" Raly said. "Why would they trade with each other?"

"They have different types, for one thing," Kech said. "Shellfish, deep sea fish, and lots of other things you don't find in other coastal areas. I think the shoals around the water temple have some interesting temperatures, which breed a variety of life here. Plus, this market is also for travelers from neighboring villages. Small ones like your own."

A man suddenly came upon them. "Greetings, travelers! Welcome to our town."

Millar and the others bowed their heads to the man, who was dressed in rich robes and a wide brimmed hat with a golden chain hanging from the back. He carried a stack of papers and a pen.

"This is a Greeter," Kech whispered to them. "They have several throughout the town as people come in. Part of what they do is to help direct people to what they need."

"Where do you hail from, friends?"

"North," Millar said. "Along the coastal path and up near Hinarum. Have you seen—"

"North, huh?" The man whispered something to a small boy, and the child ran quickly away to the center of town. "Run into any trouble along the path? We heard there might be a problem with the route there as Trades haven't made their way there in weeks. Months perhaps."

"Yes," Kech said. "I am Kech Val Onla of the Trades. A band of raiders waylaid us just south of here about a month ago, and they recently attacked a small village upon the peninsula, up in the High Ansels. They were routed and have since eluded us. We are missing one of our friends. Have you seen any people from the north in the past day or two?"

"From the north, I'm not sure," the man said. "My name is Brig, Greeter and Dock Master of Terask. The town is busy, and we don't see everyone. I do remember the Trades though. They are around. Just arrived by boat. I believe you can find them at the inn just south of this street. The Fat Walrus."

Brig pointed to a two story building across the street past the market. It had garish red window frames and a steady line of people streaming in and out of the place. It was around lunchtime and the smell of cooked fish wafted its way through the air. Millar's stomach growled.

"Have you seen a little girl, also from the north? She would have just showed up pretty recently."

The man paused for a moment, and his eyes looked down at the ground. It took him a few seconds before responding. "No. But maybe they've seen her down at the inn, too. Most people go there first when they come to town."

"Thanks, Brig," Millar said. "We'll check it out. Thank you for your help."

Brig nodded and went right back to work monitoring the docks.

The sounds of laughter and plates clattering found its way out of the inn, and the three of them, hungry and wanting to find out more about what was going on, stepped inside. Kech remained at the doorstep for a second.

"For a Greeter and a Dock Master, Brig sure hasn't seen much," Millar said.

Kech grunted in agreement. "He sounded uncertain about the Trades he's seen or heard about. But I'm more worried about this inn. The bots won't be able to monitor us if we're inside. Should one of us stay out here?"

Millar looked around the room. Groups of people clustered around the tables, eating and drinking. "I think we're safe here. It's a busy public space. Anything happens to us, the townsfolk can help. I don't see any raiders around, anyway."

"That doesn't mean they're not there," Raly said.

Kech slowly nodded. "Maybe you're right. I'm keeping an eye out, though. I'll be ready to run out here and signal them if needed. She patted her coat pocket, where she'd stored the signal flare from Two.

"All right, come on," Raly said. "I'm starving. No offense to your breakfast cooking, Millar."

Millar just shook his head.

They entered the main room, which was full of talk and the clank of pottery as food was passed around. Smoke rolled out the windows, and Millar could not quite tell if it came from the patrons, from the kitchen out in the back, or the large metal fireplace in the center of the room. It was shaped like a huge walrus and had smoke pouring out of its eyes. Most of the smoke flew up to the chimney above its head, but the smell of smoky fish and exotic spices hung in the air. The crowd turned to face the newcomers and there was a lull in their conversations. Millar waved half-heartedly and after a few seconds of sizing them up, the crowd went back to whatever they were doing before.

"Let's sit over there."

Millar pointed to an empty table near the back of the room, and they all sat down. It was dark in there, even during the brightest part of the day.

A serving girl with freckled skin walked past them carrying a tray of empty cups, and Millar tried to get her attention.

"Hello, have you seen a small girl, maybe ten, with curly brown hair?"

The girl didn't even pause, and then she was gone, right through the door next to their table. The sounds of the kitchen fought with the tumult of the customers out front.

"Busy today," Millar said. "Nice place like this, you think they'd open up a window or two to let the light in."

"Maybe people don't want to be seen here." Kech scanned the room as they waited for the serving girl to come back.

"What are you looking for?" Raly asked.

"Trades. Brig said they were here, but I haven't spotted anyone I know yet. Even if it wasn't the crew from the High Ansels, I'd recognize them."

Millar arched his neck as he looked around, too. "I don't see any sign of Bel, either, but someone had to have heard of her, right?"

He didn't say it, but he wished that Oen had made his way here with the Trades, too.

Most people avoided looking at the newcomers, but Millar made sudden eye contact with someone a couple of tables over. The person quickly broke the stare, but it made him feel uneasy. Then he noticed a hooded person sitting near the door that also seemed to be watching Millar and his friends closely.

"Anyone else getting a bad vibe from this place?" Millar said.

"It is definitely not as friendly as the last time I was here," Kech whispered. "We should go."

"But Bel is here," Millar said.

"You just said you felt something wrong, I'm sensing it too," Raly said. "I say we do as Kech said. Let's get out of here, get back to the bots and try again."

"Should have sent just one of us in," Kech said under her breath. "What was I thinking? All right. We should probably leave, but let's not make a big deal about it."

Millar shifted his chair backwards as he stood and it made a loud scraping sound and then it fell over with a clunk. He stopped and turned to see if anyone had taken notice.

Three people stood right behind him carrying large gunny sacks. The crowd suddenly grew silent, and several people stepped in front of the door to block the way out. Another group approached the table from the other side, all carrying long filet knives.

"Just come with us quietly," one of the people said. He was an older bald man with a scruffy patch of beard on his chin, and he was carrying a sack.

"Let's be reasonable," Kech said. "We're just passing through. We don't want any trouble."

The people with the knives took a step closer, herding the group closer to the ones with bags.

"Looks like they do," Millar said.

Millar's eyes shifted this way and that, looking for a break in the crowd, but they had been neatly corralled into this place with no way out. Cut off from the bots. Why though? What could this group of people want from them? They'd never met them. It seemed there was only one way out of this.

Millar made a quick move to pick up his pry hammer off the floor, but the people were ready for any move. Two of them grabbed him and flung his arms to his sides while the man with the sack readied to throw it over his head.

Kech took the momentary distraction and bolted to the center of the room. One of the knife wielders chased her, but Raly tripped up his legs and he crashed into a nearby table. For a moment, Millar was sure Kech was trying to escape and would just leave them behind.

Instead, when she reached the massive cast iron stove in the center of the room, she opened one of the lids on the surface and some flames licked out of it. She shoved something in right before someone grabbed her arms and pinned them behind her.

"Is that what I think it is?" Raly said right before one of the burlap sacks dropped over her face.

"Yes," Kech said. "We better duck."

She dropped to her knees just as a huge explosion of fire and sparks jetted from the stovetop. More smoke spilled out of the pipe leading to the roof, bleeding out through the edges from all the pressure.

"Move them out!" one man cried out. "They must've heard us."

"We're not ready yet!" another yelled out.

Millar's vision blacked out as a rough sack dropped over his face, too. Someone grabbed his shoulders and forced him along. Everyone in the room began to cough as smoke filled the air. Millar grinned, as the sack probably made it easier for him to breathe. He tried to run, but the person had a strong grip on him. They also lashed his wrists together quickly. A strange thought flitted through his head then, thinking they might have been pleased using their knot tying skills for another use besides boats and fishing.

They probably didn't have too long to wait now—the bots had to have noticed this. How could they have missed it? But the minutes passed as he was jostled along, led down a small flight of wooden steps into a cold, enclosed area, and still, no Doran or Two crashing in to save him. Millar had to keep his head lowered in the short tunnel. He even kept bumping his arms into the side as he was urged forward. There was no way Doran or Two could make it through here, unless they tore it all down.

"Are you okay?" Millar yelled out.

"Yes," both Raly and Kech replied, from in front of and behind him.

"Keep it down," the man leading Millar said.

Millar felt the blood pumping through his head, and his breath quickened as he kept walking through a long straight tunnel. Where was this? It was cold and damp, like a cellar, so he knew he definitely wasn't aboveground, but where was this leading? He was all turned around, so he had no idea. One thing did pass through his mind—despite being covered and kidnapped, the captors were not, surprisingly, too rough with them. That was possibly because they didn't want their quarry damaged, but Millar felt that wasn't the case. He didn't know how to explain it.

He also didn't know how to explain their words back in the inn. Who might have seen or heard the commotion? And what exactly weren't they ready for yet?

Chapter 31

After five minutes of walking, the ground began to slant downward. The air grew cooler and damper. Beyond the crunching of their feet upon the gravel, Millar began to hear water dripping in the distance. The tunnel widened, too. A cool breeze with a salty tang to it blew through the sack over his head. He was thoroughly confused now about where they had been brought.

"We have them," a man said.

"Were you followed?" another replied.

"No, but things are moving faster than you wanted. You have only minutes now."

Murmuring rippled among the new group of people here, and Millar couldn't understand what they were saying. After some shouting and people walking about, Millar fell and scraped his knees upon the rough hewn floor. Raly's and Kech's curses beside him let him know these new people were obviously rushing, or didn't care what happened to them. Millar was shoved into a room with his friends, and the metal door clanged shut behind him. He jumped around, trying to remove the sack from his head, but it had dropped over his hands, and he couldn't get a grip on it. In a panic, he moved around the room and hit his head upon a metal bar. He bit back a curse as he shook his foggy head. He stumbled back into the wall again and felt a bit of metal protruding. He snagged the lower edge of the sack on it and wiggled his way downward until he was able to pull the sack over his head.

The room was dark, but his eyes had already had time to adjust to darkness, so he could see through the cage around him. Dim light from above helped him to see that they were in a wide open area, circular in shape. It immediately struck him like they were being held in a cistern. Kech bumped into him.

"I'm covered up here," she said.

"Slow down," he said. "My hands are still tied, but I can help. Just lean forward."

Kech stopped and bent down, and Millar turned around to grab the top of the sack. He got a solid handhold on it, and between him pulling and her moving backwards they managed to get hers off, too. In a few minutes, all three of them stood staring at their prison.

"This has to be the water temple," Kech said. "I've seen images of this, but, like I said, they never let outsiders come in here. Or they never used to. Seems like they've been busy here."

"Are they going to sacrifice us to their gods or something?" Raly said.

"Probably not," Millar said.

They all looked down into the well below them, and could only see more rock and a deeper pit. A few levels down, a pale light showed upon a dome right in the center of the temple. Four solid stone pathways arched over the depths to reach the dome. Millar tried to pull his visor down, but then realized it wasn't even there anymore. They must have removed it before they led them down here.

A crashing sound, like that of waves from way above them, resounded through the temple. At the tail end of the sound, Millar thought he heard something else. He couldn't be sure, but it sounded almost like laughter. He waited to hear more, but nothing happened.

"Did you hear that?" Millar said.

Raly nodded. "Maybe that's what makes people think this place is haunted?"

A statue stood right outside their door. It was a large stone bot with its head hung low and its hands clasped together, one fist in the other. Millar craned his neck around to see farther into the hall and noticed a few more to either side of their room.

"Does that look familiar to you?" Millar asked.

"Just the head," Raly said. "Looks a little like Doran."

"That's what I was thinking," Millar said. He didn't know what that might mean, but it did seem a bit strange.

"What is this room, anyway?" he said. "I didn't think they'd have prison cells inside a temple."

"It doesn't appear to be a cell," Kech said. "But they've certainly prepared it to be like one for us."

Raly looked around. "How does the ocean stay out of this? It's basically a big hole in the shore line. Whenever I dug holes in the sand back home, it would always fill up."

"I don't know," Millar answered. "But we've got to get out of here. Look, it's them."

He gestured his chin to the red-hooded group of people gathering on a lower level.

"Raiders," Kech said. "And it looks like they've been here a while."

"Why are they here?" Raly said. "And where are the bots? I thought they'd be here in an instant if we got in trouble."

"We're in the wrong kind of trouble, apparently," Kech said. "They might know something is off, but the people here led us underground, and the bots couldn't track us. Not through that narrow place. This isn't easy to get to."

"They'll find us," Millar said. "Two's got that component of Doran's. That's come in handy so far for figuring things out."

"Maybe not enough to foresee this," Kech said.

"Is pessimism part of your training?"

Kech cracked a grin at that. "Just something I brought to the job, I suppose."

"They're really scrambling." Raly leaned against the bars and looked down. "Whatever they were planning, we seem to have triggered it early and they weren't quite ready. They've got us though. What's happening?"

"It must be a trap," Kech said. "For the bots. Lure them in. Capture them, or worse. Did you see any of those spears, like back at your village?"

"I didn't see any," Millar said. "I guess they might still have them after running away. But how did they get in here? And get control of the people here? What do you know about this place, Kech?"

Millar noticed that the book belt around her waist was missing—she looked strangely thin without it. They must have stripped her gear when they took the visors. Hopefully they hadn't left it back in the inn—those books were her life's work, and the inn was probably a smoldering mess right now.

"The temple? Not much," Kech said. "The people of Terask used it for religious reasons, but I didn't know they still came down here. They don't really know who constructed it, but it is one of the wonders of this world. Another of our Life Quests. There are some of the Trades who work so closely with the priests of Terask that they are not allowed to leave for years, or share any information with the rest of us. That is the level of their dedication."

"I don't get it," Millar said. "What's the point, then?"

"They're finding out the truth for themselves," Raly said. "Without caring what others think or know about it, as well."

"That's right," Kech said. "She understands. It's a stage of enlightenment for us. I have only begun on the Life Quests."

"Well, you've got two of them checked off now, right?" Millar said.

"Perhaps." Kech squinted and looked across the center of the temple. "Do you see people in there?"

Millar and Raly followed her gaze.

"Yes," Raly said. "They have Trades gear on! They must have come here from home!"

"Then maybe—" Millar cut off as he squinted his eyes. "Oen!"

He didn't care about being quiet. If his friend was here with the Trades, he had to know about it.

"Oen! Are you here?"

"Hey, keep it down," a voice said outside the cell. A figure in a hood appeared at the cage and inserted a key into the makeshift door lock. With a quick twist and a click, the door popped open. "And yes, I am here!"

"Oen!" Millar ran over to him, but with his arms still tied he couldn't return the hug his friend gave him.

"Yes, but keep it down, seriously." Oen closed the door behind him.

"What are you doing?" Millar said. "Why don't we get out of here?"

Oen busily cut each of the bonds and released their hands, and Millar and Raly each hugged him for real.

"Not yet," Oen said. "I've been in town, hiding out, waiting for you to get here. We showed up yesterday by boat, and when we first arrived the Trades told me to stay back while they went in. It was just a precaution, but it turned out to be right. The raiders knew we were coming. All of us. Or at least, they knew we'd probably be here. The Trades got caught by the townsfolk, who brought them here. I was just one person and the town wasn't looking for someone not dressed as a Trades. Not yet. They knew you'd be here later."

"Why is Terask after us?" Millar asked. "And why are they working for the raiders? They don't have any allegiance to them."

Oen shrugged. "Not sure. I think the raiders are holding someone else here hostage. Making the townspeople do all their stuff."

"So they're trying to capture Doran again," Millar said. "Great. And I led them right here."

"Maybe, but I don't think that's all," Oen said. "There's something about this place. I heard the people here talking about the temple. There's something powerful here."

"Then let's go," Millar said. "We go up there and warn Doran so he doesn't get trapped by whatever is waiting in here. Then he can get us out of here."

"If we leave now, the whole thing will be a bust, and I'll get caught too. I don't think there's a good chance of us running past everyone out there."

"How did you avoid them?" Millar said.

"Just waited for the right moment," Oen said. "They weren't looking for me, I think."

A group of people ran past the cage without even giving the prisoners a second glance—they didn't even notice that Oen was in there.

"See?" Oen said. "They don't care about us, even me sitting here. Unless we leave. Then I bet they'd find a way to make us stay put."

Millar nodded. "Maybe you're right. Are you sure you don't have a way out of here? I thought you'd plan this whole thing out. You had a lot of time to do it, right?"

Oen chuckled. "It's good to see you too."

"I bet it has to do with whatever is in there." Kech pointed to the domed structure below them in the well.

Millar started as if shocked. "Have you seen Bel? Or heard anything about her?"

Oen shook his head. "Sorry. I'm not on speaking terms with these guys yet. Why?"

"Doran and Two said they detected her around here, and this seems like the most likely place for her to be."

"*Two*?" Oen asked. "What does that mean?"

Millar laughed. "That's right, we've picked up another friend along the way. Let's just hurry up and figure out what to do. I think something's going to happen, and happen fast."

Chapter 32

"Look!" Two said. "Over there!"

Doran scanned the sky over the town and nodded. A plume of smoke belched out of the windows and chimney of the very inn that Millar and the others had disappeared into. He didn't know why they had gone in, realizing that they'd be out of range, but he could understand it. Millar was desperate. He was the child's older brother, and the only remaining family.

Doran had only met her for a short time, and he was attached to her. Even after attempting to erase her from his memory. Prism had said that she was a special girl. She was here somewhere, but he could not quite track her with the beacon.

"I see it," Doran said.

"Do we go in there? Rescue them? We could easily go in and get them out. You know, with a lot of smashing and fighting."

Doran paused. "I do not think so. Despite what it looks like, I do not think they mean them any harm. Not directly, at any chance. I think there is something bigger going on here."

He did not say it out loud, but he felt stronger flashes as they approached Terask. Nearly every step he took from the cliffs of Hinarum increased the things he saw. Yes, the storms, flashes of lightning, and the feel of wind. But this time things also included a sense of… peace? Almost like the times when he awoke to find himself in the midst of some meditation. The people of this town were not evil.

"That's no fun," Two mumbled.

"Do not worry, I am quite sure that it will come down to at least a little fighting." Doran balled up his fist and smashed it into a large boulder near his feet. The rocks broke off into tiny shards and a huge slab slid off the side.

"Oh, hello," Two said.

Two young children appeared on the other side of the boulder. A boy and a girl covered in sand. They had apparently been sitting there until Doran hit the rock.

"Did we seriously just miss two children sneaking up on us?" Two said. "Ah, this is going to hurt. Better not let Millar find out about it."

The two just stood there, eyes popped and speechless mouths wide open. How long had they been there? What had they heard?

Two waved his hands back and forth in front of their faces. "Are you both alive? Hello?"

The kids' faces turned to wonder and amazement, but still they did not speak.

"Maybe we should ask them for help?" Two said.

Not a bad idea.

"Have you seen a little girl here?" Doran asked. "New to your town. She would have showed up in the last two days."

Still nothing but stares and gaping mouths. They would probably be reliving this moment over and over in their heads for the rest of their lives. Most people in the outer villages would not see a bot in their lifetime, so for them to stumble upon two out here in their town...

Doran tried to find Bel's signal again, but he only got a vague direction and distance. She was here in this town, but where?

"All right," Doran said. "I have an idea, and I need your help, kids."

The two looked at each other and a huge smile broke out over their faces.

Doran hefted one of the raider's helmets and knelt down before them. "I need you to take this helmet and bring it way down to the other end of town. To the rocks out there."

He pointed to the jetty to the south of Terask.

"This is a very important mission. Do you think you can help us with this? We would be forever in your service."

The girl reached out reverently and took the helmet from Doran's grasp. The boy touched the helmet gently.

"Will you help us?"

"Yes!" the girl said.

"Then go," Doran said. "Go now, and hurry. Many lives depend on you."

"Oh, what are your names?" Two said. "You know, so we can remember you through the ages?" He gave Doran a sidelong glance and a nod.

"Mist," the girl said.

"Ealon," the boy said.

Two bowed his squat body and flourished a long arm.

The two kids laughed and ran off toward town with the helmet.

"Leave it there, way onto the rocks! Hurry!" Doran said.

"I see what you are doing with the helmet," Two said. "It makes me upset I didn't think of that. Especially with your strategic modulator onboard." He patted his wide metal chassis.

"Then you know we need to put one here to get a signal." Doran placed the other raider helmet upon another boulder. "And we will slowly make our way to town until we triangulate her position."

"See," Two said. "You don't need me, do you?"

"Of course I do," Doran said. "Did I say something that made you think I—"

"You're a little too serious, though, aren't you?" Two said. "That was a joke. I think I must have inherited the sarcastic module with the sense of humor update. Oh well, you're a learning bot."

Doran knew that was a joke. Right? He understood humor.

"The whole town is going to know about us in about five minutes, right?" Two said.

"Probably," Doran said. "But we are in a hurry, and our friends could all be in danger."

Even now, with the helmet on the move, Bel's signal was getting clearer. It would take just a little more and they'd pinpoint her location in no time. He and Two slowly made their way closer to town, trying to keep behind the large stones that peppered the shoreline.

"You asked me before if I got any visions. I think I'm getting some now," Two said. "Do you sense anything?"

"I do," Doran said.

"Do you know what it means?"

"If it is anything like before, it means there is something big here."

"More bots?" Two said.

"I do not know," Doran said. The visions this time were more familiar, though. Like he knew he had been here before, maybe even spent some time there. Maybe a long time ago, maybe a year or two ago. His memory certainly was not helpful in these instances.

But one thing appeared amongst the images that he did not expect. It was another bot—one he was pretty sure he recognized. His memories of her were more than just in passing.

Prism.

Millar's mother. But the images were not of her last moments in this world. It was her, in a memory. Just like the other flashes he got, this one was all over the place, but he kept seeing her face. He was supposed to know her, but he did not. Just this.

And a simple song played. One that tickled the corners of his memory.

Then a real sound brought him back to reality. A gonging sound, out from the water.

"You all right?" Two asked.

"I will be."

"Good. And let's keep an eye out for children. We don't want any more of them sneaking up on us, yeah?"

Doran chuckled.

After a few more minutes of moving closer to Terask, Doran and Two scanned for Bel's tracker again. Her direction was precise now. There was no doubt of her location. And they both looked out into the bay directly at the water temple.

Chapter 33

"Do you think they're all right?" Two asked. "Why else would they have lit the signal flare?"

"I am sure they are okay, for now," Doran said. "And no, I do not need my sensor back to know this is probably a trap."

Two sighed. "And I was just about to tell you the odds of it being a trap. What's my job here exactly?"

At this point, there was no need to hide. Their friends were in danger, and there was a clear path straight to the water temple. Two paused as he followed.

"Do not tell me you cannot swim?"

"Uh, I'm not sure," Two said. "I'm reviewing my system right now and it's not clear."

"Well, it's not like you can drown," Doran said. "The worst that can happen is you sink."

"That seems pretty bad," Two said. "How about I go right over to the main docks and see if they arc around to the temple entrance."

"It is best if we stay together," Doran said.

"I know that, I can follow the programming." Two stood still on the shore. "I'm just, I'm…"

Scared. Doran understood that. But it was not a bot trait, to be scared. Unless Two was just following safety protocols—perhaps being scared was just a basic life saving instinct.

"We are going to have to go in the water eventually," Doran said.

"Not necessarily," Two said. "But if we do, best to prolong that. Come on, let's not waste any more time."

"I am not the one wasting time," Doran said.

"I can hear you."

Two ran along the beach at a loping pace, with his arms hanging down to the sand. Doran joined him, and sand sprayed in the air with every pounding footfall. Already, the people on the docks noticed them, but they did not seem angry or even surprised to see the two bots.

"Are they… cheering?" Two said.

Once they reached the dock to the south, a large group of people gathered there awaiting them, and still others streamed in from town and the shore.

"Help us!" some cried.

"They're holding him prisoner!"

"Where?" Doran yelled as he ran.

There was no time to stop now and ask who the people from Terask were worried about. It had to be a leader, or someone important. It did not matter. He would solve that problem with Two when they got there.

"Out there!" The people pointed to the massive stone towers jutting up through the bay, around the gaping hole leading to the temple.

Doran sped up, leaving Two behind to amble along and catch up. His legs were much shorter than Doran's, after all.

"You coming?"

Two lumbered along, and the dock began to splash in and out of the water as the two huge bots ran atop it. Huge waves streamed away from them as they created a wave pool. In the back of his mind, he imagined those two children who'd helped with the helmets playing in the waves.

The crowd definitely cheered this time as they approached the temple. Doran reached the end, and without a thought he leaped through the air and splashed into the bay. A large wave radiated from him and streamed toward the towers, but before it hit, it reflected off an unseen barrier instead of falling into the unknown depths.

Just as he had made his way across the water to reach the High Ansels, Doran swam with large powerful strokes to get to his friends. Bel's signal pinged harder now. She was so close, and almost straight down. He reached the first temple tower and clung to the waterworn stones. The temple looked to be a combination of natural rocks, much like the columnar volcanic rocks back on his island, and something that was crafted either by human or bot hands.

He glanced back at the docks just in time to see Two stop hesitantly at the edge of the water.

"Come on!" Doran called. "Now is the time!"

Two stared into the depths. He didn't respond. Several fishermen gathered near him, not afraid at all, and they encouraged him onward. One or two of them jumped into the water to show him that it was all right.

"Here I go!" Two shouted.

The cry was instantly silenced as he hit the water and, instead of bobbing near the surface as Doran had, he disappeared quickly from sight.

"He's not going to drown," Doran said. "But I cannot wait for him now."

Without another thought, he hoisted himself completely out of the water and clambered along the tower until he was inside. A large hole opened up before him. It appeared as a large well, with many levels of rooms stretching out into the darkness.

"Millar?" Doran shouted into the depths. "I am here!"

He heard no response, only the sounds of the wind and water above. Doran latched onto the stony structure and began the climb down toward Bel's signal. No doubt Two would say that was where they were all being held, and where the trap would be sprung. Doran knew what he had to do.

He leapt along the wall, clinging to metal bars and swinging from arm to arm like some jungle animal, down, down into the depths. Many levels opened up before him, some containing small rooms, some wide open spaces. He didn't have time to examine each place as Bel's signal drew him ever deeper, but he got a sense that hundreds of people could worship something down here.

Several statues drew his attention on each level. They were cast in the likeness of robotic beings. They appeared regal, and powerful—majestic, almost. Some held a spear or other weapon, some stood without. There were certainly a lot of them here. Was this a temple... to them?

On the fifteenth level down, where looking up showed a much smaller view of the circle of blue sky above, Doran peered through some gates and startled a group of people. They had to be people of Terask, but while some were dressed as fishers, some were also in robes, which led Doran to believe they were religious leaders. He climbed through some large gratings and landed on the floor right amongst them. They did not know what to do. In fact, they did nothing except stare up at him.

"My friends," Doran boomed. "Where are they?"

Nothing. No one responded, even though a large bot was threatening them. Although, he wasn't really, and he knew it. Maybe they knew it too. Finally, one robed woman with gray hair and many wrinkles upon her cheeks stepped forward.

"Please," she said. "You must help us."

Some of the other people argued with her.

"They will kill him if they find out we helped them," a man said.

"Then they will kill us all!"

Doran held his hand up. "I am in a hurry. My friends, did you take them?"

The group of people looked at each other, somewhat sheepishly. "We did, but we do not have them anymore. We brought them here. We were told you would follow."

"They said they would let our leaders go," the woman in robes said.

"I will help them if I can," Doran said. "But I must find my people. Especially a little girl."

"The travelers in red brought her below. Many flights down. She is guarded, they say. At the central domed temple."

"And your people, and mine?"

"If they have them, they will be down there as well."

Doran looked back and forth. "You are trapped here? The exits both up and down are barred and locked."

"We are safe," the woman said. "But yes, they locked us in here."

Doran strode to one of the chains locking the gates across the stairway, and he grabbed onto it. In a single rending motion he pulled the links of the chains apart.

"Now you are free to do what you will."

Doran eyed the stairs but, despite the distance to the bottom, he chose not to descend that way. Too confined. He slipped back into the central area and began to drop down again, but the woman caught his attention.

"Mind the voices," she said. "They will try to tell you what to do, or what to think."

"I believe I can ignore them," Doran said.

The lady nodded. "We are sorry. Sorry for all the harm this has caused."

The whole group bowed to him and murmured softly the sound of their sorrow. Doran glanced behind her and saw one of the tall bot statues staring back at him. He nodded to the leader and walked to the edge of the central tunnel to climb down.

With each level that he dropped, more damage and decay seemed to have gripped the place. Fragments of rock walls lay strewn about the floor, and water leaked in from other areas causing small pools to gather in the halls. Even the statues were toppled—bot heads separated from their bodies like victims of some giant executioners.

With a start, he saw that amongst the stone statues there was a fallen metal one as well. A bot with its head lopped from its body. He knelt to examine it and figured it had been inactive for at least a few days.

Winds howled through the depths like laughter. Doran kept moving, though. He would not stop until he found Bel and the others, no matter what happened.

Other sounds reached his ears, too. Like the shuffling of feet. But the people of Terask seemed to be avoiding the lower levels. Who could it be then? The raiders? He resisted the urge to call out to them.

The domed shrine at the bottom of the temple was not very far now. Bel's signal hammered solidly across his system and pointed directly to the covered area. He was close enough to scan it now. It was of metal origins, but it was cleverly crafted with gray and green stones, blended together as if they were melted in a great forge somewhere and dripped into place across the temple.

And it was old. Older than the already ancient upper areas of the temple. Instead of being built from the top down, the area appeared to have been carved out first and then built upwards toward the sky. But how could that be? Perhaps it had all sunk, once upon a time.

And the sense of power grew as he approached the bottom. He felt it through more frequent visions, but he also felt the power rush through his core. This place was strong in that spirit. It seemed this temple was built upon a wellspring of the world's energy.

And with it came a sense of foreboding. Darkness crept into his body, and weakness. There was something here that did not belong, something parasitic.

But all that mattered now was reaching the dome and freeing Bel. Perhaps his other friends were in this place, too, but he had to do this first. With a final drop of two levels at once, Doran landed onto the bottom platform with a resounding crash. It should have registered as pain to him, but for some reason his metal legs absorbed all the impact, and he barely noticed anything.

He stood still for a moment, and the only sounds he heard now were the faint dripping of water falling from the temple. Hundreds of feet above, he could still see a small circle of light. The domed structure lay ahead of him. Gashes rent its surface, but whatever caused them could not penetrate deeply. Rocks or other debris had to have fallen to cause this damage, yet the people of Terask must have removed all the pieces. This was a revered and holy place after all.

"Bel?"

Doran called out and broke the silence with her name. His voice echoed in the chamber, but no one responded. He tuned his sensors to the room ahead but could not sense any human movement or sounds from within. If she was injured at all... He clasped his fist and strode forward.

The doorway was solid with no windows to look within.

Lightning flashed across his eyes. Storms. The peace of Prism looking over him. And fighting. Other bots clashed with him. He was not alone in this waking memory.

A worn-down plaque adorned the top of the doorway, and the markings upon it were barely discernible through the scratches and dents. He read the words slowly in his mind.

The way of the forgotten must not be followed.

The images ceased playing in his mind, and there was only silence.

He reached out to the door and noticed there was no handle, instead only two large recesses in the wall where handles should be. They looked just big enough to fit his hands. And they did, perfectly. Inside, he grasped two bars and twisted them with a slow steady motion. The handles slid and clicked into place, and interior mechanisms began to rumble.

He let go and took a couple of steps backwards to see it all unfurl. Metal cogs spun beneath the earth—he felt them clicking within the stone. The four connecting walls from the edge of the temple to the domed structure pulled back with inexorable motion on hidden gears. A door opened from the side of the structure now, exposing whoever was waiting inside.

"Bel?"

The dim light shone on the inside now, and Doran saw an altar, and upon it he thought he saw the shape of a person lying on their back. She did not move. Doran started for her side, and that was when the temple crashed down upon him.

Something grabbed him from behind. Strong hands gripped onto his shoulders and wrenched him aside like some child's toy. His head rammed into the doorway and he dropped to the ground. He turned enough to see a dark figure step over him into the chamber with the altar.

"Finally."

The voice was deep and old. It seemed to almost be an echo of the temple itself, with its rusty gears and scraping metal. Doran rose to face the being and saw that it was made of metal, but covered in dark slime, as if it had been waiting in some dark corner of the temple, and the depths of time had covered it. It was indeed a bot. Not quite as tall as Doran, but wider and stronger.

That did not stop Doran, though. He rose to his feet, a little slower than normal, and reached out for the other bot's arm.

"Do not touch me," the bot said.

It spun around and drove its fist into Doran's chest. The blow knocked him back several feet and he spun over, crashing into one of the retracted walls. Looking down, he saw the armor slightly dented from the attack, not quite unlike the damage that had been done to the domed structure in front of him.

"Stay away from her," Doran said. His voice sounded different in his ears. It was warbled and overlain by a hint of static.

"There is no one here."

The bot leaned over the altar and picked up something. What Doran had thought was a person had only been his own mind imagining it was Bel. The dark bot turned around, and although Doran could see the thing it held, he was uncertain about what it could be. He walked out of the domed room, and Doran could swear that it moved slightly slower now.

"But where is she?" Doran asked. "Where are the others?"

"You are too predictable," the bot said. "How could you have forgotten this?"

He held out the parts, and they looked vaguely like boots, if that could be right. Doran tried to stand, but his internals strained at the effort. He pushed through it and got to his feet.

"And persistent," the bot said. "I see you have found your armor. That was a gift."

What did he mean? He had torn it off the spider bot back at the High Ansels. That was no gift.

"One that I will take back now."

He set the boots on the floor and placed his feet beside them. A strange thing happened next. Almost like vines growing rapidly, the boots seemed to grow onto his feet.

Doran's sensors flared in his head again, visions of wind and storms. But this time, he could tell the wind wasn't blowing past him, but instead he was flying through the air at incredible speed. He had worn these boots before. They had been his.

The dark bot was wearing them now, yet something told Doran that he should not have them.

"You had your chance with them," the bot said, as if reading Doran's thoughts. "But you chose to let them go. They are mine now."

"Where are my friends?" Doran said. He planted his feet firmly on the ground and raised his fists.

"That is all you can think of? I should be worrying about your life right now, if I were you."

The boots upon the bot's feet seemed to finally finish their adjusting, and Doran heard a slight whir, like a power source activating and warming up.

"Where are they?"

The bot cocked his head a little. "You're not going to give me that armor willingly, are you?"

In an instant, even though they stood nearly fifty feet apart, the bot was at Doran's side, and he drove his fist into his head. The bot's own strength, combined with the speed of flying across the room, was almost enough to sever Doran's head from his body. Doran felt something crack internally, and he flew to the ground again.

"Why you ever let these go is beyond me." The bot jumped up into the air, assisted by the boots again, and he dove at Doran.

Despite the ringing in his head from the last blow, Doran was able to roll out from under the attack as the bot's fist struck the floor right where he had been. Glowing yellow eyes narrowed as it watched him escape.

Doran, surprising himself, sprinted and tackled the other bot. This caught him off guard, as well, and before he could react, Doran slammed him into the ground and drove a fist into his head. He reared back and swung both fists together repeatedly until a crack split open upon his face. One of the yellow eyes turned off and sparks flared from the crack.

Doran pulled his arms back to land another blow but by this time the bot had a chance to react. Simultaneously punching Doran's chest and activating its boots again, the bot slid out from under him head first into the wall. More sparks shot out into the air. He stood up, wobbling from leg to leg, and looked to the stairwell leading up.

"Get him!" the bot yelled.

A group of five red-hooded raiders ran out of the stairs now, all carrying the same spears they had back at the High Ansels. Electric bolts arced through their spears as they approached Doran. He knew that if they surrounded him, they could subdue him with that power. But why? Why didn't the bot just leave now that it had what it came for? He glanced down at his chest, at the armor. Well, he couldn't let him take that, too.

Doran remembered that the spears were powered by something else besides any internal source, as that would run out quickly. Last time the spider bot had somehow been connected to them. On instinct, he made a dash for the dark bot.

This startled him, and he could not react in time to the charge. Doran struck out at the bot's head, this time at the other eye to try to disable it as well.

The blow connected, but it did not have the force from before. Still, it was enough to cause the bot to spin and hit the floor.

The raiders stepped closer, although a bit more hesitantly after witnessing Doran's anger. The electricity arced and leapt to Doran's leg, shocking and causing him to let up on his attack.

Doran looked into the raider's eyes and did not see hate, as he'd expected. Instead, there was a fear in them. But who were they afraid of? He wasn't going to do anything to them if they chose to leave him alone. Maybe they just thought he would. Another bolt of light flew into his body, and pain leapt through his sensors.

"No!" a voice cried out, and five figures ran down the stairs out into the open.

The person in the lead lifted a hammer and smashed it into one of the raider's spears. The electricity stopped arcing through Doran as the weapon shattered in half. Millar looked up and caught Doran's eye.

"Doran!" a small girl's voice called out.

It was Bel! She threw broken stones across the room at the raiders, and they winced under the attack.

A sudden strength surged through Doran's body then, and he grabbed one of the raider's spears. Some electricity passed through his arm, but it didn't slow him. Instead, he turned and hurled it at the other bot. Stunned beyond belief at how the attack was going, the other bot did not react in time. The charged spear hit its side with enough force that it impaled his body and drove it back. It stumbled weakly and tried to yank the sparking spear from its side. It did not come out, so instead the bot smashed down with its fist and broke the spear in half.

"Finish him!" he yelled.

The bot activated the boots again, and this time it flew to the wall and it made its way up like some climbing insect, still with half the spear jutting out of its back. Doran started to follow, but he looked at his friends instead.

Millar, Raly, Kech, Oen, and Bel stood before the raiders, ready to fight to protect him. The raiders looked at each other doubtfully now, and at the retreating bot that had led them here.

"He is leaving?" one of them said.

"He'll be back for us."

The electricity in the spears had ceased entirely now, as its main power source was escaping the temple. Another group of raiders appeared out of the stairwell with their cudgels and clubs drawn.

"What do we do?" Raly said, and she ran to Doran's side.

They all grouped together and faced off against their enemies, who didn't seem to know what to do themselves. Everyone stood in silence. Doran reached his hand down and laid it upon Bel's brown hair. She clutched it with her own tiny hand and smiled.

"You came for me!" she said.

"And you for me." Doran stood in front of his friends to face the raiders.

They all took a collective step backwards toward the stairwell. But instead of them escaping as well, a huge chunk of stone fell from above and smashed into the ground in front of them, blocking the way up. Explosions from above sounded, and pebbles and stones began to rain down. A chunk of metal, seemingly a portion of the wall, smashed down, and this time one of the raiders screamed out in pain.

"This temple is collapsing!" one of them shouted.

"He is tearing it down upon us," Doran said.

"He would not do that," a woman wailed.

More debris struck others. Doran stood tall and gathered everyone to him. He tracked a piece of stone as it fell through the air and swatted it out of the way, causing it to erupt in a shower of broken stone. The raiders looked at each other in fear, but they did not leave Doran's side.

"We've got to get this cleared," Millar said. "It's our only way out. Come on!"

He used his pry hammer now to dislodge rocks and chunks of metal blocking their way. Doran tried to help, but he had to keep watching for falling rocks that threatened to crush the people. He flailed his arms to knock the pieces out of the air as they worked. Spears became levers, and soon the two groups cleared a small area that the smallest of them could crawl through.

"Make it bigger first!" Bel said. "That way we all get out at once!"

Everyone kept laboring, but then a few drops of water hit Doran's head. They all paused for a moment to watch what looked like rain falling upon them. But it wasn't rain. Bigger streams of water poured down until it was a deluge. The rocks had stopped falling, but now it appeared that the bot was forcing the ocean down upon them.

Doran swept everyone out of his way with a big motion of his arm and then began on the rock pile. With his full attention on this now, it didn't take long until he had cleared a way for all of the humans to escape.

"Come on," Millar said. "You too!"

"It is all right, I can climb the wall. You just concentrate on going up all those stairs. There will not be much time if he brings the ocean down upon us. Do you have enough energy to do that?"

Millar nodded. "We can do it. You be careful."

"Go!" Doran said and his friends began their way up and around the temple.

Bel was the last to turn the corner, and she sent back a reassuring smile as she left. That was when the largest of the rocks struck Doran and pinned him to the ground.

Chapter 34

"Just go!" Doran shouted, unable to move.

His friends had returned after the crashing had ceased to try to wedge the chunks of rock off of his legs and arms. Already the water was up to everyone's shins as they worked to free him. The water began to pour down much faster now, as if a new hole had been smashed up above.

Still, the dark bot did not descend to pick the armor from Doran's frame. Perhaps it would wait until the end.

"I will not drown," Doran said. "But you will if you wait much longer. Do not worry, I will get out of this myself."

The water poured in even harder, and still the humans ignored his words and worked faster to clear any rocks off him. His gears and servos ground in resistance against the weight of the rocks, but he could not budge. The water level rose to his chest, and then another chunk of masonry crashed onto his head, covering him almost entirely with debris. Through a crack in the rocks, he spied someone coming through the stairwell.

"Behind you!"

Millar spun around as quickly as he could, wading in the deep water with his hammer raised. A single raider ran at them with a spear and jumped onto stones to stay out of the water. Bel shouted and threw a stone at them, but they kept coming.

"Stop!" the raider called out. "I want to help!"

This did not compute—the raiders were only there to remove his parts for that other bot. But there was something familiar about the girl.

"You?" Raly said. "Liar! You only want to destroy him!"

Doran remembered now. It was the same girl from the High Ansels. Doran could not see much, but he could hear them arguing beyond the rocks that covered his head.

"Will you stop, the water is rising too quickly, we need to move faster, together."

"There's more of them," Millar said.

Through the single space between wreckage, Doran saw a few more raiders gather with the others and splash into the water with their spears.

"All together!" the girl shouted.

Doran felt the rocks strain and flex on his head as he registered the pressure release. The water fully covered him now and the sound cut out. He could feel the people climbing atop the rocks to stay above the water. With the added weight of everything, it was harder to lift the rock off his head, but with them all straining the debris shifted slightly.

"He came back!" one of the raiders screamed.

Another huge splash made a great wave sweep across the room. Something else had entered the chamber, and the raiders were calling to it. He would be easy pickings now. The water blurred his vision, but he could see something standing above him. Its eyes glowed and narrowed as it focused on him.

Three blue and red flashing lights.

Massive fists splashed into the water and pummeled the stone on Doran's back.

"I did not know how, by the way," a voice shouted through the water.

The rocks cracked and shattered and were finally lifted off his back. The water flowed away for a moment, clearing Doran's face.

"Know how to do what?" Doran said.

"To swim!" Two shouted.

With his arms freed, Doran was able to help Two pry the remaining rocks off of his body so he could stand up. He clasped his arms around Two and lifted him out of the water with a massive hug.

"And that was a pretty long drop down here," Two said. "I had to climb and jump off the wreckage when that other bot left. Did you see that thing? I'm sure you did. He left in a hurry."

"Did he see you?" Doran asked.

Two paused. "I think so. It all happened so quickly. But let's get these people out of here."

The water level was high enough that the humans had to tread water to stay afloat.

"We could let them swim up, as the level goes up, right?" Doran said.

Two parsed that for a moment. "Nah, based on their fatigue, and the fact that more water is coming down, they could get trapped on one of the adjoining levels."

"All right, all of you climb atop us, and we will carry you out." Doran drew himself out of the water and clung to the wall next to the last remaining chunk of stone out of the water.

Millar picked up Bel and lifted her onto Doran's back. She gripped onto his neck, and then Millar made sure his other three friends were aboard before climbing on himself. There wasn't much room, and they clung tightly. Doran began to scale the walls steadily, trying not to shake too much or endanger the others on his back.

"I guess I got this lot." Two pointed to the three raiders that had stayed behind to help. "Don't do anything stupid, or we can check to see if I really know how to swim."

The girl scrambled onto his wide body and gripped onto a makeshift handle atop his head. The other two raiders latched on as well, and Two, not as carefully as Doran, began the ascent

After thirty minutes of climbing and recharging along the way, the two bots finally made it all the way to the upper levels of the water temple. Here the damage was the worst, and the water streamed over like a waterfall into the depths.

A group of people from Terask, surprised at the bots popping over the edge of the wall, called to them.

"Here! You can escape from here!"

Doran and Two swung over the ledge, and their tagalongs, exhausted from holding on for so long, dropped to the floor. Doran noticed that the twenty or so Terask religious leaders had the other raiders tied together in a line. They started when they saw the raiders come off of Two's back.

"Traitors," one of the captured people called out.

"He was leaving us, he was betraying us," the girl said. "Who ended up saving us?"

"That does not matter," the first raider said. "Entity is the way. We do not question his way."

One of the Terask guards shoved the raider. "Silence."

The three raiders who had helped free Doran held their hands up and fell into line with the others. The guards bound their hands and pushed them forward.

"We have to leave," a man in golden robes said. "This whole place is collapsing. We are not safe."

"Two," Doran said. "Do you think you can help patch this place up?"

Two scanned the structure for a moment. "It looks trashed, but I think we can slow the water flow for now."

"You go on, we will follow you when we are done here," Doran said.

"Yeah, you're not going to trap our friends again, are you?" Two said.

The people of Terask looked up at the two bots apologetically and reverently. "They had captured him and held him hostage. We had no choice but to—"

"Yeah, yeah," Two said. "Just go!"

The group of people hurried down an adjoining hallway heading toward the shore. Millar and the others all waved with relief in their eyes. Bel clutched her brother's side with a huge smile on her face.

Two watched them leave and looked up at a giant bot statue.

"Hey, did you notice? He kind of looks like you."

"I had not noticed. Let's get to work." Doran jumped to the edge of the temple opening and began to size up the damage.

Chapter 35

It took hours before Doran and Two finished reinforcing the temple. Terask had a few loaders that they put to work excavating the lower levels and setting up a drainage system, and they scurried up and down the levels following orders. Doran looked at their lifeless eyes. They did not have thoughts like he and Two had, not that he knew about, anyway. They were just programmed to do a job and then await the next one.

"Don't worry about them," Two said as they finished slamming the supports into place. "They don't mind. Seriously."

Two waved one of his large hands in front of a loader's face as it returned from the depths with some wreckage. It barely registered the interruption and it merely walked around and resumed what it was doing.

"Do you think they have it better than us?" Doran said. "They have a job, they do it, then they await the next orders. You do not see anyone trying to dismantle them and take their inner systems."

Two covered his torso reflexively. "Oh? You think that's good? Although, I guess worrying you'll gut my brain case does keep me up at night. But seriously. Being able to think is the best."

"You have been sentient for a short while now and you have enough data to make an assessment?" Doran walked to a giant cable suspended over the temple opening.

"That's right, keep resetting your memory, you'll make sense someday. Plus, didn't you say you saw a bot in the lower level with its head removed? Seems like the haunted temple got the best of that one."

Doran grunted and pointed to the cable.

Two gripped onto it. "As you wish. I am a pre-programmed loader awaiting your orders, master. No offense, guys."

The loaders just walked right on by without pausing to consider him as they both climbed up to the surface.

"Well, I thought it was funny."

***

Evening settled over the town, and the chaos from the earlier explosion passed. The group had been brought to another temple, this one along the main street with no danger of water collapse. The room was big enough for the two bots to enter and sit upon stone steps while the others sat at a large round table. Doran took this moment to rest and look at the people that gathered.

The people of Terask returned Kech's journals, and she was silently going through a few to make sure nothing was missing. She stood up and walked over to the rest of them with a limp now. She couldn't wear the book belt because of the injury, but Raly tried it out to see if she could carry it. The thing nearly weighed as much as she did, but the straps on it were fastened in such a way that the weight was evenly distributed and she could at least walk a few steps. How Kech had been able to run around with it on was beyond him. Maybe it was a custom fit.

The leader of Terask, an elderly man named Vo'Sav, sat before them.

"You saved us. You saved me." He gestured to Doran and Two, and then to the Millar and the others. "We apologize for all that happened. We were being held hostage, and my people did what they could."

"By kidnapping Millar and the others?" Two whispered to Doran. "Seems like they could have found a better way."

"I think they tried sending one of their programmed bots to get them first," Doran said. "Remember…?" He mimicked cutting off his head.

"Oh yeah."

"What was that thing?" Millar asked. "They called it 'Entity.'"

Bel was barely awake next to him, and she bobbed her head as she tried to listen.

"It was an evil spirit that haunted our temple," Vo'Sav said. "For that reason we did not allow others down there. You have cleansed our home. Now people from all over can worship there again."

"So, I am free to speak of it now?" Kech said.

"Yes, indeed," Vo'Sav said. "In fact, you can spread the word. The Cora'chan has returned and cast out the darkness. You have claimed what was rightfully yours."

These last words were directed at Doran, and the people of Terask bowed and touched their hands to their foreheads.

"You have lived with the Entity for a long time, what did you learn about it?" Millar asked. "Because it may have left you alone, but I don't think it's finished. Many other towns will be destroyed by it."

"We know very little," Vo'Sav said. "Only that it lived in the Cora'chan's shadow. It will do whatever it can to be like him."

"It took a very powerful artifact from the main chamber," Doran said. "Why did it wait for me to take it? Why not before?"

Vo'Sav stood from the table. "Did you not see the savagery it beat upon the central walls? Every night, the people of Terask would fall asleep to the sound of the Entity lashing out at the doors, trying to rend the metal. For years. In fact, you were the only one who could open it, because you were the one to close it."

"Are you getting this, Kech?" Two said.

Kech was wasting no time recording everything that Vo'Sav was saying about the temple. If this was one of her Life Quests, she wasn't going to miss a thing.

"Where did it go?" Doran asked. "I must stop it."

Vo'Sav shook his head. "Little is known about it. Other than it will do anything to be like you. It wanted us to praise it—it pretended to be the Cora'chan. But we did not worship him. He is false, but we knew not to anger him. So we made sure no one else came to the Temple and we appeased him in falsehood."

He shifted in his seat.

"Although some fell under his sway."

"The raiders," Kech said.

Vo'Sav nodded slowly, hesitantly, as if he did not want Kech to record this portion. But it had to be known.

"They took the preachings of the Entity as truth, and passed it on in secret. A religious sect grew, until it was like a cancer in our town. We did our best to stop them, but they carried out his orders, it seems."

"How long has it been here?" Doran asked.

"A long time. Before my own."

"But it has not always been here, do you think?"

Vo'Sav nodded. "No, it came from beyond, it is written. Seeking out what you had hidden."

"It needed this artifact to move on," Doran said. "There are other pieces out there. Why did it need this first?"

"Do you not know? They are yours. You put them in places none would find for a reason."

Doran's head sank. "I made myself forget."

"Maybe the raiders will know!" Oen said.

"Perhaps," Vo'Sav said. "But will they share that with you?"

"It's our only hope of stopping him," Millar said. "They have to tell us. But maybe Raly should stay behind."

Raly nodded, and she wiped at her eyes with the back of her hand. Doran placed a hand on her back to comfort her.

"You carry a heavy burden," he said.

"You can't make me forget that, can you?" Raly looked up at him with a sad smile.

Vo'Sav stood and his people followed. "They are being held within the prison. Come. You shall question them."

"We've called them the raiders," Millar said. "But who are they?"

"They call themselves the Soldiers of the New Sun," Vo'Sav said. "And they hope to bring the Entity forward as a new god upon this land. As you have seen, there is already dissent among their people. Follow me."

The prisoners were being held in the town hall, a squat stone building in the center of Terask. Millar and Oen stood beside Doran and Two to question them, but Raly stayed behind with Kech. Kech was injured and was busily writing notes down about the events under the temple, but she mainly stayed behind for Raly. Millar asked Bel to stay there, too, as he didn't want her near the raiders anymore.

"But I want to be around you and Doran, and Two!" Bel waved again to the new bot.

Two chuckled and waved one of his huge hands back at her.

"I cannot wait to hear about your adventures," Doran said. "Do not go to sleep yet. We will be right back."

Bel yawned. "Okay, but hurry!"

Vo'Sav led them in. Doran ducked his head to enter the doorway and instantly noticed all of the raiders clustered together in the same room.

"That may not be a good idea," he said.

"Why is that?" Vo'Sav said.

"Some things happened within their group that might not befit a radical religious sect," Doran said.

Vo'Sav gave them a questioning glance.

"Part of the group has jumped ship," Two said. "They might kill each other over it. No big deal."

"He is nothing!" one of the raiders shouted.

"False!" another yelled.

The group of raiders began to argue with those that had helped free Doran from the wreckage. They cornered them in the room, and even though their hands were bound they were clearly becoming angrier and more violent. The Terask guards stationed around the room grabbed them and separated them.

Doran approached the young girl and the two hesitant raiders beside her. They looked sheepishly and fearfully at the others.

"Will you speak with us?" Doran asked.

The girl nodded, and the group of others yelled. They swarmed closer and it took the guards' collective efforts to push them back. One of them took the girl's bindings and led her away from the others.

"Did you not see Entity abandon us?" she said.

"Do not speak his name," someone called out to her. "Heretic!"

The group surged again in anger at her and the others, and the guards struggled to pull her away from them. It took the lot of them, and more than one was knocked unconscious in the process. They removed the girl from the building as the fighting quieted, and together they sat alone in the main square. A fire blazed in an open pit before them as they stared at her. Now that they had her in front of them, Doran realized that the girl was about the same age as Raly.

"I am Kindra," she started.

"We don't care," Oen said. "You destroyed our home. Killed Millar's and Raly's moms. We're not going to be your friend."

Kindra looked down at her shackles. "I know that. I… I am sorry."

"You think you can apologize for all of that?" Millar said. "How can you possibly justify what you did?"

Kindra didn't say anything.

"This is not what we came for," Doran said.

Millar and Oen calmed down a bit, but it was clear they weren't done with her. It was also good that Raly didn't come along.

"We need information on this Entity," Doran said. "What he wants. What he was doing here at the temple. We need to stop him. Who is he?"

"He is our guide." Kindra sounded almost loving when she said that. "Or, he was. He was going to just leave us all at the bottom of that well. How could a god do that to his people?"

"There weren't any clues before that?" Two said. "You know, that he was bent on genocide and would do anything to get those artifacts? Those were yours, right Doran?"

Doran nodded. "I believe so. I lost them. I lost them all."

No wonder he did not appear to be the Cora'chan as everyone believed him to be. He was a weak shell of his former self. Not that he remembered.

"He's been collecting them," Kindra said. "But he has been here for years. Waiting. He told us how we could draw you out, so you could unlock the traps you set here."

"Wait," Two said. "He told you this? If he has been here, how could he tell you?"

"He has Ghosts he speaks through. Shells of bots that need a voice. One of them was the one at your village, who had the armor you wore."

"Where did he find that?" Two said. "That would be very helpful information."

Kindra thought for a moment. "I don't know for sure. Somewhere to the south of Metlar. In a desert."

Two computed this data.

"What did he say would draw Doran out?" Millar said. "No one knew about him. And he just recently got off of his island. How would he know this?"

Kindra shrugged. "He knows much. For sure he needed these boots to get a weapon. It is said that with it, nothing will stand in his way."

"Great," Oen said. "What are we going to do about that? You two aren't exactly the arsenals of destruction."

"We could get there first," Doran said.

"But the boot thing," Two said. "Seems like it's a mobility issue. You were pretty smart, it seems. You hid the parts in a specific order. I can only imagine that it is someplace you'd need those things to get to."

Kindra seemed to be thinking about these words. "I believe to the east, there were whispers of mountains and cliffs over frozen plains. Maybe there in the Blue Ice Mountains."

Two nodded. "That would make sense. I'll start reviewing the data and see if I can make a plan. I'm guessing Kech could also give us a hand."

"Or we could get the other parts first," Doran said.

"There's that." Two held his hand to his head in thought.

"But he could use that weapon to kill others," Kindra said. "And any other locks you might have left for yourself could be possibly destroyed with it. If you wait too long, he will become too powerful."

"Are there more of you," Millar said. "Your *Soldiers of the New Sun?*"

Kindra nodded. "We are travelers, but we have a stronghold within Metlar. It would be wise to avoid that place."

"Any other places we need to avoid?"

Kindra did not answer.

They all sat in silence for minutes, pondering their next steps.

"Have you anything else to say?" Doran said. "Anything that could help us?"

Kindra looked down. "Entity is already powerful, and dangerous. The longer you wait, the worse it will be. For everyone. I believe he is stronger than you are. There is only one way to stop him, and that's to get your parts first. The Soldiers are growing in strength and number. Their belief is that, with Entity behind them, nothing can get in their way."

"You certainly turned quickly," Millar said. "You expect us to believe you? That you'd turn your back on your 'God?' How can we believe anything you just said?"

"I didn't turn quickly," Kindra said. "But it did start with you."

Millar looked like he was about to say something but only bit his lip.

"Thank you for assisting us," Doran said. "Back in the temple."

Kindra smiled slightly. "I said he was stronger than you, but you still fought him. I did what I had to do. And I would do it again."

"Is there nothing else you can tell us?" Doran said.

The girl shook her head.

"Then we leave at dawn."

Doran motioned to the guards and they led Kindra away.

"Do not put her with the others," Doran said. "I fear for her safety."

Not too gently, they shoved her in front of them.

"I am sorry," Kindra said. "It may mean little, but I hope I have helped in some small way."

Chapter 36

"Bel!" Doran said.

Bel sat up quickly and rubbed her eyes. "I'm awake!"

Millar walked over and gave her a kiss on the top of her curly brown haired head.

There was still a contingency of guards around the town, but with Two and Doran around, they seemed unnecessary. A fire crackled happily in an open air fire pit, and the group, including the two bots, gathered around its warmth.

"So tell me, from the beginning, what happened to you," Doran said. "If you do not mind telling everything again."

"Oh I don't mind," Bel said. All signs of sleepiness were gone. "If they don't mind."

Millar waved her on with a smile.

"Starting from when I left you?"

"Yes, from when you left the island." Doran had not remembered a thing from before that, as he had forced a memory wipe when she departed. "I am sorry. I do not know how to tell you this…"

"That you wiped your memory after we met?"

Doran flinched as he awaited some sort of negative reaction to this.

"Millar told me all about it, don't worry! I'm just happy to see you! And now we can start all over. Just don't do it again." She shook her finger at him, but her wide smile betrayed any seriousness.

Doran was holding the black rock she had given him, and he turned it over in his hand.

"He remembered something about you," Millar said. "Something he couldn't quite delete."

"I saw a cat," Doran said. "Or I thought I did."

This made Bel laugh. "Well, Raly's boat got me back safely through the bay. I don't know how. That's a good boat."

Raly smiled. "My mother helped me build it."

"I am sorry about her," Bel said. "She was a real nice lady. She used to give me spiced licorice candy she'd make from stuff on the cliffs. It was real hot. But real good."

"Thank you, Bel. And I'm sorry about your mom, too."

Bel walked over and they gave each other a big hug. "We'll never forget them."

Raly looked over at Doran and gave him a knowing look.

"Mom acted like she was not going to make it, and made me promise to go somewhere safe. 'To the island?' I said. 'No, that's too dangerous. You barely made it across there once, no chance in trying another time,' she said. I had to go, by myself, and that would be tough, she knew. But there was something bad coming. She felt it, she said. I said to come with me. Take care of me."

Bel paused and her voice choked up.

Millar sat next to her and held her close.

"It's okay, I'm okay. I didn't know any other place else. Only the High Ansels, really. But she made me promise to go. Take Raly's boat and ride the shoreline as far as I could get. To Terask. Gave me food and water and made me run. Run, she said. Don't look back! But I did. I couldn't help it. I looked back and saw her, Millar. She looked strong. And sad. It made me cry, and I almost ran back to her."

"You were strong yourself," Doran said. "I do not know if I could have done that."

Bel looked up at him. "You're still silly. Of course you would have, you're the strongest one here, even though you don't always look it. Don't p… p… what's that word Millar?"

"Patronize."

"Yeah, don't patronize me!"

Doran chuckled and apologized. "Never again."

"Well, I got here and they were super nice to me. Hid me in their temple in the water. That place is something. Put me in a room by myself and told me to be quiet, since there were bad people about. I had to hide from those red hoods, I call them. They were in the temple too. They were waiting for me and knew I was coming. I think they were pretty close to finding me, too. These people helped me hide in their walls, though. There's some hidden tunnels in there not everyone knows about, they said."

"I do not doubt they would have found you soon," Doran said. "But I am wondering how they made it seem like you were in the bottom-most room. I thought you were trapped down there. I followed your signal."

"My signal?"

"Prism—your mom—placed a tracker on you, and we used it to find you."

"I didn't find one on me." Bel turned around to look at her back side and felt along the bottom and top of her shirt.

"Maybe the townspeople took it somehow," Two said. "To keep you safe?"

"Then how would it be where I thought it was?" Doran said.

"It was a trap," Kech said. "They needed you to open the dome, right? The raiders knew you would follow. They knew you were following Bel, somehow, and they must have gotten her signal and set it to the chamber below. Maybe the people of Terask gave it to them to protect her."

Bel shrugged. "Maybe. Maybe that's why the red hoods took the town people and hid them there, too. They made sure I was safe over their own people. That was really nice of them. Anyway, all I know is Millar showed up after Oen broke them out."

Oen flourished a bow, and they laughed.

"I hugged him so hard I thought he'd split. He told me you needed help next, and we all went down those long stairs even though Millar said I should stay up there. I told him there was no way I would leave you alone, and then we heard you fighting hard with that mean bot and those others. Well, you know the rest. Thank you for getting us out of there!"

Doran copied Oen this time by mimicking his bow, and he gave Bel a pat on the back.

"You liked that name, I see." Bel smiled.

Two cocked his body sideways. "What name?"

"Doran. He forgot his name, so I named him after my old cat."

"After your cat?" Two began to laugh.

"He was a really good cat! And where'd you get the name Two, anyway?"

Two stopped laughing and stared at the ground.

"Because it's a great name!" Bel said. "I love it!"

Two's red eye glowed a hair brighter. "Me too."

"Me Bel!" Bel said.

"What?" Two sounded confused.

"Me Two. That's funny!"

Chapter 37

"They're dead."

"What do you mean?" Millar said.

"Who's dead?" Bel said.

"The ones that helped you at the bottom of the temple," the guard said. "Those soldiers. They were murdered last night."

"All of them?" Oen said. "The girl, too?"

Raly looked up at this.

The guard shook his head. "She never went back with the others. Vo'Sav agreed with you and had her sent to another building to be held. Lucky for her."

Raly turned back to finish packing her bag.

"What's going to happen to the rest of the soldiers?" Millar said.

The guard shrugged. "We don't know yet. They're too dangerous to keep here. We can't risk holding them for too long. The rest of their cult might think of it as an act of war. We can't hang them all, either, for the same reason."

"So you're going to let them go?" Millar scoffed. "Back out there? You know they're just going to kill more people."

"There is not much we can do about them. We're just not big enough to stop an attack from their army."

"Do you know where they come from?" Doran said. "The girl said they had a group in Metlar."

"They come from all over. Somehow they receive word and come together. That spirit told them to form their soldiers. What to believe. It is a dark presence in our world."

"It is only a bot," Two said.

"An old one," the guard said. "And some think it is a voice of the earth." He looked out the window toward the sea. "I have to get back to my duties now, is there anything else you need? Before you go, Vo'Sav will speak with you and send you with fresh supplies."

"That is good," Millar said. "And thank you for your help."

The guard bowed and left them. He shut the door to the smaller temple behind him.

The group packed their gear and ate the rest of their breakfast.

"What do you think they are going to do with that girl?" Bel asked.

"It doesn't appear she wants anything to do with the rest of her people," Kech said. Her arm was bandaged up now and in a sling. She wasn't able to carry her book belt yet, so she helped Raly to put it on.

"Maybe they'll just leave her here. Or send her away. I know that guard said they didn't want to keep them imprisoned. Maybe they'll just execute them all."

"Her too?" Bel asked. "She's just a kid."

"She did bad things," Millar said. "Even if she wasn't the one who hurt Mom, she didn't stop them from doing it, either."

"If I did bad things, would you want to hurt me?" Bel said.

"Of course not," Millar said. "But I know you."

"Maybe you just don't know her enough. And plus she did try to stop bad things, weren't you paying attention in the temple?"

"You're not going to make me feel guilty about this." Millar rubbed his arms.

"Looks like she is," Two said.

"Ooh nice work," Oen said. "Is that social cue detection from Doran's part?"

Two shrugged in a coy fashion, and Bel laughed.

"We need to just leave this town." Raly hoisted the books on her back and grunted. It was heavy for her, but she wasn't about to complain about it. Kech readjusted a few belts for her to even out the load. That seemed to help, and Raly was able to walk around with relative ease.

"But what will they do with her?" Bel said.

"It's not our problem," Millar said. "We can't just take her with us, anyway. The people of Terask will figure it out."

"It's sad." Bel kicked the ground. "I think we should figure it out and bring her with us."

"You're lucky I'm bringing you with us." Millar tried to give her a hug but she ducked out of his arms. He smiled, but it was clear he didn't know if she was joking or if she was legitimately mad with him about this.

"I do not think it is a good idea for any of you to come with me." Doran stood up in the center of the group and looked around at them all. "This is my fault. If I had hidden things better, or better yet, destroyed them, there would be no problem. This Entity is powerful, and growing stronger, still. He has an army behind him. Your loss would be devastating to me. Go back to your village. Wait with your village until I finish this myself."

He stood still, and no one moved or said a word for several seconds.

"Phew," Two said. "I was wondering when someone was going to say that. I've been thinking of heading home since I left. And now that I have your permission, I can go back there and wait for you to die alone. Thank you so much, Doran."

Millar stood up. "I think what Two is trying to say, if I can get through his sarcasm, is that we all want to fight with you. Come on. You would be at the bottom of that temple underwater right now, with Entity picking your frame for parts if it wasn't for us."

Bel jumped up too. "It's scary, but I'm not leaving you. Friends don't do that. I'm still sad I left Mom when I did. What if I had stayed with her? Would she still be alive?"

"Don't say that," Millar said. "There was nothing you could do. And you might have been hurt. That's why she made you leave."

"See? That's what Doran is saying to us right now. Go away and hide, because we can't help him. I don't want to believe that." Bel crossed her arms over her chest and sniffled a bit.

"We will do what we can to help." Millar hugged Bel close to him. "We may not be able to fight Entity like you do, but we can all work together and help figure out what to do."

"Together we are stronger," Two said.

"Is that another of Prism's sayings?" Kech said.

"That one is all me. See? I'm getting wiser in my old age."

"You're literally one month old," Oen said.

"And just imagine what I'll be able to do in another one." Two flexed his arms in the air. "I'll be stronger than old Doran himself."

Doran nodded slowly. "It does make me glad to stay together. The road ahead will be difficult. I will do what I can to protect you."

"And I'll do the same!" Bel flexed her arms just like Two.

***

257

The group walked in silence to the center of town where Vo'Sav awaited them. Many people of Terask stared up at Doran and Two as they passed by. They had seen Entity, or had at least heard tales about him as the haunted spirit at the bottom of their temple, but there was something different in these stares. They weren't frightened. Doran overheard some of their whispers, and they spoke of them as heroes. Or saviors.

Some women and children threw white flowers on the ground in front of them as they passed. Whenever Doran caught the eyes of the children, they all smiled and waved at him. Bel skipped along around the bots and didn't mind waving back. This was pretty amazing for her, and she wasn't going to miss out on any of it.

Vo'Sav greeted them with a smile and held his hand before a stack of supplies.

"Food for your trip. And extra blankets. The guards tell me you seek the Blue Ice Mountains. They are treacherous, and the ice and winds are fierce."

Millar bowed. "We thank you. And tell us, what will you do with the girl, Kindra?"

"It is undecided."

"Can you at least wait to decide what to do with her?" Millar said. "You know, really think about it?"

Bel looked up at Millar with a smile and held his hand.

"We will at least do that," Vo'Sav said. "You are wise to not make a decision in anger."

"Well, I have someone to help keep me wise." Millar rubbed Bel's head.

Within an hour, the group had packed up, and waved to the great line of people as they began their journey to the east to stop Entity.

Chapter 38

"I don't understand," Bel said. "This Entity. Is he like you? Was he one of your friends or something?"

Doran shook his head and looked down at her as they walked. "I wish I knew. It is not in any of my memory caches. Not much is. But it sure does feel like we knew each other, no? Perhaps I did something very wrong to him."

"I can't imagine that. You're such a nice bot."

"Yeah," Two said. "Even when you defended yourself from my village and almost ripped my head off you were still such a nice bot."

"You know what I mean," Bel said. "He always does the right thing. Something like that can't be programmed or forgotten."

"What did happen to you, Two?" Oen said. "Your sarcasm level seems to have been turned up pretty high. From what Millar told me about your people, they all seemed pretty serious."

"You never had breakfast with Intari," Two said. "She may seem like a wise old lady, and she is, don't get me wrong. But she has another side to her."

Two stared off to his left in a longing kind of way.

"You miss home," Bel said. "I know what you mean. I miss my mom, too."

Two picked Bel up and placed her atop his wide head. She giggled and grabbed onto the antenna off to the right side and held on as he loped along.

"She had some very nice memories of you, too."

"What do you mean?"

Two tapped the panel where he put the memory cube. "Latest upgrade, and a gift from Prism. Here, walk with me and I'll share some things."

Both of them walked off a bit from the others and talked so only they could hear.

Doran walked beside Kech, who had started to fall behind.

"Are you all right? You sustained some damage back at the temple."

Kech nodded. "I'll be fine. It's this kid who might need a hand. Right Raly?"

Raly huffed and reshifted the book belt on her back. It didn't actually move—the thing was supported by its complex strap system—but she acted like that would help her settle it better.

"I got this."

"Of course you do," Kech said with a smile. "Now Doran, what do you want to know about those mountains?"

"I just want to know if that's where he is."

"Based on what that Soldier child told you all, and what Two and I have discussed, the Blue Ice peaks more than likely hold the next piece. Who knew you were such a sought after collection?"

"Not me. Not anymore. But that makes me wonder, again, why I did this."

Kech stopped to collect her breath. "You erased your memory, presumably after getting rid of all those things, so you couldn't find them again. Maybe you were just waiting for the right time to reclaim yourself. Each of those artifacts is extremely powerful. Just one has made you nearly indestructible."

"Too powerful, it seems. Even in the hands of someone else. Why did I not just destroy those things and get rid of them? I appear to have only made matters worse, now."

"Perhaps something about you made it so you couldn't. Maybe you knew you could get them back."

Doran nodded. "Perhaps. I can only imagine I was tired of that life and everything it brought."

"That may be true, but it appears you must reclaim your power and destroy this Entity."

Doran stared out at the rest of the group as they laughed and talked with each other. "I like this, what you all have. This is what I want."

"Maybe you weren't meant to have it," Kech said.

"That should be a choice for all beings under the sun."

***

The next morning, Doran awoke to find himself staring at the sunrise through the peaks of the white-topped mountains. It had happened again, where he was already in a meditative pose, and what's more, there were others by his side now, all standing the same way he was. Raly, Two, and this time Kech, were silently by his side. Focusing on the day.

This wasn't the first time he'd awoke without knowing what he was doing, but this was becoming an unintentional ritual. Raly gave him a gentle glance and urged him to continue. At this point he felt a little awkward in the poses, but his confidence in letting go and listening to what the land had to tell him had grown.

Bel woke up and got to her feet quickly. She stood on one foot and held her hands out to mimic Doran. "What is that? That looks like a picture I saw! Are you doing magic?"

"I do not know what magic is," Doran said.

261

"Oh you know, the stories. Of monsters and bots and the wonderful things they could do."

"Intari told me stories like that," Two said. "I liked those stories."

"Teach me, teach me!" Bel got behind Raly to watch her. "You're good. You've been practicing!"

"It helps," Raly said.

"Helps what?"

"The hurt." Raly didn't say more. She only breathed deeply and copied Doran's movements, although at times it appeared she might be leading him.

Bel jumped in, and they practiced some forms, repeating them in a cycle as the birds awoke and the sun broke out through the tips of the mountains. Oen and Millar woke up too to see the rest of them practicing.

"Join us," Bel said.

Oen and Millar chuckled. "We don't know how to dance."

"It's not dancing," Bel said. "Don't be that way."

Millar threw a log onto the fire. "Maybe tomorrow."

Oen, who had been mid-pose, shrugged it off as a stretch and a yawn when Millar looked at him. "What?"

"Tomorrow is forever," Bel said. "Start something today."

"You keep quoting her," Millar said.

"Two reminded me of some of the things she said. And it's a good quote."

"It is," Millar said. "But I'm hungry. And I bet you're hungry too."

Everyone else agreed that they were, as well, and so Millar started cooking up the mash. He was getting better at it.

"Tomorrow. I promise I'll try it."

***

"I think I might have something," Two said. "Something that might help us track down the parts. It all started back when Doran and I got those flashbacks. He thought it was just a memory thing, but I realized that's something that could be tracked, if we could pinpoint a signal. I think I can boost this enough to track him down. Entity has also taken on some parts, and the combined memories will make it easier, too. If I can muster the reserves."

"What kind of energy source do you have?" Oen said. "Doran is one thing, his energy system is unbelievable, I wish I knew more about it. But he is pretty closed on the subject. What is yours based on?"

"Heavy absorptive solar cells keep me topped off." Two patted his metal chest. "Lots of panels with high solar interlace quality. Not sure how Intari and the others got a hold of it all, but I bet they paid a lot tracking it down."

"You sound uneasy though," Oen said. "You're not joking around as much. You get serious when you're worried."

Two nodded. "You have an empathic upgrade?"

"We all notice different things."

"Truly. Anyway. Battery life is unstable with the high daily input. Degradation is a thing. I don't know how much time is left on the current charge."

Doran listened carefully to his words. He knew Two pretty well now, and the bot was really good at making predictions with his strategic subsystem. He probably knew exactly how much charge he had left on this battery.

"Doran has been… showing me a few tricks though."

"What kind of tricks?" Oen asked.

"Our dancing, as you put it."

Oen started laughing, but he stopped when no one else joined him. "Seriously? You really think that will do anything?"

Two shrugged.

"That's got to be a load of…" Oen trailed off. "More fairy tales. But really, it looks good though. When you do the wavy arm thing."

"Say what you want," Raly said.

"Yeah, you eat what you want, and I'll do the same," Two said.

"I'm confused," Oen said with a laugh. "More quotes from Millar's mom? You're full of them. All right, I didn't mean anything by what I said about your *dancing*. I'm just worried about standing up to that bot again. Doran took a beating down in the temple, and he had that armor on. Why wouldn't that Entity take it from you, if he wants all of your parts? And Two, you don't have any extra armor to protect yourself."

"I'll be fine," Two said. "Plus, Doran is there to protect us all. Entity didn't want to risk putting himself in danger by getting too close, based on what you told me. He seems to be more of a picker of bones."

Doran nodded. "He probably would have waited until it was certain I was shut down before taking this off me."

"That would have been tough," Bel said. "It's on there good."

"You ought to know, little one." Doran rapped on the armor. "I heard you were the one to find the binding part in here."

Bel smiled and kicked some of the rocks at her feet. "Those things could be anywhere!"

"See, we do not need Two to track them down," Doran said. "We have the Great Diggoo in our presence."

"I see that name has stuck." Bel smiled proudly and kept turning over stones.

"Hey," Two said quietly to Doran. "What did you mean by that?"

***

They walked the rest of the day, and the road grew steeper and steeper until they were high above the coastal plains. Looking back, they saw the ocean far behind them, Terask barely a dot on the horizon.

"We are definitely going in the right direction," Two said. "Can you see the readings? We're very close."

Doran nodded. "Yes, you are still a good tracker, Two. I was just joking earlier."

"Well you never joke, so you can see why I might be worried."

Kech stretched her arms out hesitantly and tenderly, wincing as she did so. "We won't see much along this way. Nearest encampment or village is to the south from here, another day or so away. Here, Raly. I can take my belt, I think."

"I can carry it," Raly said.

"I know you can, but I can too. I feel safer carrying it, you know? For both of us, in case we run into any trouble."

Raly nodded and knelt down to start unbuckling the harnesses. Doran noticed Raly sigh a little as she removed it. She didn't show her discomfort, however, and helped Kech put it on.

"Whenever you need me to carry it, I will."

Kech smiled as she laced it up and yanked the straps tightly. Her stature seemed to grow despite the weight, like she was remembering her old strength as she put it back on. Instead of a burden, it made her appear more powerful.

"That's more like it." Two patted her back. "You look solid now, like me!"

"Thanks," Kech said. "And thank you, Raly. You made it look easy. We'll need to construct you a set sometime, if you want."

Raly beamed, despite the popping her back made as she stretched out.

Millar squinted ahead and drew his visor down. "I see a small pond at the base of that hill. Near the rocks. Do you see anything there?"

Doran and Two scanned the area. The steep mountains deposited a rocky pile of debris at their base for about a hundred feet below a small tree line. A clear pool of water sat at the bottom of it all, surrounded by a few dark tree trunks. Doran fine-tuned his scan again.

"Something is waiting for us," he said.

"Yeah, a couple of bots," Two said. "I'll keep looking for others."

Doran held his hand out. "You all stay here, Two and I will go see what they want."

"What kind are they?" Bel reached for Millar's visor to take a look, but Millar gently pushed her hand away.

"Just a minute. Guardians, looks like. Two of them. Be careful, they look paired."

"Guardians?" Bel said. "Really?"

Doran nodded. As he and Two approached he saw that the pair of bots may have looked the same, but they carried themselves differently. One of the taller, thin humanoid bots stood straight and tall as it held a metal staff at attention. The other sat upon a large boulder in a more casual pose, resting its staff on its knees. It wore a gray strip of cloth around its head as a bandana. Despite it appearing more relaxed, Doran sensed a coiled up power to it. Like a snake.

"Watch out for that one," Two whispered.

"Which one?" Doran shot back.

"Yeah, both of them, I guess. Nevermind."

Doran raised both of his hands, palms outward as they approached. "Greetings. What are two Guardians doing on the road?"

"You know," the sitting bot said with a low voice, but with a female setting. "Those could be weapons you're pointing at us right now. That could be considered rude, and dangerous, don't you think, Brother?"

The other bot did not move.

Doran lowered his hands. "These are not weapons. We are seeking a way through this land. Do you mean to hinder us, or let us pass?"

"How pretentious, thinking we care about a couple of broken down bots coming along the road."

"So, you're going to let us pass?" Two said.

"How pretentious, thinking we would let you both go." The bot passed the metal staff from one hand to the other in sweeping arcs. She increased the arc range until it formed a circle.

"These guys," Two said. "I do believe they are intentionally wasting our time. As Entity goes for the weapon."

"Do not speak His name," the female bot said.

"Then what are your names?" Doran said.

The staff faltered in its spinning and the bot caught it before she dropped it. "I am Willa, and I am your undoing. But we did not wait here for you to talk."

"Sure seems like it," Two said. "Willa."

Doran stifled a chuckle as the bot tightened her grip on the staff. "Then what are you here for? Surely not to fight us. That would not end well for you."

The second bot snapped to an attacking pose and held the staff out.

Willa stood up. "Oh, you've made Enriss upset."

"Willa *and* Enriss?" Two said, casually gesturing to Doran. "See, those are both great names. I wonder what the laws are on changing a bot's name."

In an instant, Two reached down and grabbed a large boulder with both hands, spun around and launched it at Enriss. The robot quickly ducked, but there was no need. It flew well over his head.

"Perhaps you should work on your aim," Willa said.

"I'd say it's pretty good."

A deep rumbling emanated from the hillside as a large pile of rocks rolled down toward the bots. Enriss tried to jump out of the way, but not before a knee-high boulder rolled over his leg and knocked him down.

Willa sidestepped all the debris as she evaded the pile, but she didn't watch where she ended up. Doran, not waiting to survey things, tackled Willa from behind and dropped her face first into the water. Still clutching onto the staff, she twisted her body and swung it around at Doran's feet. She caught his heel at the right angle and he tipped to the side to regain his balance. Before he could attack, Willa was back on her feet.

Meanwhile, Two spun his arms round and smashed Enriss square in the face. Enriss's head twisted at an angle that didn't seem normal, but it didn't slow him down. Two reached back to swing again, but the staff drove right up into his middle eye. The red light on it flashed out and he stumbled backwards, waving his hands in front of his face before another strike of the staff swept for his legs. Two was much too solid and low to the ground for this to have any effect, and Enriss dropped the staff.

"Stupid bot, with a stupid name." Two stumbled blindly for a few seconds until his center eye blinked on again. "There we go. Where are you?"

Doran held his arms up and blocked Willa's blurring attacks. Under the repeated hits, his forearms started to wear and dent slightly. He switched stances in between her blows and shifted closer to her, well within her reach. This made her step back reflexively but the ground was uneven. She missed a beat as she slipped on a rock, and Doran took that opportunity to punch her twice in the head and follow up with a blindingly fast kick to her midsection. She crumpled forward but still clung onto her staff with two hands. Doran drove his leg up high and then down again upon the staff. She tried to keep her grip, and that was her downfall. The force of the kick was so intense that it ripped her hands off in a quick pop. Sparks bled out of her wrists and she groaned in pain.

Doran picked up her staff and assumed a new pose to fit the weapon. Willa's head twitched as she looked up at him with what could have been fear in her robotic eyes.

"Willa!" the other bot yelled out in a gravelly deep voice.

Doran did not look away. He knew better than to do that with a dangerous enemy. One blow could finish her then. He gripped the staff tightly and his blue eyes narrowed.

A loud clang and crash from behind made him pause, though.

"It's over, Doran," Two said.

With a step backwards, Doran moved so he could see Willa and Enriss at the same time. The other bot was missing a leg, and Two held it out in front of him like a weapon. He quickly put it behind his back and dropped it with an awkward chuckle. Enriss crawled over to Willa by pulling himself along and pushing off of his one remaining leg.

"Where has your master gone?" Doran said in a booming voice. "Where is Entity?"

Enriss reached Willa and scanned her with his still-bent head. She was twitching uncontrollably.

"Do not end my sister, please," Enriss said.

"Tell us where he is." Doran's voice no longer held the malice and threat like before. "We won't end either of you. But tell us where he is."

"Not a good idea," Two whispered. He pointed to his head in a knowing fashion to where the artifact was embedded.

Enriss held Willa's head in his hands and tried to stop the shaking motion. She managed to force her head into a singular nod though, and Enriss looked at them.

"Up this road. There is a path to the right that leads up into that mountain." Enriss pointed to that peak. "There is a cave. It will lead you to him. It will do you no good though."

"Let us handle that," Doran said. "Do not hinder us anymore."

Enriss bowed his head and went back to care for his sister.

Chapter 39

"They were brother and sister?" Bel said. "Like me and Millar?"

"Something like that," Two said. "Maybe they were built at the same time."

"But they talked like real people?" Bel said.

"Bots do that," Two said. "Look at me. I practically feel like Doran is family. Right, Doran?"

"Hmm? Oh, affirmative."

"Wow, we're just like real people," Two said in a lower voice.

"That's sad." Bel kicked a stone and it skipped around before coming to a stop on the mountain path. "But you let them go?"

Two nodded, which he did by moving his entire upper body. "I even recommended that we shut them down. That's what the implant suggested, anyway. But Doran had nothing to do with that. After they told us what we needed to know, he just let them be."

"That's good," Bel said.

"We had to watch that from a distance," Millar said. "You both seemed to handle yourselves just fine against them."

"Yeah, we did a great job, right?" Two nudged Doran's side with his elbow. "Affirmative? You're tough today. Anyway, maybe that's part of Entity's plan. To draw us in after letting us feel strong."

"Either way," Doran said. "We must stop him."

"Remember the last time," Two said in a sing-song voice.

"We did just fine."

"Right, being buried under the water was fine," Two said. "I know, I know. We've talked about this before. Kindra said he's going after a powerful artifact. Some weapon. And he was already pretty strong to begin with."

"But we did not know he was there. Now we have that advantage. He's never been to this place, at least where he needs to go with those boots. And maybe he won't have the weapon yet? Maybe I need to be here to unlock some door as well."

"Okay, so we're more even with him. We've got to have a better plan than charging in."

"If you just stopped altogether, maybe he wouldn't be able to get the weapon," Raly said. "If you hadn't opened that shrine under the water temple, where would he be now?"

"Still there," Doran said. "Waiting. Building up his soldiers. Getting stronger."

"Maybe," Raly said.

"I could beat him to this weapon," Doran said. "Destroy him. Then, it will truly be over."

No one spoke against him after that, and they walked up the mountain trail in silence.

***

The treeline thinned out as they ascended until there were only scrubby brush trees, stunted by the constant wind. Up ahead, a cliff appeared, rising through a cloud bank like the walls of some ancient fortress.

"You sure picked some good places to hide your things," Two said.

"Too good," Millar said.

A sudden vision flashed before Doran's eyes. These steep cliffs at night. Rocks crumbling and falling. Followed by a peaceful feeling of release. These were his own memories coming back to him. He had been glad to get rid of this weapon. He looked over at Two walking beside him. The bot gave him an understanding nod.

In his own hands these things were dangerous, he could not allow someone else with evil intent to possess them.

The trail narrowed so they could only walk single file. Doran led the way, and Two walked at the back to make sure no one fell behind. Rocks near the edge of the path loosened and slid down the steep walls. None of them spoke, and they focused instead on their footsteps, walking bent-over in the wind.

For an hour they trudged, taking breaks here and there beside large boulders that had broken loose and fallen sometime in the past. No matter where they sat, the wind always found a way to hit them. Two and Doran tried to position themselves to help block it, but that did little. Raly offered to take Kech's book belt again, but she refused.

"We have to be almost there," Oen yelled, which only came out as a whisper.

"I have not seen any tracks," Doran said. "Not much could make a mark on this ground, I suppose."

Two held out his hand forward, as if pinpointing something. "We are getting closer. Not much longer now."

Another hour of inching along the bare terrain, and the sun disappeared behind the clouds. The day seemed almost at an end because of the sudden darkness, but it was only early afternoon. They put on the extra layers of clothing—which the people of Terask had given them—but still Bel huddled close to Millar's side with her teeth chattering. Luckily, with the first vestiges of spring, the ice storms which normally covered the mountains were absent, at least that day.

They reached a spot where two steep spikes of rock seemed to have been driven into the mountainside. A large hole opened into the mountainside like some gaping maw. Jagged black rocks all around the entrance made it look like the fangs of some giant creature. White and blue patches of ice lined the ground.

"This is it," Two said. "The signal is the strongest here."

"Watch your footing," Doran said. "Two and I will go first here. The path looks narrow, and we do not want you in danger of sliding down a crevasse."

"Ooh, crevasse," Two said. "I always find it interesting how you can still have a wide vocabulary after having deleted yourself. Bravo."

"Smart ass," Doran said. "Is that better?"

"Ah, there's the dumbed down language I came here for. Thank you."

The inside path was covered with both rock and ice and, despite the respite from the wind, they still had to walk slowly to avoid slipping. Doran and Two pointed out where the main dangers were, but since they were so much bigger, sometimes they missed the smaller ones that would cause problems. Millar led the way for the humans and held out his pry hammer with the pick side ready to jam into the ice if needed.

The path wound its way straight into the mountain, neither going up nor down. It was tall enough for Doran, but occasionally he would have to chip a huge ice chunk hanging from the ceiling to clear the way. The room opened up a bit sideways with a couple of pathways going in different directions.

"It's snowing!" Bel waved her hands in the shower of ice caused by Doran's smashing.

She stepped off to the side, still playing in the snowy mist, and suddenly slipped. In an instant, she fell through a small hole in the ground. Her short shriek faded as she slid away.

"Bel!" Millar shouted as he flattened himself on the floor to peer into the hole.

After a few seconds, they heard her reply.

"I'm all right!" she called from a distance. "That was fun!"

"Stay there," Millar shouted. "We're coming."

He opened up the pack given to them by Vo'Sav and pulled out a coiled-up rope. He looked for something to tie it on to, but there were no clear outcrops of stone.

"I can hold this," Doran said.

Millar drove the hammer down into the ice, and the sharp pick drove in deeply. He lashed the rope to it and let the coiled end through the hole.

"I can do this, you won't know if something comes along and you have to let go. This is safer."

Millar tied the rope around his waist and climbed into the hole feet first.

"You shouldn't waste time," Millar said. "Go ahead, I'll be right back with her."

Doran thought about it. The boy was probably right, but he did not feel comfortable leaving him behind.

"Slow down," Two said. "We need to stay together. I say we just wait here for Entity to come out. He will have gotten the weapon by now and will be waiting for us. Better for us to be prepared here."

"I've got to go." Millar's head bobbed up and down in the hole as he started to lower himself down. "Bel may say she's all right, but I've got to check on her."

"But…"

The pry hammer shifted in the ice just then and slid out of its hole. Millar cried out and sped away just as Bel had. The clattering of the hammer followed him as he disappeared.

"Millar!" Raly shouted down the hole. "Was that the only rope we have?"

Voices echoed back as both Millar and Bel talked at the same time. Oen and Kech shook their heads after checking their packs. "No extra rope."

"We've got to get them," Raly said. "There's no way back up there without a rope." She ran toward a branching tunnel that appeared to be sloping downwards, checking her feet as she did.

"Wait!" Two said. "All right, everyone stop!"

But Oen had already followed Raly away, and Kech stuck her head in the hole in the ground.

"Fine, that's fine," Two mumbled. "Why follow a perfectly good plan? Wait. Here." He emphasized these words and pointed to Doran just before he went after Raly and Oen.

In the chaos, Doran heard something in the distance. A faint melody drifting through the biggest tunnel. A familiar melody. It called to him.

"Do you hear that?" he said to Kech.

Kech just cursed something into the hole.

This was it. It was the tune that had eluded him for so long. Whisps that had only briefly lit into his memory were now a song he knew in his core. A soft flute played the haunting song somewhere in these caves.

An image grew in his mind, another flash of a memory. Bits and pieces, this time of other beings in his life. His friends and family. One small human, a tiny girl he once knew a long time ago. She'd played the song for him. The comforting melody wrapped itself around him. He knew he had to let go of everything.

He opened his eyes, and he found himself in a different room. How much time had passed, he did not know. This place was a vast chamber filled with a bright light emanating from deep pockets in the ground. Instead of dark stones like outside, this area contained mostly white ones, and the lights from all around made everything glow. He overlooked it all from a singular platform that ended abruptly like a broken bridge. Across the chasm, well beyond reach, the path continued on through a darkened passageway, and Doran knew that in there was the chamber that Entity sought.

Did he already possess the weapon? Was he waiting up there? Or had he already left?

Something told him, however, that the weapon was unclaimed. He felt it to be true. And he knew he had to get it before Entity did. He would not lead him to it like in the water temple, however. Nor would he lead his friends into danger. He had to make a better plan. The easy way, and the only one possible, it seemed, was to use the boots he had hidden in Terask to easily reach the broken path. There did not appear to be another way. At least not from up here.

So he slowly climbed down the steep walls, down onto the glowing valley floor. He drove his fingers into the stones to stop from sliding down too quickly. Bits and flakes ground off as he slid on the white marbled stone. Faint purple and red veins flowed through the rock, as if they were blood vessels.

The room felt alive. The throbbing of the lights increased from below and cascaded through the room. Doran reached the bottom and he stood still for a moment as the crumbled rocks settled at his feet in neat piles of chipped stone.

He shifted through them and they slid off in pleasant, tinkling sounds. Some rock slid over the edge into the lighted pools of water. Instead of piling up in them, the surface of these pools bubbled and consumed the stones.

Doran took a hesitant step back from the nearest pool. He held his hand over it to get a sense of what was happening inside, but it did not appear to be hot. It was a strange mix of light and rock in a fluid mixture, unlike anything he had ever beheld. It mesmerized him, but he quickly snapped out of it to plan a path across the room to where he would need to climb.

He tried not to think of how steep that last wall had been when he slid down it. It would take some effort to climb up that again.

Once again, the song floated into the air and called to him. He followed the tune until he was in the center of the room. The melody made him want to sit on the floor and just stay there, but he gripped his fists tightly. Was this trying to slow him down? He needed his speed and energy. He needed to be ready.

But he realized too late what was happening. The song cracked in fragments as a dark shape struck him in the side and knocked him off balance. He fought to regain his footing, but the shape flew off and in a circle so quickly he could barely see it, and so he could not defend himself when it hit him again.

One of his feet stepped back into a lighted pool and he felt its power. It was not hot, but cold. Freezing. The energy drained from his leg in an instant before he could yank it fully from the pit. He regained his footing and placed it on the solid ground again, but he could barely sense the receptors in his foot.

He saw the being now before him. The black twisted shape of the bot he saw in the temple, with its one yellow eye glaring at him. A burnt ridge covered the place where its other eye had been.

"Predictable." Entity burst forward again from the drive of the boots. Their blue energy trailed behind as Entity dove at him again.

Doran held up his hands to block the attack, but his footing faltered. This time when Entity struck him he was barely able to stay up. Another pass hit him, and he fell face forward. Bright flashes of light flared as he struck the stone, and his vision blurred out for a few moments.

He got to his knees and looked around. The dark bot stood twenty feet away on the other edge of a large pool, no longer hovering. Instead, he held out his right arm at Doran. His hand had a device attached to it. The barrel of it sat above his fist, and it began to power up with a quick whine.

Entity had found the weapon. He had drawn Doran in and was now going to eliminate him. The light on the gun pulsed a fraction of a second before releasing a bolt of light. Doran leapt before it fired, and the blast exploded into thousands of shards. Doran hit the ground, but he still wasn't used to his foot being inoperable, and he fell again. He propped himself up just in time to see Entity speed toward him.

His fist connected with Doran's jaw and drove his head sideways into the ground. More pain spread into his body now from his leg. He managed to look over and see that he had slid into the pool again, this time up to his thigh. The sensors all cut out in the appendage and he scrambled to pull himself out.

Entity stood over him and reached back to punch him again. Doran rolled out of the way as his fist crashed into the floor. He dipped his already numb foot into the pool and swept out a spray of the liquid, and Entity held up his hands as the glowing substance hit his face.

He screamed and cursed as the material froze on contact with his missing eye. The exposed wiring turned dark with the liquid. Enraged, he pointed his charged weapon at Doran's chest and fired. The shot hit him square and direct, and although he wore his ancient armor to protect him, the momentum of it sent him flying into one of the liquid pools.

Doran scrambled and flailed his arms about, he even grabbed the ledge of the pool to pull himself out, but soon the freezing material seeped into his body. He could fight it no longer. He fell in and could sense no more.

Chapter 40

Through the frozen fog that covered his mind, Doran heard the song. Slow and weak at first, then it grew. It called him back from the edge of darkness. He was surrounded by light, and it flowed through him. The coldness penetrated his body, and he floated there, still and calm. This was the source of that song.

He was barely aware of the world outside of the light now. Only shades of images swept past him. And nothing felt important anymore. Nothing drew him… anywhere. He just flowed.

Entity dragged him out of the liquid and he did not care. The other bot moved quickly, and often swung his hands away when the cold of his touch was too much to bear. Doran's body jerked as Entity stripped the armor from his core and exposed his old circuitry beneath. The bolts pinged off his body as the first half came off, then the back side. His body felt as light as snow now, drifting this way and that as Entity removed his parts.

His yellow, glowing eye grew close to his own face and his words came from beyond.

"You took something from me, let me return the favor."

Doran's head jammed back into the stone but only barely registered the scraping against the floor. A bright light flashed once and then fell black. Entity yanked his hand back from Doran's head with a long string of wire and a plug. It only briefly registered to him that that was his eye.

"Always drawn to the helpless. Weak drawn to weak. I can see things you know. Things that come from your parts."

Doran felt his ribcage pried open. Streams of pain appeared, but they never registered to him—he only sensed them happening now, somewhere else.

"I hate your cursed parts—all the things they show me about your stinking past, the things you want to forget. But I will not be forgotten. You are always trailing after a song, or a family. And that is something you will never have again."

Doran felt Entity root around for something in his chest, and then he wrenched it out. Doran's consciousness faded quickly now. Whatever Entity needed, he had taken it. His foot drove into Doran's gut and pushed him back into the liquid with a splash. He didn't sink immediately, however. He got hung up in the fluid and the rocks jutting out from the surface. His one remaining eye watched Entity assemble the removed parts onto his own body. First whatever he had removed from Doran's chest, then the armor, and then finally he plugged the eye into his own socket. The light flickered briefly and then glowed a soft blue.

So this was it. This was how he was going to go out.

It didn't matter now. Entity had gotten what he came for, and it somehow didn't matter to him.

Until he saw another figure appear from above.

It was Two.

Doran heard him shout a challenge to Entity from a far distance, but it was loud. Loud enough to vibrate the liquid surrounding Doran's body.

No, Two! Don't do this!

But he couldn't speak even if he wanted to at this point. His parts were nearly completely frozen. He struggled to move, to grip on to something, but he couldn't find anything to hold. His vision slipped away until it was almost fully dark.

Two landed on Entity's back and drove him into the ground. The fallen bot scrambled its arms to try to get up, but Two's weight pinned him down. He pounded relentlessly, but the new armor turned back every hit. Two repositioned himself to hit Entity's head, and in that moment he swung around his gun arm.

There was a whining charge followed by Two's right arm blasting into bits off of his body. Two stumbled backward and looked over at what remained of his limb. Entity took that stunned moment to get to his feet and quickly attack Two.

Terror overtook Doran now. He had almost settled into a peaceful state of forgetfulness, but with his friend in danger he tried to escape. The uselessness of it hit him. He could not move. He could only lay there and watch his friend take hit after hit from the dark bot.

Why didn't Entity fire his weapon again? Why did he take his time, nearly relishing each strike of his fist against the one-armed bot?

Doran knew why. It was all a show. Entity gloated in his victory over the both of them.

Two crumpled to his knees, and his eyes faded behind his cracked faceplate. Entity split the glass with one more blow, and the lights faded entirely. He rooted around in Two's body frame and pulled out the part that Doran had once threatened to take from him. That was it, that was the final part he needed.

He claimed the piece and let Two's body drop onto the ground, inches from Doran's face. With his final moments, Doran watched Entity use his boots one last time to reach the pathway up above, and then he, too, lost his vision to the blurry depths surrounding him.

Chapter 41

But the light did not fade entirely, and the song had not stopped. A clear, ringing tone played in the distance. Something still called to him from below. Doran let go of the side of the pool, and the light consumed him.

The bright center of the pool beckoned him in with its song. And a voice. Yes, he clearly heard a voice through the pool. Someone called a name. He did not recognize it, nor did his mind comprehend the word, but he felt it was his name.

"You came." It was a female voice.

"Who are you?" Doran didn't think he spoke it aloud—maybe it was in his mind.

"You know who I am. I have been waiting for you to return."

"You," Doran said. "I do know you."

He felt her smile—it was so much like that first glimmer of daylight upon waking in the cave, back on the island. She was there with him, and in him. She reached out her hand, and he clasped it.

And then he remembered. He knew why. He knew who he was. He knew who she was. And he remembered why he'd needed to forget.

It had not been his fault, not really. But he'd had no one else to blame.

The Cora'chan were there to help others. To fight for those who could not fight. He was their leader, and they were powerful. But in the end, they were too powerful.

Lands had burned. Buildings fell. People died.

His friends twisted and turned on each other.

And he was the only one to stop them.

In the end, he was alone. And that was why he had to forget.

"I don't blame you for forgetting me. I know why. I forgive you."

Doran could clearly see Prism's face, and he thought that if she could, she would be smiling. He certainly felt the warmth of her smile.

And then his heart dropped. All these memories, the forgotten life that he'd lived, all his memories with her—and he never was able to say goodbye before she died. Instead he had just watched her pass like some unknown thing.

"That was one moment," Prism said. "You know we shared more than just that. And there is still more for you to do."

All of what she had done flashed back to him now, and he drank it in. She had saved the royal line from the war of the Cora'chan. The ones that they were bidden to protect with their lives.

She had watched over them throughout the years. She had kept them safe throughout the long ages. She had carried on when he had forgotten. Many lifetimes, many bloodlines, until she protected them even in this time. Even the youngest of all of them.

A little girl.

The grip that held onto Doran's hand loosened, and his vision slipped for a moment. But seeing Bel, clear in his mind, made him grip even tighter.

"Come back."

As light as a child, Doran was brought back through the pool. He landed on the ground and the icy waters passed from his body. His life still hung on by a hair.

Through his one good eye, he saw that Two clasped onto his hand. How long had he been holding on? Had he pulled him up?

Two's red eye blinked twice.

"I want to go home. Take me home."

"I promise I will."

And with that, the red light blinked one last time and then disappeared.

Everything seemed to move slower as Two faded. Doran felt like he was on another plane from all of this, like he was watching another vision pass before his eyes. His voice was gone, despite all he wanted to shout to his friend. The cave spun around. Seconds passed like hours as his life spilled away. Out of the corner of his eyes, he spied motion from up above, again. Had Entity come back to finish him? To push him back in the waters?

***

"Doran!" Millar yelled. "Two?"

Millar tried to slow his sister down, but she started to slide down the steep walls of the white room before he could stop her. She jumped into giant grooves left there, possibly by where one of the two bots had carved a path, not caring about how to get back up.

He couldn't believe it. Were both of his friends… dead? How could they be? They were the most powerful things he could imagine. But they weren't moving.

And had that blur that wound past them been Entity escaping? Did he have the weapon? He had to. Nothing else could have stopped both of the bots down there. But none of that mattered now. Millar jumped down into the debris after Bel without another thought.

Oen, Raly, and Kech followed them in a heartbeat. No one said a thing, but Millar thought he heard crying coming from behind him. Bel was surprisingly quiet, but that was probably because she was dead focused on reaching the bots.

The bottom of the room opened out into an area pocked with giant pools of some liquid. Something told him not to touch it, though. Luckily, Bel thought the same thing and wound her way between the glowing pools.

Bel reached the bots first and climbed up onto Doran's chest to peer into his one-eyed face. He looked bad. His armor had been ripped off and something had been torn out of his chest. Was that his power source? A strange but familiar part lay on the ground in front of him. Millar recognized it as the one Bel had found long ago, the one that had led Entity to their town.

Bel sat beside Doran's neck and held his face. She shook him gently as she stared into his remaining eye.

"Come on, wake up!"

Her voice wavered as she repeated herself.

Millar looked over both bots. Two still clung to Doran's hand. It looked like he had pulled him out of the pool in his final moments. Doran's other arm lay twisted behind him, out of sight, and dangling below the surface of the liquid. Millar checked on Two's vital components and found that he was completely shut down. One of his arms had been blasted off. Bits and pieces of it lay behind him.

His faceplate in the center of his body frame had been smashed and a hole showed into his head.

"He took it," Millar said. "Doran's old component. If he has that processor, and Two's thoughts were all through it, then there's a good chance he knows how to track any remaining pieces."

"Are they both dead?" Raly said. Her voice was lifeless. She had witnessed too much loss in such a short time. They all had.

"No, no, no," Bel repeated as she turned Doran's head. "Please, no."

Oen scanned Doran's split-open chest without saying a word. There was a space in the very center, which looked to be where a heart would be in a human, and there was an empty hole.

"We always wondered what his power system was." Oen traced the lines with his fingers. "This is it. I've never seen anything like it. With this wiring. What is that made of? And those marks? Is that writing? This is incredible."

"Can you do anything about it?" Millar said.

"I wouldn't know what to do. No one would. But it doesn't look like Entity ripped out the whole system, just the power supply."

"He took your heart," Bel said in a low voice.

Suddenly, Doran's hand twitched and his head bobbled, but his eye never looked away from Bel. A faint blue glow appeared in its depths, almost it looked like a reflection of the glowing waters.

"You moved!" Bel said.

Millar waited a moment, but nothing else happened. He let out a breath he didn't know he was holding. "Just a death twitch, or something. There's nothing left. Entity took it all."

"No, it's not, look!" Bel pointed to Doran's hand. "He's pointing at me!"

"No, Bel," Millar said. "He's not."

"He is! What is he telling me? What does he want?"

Bel looked into his chest at the opening where something that powered him used to sit. It was roughly fist sized. She smiled widely, pulled her pack off, and began to rummage through it.

"What?" Millar said. "What is it?"

"You'll see! I meant to show you before, but I never got the chance."

She pulled out a cobalt blue stone, the size of her hand. "This! He gave it to me a long time ago, on the island."

She reached into Doran's chest and placed the stone in the center spot. It was a perfect fit. They all waited expectantly for something to happen, but nothing did.

Oen inspected the casing again and began to straighten out bent wires and metal shards that had been ripped open. Anything to try to connect the power to Doran's system. He worked for several minutes, but nothing happened. He hung his head.

Millar put his hand on Oen's shoulder. "You did your best."

Bel began to cry.

Millar heard a shifting sound behind him and turned to see Raly standing on one foot. She twisted and waved her arms in a flowing motion, just like Doran had shown them. The pattern completed and she started again. This time Kech stood beside her, and so did Bel. They each breathed in deeply and flowed with their breath.

Bel began to hum a simple tune that fit with the forms. A sad, sweet tune that Millar thought he recognized. He looked at Raly, and she smiled back, waving for him to join.

It didn't feel silly to him now. It felt right. Bel's tune resonated with the cave, and the waters pulsed out in rhythm to her singing. Millar and Oen joined them as best they could, following Raly's lead, until the music and the forms became one.

The glowing of the cave must have clouded Millar's eyes, because it now shone brighter and seemed to be growing inside of Doran's chest. He rubbed his eyes and stared again. This time there was no mistaking it. The stone inside Doran's chest throbbed like a heart beating, and wires of light seemed to grow like vines within the casing to envelope his new heart. They all stopped moving now, but Bel continued to hum the tune.

Doran's body shifted. A perceptible murmur of motion flowed across his body, like a ripple across a pond. His eye began to glow with a blue light again. His arms straightened and he brought them to his sides.

"What's that?" Kech pointed behind Doran's back to where the other arm had been twisted up.

Doran brought forth a blade of pure light. Millar could only guess that he had retrieved it from the pool. That was the only explanation. It was a thing of power. And it felt like it belonged in Doran's hand.

For the first time, Millar knew for certain that Doran was the Cora'chan.

Chapter 42

"Bel?" Doran said. He then looked to his other friends and breathed a sigh of relief.

Doran rose to his feet shakily. That freezing liquid had sunk into his frame and slowed his movements, and also his reactions. Everything seemed to still have a trace of glowing as lights moved past him like fireflies. Freezing liquid dripped from his left hand after pulling it free from the pool.

Everyone stared at the glowing metal sword. He turned it over and then held it aloft. Was it glowing, or merely reflecting the light? It was the most beautiful yet simple weapon he had ever seen, and he knew when he held it wasn't his first time looking upon it. As soon as he had found it beneath the surface, memories had bubbled up with it.

He had remembered much, but also some things that he knew he couldn't have remembered. Like how Prism had found Bel amidst the line of the fallen royals. How could that be possible? And where did that memory come from? That wasn't his own, and any images trapped within the sword were too old, as well.

Two! His friend had used his last remaining energy to pull him out of the liquid. It had to be the connection there that showed him Prism's memories. He reached down to his fallen form and put his hand on his back. Gently he pulled him to the side so he could look inside his chest panel.

Entity had ripped through there to get his old part, but he didn't take everything. He did not appear to want to know about any personal feelings that Doran had. It was like a curse to him, and he revulsed from any touch to it.

Doran gently reached into Two's exposed faceplate and saw what he was looking for. It was the small, glowing cube that held Prism's last memories, and probably more. Touching Two had shown Doran some of Prism's very powerful core memories.

He took the cube and cupped it gently in his hand. He would hold onto this forever since it held memories from his two favorite beings in the world. Doran didn't have all his old memories, but he certainly remembered Prism now, and how she had helped him and sacrificed much for him.

He nearly fell over. Not because of the cold, but because of all she meant to him. She had said it was all right that he had forgotten her, but he did not feel that way. Part of him died because he had to forget her in the first place, and the next, and last, time he saw her, he had no idea who she was, or what she had done for him…

Doran pounded the ground with his fist. He placed the sword down and gently straightened Two's body.

"Is there anything you can do?" Doran asked Oen.

Oen quickly scrambled onto Two's frame and inspected his systems.

"This is something more manageable than yours." Oen traced wiring and circuits through different boxes. "But he is badly damaged. Nothing is responding."

"Even his power?" Bel asked. "That was what was wrong with Doran."

"This shows there's a power supply." Oen used a device to show everyone. "It's just not connected anymore. Main circuits are down. Memory banks are dead. Poor guy, he's not coming back from this."

"He saved my life," Doran said. "Many times before today, yes, but I mean today. He pulled me out of this." He gestured to the liquid with his metal blade.

"That is some weapon," Kech said. "Are you telling us that you just happened to find it beneath the surface there?"

Doran nodded. "It's true. I did."

"Then I don't think it was just luck, you finding that," Kech said. "You had to have known it was there, somehow."

"If only I had known earlier, I might have been able to stop Entity here. But now that he has that powerful weapon, and Two's memory, and the strategic subsystem, he will be able to track down any remaining parts."

"I think we can find him," Kech said. "And I think that you can stop him."

"Me?" Doran said. He still moved a little awkwardly and pointed to his chest cavity. "Look at this."

"You can do it," Bel said. "It doesn't look that bad."

"Maybe you are not seeing what I see right now," Doran said.

His chest was still exposed since all the metal had been pulled back. Interior lights coruscated like blood flowing through his body away from the blue stone. It appeared like some of the connective parts had somehow grown in him and, despite having no new wires installed, the pathways were all connected.

"Your heart works again," Bel said.

Doran knelt down beside her. "Thank you for hearing me, little one."

Bel smiled. "You looked at me and showed me!"

"I did." She may not have known, but that was probably the last bit of movement and thought that he would have been able to do.

"What are we going to do about Two?" Raly said. "We can't just leave him here."

Doran placed his hand on her back. "I will do what I can to lift him, but I do not know if I can make it back up."

"We could leave him here," Millar said. "He would be safe. If the weapon and that sword were safe here, he can stay here a while until we figure out what to do with him."

Doran nodded. He placed the sword down on the ground and gently straightened Two's body like he was lying asleep. He placed his one arm reverently across his chest. Bel and Millar gathered the shattered pieces of his other arm and laid them beside him.

"He looks like an angel," Bel said.

The light glowed brightly around them and reflected off of Two's body and remaining faceplate. He did look peaceful now.

"We will miss you," Bel said. "I wish I had another heart for you, too."

"For you, Two," Millar said.

Bel smiled and held Millar's hand.

Doran placed the six-foot long blade behind his back, and a magnetic panel locked it into place.

"I didn't know you had that." Millar marveled at the weapon, which seemed to float a few inches away from Doran's back.

"I am learning new things all the time."

Doran limped behind the others as they went back to the wall. Sliding down had been considerably easier than what it looked like they had to do to go back up. There were grooves aligned in the slanted rock that Bel first tried to scramble up, but the pieces kept sliding, and it took a lot of effort to make little headway.

The rest had to constantly move out of the way to avoid getting hit by any of the white rock debris sliding back down. All told, it took them over an hour to find their way fifty feet up the wall and back to the pathway. They did it, but their fingers and legs were all banged up and bruised, and more than just Doran were limping by the end of it.

They looked over the edge and saw Two's gray body peacefully lying between the pools below.

"Bye, Two." Bel waved down to him. "We'll see you again someday."

"Better bring some ropes for the way back up," Oen said.

Besides saying that, he grew pensive, but he was obviously doing some mental calculations on how to get Two up out of there.

"It is a good resting place," Kech said.

"No," Raly said. "I think he'd prefer to be back with his people."

Doran nodded. It had been Two's last wish to go back home, but he did not tell them this. There were many things he had to take care of first.

"Are we ever going to talk about what happened down there?" Millar said. "Are we just going to pretend we did that?"

"What happened?" Doran asked.

Raly turned to face him but gave Millar a sideways look that warned him not to joke. "We did what you taught us," Raly said. "When you were powerless and needed our help."

"Come on," Millar said. "There's no way that did anything. Bel just gave him the stone and it finally powered him up."

"I have been up and down these shores my whole life," Kech said. "I have read many stories. Heard many tales. I believe in what we did."

"When you walk along the Way, you will see many strange things." Doran limped along back up the icy pathway.

"Why didn't it do anything for Two?" Oen said.

No one responded. Doran trudged along and scraped his foot against the ground every time he stepped. He knew they had failed to stop Entity from getting the weapon, and now he was even stronger because of his and Two's pieces.

Everything he did made Entity stronger.

"Where do we go now?" Raly said. "Back home?"

"We need to go somewhere to get Doran fixed," Millar said. "He's in no shape to go after Entity now."

Doran stopped walking and they turned around to face him. "I am going after him. I need to stop him."

"You can barely walk, you can't see straight." Oen waved his hand in front of Doran's missing eye. "If you go face him now you're going to get destroyed."

"I did not trust myself to keep my parts, I will not trust anyone else to do it, either."

"Wait," Millar said. "How do you remember that?"

Doran paused for a moment. "I am remembering more now. I saw things under that pool. Things I know from my past. I think that they came to me when I held this."

Doran pointed to the sword on his back.

"So that was yours," Kech said. "You put that there, too. Like the weapon that Entity has now."

Doran began to walk again, and they all continued on the path out of the mountain. "I remembered what I did. I grew too powerful, and less careful about that power. People died. Friends died. I needed to let it all go. I only wish I had destroyed them."

"Did you remember anything else," Millar said. "You know, that might be useful against Entity?"

But Doran did not speak. Instead he turned Two's memory cube in his hand. He focused on each step but also upon the last memories of Prism that he had when he was under the pool.

The sun was still out as they exited the mountain tunnel, but they watched it set far off into the ocean, and then everything hung in the grayness of twilight.

"Where do we go now?" Bel said. "Do you remember where your parts are now?"

Doran shook his head. That was something he would not remember. He looked down at Bel. Should he tell her she was the daughter of ancient rulers? She flipped over a flat rock that lay beside the path and she smiled up at him.

Not yet.

Doran felt the skeptical stares everyone gave him, and he knew it was because of how weak he appeared. No matter what they thought, and no matter the truth, there was only one path for him to take now.

"The two bots we left outside earlier might have something they can share with us. If they are still there."

He and Two had damaged them enough that they probably had not left yet.

When they arrived at the water, Doran walked ahead and held his hand back to ward off the others. In the dim dying light, he saw first an arm, then legs, all in pieces. He drew the sword off his back in a smooth motion and held it in both hands. Dim lights reflected off its polished surface.

He scanned the ridge line and the pathway in the distance, but it was empty. Entity had finished them when he exited the mountain and made his way somewhere else. On his way to the next part.

"Why would he do that?" Millar said. "They were his followers, weren't they?"

Doran replaced the sword and scanned the ground. "They could have told us where he went. Since they could not go with him quickly, he did not want to leave any clues behind, even if it meant destroying his own."

Millar inspected one of the arms and the scoring on it from the weapon. "We should probably camp here and think about our next steps. What do you think?"

Doran finished walking the area and nodded. "Nothing more we can do tonight."

"Except rest," Bel said. "And we all need it, you the most, Doran."

Chapter 43

Millar awoke before dawn and saw Doran standing off from the group's smoldering fire. The giant sword lay propped against a boulder. He expected the bot to be doing his forms again this morning but he just stood there staring into the darkness. Bel had given him a bit of cloth and he had used it to tie around his head to cover up the hole where his eye used to be.

"Hey, are you all right?"

Doran didn't move. "I am worried."

"You? You're never worried."

"I mean, the longer we wait, the more danger this land is in. Look at what he did to his followers. He blasted them to pieces and he even left his own disciples at the bottom of that temple to drown. When he regains all of my former pieces, what will he do to those who oppose him?"

Millar nodded. "How many more pieces do you think you hid?"

"I believe only one more."

"And what is that? He already has that weapon, and the armor, and boots. Two's system."

"I forced myself to forget everything, even my closest friends. I remember much now, but I do not know what remains. However, it must be powerful. But if we can beat him to it, we might have a chance of stopping him."

"But how are we ever going to do that? He's got a day's lead on us, and probably used Two's programming to figure out the location."

Doran reached up to his exposed chest cavity where the blue stone throbbed its energy. "I have seen things."

"You always have visions, is this one different from those?"

"Ever since that last battle with Entity, I am seeing flashes, but they are not like before. They are not of the past. These images are from right now."

"How is that possible?" Millar said.

Doran tapped the cloth wrapped around his head. "He has my eye."

Understanding fell on Millar. "You can see what he sees!"

Doran nodded. "It has grown faint though, as he has moved further away. It is not a steady stream, either. Only bits and fragments as the system is adjusting to his body. I fear if we wait too long, I could lose all contact with it."

"And we're very slow," Millar said.

"You mean me."

"No, I've got short legs, I can barely keep up with you."

"Now you are patronizing me."

Millar smiled. "Maybe we can do some of your... dancing... before anyone wakes up? That seems to help you."

Doran turned and bowed to Millar. "You honor me."

Millar bowed back.

The two of them quietly focused on the forms as the sun rose behind them.

***

"The ocean."

Millar breathed out as he finished dropping his hands and looked up at Doran. "What do you mean?"

"I saw the ocean. In one of the images."

"Just the ocean? Anything else?"

"No. But it was only a flash. At least it tells me where to go next."

"You mean 'us,' right?" Millar said. "Not just 'me?'"

Doran picked up the sword and attached it to his back. "We are most likely heading into the territory of those Soldiers of the New Sun. Entity got rid of these two bots, probably not to his liking, and will need more support. He is not so proud yet, unfortunately."

"Unfortunately?"

"Yes, if he were alone, this would be much easier. For all of us." Doran pointed to the others just waking up and moving around. His eye settled on Bel.

"We know what we're getting into," Millar said. "And besides, are you too proud to accept help from others?"

"If I did not care about you, that would make the decision easier. Entity does not care. He will use his people as a shield to get what he wants."

Raly walked up to the two of them and stretched. "You got up early today, sorry I missed out. What are you talking about?"

"Doran here was just saying that we're all heading to the sea, today. Weren't you?"

Doran waved his hands in defeat. "I accept your help. I just do not want to lose you, any of you, like we lost Two."

Bel came over and held his hand. "We don't want to lose you, either."

They spent the rest of the day walking back to Terask, and the going was slow. There wasn't any noticeable change in Doran's walking. He still dragged his foot with every step. Every other time he'd been injured, a day had made at least some difference in healing. Perhaps this time the damage was so great that any change would be hard to notice. He looked emaciated without that armor, and the ripped-open chest cavity made him look like a bot awakened from death.

They were lucky he was even walking at all.

As the sun traveled overhead and started to pitch into the ocean, they saw Terask. Great plumes of smoke rose from the tiny city.

"The people!" Raly said. "The people of Terask! They still have the raiders in there. Entity would have known that and would have gone to free them."

"Leaving those who opposed him to die," Kech said.

"Do you think he'd hurt everyone?" Bel said.

No one spoke their thoughts aloud, but the ever-growing plumes of smoke made them more and more terrified of what he was capable of.

"What do you think he wants from all of this?" Millar said.

"It's hard to tell," Doran said. "I do not think he is following a base programming. Mine was to defend the royal family and their realm. From our limited interactions, he is on path to gather all the parts, no matter what. When he spoke to me last, he had said that they are a curse to him."

"And yet he still takes them," Kech said.

"Yes. My guess is he has gone mad from the images and the power that they bring. He will only deliver death to everything he touches." Doran clenched his fists.

"We can stop him," Bel said.

"It is not that I am worried about," Doran said. "It is the fact that I led him to these things. My things. Why did I have to get rid of them in the first place?"

"You know why," Kech said.

Doran nodded. "In my hands they were a problem. In his… If Terask is in pieces I blame myself."

Despite the hitch in his stride, Doran pushed the pace of their walk back down the long hill to the ocean. With each passing mile, the smoke grew darker and the destruction seemed greater. No boats were out in the bay. No carts rode in from the docks. When they grew close enough, they saw a long train of people winding out of the town, escaping the fires, which were growing out of control.

"Are they going to want to destroy me?" Doran said. "This is my fault."

When the people saw Doran, a collective cheer arose.

"He has returned!"

The group was mostly made up of the elderly and the very young, because they had been removed from the town first while the others remained to fight the fires. Doran shuffled by a little faster, despite the creaking and groaning in his gears.

"You are injured!" one of the elders said and pointed to the cavity in Doran's chest. "Come, we will tend to you."

"Thank you, but I have things to do first." Doran, carrying his head a little higher, broke into a painful jog toward the town center.

The people let loose another cheer as he passed by. Bel and the others had to nearly sprint to keep up with him. Soon, Doran had reached the edge of the blaze where a group of soldiers were battling the flames with a water brigade.

"Are they still here?" Doran shouted.

"They're gone," one villager said. "And Entity escaped with them."

"It would have gone a lot worse," a soot-covered elder said, "but they fought with each other as they left."

"Tell me what to do," Doran said. At this point the rest of the group arrived. A little breathless but ready to lend a hand, as well.

"The fire is raging through the middle of the village," the elder continued. "That is where Entity first struck, and hit us hard at the town center."

"You should go after him," another villager yelled. "He just left, and you can stop him!"

A vision came to Doran then, of the town of Terask. It was from his other eye, for sure. There was no feeling associated with the sight, it was only a glimpse of what Entity was doing, not what he was thinking or feeling. The view was from the south, and perhaps a mile or two out, watching the city burn.

He could run now, and try to stop Entity, but that would not help these people. And everything that Entity did to them was his fault.

"That will have to wait."

The next hours were spent running back and forth from the sea, carrying buckets of water and dumping them on the houses near the blaze. Some were beyond saving, but Doran tried anyway. Wherever smoke blinded others and seared their lungs, Doran went.

People watched him go where the fires were the hottest, but nothing slowed him. Sometimes it appeared that he slowed down to focus, like he did during his morning forms, and when he did that the flames closest to him miraculously disappeared. If anyone noticed, they never said anything.

The screams of a mother drew them all close. She wailed and pointed to a burning house that was on the verge of collapse. It was surrounded by several houses that were also on fire. The main door to the house was blocked by a large flaming beam fallen from another building.

"My child!"

Doran didn't pause. Instead, he drew his sword and approached the blaze. The crowd drew back and watched him neatly slice through the wreckage with one swing. He pulled it away from the door and went inside. After a few seconds, Doran came back through the doorway with his back arched and his arms cradled in front of him.

He was carrying a young girl, and also an excited dog that had not left her side. Doran's body was covered in soot so that his glowing blue eye was the only thing that appeared. He placed the two on the ground near the mother, who thanked him through tears and began tending to the coughing child.

Doran didn't stop to talk. He went back into the fiery fray and kept working. Wherever he went, the crowd followed, for he would brave the most flames and leave a swath for the firefighters to follow.

Night deepened, and the fires abated, so that only the smoldering embers of the buildings lit their surroundings. Groups of the townsfolk wandered the streets as the fires disappeared, and when they met, they rejoiced and hugged each other. Many cheers went up for Doran. Food and drink were broken out for everyone.

Yet despite the cheering, sounds of dissent arose from one corner of the town. Doran and his friends met there, expecting a fight between the people. They found a ragtag group of red-hooded figures that had to be the Soldiers of the New Sun. A group of people from Terask were standing off against them and seemed to be only seconds away from a fight. A young girl stood there holding up her hands to ward off the fighting. It was Kindra.

"Stop!" Doran strode into the center of the two groups.

"They are the enemy!" a man from Terask shouted. "They burned our town!"

"We are trying to help," Kindra said.

"It is true," an older woman said. "They could have left, but instead helped us."

Vo'Sav, covered in ashes, walked into the open area. "I heard you stood up to your own people."

Doran counted them, and there were more here now than there were when the raiders were taken. Kindra had obviously been busy in their short time in prison together, convincing who she could about the other side of their new religion.

"Things could have gone worse, if not for your help." Vo'Sav bowed to Kindra. "And to you, Doran, and your friends, we owe our lives and our town."

Doran limped to the side of the area and dropped to the ground unceremoniously. "I need to rest now."

"We are at your service." Vo'Sav directed some of his officials to gather food and supplies for this group, and then he left to deal with the destruction of half of his town.

Despite Vo'Sav's words to the soldiers, the townsfolk still eyed them suspiciously.

"We should stay here with them," Bel said. "Remember? We should be friends with her."

Raly shook her head and left with Kech.

"We will be back here in the morning," Kech said.

"What happened to sticking together?" Millar said. He caught Raly's eyes and she pleaded with him silently to come with her.

"I can't believe they're just going to let them stay here." Raly looked them over. "They should leave."

"They did help," Doran said. "Plus, where would they go? They are outcasts now. And we could ask them where Entity could be going next."

Millar appeared torn. Doran knew he wanted to go with Raly and Kech, but he also felt the need to remain with the raiders.

"You stay," Raly said. "But thank you."

She smiled at him and left with Kech to get shelter elsewhere. Kech lingered for a moment.

"I saw some Trades here, I will question them about what they think about Entity and where he might have gone." Kech raised an eye at Kindra. "Take good notes on what she says."

When Raly and Kech were both out of sight, Millar, Oen, and Bel sat down across from Kindra and her people. Vo'Sav also joined them. Doran sat apart from them, but still close enough to listen. The more Doran looked at Kindra, the more she reminded him of Raly.

The air was still charged between the two groups. Doran felt Millar wanting to ask a question, but his anger still burned in him. Oen wasn't any closer to having another conversation with them, either.

Bel was the first to speak. "We're trying to stop him—Entity. Have you heard where he is going next?"

Kindra bowed to Bel. "It appears he went south. Metlar is that way, so perhaps he is going to regroup with others."

"After cutting ties with you, it seems," Oen said. "I see you got more friends on your side?"

Kindra nodded. There were ten others there in the Soldier garb. "During the night, we snuck into the prison and talked with them. A few became sympathetic, after seeing what he did. And after he came to free them all, some broke out and joined us instead. He was enraged. He could have destroyed everything, but he left instead."

"Tell me more," Doran said.

"He got the weapon, I see. He used it here several times, but stopped when the flames began to consume the village. It is powerful. He seemed... confused at times. It was strange—it appeared like someone was talking to him, but we saw no one."

"Great," Oen said. "Unstable, murderous, unstoppable. More things to add to the 'reasons to worship him' list."

"Fear is often a great motivator," Kindra said. "But fear is only one thing. Killing anyone who gets in his way, including his own people, is another. So he is gone now. And unfortunately the people of Metlar will welcome him back."

"What other parts are left?" Millar asked. "Do you know, Kindra?"

"I am not sure. Not many, and maybe even one. Or only one that matters to him. He said there is some sort of test for those who seek it, so I am guessing it may be the last. It seems like he was gathering all the pieces so he would be able to pass that test."

"And I'm guessing he didn't share that location?" Millar said.

Kindra shook her head. "We could follow him to Metlar. See where he goes."

Doran nodded. "Do you think he will try to attack this town? Against those who stood up to him, and those who turned their back on him? It seems like the logical thing for him to do."

"Crush any spirit of rebellion against him as a god," Millar said. "Could be. But it seems like he would finish all of his part collecting before he came back."

"He might send more Soldiers, though," Kindra said. "He's got enough of them there."

"Can you stop them?" Bel said.

Kindra shook her head. "Most of those we convinced to turn against him saw what he did. I'm not sure we can convince others who haven't seen."

"We'll get murdered, burned for heresy," an older man from her group said.

"We need to just leave," another said. "Do you see the way this town looks at us?"

Doran scanned the area. Indeed, the people of Terask eyed them suspiciously as they passed by on their way to repair the burned structures.

"We're targets, no matter where we go now," Kindra said. "We have to start small. Some of Metlar's neighboring camps. We would tell them about him." She motioned to Doran.

For the first time, Doran noticed them staring at him. Almost how Intari and her people looked at Two.

Kindra began to talk to her party in a hushed voice now as she gave them orders. Millar grouped with Bel, Oen, and Doran.

"She seems smart." Bel watched Kindra speaking. "I bet that people would listen to her. Look at what she did in just one day."

"We could travel with them," Millar said. "To Metlar. They could tell us of any dangers along the way."

Oen squinted. "You trust them? After what they did?"

"Actions define character," Doran said. "And they have done enough to earn my trust. But for you, I assume it will take more time?"

"Time we don't have," Millar said.

"Or never will," Oen said. "Raly won't go for it. And if we do go with them, what's to say they won't turn Doran over to them? I know, I know. 'Actions define whatever.'"

"Character. If they wanted to turn me over, they would have already sided with Entity and turned back."

"Well, maybe they couldn't. You know, he would kill them or something after turning their backs on him. He seems like the judgey type. Maybe this would be the perfect in with him. Serve up your remaining parts on a plate. That sword would be a nice gift. I've seen them looking at it."

"They like Doran now," Bel said. "They've seen how a bot can be good, and powerful. I think they'll want us to go with them."

Millar patted her back. "Doran, what do you think?"

Doran stared out to the south. "He is looking at the town now. From a distance. Watching the fires burn out. I cannot feel what he is feeling, but I imagine it is hateful. I think that our road ahead will be dangerous. Perhaps he does not know I am alive, and that will be to our advantage. The longer we wait, the more word of my survival will spread. I say we ask Kindra for her help."

"Yes."

Millar and the others stared back at Kindra, who was already moving closer to them.

"We heard you, and yes, we will guide you to Metlar," she said. "We know of the back trails that will not be guarded. It will be an honor to bring the savior back."

"If Raly and Kech will come, too," Oen said.

"They will," Millar said. "We should warn Vo'Sav about the possible attack and leave in the morning."

"It would probably be best if we left under the shadow of night," Kindra said. "And we should not tell anyone."

Doran stood up. "We shall gather our friends. Thank you for your help."

Kindra bowed low. "It is to you whom we give our greatest thanks. If not for your mercy, we would not be here. We are forever in your debt."

Chapter 44

"I can't believe you would agree to go with them," Raly said.

"It's our best way of getting there," Millar said. "And figuring out where he went."

"He is right," Kech said. "I understand your reluctance to go anywhere with them, however. And you feel this way too, yes Millar?"

Millar nearly tripped over his words to respond. "Yes, I do. But we need everyone. We need you to be there."

Raly stared into the fire pit. She didn't say anything.

"We might have found some clues," Kech said. "The other Trades here who have ventured around Metlar's Keep talk about quarries to the east of the city. The rocks from these quarries are used to build there, but rumors say that more of the workers have gone there in the past months than are needed for just digging. It may be that they uncovered something."

"It's a start," Millar said. "And maybe the raiders could tell us more."

"I'm surprised they didn't mention any possibility of it before," Raly said. "If they are wanting to help us, that is."

"Look, I don't want to be around them either," Oen said. "The whole thing stinks. But we have a chance to stop this thing before it hurts more people.

And it can get a lot worse, if Doran's hints about what his old powers could do are true. Entity needs to be stopped."

Raly looked to Kech. "Will you come if I do?"

Kech nodded. "Of course."

Raly sighed. "Then I guess I'll go."

Millar squeezed her shoulder. "I know what this means for you. I'll do what I can to make sure you don't have to look at her, or talk to her."

Raly smiled. "You have every right to feel the same way I do. You lost someone to them, too. Both of you."

Bel walked over and gave Raly a hug. "'Hate is a poison for the soul,' Mom used to say. Together we can make this better."

"What are we waiting for then?" Raly stood up and dusted off her pant legs. "Let's make things better—by overthrowing a crazy bot tyrant."

Doran, who had been sitting nearby listening to the whole conversation, stood up and clapped his hands. "Together, then."

The people of Terask were still putting out smaller fires when the two groups walked out of the town. None but a few people saw them leave, and they stood in awe of Doran as he passed by.

"What did Vo'Sav say about the potential for an attack from the south?" Oen said.

Doran, still limping, looked down at him. "They do not have an army to withstand them, he said. But the water temple can protect them from an attack for a time. Stores of food are there for the people. They can stay there while we complete our mission. Hopefully with Kindra's efforts, they can turn away some of the soldiers."

"How long of a journey is it to the Keep?" Oen said.

"Days," Kech said. "And with Doran in his state of disrepair, maybe more. How are you feeling, Doran?"

"Better than before," Doran said. "Not as good as I have been. Thank you for covering my chest."

He straightened the blanket that was tied around his front side, covering the exposed chest cavity and the stone within. A small glimmer of light shone through the dark fabric.

"The people of Terask provided it," Kech said. "They would do anything for you. You saved them. Twice now."

"I had help," Doran said.

After a minute of walking he spoke again. "Should we do more to stop the attack? I worry for them."

"What could we do?" Kech said. "We couldn't stop them all, and then they'd just send more to die if we did. No, I think Vo'Sav will handle this in his own way."

Doran nodded hesitantly. "Plus, what can I do?"

"More than any of us," Millar said. "And you're getting better, right?"

Doran straightened out his arms and tried twisting them, and then each of his legs. "Maybe."

Kech had started a new journal and had been filling it up with her neat handwriting ever since they left the town. To help her write and walk at the same time, she propped the journal upon a metal stand that protruded from the book belt. She walked with a candle flame and a glass that caught its light and amplified it upon the book.

"That for your Life Quest?" Bel said.

Kech smiled deeply. "Indeed. I was granted permission to write about our adventures in the temple's depths. Now that the Entity is cast out, things have changed. Vo'Sav shared many things with me, but there is much more to learn and record. So I am adding to what little I had written years before in hopes of more knowledge."

"What are your other Life Quests?" Bel asked.

Kech chuckled. "How about I focus my energy on this one, finally? There will be time for us to record more. I want to finish my thoughts now, and then plan ahead for when I will go back to uncover more." She gave Raly a sidelong glance.

Raly gave her a small grin as she walked.

***

The moon arose over the mountains, and it lit their path upon the main road. Soon they would be taking a road that led farther inland, which would help them avoid any soldiers that might be coming back north. Their own group of converted soldiers walked a little farther apart from them under the starry sky, while Kindra still stayed close enough to speak.

"What can you tell us about the quarries?" Millar said.

"The quarries," Kindra said. "That is closed information. I was not privy to that, but perhaps a few of us know of them. All I know is there is a vast range of mountains that were mined for various ores throughout history. Most have collapsed over time. But some are still used, just to the east of the Keep, perhaps a day's march or more. The soldiers have mined there for the metal that was used to make our helmets."

Millar glanced around their group. "Not many of you have those."

"The materials for them are rare," Kindra said.

Another raider walked over from the other side of the camp. "And only certain levels of the Soldiers can attain them." This man did not wear a helmet.

"Levels?" Oen said. "You mean like rank? How did you have one?"

Kindra scoffed.

"She happens to be the dahter of a high ranking Soldier," the man said. "They don't look too kindly upon people losing their helmets. You do not happen to have hers anymore, do you?"

Doran ignored that.

"It's not like she can go back now," Raly said. "What's the use of finding it? It's probably well known that she's turned away from your path, so why would they care?"

"Our reach has grown far and wide." Kindra walked with her head facing down.

"Well, can you use your rank to help us out?" Millar said. "Get us clearance at the quarries? It will probably take some time for word of this to get out to all the places."

Kindra kept walking in silence for several seconds. "I must help spread the word. I cannot assist you there. I am sorry."

"Well, it's not like she can cover up a fifteen foot tall bot anyway," Oen said.

"I can help you with maps, however." Kindra motioned to one of her companions.

The man hesitated.

"Do it," she ordered.

The man, at least ten years older than her, only paused a second before retrieving them from his pack. He rolled open the map and handed it to Kindra.

Doran walked beside her. "May I have a look?" he asked.

Kindra nodded.

Doran gave the map a quick scan.

"I know you've got it now," Kech said. "But may I? I would like to update what we've never been able to explore before."

Kindra handed her the map next. She gave it to Raly so she could get out another journal and her pen and then she quickly started scribing the map within it.

"Your craft is wonderful," Kindra said. "I've never seen anyone draw or write like that."

"If you'd only have met with the Trades instead of trying to kill them," Raly said under her breath.

Kindra had obviously heard her, but she did not react to Raly's goading. She was taking her punishment silently.

Kech copied the map over into her journal and handed it back. The man carefully rolled it back up and put it into the leather tube.

"We will use this well," Kech said. "Thank you."

Kindra smiled and then went back to walk with her group while Doran and the others gathered together.

"Have you seen any of Entity's sight yet, Doran?" Millar said.

"Over the past hour, the images are coming more frequently. It is dark out, so I barely see anything in detail, but it still appears he is taking the straight route back to the Keep."

"Then we might be able to beat him to the final piece?"

"We are assuming the piece is in a quarry," Oen said. "What about those stories your mom used to tell us about the mines?"

Millar laughed. "I'm sure we have nothing to worry about. I'm more worried about tracking down the final piece than old tales about demons. Do you have a plan to help with that, Doran?"

"Two devised a system to track down parts. Unfortunately, I let him handle that by himself. I can mimic his ideas, but I did not have the subsystems to actually do what he did."

"Seems like each of your parts was found at a special place," Bel said. "You know? Powerful places? The water temple, the mountains. Seems like Two's home was also like that, from what you told me. Do you remember if you chose those places because they were like that?"

"Or did they become energy focal points after?" Kech said.

Doran did not know. "It seems to be a coincidence that the two are together. A nexus. If there is a book or a mind that remembers any of this, I know it not."

"Trades keep and tell stories. Lots of stories. Ones of the origins of the bots. Yes, people helped to craft them, but there are tales of people finding ways to manipulate the forces of the land to create them. And some even say that the first bots came directly from the land itself."

"The Cora'chan?" Bel said.

"They awoke. That is the legend."

"Huh," Oen said. He seemed to want to say something more off-handed about it, but the look he got from Kech made him bite his tongue.

"A child of the land," Kech said. "It may be that the land was reaching back up to the parts it created, and these areas are the extent of its grasp."

"But why would it create Doran in the first place?" Bel said. "I mean, I'm glad it did. But why? And how could it?"

"They awoke when they were needed," Kech said.

Bel normally would have raced around and asked more questions, but a huge yawn split across her face.

"We should probably stop for now," Millar said. "We could all use the rest."

Doran kept limping forward. "I can carry her."

"No you can't," Millar said.

"But I must go on anyhow," Doran said. "Entity will not rest, and neither should we."

He weakly picked Bel up, to her utter enjoyment, and placed her on his shoulder.

"I could've used a rest," Oen muttered.

"Did you see anything new?" Millar said. "From Entity?"

Doran nodded. "As he approaches Metlar's Keep, I see more and more of the soldiers. They gather and prepare. It is not only for the people of Terask, but for the entire countryside. From Hinarum and the High Ansels. Everywhere that has heard of me. He wishes to truly make me be forgotten. As I should have stayed."

"He drew you out," Millar said.

"No," Doran said. "I was awakened and chose to come out on my own. I should have stayed."

Bel leaned sideways against his head. "But you would never have met us. Aren't we something to you? A family?"

Doran turned to her. "More than you will ever know. But I should not have ever been made. Then none of this would have happened. We would not have lost Two."

"We wouldn't have had Two at all, if not for you," Millar said. "Remember, he had some of your parts. This is all just too much to discuss and argue. You are alive and this is what we have to face."

"We must go on as much as we can tonight," Doran said.

The entire group turned eastward at a crossroads soon after. After a few hours, the moon began to dip over the ocean, and their light grew dim. They set up a quick camp to eat a little food and then to sleep for the remainder of the night.

***

The gray sky of dawn came too quickly for everyone, but within an hour they were packed and ready to walk again. No one had woken early to practice Doran's forms, and it felt strangely sad. Perhaps it was the danger of the journey, or maybe the present loss of Two, but no one said much over their meager cold breakfast.

318

Doran's limp had grown a little smoother, but he was not yet to his former strength or speed. The sunlight crested over three of the tallest peaks in the mountain chain and shone on their path. Their goal was to find the hidden quarries in the mountains. Miles still lay east before them and also farther south to get to where Metlar's Keep got their building resources. Everyone dug in and started out the day with a quick pace.

Doran had not seen many more images through Entity. As he had guessed, Entity never stopped to rest through the night, and the distance between them must have made the connection weaker. For now, Doran could only assume that the other bot would reach the Keep soon, within a day perhaps, and then head to the final part.

Their success stood upon two things. First, Kindra had to rally her own soldiers to her side, and second, they needed to reach the part before Entity. Would Doran have the strength to face him there, at the end? He had nothing left. Nothing but the sword and perhaps the surprise of him still being alive. But given Kindra's plan, that secret might be out before too long.

At midday, Kindra's people reached their crossroads. There was little speaking between the two groups. The soldiers were in shame of the actions their god had brought to the others, and Raly was still unwavering in her anger. She seethed as Kindra spoke to them in parting.

"May you succeed at your quest, Cora'chan. We will do what we can to stop the others. It will take more than just us to do what we speak of, and we may not survive. If this is our final parting, know that we regret everything."

Doran bowed to them but did not speak, and neither did the others. Except for Bel.

"'We all make mistakes. Then we must fix them.' My mom said that."

Kindra smiled. "Then she was a very wise mother."

Her group stepped onto the southern path and within minutes they wound along through trees and hills and were lost from sight.

Raly didn't realize she was staring off at them until Doran prompted her to walk again.

"I… I don't know what to think," she said.

"Maybe you are not supposed to," Doran said. "Not yet."

"I don't even know who killed my mom. Maybe it wasn't anyone. Maybe the house fell on her. Or it was that bot you already destroyed."

"I think the important thing is that Kindra is alive."

Raly scoffed and walked forward again. "Is it?"

"Look where we are now. Look where you are. You were devastated by almost killing her back at the High Ansels. Perhaps if you had killed her, we would not be on this path. Perhaps we would all be dead."

"Or perhaps none of this would have happened. Where does it all begin? Whoever put Entity on the path will have some questions to answer."

Chapter 45

"According to this, there are three major areas we could explore." Kech opened her map journal and showed it to the others over a short break. The areas were spread out from each other, each in different mountains throughout the chain. One was directly east of the Keep, and the other two went farther north and east. Kech had said that the northernmost quarry was completely abandoned now.

"Which should we go to first?" Millar said. "The closest? That seems to make the most sense. Doran, what do you think?"

"I have thought about this. I cannot get a clear reading based on Two's calculations, so we will have to be systematic. Although I…"

"You what?" Millar said.

"I get a sense from a little farther east. It is almost like I can feel something, like a signal."

"Well, the nearest one is a day's march from here," Kech said. "It is a large quarry, with multiple mining entrances around it. We could go there first? Just to eliminate it? Then I suppose you could try to sense something when we get there?"

Doran stood up to go. "No. We need to move. With each moment, Entity will get closer to finding everything. I do not know how much time I have left."

"Do you mean how much time you have left?" Millar said. "Or how much time we have until Entity finds what he is looking for?"

"Either way would be bad, so let us hurry."

Bel, usually spry and ready for adventure, dragged a little bit.

"You going to be all right?" Millar said. "We could maybe rest a little longer?"

"I'm all right! If Doran can do it, then so can I."

Doran reached over and picked her up despite a major hitch in his stride when he did so. "I have got you, little one."

"I'll be ready to run in a bit," Bel said.

"It's okay," Oen said. "Even us older ones are getting pretty tired, too. I don't suppose there's room up there for me, too?"

Doran gave him a side glance and then began to laugh.

***

"How much farther south is the Keep?" Raly asked. "If we turned now?"

"We've reached the major road to the first quarry east of the Keep. See that mountain?"

There was the first major mountain peak off in the distance, east of the ocean. It wasn't as mighty and frozen as what they had climbed near Terask in the Blue Ice Range, but it still had a peak tipped with snow.

"That's in line with the Keep, and it's maybe twenty miles away. The next quarry on the map is closer."

Raly squinted her eyes. "You've been here before?"

"Not often, and not in the past ten years. It had already started to become dangerous, even back then."

"So are we going to see many soldiers along the road?"

Kech shook her head. "Probably not. With the call to arms along the coast that Entity has surely already begun, that should make it easier for us."

Eventually, Doran put Bel back on the ground, and she was back to her old self. Doran, on the other hand, still seemed to suffer from the damage to his leg. It was slightly better, but not as strong as it used to be.

They stopped infrequently, as Doran seemed to be in a rush to get to the quarry by the next day. The endless, rutted old quarry road ran straight to the hills. No one spoke more than a few words for the remaining daylight, and even the fireless camp at night was a sullen, silent time. They hadn't seen another soul the entire day.

The next morning, Doran immediately awoke and urged everyone to get on the road. Raly, however, had gotten up early in an effort to have a word with him.

"You haven't practiced in days," she said. "Not since Two left. Even when I start, you ignore me."

"We need to move quickly," he said. "There are more important things than this."

"That never stopped you before. Come, lead us. I've seen it help you. We've helped you, using it."

"The longer we wait..." Doran said.

"Is okay for now," Raly said. "You are not thinking. It will help us, in the long run."

"It feels wrong to do it." Doran sighed. "Without Two."

Bel came over and leaned against his leg. She yawned. "It feels wrong not to do it anymore. It used to wake me up a bit! And plus, wouldn't Two want you to keep doing it?"

Doran didn't respond to that.

"It's okay to think about him, and to miss him," Raly said. "Practicing with you was what helped me to think more clearly about my mom. I miss her, but I don't want to forget her."

Doran knelt by her side and placed his hand on her head. "You have been through a lot, too. I was not thinking about that. I am sorry. You cannot just erase your memory."

"No, I wasn't blaming you for anything, I just know it has helped me. Oh, and you better not be thinking about erasing your mind again. Don't take the easy way."

Bel gave a big nod.

"Well then," Doran said as he stood with a creak. "We should probably get to it, yes?"

As a group, they welcomed the morning sun with their slow, meticulous movements. The mountains turned from black to gray, and then to white as the light touched their peaks.

"This is it," Doran said. "The way."

"Yes!" Bel made some extra motions, with an added kick for flare. "It will help us."

"No," Doran said. "But yes. I only meant the way we are going is correct. I hear a call."

"More images?" Millar said.

Doran shook his head. "It is different this time. The images I would get as we approached one of my old pieces were a series of flashes. Like memories. This is a steady call, almost like a message."

"That's a good sign," Oen said. "Right?"

"Very good." Doran twisted his neck and then rotated his arms.

"You look better," Bel said.

"I feel better. Are we ready? Today is the day we will finish this, I am certain."

They packed their bags and then took to the rutted tracks in the old quarry road.

***

"Should we be sticking to the main road?" Oen said. "Anyone on it is going to easily spot a big bot from a mile away."

It was true. The road from the mountains was a straight shot to the coast, which had probably been the easiest way to haul materials to the Keep, or wherever it was going from there.

"If there had been anyone on the road yesterday they would have seen us, too," Kech said. "I think we're safe. By now, Entity will have reached the Keep and done what he needed to. All eyes will be focused on the coastal route."

"Poor Kindra," Bel said. "She's trying to stop them. Do you think she'll be okay?"

"She will do her best," Doran said. "As shall we."

That didn't seem to make her feel any better, though.

"We should have taught her what we do," Bel said.

By late morning, they reached the first path going up into the mountains to the south. Doran looked up at the peak and saw remnants of old towers which were now a series of crumbled stones.

"People used to live up here?" Bel asked. She pulled Millar's visor over her eyes to get a better look. "There sure are a lot of ruins!"

"Some of the oldest cities are around here," Kech said. "This whole area was a thriving civilization. The pinnacle of human and bot existence."

"Where did they go?" Bel scanned the mountains, as if she would find the missing people who used to live there.

"They were fraught by wars, and so they left."

"That's terrible," Bel said. "Wars are stupid."

"They are," Kech said. "We're here now, and there is a quarry beyond the mountain, to the south. Are you sure we should not go check it out first?"

Doran shook his head and continued walking eastward. "We must go."

They walked toward the next mountain, still miles away, which was more worn down, and blasted in gray ash. Remnants of a great cliff face opened before them, filled in with landslides and piles of dirt and debris.

"This whole area is desolate," Raly said. "How did people survive out here? If they had big cities they would need a constant water source, right?"

Kech nodded. "They wasted it all. Rivers disappeared, possibly running into underground areas, from the vast mining they used to do. When a civilization runs out of their own resources, they often reach out to other areas."

"And by reach, you mean…?" Oen smacked his fist into his palm.

"Pointless," Millar said. "What a waste."

"Yes it is," Doran said.

"How's the signal now?" Millar said.

"Practically screaming at me," Doran said.

"Yeah, I figured. You want to slow down a bit? We're having a hard time keeping up with you."

Doran glanced back and saw the others lagging behind. He slowed a bit, but not much.

They climbed up the path from the main road toward the mountain. As the road turned a corner, they looked nearly a hundred feet down into a huge pit. Vast waterways appeared at the base of it, beautiful clear blue lakes.

"Are those the quarries now?" Millar asked. "All filled in?"

"Possibly," Kech said. "I know very little of the specifics of this area."

"It is down there." Doran pointed at the base of one of the tall cliffs that appeared to have been carved out by people or bots as opposed to anything natural. There were debris piles all around, however, at the level of the water. A stone archway looked to be a way into the mines, however they could not tell from here if the way was blocked.

"That water looks deep," Oen said. He pitched a stone into the air and it took about six seconds for it to hit the water's surface. "That's one way down there, huh?"

"Not funny," Millar said. "Don't get too close to the edge."

There was a stone fence between them and the cliff's edge so they felt safe, but it was still a sheer drop down.

"How are we going to get down there then?" Oen said. "Not that I'm seriously considering jumping. Maybe."

"You would not survive," Doran said. "I am not even sure I would make that fall."

"Ah, so you still have basic survival skills working in your memory. Thanks for the tip."

"It looks like the path winds away up there, and then down to the base, one level at a time." Millar adjusted his visor and scanned the quarry walls.

It took them another hour, and the sun seemed to set because of their descent into the pit. Stones slid, gravel piles threatened to drop from above, but they slowly made their way to the bottom.

"Why isn't anything growing near this water?" Bel asked. "It looks beautiful. But dead."

They stared into the depths of the clear blue water and at the sparse and scrubby plants growing near its edge.

"It's freezing!" Oen said after sticking his hand in it. He reached for his water bag.

"Do not drink it," Doran said. "More basic survival skills have told me that the water may be poisoned this close to a mine. You are welcome."

Oen nodded his thanks and quickly wiped off his hand. "Now, about getting in there. If you're sure?"

Doran approached the gateway, and it indeed had collapsed, or at least the cliffs had spilled down to fill it over time.

"I am certain."

"Well, then I guess there's only one way in." Oen threw down his pack and began to haul material away from the doorway.

Millar hoisted his pry hammer and joined him, as did the others.

Doran surveyed the gateway, which was a little over ten feet wide and the same high. "We must be cautious. Do what you can here, and I will remove the bigger material closer to the entrance."

Despite his scrawny form, he was still able to lift and roll massive stones away in short order. The hillside dropped small material as he cleared it, but there did not appear to be any major rumblings as they worked.

"See?" Oen said. "I look like the good guy now, offering to help first. And he's doing most of the work."

"Just keep hauling," Millar said with a smile. He pried apart a boulder and it rolled away from the gateway.

***

"What do you think the part is?" Oen asked.

"Not sure," Millar said. "I'm more worried about this entrance. We've been digging in it for a while now and we've made it several feet, but how much farther will it go?"

"Yeah, I was thinking it was like a neural scanner, or a bot control system. Or maybe a laser mining beam, which ironically would have made all this digging unnecessary."

Millar shook his head. "You're very focused, you know?"

"Or a strength enhancer, power knuckles…" Oen trailed off as he rolled another boulder away.

"Stand back," Doran said. "I hear something."

He grabbed onto a boulder at the base and yanked it out, causing others above it to pull free and slide down in a rumbling pile of dust. They waited a moment for the dust to clear, and then Doran flashed a light inside.

"That's it!" Millar said. "We're in!"

They had to crawl over the top of the pile, but Doran made it easier to fit through by first scooping out a few handfuls of debris.

"You going to make it through?" Bel asked from inside.

Doran pulled himself through the narrow gap and scraped the sword against the ceiling. More bits pulled free but didn't collapse the exit.

"Yes."

Doran's blue eye lit up brighter in the lightless hallway, exposing the vast stone corridor beneath the earth. It was quiet. The only sounds they heard were the echoes of their feet upon the stone path, and the occasional drip in the distance. The light from the outside faded quickly as they walked through the mine, leaving only Doran's light to see by.

"This doesn't seem like the other places," Raly said. "They felt different than this."

"This feels more like a tomb," Millar said. "Like whatever he buried here wasn't supposed to be opened again."

"It is here," Doran said. "I can hear it."

Everyone strained to hear something, anything, besides the dripping and the echoes, but there was nothing.

"I'm cold," Bel said.

"Me too, kid," Millar said. "It's definitely a tomb."

They followed the tunnel as it started to dip downward even deeper into the earth, and the walls seemed to close in on them.

"I don't like this," Raly said. "I can hear my heart thumping in my ears. I just want to scream."

"It is down here," Doran said.

He was moving faster now, as if the call to whatever lay beyond these tunnels was more insistent.

"What is that?" Bel said. "Looks like a tool or something."

They stopped and all gathered around the thing on the ground. Millar flipped down his visor and turned on the light that was on there, too. Doran's blue light helped to see the path, but a whiter light would help with the details. It was made of black metal and shaped like a hand.

Doran picked up the object and turned it over. "It looks to be from a bot. Here. An inscription. Model NT."

"Miners?" Millar said.

"A mining bot?" Oen said. "Oh man, are they down here? Those things…"

"It's been here for a long time," Millar said. "We've got nothing to worry about. They'll have been gone forever."

"It looks like some of them are still here." Oen checked on the tunnel behind them. "Come on, you know those stories."

"All meant to spook out kids, right? And look. It worked on you." Millar glanced back and forth as well, though.

"Come on, you're not scared either?" Oen said. "They never see the light of day. They're blind. They drag kids down at night into the mines to feed on them."

"Stories may have embellished that last part," Kech said.

"I don't know," Oen said.

Millar flipped his light off to save on power and they began along the tunnel again. It wasn't too long before they found another hand. And then a metal foot, too. And then a pile of both of them.

"Does anyone else find this a little disturbing?" Oen said.

"Maybe they leave their broken parts here," Raly said. "Kech says they didn't have tools beyond their own limbs to work on the rocks. Maybe they got so damaged they just scrapped them here?"

Oen shrugged. "I guess that makes sense. Doran? Does that make sense? Please make it make sense."

"I do not know about miner bots. But that sounds like a perfectly reasonable explanation. There, does that allay your fears?"

"Not if you're just trying to make me feel better."

Doran pulled the sword from his back and held it in front of him.

"Okay, now you're really not making me feel any better."

"The call is stronger here. I feel that something bad has happened." Doran walked forward a couple hundred more feet until they reached the end of another blocked passageway. "This is it. We are here."

"I guess it's safe to say that we beat Entity here," Millar said. "Unless he found another way in, that is. Or he trapped himself inside."

"He is not here," Doran said and then replaced the sword.

"You did a really nice job of sealing these entrances." Oen rolled up his sleeves and reached down for a rock on the ground. "Here we go again."

"No," Doran said. "I have this."

He acted like he was reenergized now. His blue eye glowed even brighter as he moved, and he quickened his motion with every second. Huge boulders moved like nothing and were scattered along the hall behind him. Everyone took several steps back to avoid any of the flying shards.

"Where did these rocks come from?" Oen said. "It's not like they fell. Look."

He pointed above to the ceiling which had not been greatly marred, at least not to the extent of the number of rocks that had been piled here.

Doran slowed down when he reached two metallic surfaces, like a door or a gate. It had been scratched by the rocks, but there were rounded dents on it, as well. Once all the rocks were removed from the door, Doran inspected it and saw a metal bar across the two panels, blocking it from opening outward.

"Are you sure we should be opening this?" Kech said.

Without a second thought, Doran wrenched the metal bar free from the door and flung it to the side. He gripped onto the handles and strained to pull the doors outward. They slowly moved with a huge creaking and scraping sound, leaving deep rents in the stone floor.

Clang. The doors struck the walls and shivered on their hinges.

Then there was silence.

Doran stepped first into the chamber.

Chapter 46

Doran walked cautiously into the chamber. He couldn't see how wide it was, but he felt it.

"Is the signal here?" Millar asked.

"It has stopped."

"That's not good," Oen said. "Something led you here, and now it's gone? Are we sure these doors aren't going to just close back on us?"

Millar flipped on his visor light and shone it upon the opened passageway. What had been smaller dents on the other side seemed to have been caused by multiple blows to this side.

"Something was trying to get out of here," Millar said.

"Did he close something in here when he sealed it up?" Oen said.

"He wouldn't have done that," Bel said. "Not on purpose."

Doran focused his lights farther into the room. A few short steps led up to a platform and at its center sat a stone altar.

"It has to be up there!" Oen said. "We beat him to it!"

They all went up the steps, but slowly, and with Doran at the lead. The altar was empty except for dust and pebbles. Doran looked around the back side of it but there was no opening there.

"Nothing. There's no part here."

"Did he already take it?" Oen said. "Great."

"There's no way he could have," Millar said. "This place has been closed off for years."

Scrape. They all heard the slow movement of metal upon stone from behind them.

"The door!" Raly said. "We're going to be trapped in here!"

But it wasn't the door. The scraping sound first started off to one side, then the other, and then both. Doran drew his sword.

"Stay close to me." Doran walked quickly back to the door with the others behind him.

The sound grew louder and faster as they approached.

"I don't like this," Bel said.

Millar turned his visor light on as bright as he could and its beam pierced the darkness. Masses of dust-covered shapes struggled to pull themselves toward them with reaching, twisted limbs. Worst of all were their faces. Empty eyes stared out into the void, and where their mouths should have been, only stripped-out wires and hanging jaws remained in a perpetual, voiceless scream.

Bel cried out and clung tightly onto Millar. Oen backed into him, too.

"Get them, Doran!" Oen shouted.

But Doran stopped running and lowered his sword.

The metal monsters kept crawling.

"Not a good idea!" Oen said.

"Wait!" Millar said. "Look at them."

Bel let go of Millar. "They don't have any hands, or feet. And they're in pain. How are they still alive?"

Doran put the sword on his back and knelt down next to the nearest bot. The bot reached out a wavering arm in Doran's direction and the rest of the crawling bots joined him.

"What's going on?" Oen said. "Why are you putting down your sword?"

"The signal. I heard it again. It was them."

"What was the signal saying?" Millar said.

"Help."

Doran reached out and touched the arm of the closest bot to him.

***

"Mining bots," Oen said as he hauled a broken hand back to the main chamber. "I can't believe it's mining bots."

"They're hurt, Oen," Bel said. "It doesn't matter what they are. Mom always said to help anyone in need, because it could be you someday, and wouldn't you want someone to help you?"

Oen just grunted and kept moving.

When they got back to the bots, Doran was already replacing hands as quickly as he could. The bots struggled to stay still as he reattached them, which made the work that much longer. The slow-moving bots pointed their stumps of arms as a group to one bot, the one who'd first approached Doran earlier. His vacant eyes stared out, but he reached for his gaping mouth, holding a jaw in his newly attached hands.

"Millar," Doran said. "You must have had some practice with bot repairs on fine motor parts like this. Could you repair this one?"

Millar nudged Oen with his elbow. "Help me with this, will you? You've got some tools."

The miner turned to Oen, and its damaged face appeared to be smiling at him.

"Great, now I'm not going to sleep for weeks," Oen muttered.

335

Oen opened his pack and handed tools to Millar when he asked for them. The bot held out its jaw until Millar took it from him. He turned it around under the light from his visor.

"Are we really thinking that reattaching the jaw will help them speak again?" Oen said.

"No, but it won't freak you out as much to look at them, and we need you to calm down, so I'm going to reattach it and fix their vocal modulator. Here, hold this."

Millar handed the jaw to Oen, who held it with two fingers before placing it carefully on the ground.

Millar inspected the bot's mouth for a few moments. He gently pulled back the wiring to see the connections and test the power in them. After feeling confident, he held out his hand for the jaw piece. Oen daintily picked it up and handed it to him.

Millar reattached the wiring as best he could and then locked the jaw in place with a click.

"Self-wiring should seal in a minute or two. This is an older model, I mean really old, but that function should still work."

"I'm just surprised they have enough power," Raly said.

"Not much," Millar said. "Look, they're barely moving around. They must be running low on it."

"Look at them," Oen said. "All beat to a pulp. Doran didn't do that, right?"

"Of course not!" Bel said. "Poor guys."

She had attached many of the hands already. One of the bots crawled over to her and laid its head on her lap. It seemed so tired. She just stroked its head and hummed a tune.

In one great motion, all the bots turned their heads toward her and froze in a sightless stare. Bel stopped humming for a moment, and the bots' heads began to wander again, lost in their blind pain.

"Do not stop," Doran said. "Please."

Bel quickly began humming and their heads once again centered on her music. She smiled and kept singing to them as the rest of the group worked on the now-docile bots. Attaching their hands and feet was easier, as their attention was fully on Bel's song.

They lost track of the number of bots they repaired, mostly because they couldn't see all of them in the pale glow of their lights. Their eyes were irreparable, having been smashed or ripped out long ago. Oen shied away from them whenever they faced him as he attached a limb but the bots didn't seem to care—they just waited patiently for someone to help as they listened to Bel's humming. When a miner had its limbs reattached, however slowly it moved, it tried to assist others.

"You came back to us."

The voice was low and soft, and everyone turned to face the bot. It was the first one that Millar had helped, and apparently its voice box had come back online.

Doran stood beside the miner bot, almost eye to eye with it. "Did I cause this to happen to you all?"

"You did."

Doran took a step back. He looked around at the other miner bots, expecting them to exact their revenge. But they did not move—they only stared blankly at him.

"That can't be right," Bel shouted. "He wouldn't do this to you. Take off your hands and legs, block you inside? He would never do it! Even if he can't remember, he couldn't. I know him."

"We know him, as well. It is not his fault, but he set in motion the things that happened after he left us." The old miner bot reached out to Doran. "But we do not blame you. Come. Sit. For we are weak, but if you returned there is much you need to know."

The group gathered together on the steps and sat. Oen's darting glances shot to all sides.

"Yeah, get us in the middle so you can eat us," Oen whispered.

The main miner bot chuckled. "We may not be able to see, but we can hear much. We heard the Cora'chan approaching long before he arrived."

"That's because we were leveling the mountain path," Oen said. "I bet even the people in Terask heard that."

Millar slapped him on the back of his head. "Come on, don't encourage them to eat you."

The bot chuckled again. "I am NT-N1."

"Two would have felt better about his name after hearing that one," Oen said.

Millar shook his head and urged the leader to go on.

"Your coming has been expected. The last time we saw you was long ago. My memory cycles have indicated many years have passed."

"In here?" Bel said. "All this time?"

"All this time," NT-N1 said. "Time has worn us down, both in body and in mind. Some did not survive the long sleep as we waited."

"You're miner bots, couldn't you have found a way out... oh." Oen realized what he was saying as he looked upon their newly attached hands and feet. "I'm sorry."

"Some dashed themselves to scrap on that gate. Some lost their programming. Others just stopped. But those who survived the betrayal entered this sleep until your signal awoke us."

"The betrayal?" Millar said. "What happened here? What did Doran do?"

"Doran," NT-N1 said. "You may have forgotten your name, but your deeds are still the same. Yes, little one, you do know your friend."

Bel walked over and plopped into Doran's lap and looked up into his face with a smile.

"I told you."

"But what did I do to betray you?" Doran said.

"Not you. We met you when you were on your quest to lose yourself. To bury and hide your parts. You came here, in an abandoned section of the mine, not expecting to see any other bots. But this was our domain. Commanded to work here without ever leaving. For that was our programming."

"Lousy programming," Oen said. "That's not right."

NT-N1 nodded. "We knew nothing but what we were told to do. You, however, came here from the outside and told us we could be more. That we could escape. We asked for your help, but you were incapable, you said. You had caused destruction. You hurt people you cared about, and you had to escape. That, we understood. We felt your pain. We heard it. You had already removed your first part. You never told us what it was, but we could sense the power in it. We told you we could watch it for you, but you said it was too dangerous for anyone to possess. And so you left us."

Doran sighed. "I am sorry I did not help you."

NT-N1 put a hand out and laid it upon Doran's shoulder. "You are here now. And you have helped us."

"What about the rest of your story?" Millar said. "Something has to explain why all this happened to you."

NT-T1 looked down. "We still heard you, after you left. We could all sense the part, for it sang to us. Even days later. Your words of freedom and escape haunted us. Some more than others, and one in particular. He begged us to locate the part precisely. He could find it, he said. He could return with it and be strong enough to lead us all to freedom from these mines. So we agreed. As a group we located where you hid it, and he managed to escape from those that held us prisoners.

"And then he returned, but he was changed. He had gotten stronger. He said he could save everyone himself if we helped him find more of your parts. He wanted to be a savior, like you were. But we denied him. Called him a heretic. And so he said he did not need us anymore and that he could claim all of your parts. And then he did the unspeakable."

The bots around him moaned as they remembered.

"He would make sure we could not escape to stop him. Or to tell anyone. He allowed us to live all of these years. Trapped."

"He did this to you?" Bel asked.

NT-N1 nodded and the other miner bots moaned. Bel held one of the bot's hands and patted it.

"What was his name?" Doran said.

"His designation was NT-T7."

"Entity." Doran stood up.

"Wait, *the* Entity?" Oen said.

Millar nodded. "He is still alive. And he has almost finished his task. We have been looking for one final part so we can stop him."

"Still alive," NT-N1 said. "This is why you have returned."

"We must find this," Doran said. "It has to be close."

"We could find it for you," NT-N1 said.

"But do you have enough power for that?" Doran said. "You barely have enough to move."

"For you, we have enough."

"You have got to get out of these mines first. You must get to safety."

"We will, in time," NT-N1 said. "It may have been our prison, but this is also our home."

He gathered the mass of bots, and they linked their hands together, forming a giant connected ring. They swayed as a group, mumbling together as well.

"We can hear it," NT-N1 said. "And we can hear NT-T7. He is approaching this part you speak of. We will focus on its location and transmit it to you while we can."

"Thank you for all you have done." Doran walked, now with only a slight limp, and headed to the exit. "I am sorry there is nothing more I can do for you now."

"You have saved us," NT-N1 said. "And we will do all in our power to help you."

Chapter 47

"Feel better about them now, Oen?" Raly asked. "You kind of acted like a baby in there."

"I'm fine," Oen said. "Now that we're leaving. But I'll feel better once we're back outdoors."

"They were nice," Bel said. "And very helpful. Right, Doran?"

Doran turned his head to the signal in his brain. "I am getting a direction from them. It is not far from here."

Kech got out her map journal. "Let me know which direction, and then I can help you figure out where to look next. It's only a matter of time before Entity reaches it."

The two of them walked together through the tunnel and discussed the possible locations.

"I can't believe that Entity was one of them," Oen said. "NT-T7. I wonder who came up with that name for him? The people of Metlar's Keep?"

"Maybe," Millar said. "It's sad what happened to him. Twisted by the very things that Doran tried to get rid of. He really only wanted to help out his people, it seems."

"At first," Raly said. "And now he is chasing down the one thing that he hates and blames for what happened to him."

She walked in silence after that.

When they reached the end of the tunnel, they could barely tell the difference because it was a dark night. Clouds rolled past, blocking the stars. A deep rumbling shook the ground from faraway thunder sounding in the hills.

"Maybe we should stay inside tonight," Millar said. "If it's going to rain like I think it will then we'll have some cover here. Doran, have you and Kech figured out anything else?"

Doran moved his arm around, pointing in a direction as he centered on the signal. "It is strongest this way, but I am not sure about the distance."

It was too dark and cloudy to see anything. The moon had not risen yet, but Doran peered beyond the walls of the quarry.

"Even though we didn't find your part, it was good we went there," Bel said. "Look at what we did for all those poor bots."

Doran did not look away from the quarry. "If I had not gotten them into that position in the first place, we would not have had to. And we might have reached my final part sooner."

"It wasn't your fault," Raly said. "They even said so. We can't be held responsible for all the outcomes of what we do." Raly's eyes seemed to focus far away.

"Everyone I am around eventually gets hurt," Doran said. "I do not want to lose you all like we lost Two."

"We're all in this together," Millar said. "From the very beginning when you woke up, Bel was there, we were there. You've needed our help before, and you know we're not useless. And we're not going to leave you now."

Doran placed his hand lightly upon Bel's head. "You must be kept safe, little one. You are more important than you know."

"You're important to me, too!" Bel said. "And I want to protect you!"

Doran looked back up. "Yes, we should camp here. It is too dangerous to travel out there at night."

Thunder boomed and the rain began to pour outside the tunnel entrance. Lightning crashed, thunder boomed. To Doran, it felt like one of the old visions had come to life. Maybe all the memories of what he did were close by.

The rain began to splash inside, and Doran ushered them back further in the tunnel.

"It will be safer inside."

Oen glanced nervously back into the mountain. "There's sounds in there. I think they're coming out this way."

"Better to be in here than out there," Bel said.

"Hmmph," Oen said. "Well good night then. I'll just be over here not sleeping."

Doran sat at the entrance and watched as sleep took them.

***

The next morning, they awoke without the sounds of the pouring rain. Just the silence of a new day. Gray light came into the entrance.

"Let's get moving." Millar gently shook everyone awake.

Bel's eyes shot open, and she nearly jumped to her feet. She looked around and then ran to the entrance. "First I want to practice with Doran out there this morning!"

"She has too much energy," Oen said with a stretch.

Millar nudged him with his foot. "This is it, the last day. You can rest when it's over."

"Ugh." Oen sat up and then stumbled to his feet. "We better not be having any of your mashed cereal."

344

"Thank you very much," Millar said. "But we don't have time for it. We'll be—"

"Doran?" Bel shouted from outside. Her voice sounded a little panicky to everyone inside, and they raced to the exit.

He was gone.

"Where did he go?" Raly said. "He left without us?"

"I should have listened more to what he was saying," Millar said.

Bel was beside herself and could do nothing but cry. Millar ran to her side and tried to comfort her.

"Let's go, he can't be too far ahead."

"Are we sure we even know where he is going?" Oen said.

Kech strapped on her book pack and hefted it once before heading outside. "We made plans together with my maps."

"Was he lying to you, though?" Oen said. "Because he really seems to have wanted to get rid of us."

Kech thought about it for a moment. "That's all we have. And it makes sense that he was serious when we were talking. I don't think he thought too much about going alone, not until we were ready to go out the door last night."

"He just thought he was doing what was best for us," Millar said to Bel. "He still likes you. But now we've got to go help him."

That seemed to help. Bel sniffled a few times and dried her eyes. "He's my friend."

"I know," Millar said. "He's mine, too."

Bel took a deep breath and ran back inside to grab her things. In minutes they were packed and on their way up the steep quarry slope.

***

Doran sighed and looked back toward the old quarry as the sun rose. It was many miles away and beyond his vision now, and his heart still hung heavy from leaving his friends behind. He had to end this himself, and without endangering anyone else. Too many were hurt because of him.

The mountain peak loomed tall above him where the miner bots' signal pointed. There was no clear way up its slopes from this direction—perhaps the road they passed yesterday that headed south would present a way. Many years had passed since he'd hid whatever part was up there, and much could have happened to the countryside. Earthquakes, ice, and rain.

Fresh rock piles at the mountain's feet spoke to that. Would there be any path for him? Or would he have to forge a new one? Or would he even go up at all? Maybe he just needed to stop Entity before he could get up there. He pushed on to the road that would travel around the mountain to find the way somehow.

He off-handedly began to hum the tune that Bel sang yesterday, and it lightened his mind, if ever so slightly. He kept trying to convince himself that he had left his friends for the right reason.

Memories for him were easily erasable, but he was not certain if he could do a partial wipe. To eliminate certain harmful memories would be ideal, but he could not chance it. What if he lost the reason to complete this task?

And what if he forgot his friends? He could not lose them.

But was it better for him not to know them? To keep them safe?

These ideas fired away in his mind until he tried to unravel all the thoughts and actions he had ever done, to find a reason why he existed, and to wonder if he had ever done any true good in this land. Or if everything he said or did ended in ruin.

He eventually came to the southern road and set foot upon it.

"This is it. The end of all of my travels. Here I will be tested and my actions weighed."

With these thoughts, he focused on what he must do and began the final journey with a single step.

Chapter 48

The day crept on as Doran walked along the path. The area was quiet except for the songs and sounds of the small birds that skittered between the rocks and swooped in the air picking at the many bugs flying around. Oen surely would have complained about them by now.

The miners still sang their song that pointed him toward the mountaintop. Images began to swell within him as he approached, much like the other places where he'd hidden his parts. Still there were storms and fires, but this vision felt different somehow. It was less abrupt. Maybe it was because he knew what to expect now after unearthing the pieces, or maybe it was because they were all exposed except for this one last one.

And it was almost back in his possession.

Entity was approaching this same location. Whatever Two had programmed in his circuits had worked and was leading him here. The visions from his stolen eye were becoming more frequent and clearer—he looked upon the same mountain but from the west. He followed a well-traveled road and he stayed focused on the peak. If there were any soldiers with him, he was not looking behind him for Doran to see.

He walked steadily, but not racing. Although Doran could not get a sense from any emotion he received, the sight made Entity appear confident but not rushed. That made Doran move quicker.

There still were no easy paths up to the peak on this side, but there had to be something soon. The road dove into a small canyon with steep cliffs to either side that stretched upward a hundred feet. When he turned a corner he saw something that he had not expected, but he should have.

A Soldier watch station along the road. And it was occupied.

A clanging of an alarm echoed in the small canyon. How could he have been so foolish as to think no one would be on this road? No one had been on the path to the abandoned quarry yesterday, so he simply had not thought about it.

Ten guards in red hoods ran out of a small building, all confused to see a lone bot wandering down the path. They must have all seen a bot before—they all followed Entity, after all—but no one had seen one in his condition, with a patch over his missing eye, a cloak over his ripped-open chest, and a huge sword on his back. He thought about it and wondered how he was still able to walk after all that had happened.

Most of the soldiers stood there staring up at him as he came upon them, but a few scrambled for their weapons. The only thing that could have worried Doran were the spears they had back at the High Ansels, but with nothing around to power them, they were left with only clubs and hammers and a few bows.

"Let me pass," Doran said. "My business is not with you, unless you make it so."

A thought passed through his head. Did these people have a communication device that could allow them to send word of him back to Entity? He reached for his sword and drew it slowly.

A few guards fell backwards on the ground as they hustled back inside the guardhouse. They were not elite guards on the front lines going to war— these were the ones left behind at the farthest reaches of guard duty in the mountains, just in case someone happened along the path of an abandoned quarry.

The guards who stayed outside must have known that, too, and did not approach Doran to stop him. To show they were not completely disloyal, though, one lone arrow whined in the air and plunked off of Doran's metal body. There was a moment of silence and dread as the soldiers waited to see what Doran would do about it.

Doran made a sudden move, and the soldiers leapt for cover, but he only returned his sword to his back. He began to walk past the station when suddenly a large arrow shot into the air, high above them all. When it reached its peak, it exploded into a flash of red flames.

Within seconds, another arrow, this one further along the path, shot up and exploded as well. The guards might not have been willing to fight an unbeatable foe, but they were not stupid. The threat of invasion was being notified along the road and would reach the Keep's walls in a short time. They would not know who, specifically, was invading, unless somehow red flames meant a bot assailant. But at the very least, they would now be aware of something here. Perhaps that would not mean much if the entire army was marching up the coast, but maybe some of that force would be diverted this way for a time.

Doran began to shuffle along as close to a run as he could manage with his malfunctioning leg. The soldiers followed him with their eyes as he passed by. Doran thought that Bel would have laughed at that. He began to hum her tune again as he marched along.

The guards were not dumb enough to attack, but that did not mean they would not pursue him from a safe distance. And so nearly all of that force joined behind him, not quite able to keep up with his pace, but they would follow him and arrive where he was going eventually.

***

For two hours he sped along, right along the base of the mountain. Only then did its surface appear somewhat passable. Entity's sight now came into his own eyes almost constantly, and with such clarity that it appeared he was looking at two different locations at the same time. He parsed the information so that it would not interfere with his ability to walk. What started out as two different visions, he realized, was both of them looking upon the same mountain, but from different angles.

They were here together. At the same time. Doran laughed. It could never be easy, could it? At any moment, Entity would emerge around a corner. Doran felt the weariness finally settle upon him from all the running. His core was drained, his body was still weak and damaged. He climbed a few feet up the mountain. Entity approached from perhaps a mile away now, and he turned to face him. The area was flat, with some large standing stones surrounding it like barriers around some sort of arena.

He removed his sword and placed it gently upon the ground. This mountain was different. Images flashed into his mind again, memories of his past life. Storms, fires, but also peace. There was more to his past than destruction and death. There was a power here, deep within the stones.

He closed his eye and planted his feet firmly on the ground. The forms came readily to him now. He was aware of all his movements, and he settled his mind to reach for the power. Who had taught him that? He did not know. He did not even know if anybody did. He lost track of time as he stood upon one leg, then the other, swaying with the wind as it blew past his body. New energy crept into his frame, and he felt his chest warm.

After a time he finished and sat down upon the ground with his legs crossed and the sword over his knees. He rested both hands upon the metal blade and waited. For better or for worse, it would all end today.

***

"You're still alive!"

It was Entity. Doran focused on the other bot upon the field and now he could see the similarities between the other miner bots, although the additions he'd made to his body had altered it somewhat. At his core, that was what he was.

"I don't know how you managed it."

His two eyes, one yellow and the other blue, brightened and refocused on the sword upon Doran's knees. His pace faltered.

"Where did you find that?"

"It was in the waters where you left me to die," Doran said.

Entity glanced at his gun, now attached to his right arm.

"You tricked me. I should have known when there were none of your accursed memories attached to it. But it matters little, it still works just fine and will do its job. We will end this now."

"Indeed."

"Enough." Entity fired a blast from his arm.

The aim was true, but Doran moved with a blur out of its path. Stone shattered from the exact place where he had been sitting, and the blast left a fissure in the ground. Doran leapt to the top of one of the standing stones like an insect springing, and he held his sword with two hands over his head.

"I passed into death and returned with my sword. It will be your undoing."

Entity grunted and fired again. The stone erupted in a shower of fractured stone, but again Doran leapt away from the bolt, this time flipping neatly to the ground. He was a few feet closer to Entity and held the sword in front of him.

The sound of people shouting came from behind Entity. The soldiers who had followed both him and Doran had finally arrived and were all moving into position where they could see the battle.

"Your people will see you fall. What will they do then?"

Entity looked back at his troops along the mountainside.

"He is not dead," a soldier said.

"He survives!"

"Just like Kindra said!"

Entity yelled and aimed his arm at them. Before he could fire a shot, a large stone hit his arm and caused the blast to fire sidelong into a cliff. The soldiers scattered like ants to get out of the range of their angry leader.

"You would protect them?" Entity said.

Doran was only twenty feet away from Entity now, and still held the sword up defensively. The gun whined upon Entity's arm as it charged up again and he aimed it right at Doran. He couldn't miss now—he was so close.

"I will protect everyone from you."

Even as Entity fired again, Doran moved out of the way of the blast before it could hit him. Entity grunted and fired twice more in succession. Still, Doran moved out of the way seemingly before he even fired.

"You're half-blind, how are you doing this…" Entity said. Then he jumped away onto a rock. He scrambled a bit to get his footing and then shook his head.

He gripped onto Doran's blue eye embedded in his head and yanked it out amidst a shower of sparks. He threw it to the ground and stamped on it. "Clever. No more free shots now."

The gun whined again, this time taking a bit longer. Entity shook his head and slapped his face as if trying to wake up.

Doran now took a few steps closer to him, still holding the sword in front of him.

"A gun is always going to win in a sword fight," Entity said. "Why don't you just give it to me now?"

Doran did not falter and walked closer until he was right upon him.

"Your loss." Entity fired the weapon. Not just a single blast, but a full, massive beam of energy.

Doran did not move out of the way this time—instead he took the full brunt of the weapon. The sword flew to the side and the beam punched him right in the chest. He flew back along the ground and hit a rock so his body twisted at an unnatural angle. The cloak covering his chest caught fire and exposed his energy core, which glowed with a fierce blue light.

"You had a chance to get the final piece before I came here. Why didn't you? Look at you, you've lost." Entity stumbled as he tried to get his footing. "You know nothing of power. You gave it all away."

Doran did not reply.

"And now look. You are a shell."

And then Doran stood in a calm but powerful stance.

"You have nothing," Entity said.

"I have them." Doran pointed above and behind him.

Entity glanced above at the mountain. There were Doran's friends standing in a line with a group of other bots, nearly fifty of them. Their black metal shone in the sunlight as they shifted in slow, deliberate motions. All of them moved as one in the practiced method that Doran woke up with nearly every morning.

"Them? How did they get here? What are they doing?"

Entity pointed the gun at Doran and pulled the trigger. Nothing happened. He clicked it again and again, but the slow whining of the gun never charged it fully.

"You have forgotten everything," Doran said.

The sword leapt to Doran's hand and he brought it down in one swift motion, straight through Entity's body, cleaving him in half. The two pieces dropped to the ground and his remaining energy coursed out of him in a torrent of sparks until there was nothing left.

Chapter 49

For a moment no one moved on the mountainside. Then the raiders all started talking at once and running about. Many ran up the hill to where Entity had fallen, but when they realized Doran still stood there with his sword poised to strike again, they faltered. But Doran was not concerned with them. He turned to face his friends and raised his sword to the sky. Sunlight glistened off its blade.

They waved back, and little Bel jumped up and down with her hands in the air. He could imagine she cheered, but he could not hear her from this distance. In a moment, he bowed low to them and they, as an entire group, even the miner bots, returned it.

The black bots wound their way down the mountainside, much quicker than Doran expected, considering they could not see anything. But no one outpaced Bel. She nearly sprinted toward Doran with a triumphant smile on her face.

And then the pain struck. The last blast that Entity had fired had hit him directly in his chest, and only now did he glance down to see the full damage. The metal still glowed orange from the heat of it, and circuits seared and sizzled from his insides. He dropped to his knees, and the sword clattered to the ground.

Bel's smile fell quickly as she reached his side. "No, no, no!"

The others soon joined her and knelt around him. Only Bel's soft sobs could be heard. Doran placed his hand on her head and he began to hum her song.

"Can't we do something?" Raly said. "Can you fix him?"

NT-N1 reached down and felt the wounds on Doran's chest. The metal began to cool into a gnarled melted form, and the glow faded. Even the fire of the blue stone within his chest began to dim.

"We could use some of the other one's parts to repair him."

Doran reached up and grabbed NT-N1's hand. "No."

Entity's remains lay strewn upon the ground in a pile of unrecognizable scrap. Even if there were working parts, Doran did not want them.

"I understand. But then there is nothing else we can do but wait and see what will happen. Rest, Doran."

Doran laid his head upon the ground and, with his hands, covered his exposed and damaged chest.

The noise from the raiders grew as they approached the hill. Millar reached for his pry hammer reflexively and stood over Doran. The men removed their helmets and held up their hands.

"We will not fight you. We only mean to see what has happened to Entity."

Millar did not waver. "He was destroyed, if that wasn't clear."

"He tried to kill us," one of the soldiers said. "Like Kindra said he would."

A man with a long gray beard, possibly the leader, quieted the other with a hand gesture and then stepped forward.

"He is dead. It is over."

He hung his head and turned to those who came with him. They spoke softly to each other but only when they walked back to the main group did Millar lower his weapon.

"Tell me how you came here so quickly," Doran said.

Millar laughed. "You left us alone. Well, not alone."

He gestured to the miner bots around them. Some stared blankly toward the mountains while others inspected what remained of Entity with their hands.

"They were more than willing to help us, despite Oen's refusals."

Oen smiled meekly.

"They guided us to you, using their mining skills to find pathways through the stones on the mountain. They said you were taking the long way around, but we just went straight over. It was amazing. They saw things even though they couldn't see. And you must have distracted all the guards along the way. Otherwise, we might not have gotten here in time. But anyway, here we are."

Doran nodded and went back to resting. "Thank you for coming here. But how did they know how to help you with the forms?"

"You forgot many things," NT-N1 said. "When you first came to us, these forms were something we taught you. We reminded you how to connect to the powers of the land beneath us. It was something passed down to us from the beginning. And this was something you never forgot, apparently, when you forgot everything else. Even he forgot what he always knew."

He bent over to touch Entity's remains.

"He was once my friend. But even the most noble of intentions can be twisted."

Doran reached for his chest. "I know this. I could have been this. In fact, I may have been this before."

"But you are not that now. Nor will you be again."

Doran nodded. "Then I must go to see what lies atop this mountain, to see what I left behind."

NT-N1 faced the peak to where the final piece lay hidden. "Go then. We will be waiting here for your return, no matter how you come back."

Doran struggled to his feet with the help of the sword as a crutch.

"Let me go with you," Bel said. "To help."

Doran shook his head. "You will always be with me, but this I must do alone." He touched her head lovingly.

As he stumbled up the mountain, he looked behind. The miner bots gathered around their brother in pieces on the ground.

"What will you do with him?" Millar said.

"We will give him a proper burial under our mountain. And we will make sure he is taken care of so no one will ever use these parts again."

"Perhaps you could save one part in particular." Doran caught Millar's eye. "In the end, it did not belong to me anymore."

"As you wish," NT-N1 said.

Millar smiled and knelt beside Entity's body. "I know what he's talking about."

Doran took another step, this one with a little more confidence. "I will be back soon."

"We will wait for you here!" Bel said and waved to him.

***

The rest of the day passed, and the sun set behind Doran before he reached the peak. He turned around once again to see how far he'd passed, and to see his friends. Only small flickers of light let him know they still existed in the valley below, camping along the slopes as he climbed.

The miner's song of guidance still sung in his mind, stronger now as he approached the way in. Near the summit he saw a dark passageway between two crags of rock that led inside. He did not need the song to tell him that this was the way. The strength of the visions surrounded him, and he walked between two planes, the path of now and the path he'd walked an age ago.

When he entered the stone halls, a light glowed from within the walls, as if it sprang to life. The lights shimmered like reflections off a pool of water. Doran's stride grew stronger, more confident, as he approached.

The pathway ended at a great metal door. He reached for the handle, but it would not budge no matter how hard he pulled on it. The door was smooth and unadorned except for a single, wide keyhole in the center of it. He knew what had to be done.

He pulled the sword from his back. The blade inserted into the keyhole with a metal ringing sound and clicked fully into place. He turned it and the door suddenly began to open outwards until it came to a rest without a sound. The thought that he'd sure made a big deal of hiding these things a long time ago crossed his mind and made him laugh. Prism would have thought it funny, too.

The lights grew as he stepped inside, and he was immediately aware of the pedestal in the center of the rounded room. A single, tiny metallic component lay atop the platform. Doran approached it.

He knew what it was even as he entered. This was his core memory system. It contained all the knowledge he once possessed. This much was made clear to him. To take it he would become who he was before.

"Do I claim it?" he said. His words amplified in the room as the sound redirected back to him off the walls.

"What will happen to me? Will I forget everyone I know now? Is this my final test?"

No one answered. He had no response to this. Nothing in his deepest memories gave him any insight.

He stood for a while, staring at the device, and then he sat upon the floor and placed the sword across his legs. And he thought.

***

Sun broke the next morning across the slope of the mountain and upon Doran's upright metal form as he came back down to his friends. Bel, in the midst of practicing her forms with Raly and one of the miners, was first to see him from a distance. She ran up to meet him and he picked her up onto his shoulders.

She patted his head in beat to the steps he took like some ship drummer to keep them rowing in rhythm. "Did you find what you were looking for up there?"

"I did."

"Good!" Bel resumed her drumming.

When he reached the group, he became aware of a new gathering of soldiers.

"Who are they?"

Millar came to his side. "They arrived late last night. It's Kindra. That man we saw yesterday who spoke for the raiders? That was her father."

"So will I need to stop the Soldier's march upon the coast?" Doran asked.

Kindra bowed low when he approached, and those with her did as well. "We spread word of Entity's betrayal. The army halted well before it had a chance to reach Terask. They have returned to Metlar's Keep, but no one knows what will happen now. If you come with us, I am sure my people will welcome you home."

The Soldiers of the New Sun all dropped to one knee before him.

"Great," Oen whispered. "These people go from one deity to another pretty quickly."

Doran placed Bel on the ground beside him. "I am honored you feel this way."

"You would be helping our people find their way," Kindra said.

"For now, they will have to find it themselves, I am afraid. I have my own family."

"I understand," Kindra said. Her voice did not sound like she understood, but she bowed even deeper and rose to her feet. "Your legend has gone on before you, and if you ever come to the Keep, you will find that you are most revered."

Kindra turned to her people and they all arose. She took one last look behind her and caught Raly's eye. "I know you will never forgive my people, but we are forever in your debt."

"I have seen what happens to a life guided by vengeance," Raly said with a wavering voice. "I choose not to follow that."

Kindra bowed to her and then turned away to follow her people back to their home.

As the soldiers left the group on the hillside, Doran noticed that Entity's body was missing.

"Some of our people already brought him back home for burial."

"Don't worry." Millar patted his pouch. "I took what you asked for."

Doran faced the sun. "Then it is almost finished."

"Almost?" Oen said. "I'm ready to go make sure everyone is safe back home."

"I think we all are," Millar said.

"I have one last thing I must do. The last words of my dying friend were that he wished he was back home. I intend to honor his wishes."

"Can we come with you?" Bel said.

Millar looked up at Doran to read how he felt about that. "This is something he needs to do on his own, I think."

"He sure needs a lot of alone time," Bel mumbled.

Doran chuckled and nodded slowly. "When I finish, I will meet you back at your home."

"*Our* home!" Bel said.

"Yes. Our home."

Chapter 50

Two opened his eyes. Doran looked upon him without saying a word. His main eye, shining red behind his newly installed faceplate, focused on the taller bot. Two humans finished working on his chest. The older one, Intari, guided a younger woman to fasten the bolts around its edge.

"The parts you gave us are installed," Intari said. "It may take time."

"Will he…?" Doran said.

"Remember? It is hard to tell. He may never remember who he was, much less anyone else. He was hit hard by that bot you spoke of, and many of his pieces were too badly damaged. We had to make due with those replacements. He was lucky, for several things. One, for you. How you were able to bring him out of those mountains and all the way here in the shape you're in is a miracle."

"I made him a promise."

Intari smiled. "A promise from you wields great power. He is lucky to have you. And there was also something about those caves. A true connection to the powers within the land. I believe that he was preserved somehow by that place. It seems to have helped you, as well. I would very much like to travel there someday."

"I'd rather not go there again," Two said.

His voice sounded… different. Calmer, perhaps.

"You remember?" Doran said.

Two shook his wide head. "I don't think so. The way you spoke of what happened to me there… I don't think I would like to see it again."

"The danger has passed." Doran sat down on the stone floor. His system registered to him that he had not moved from Two's side for many hours. His body settled into place and the exhaustion hit him.

"Still, I suppose I'd just stay here instead. It looks like a nice place."

Two examined his body, specifically both of his arms. He held them out before him.

"So, you've made the right one shorter than the left. Bold choice."

Intari smiled and bent over to kiss him upon his forehead. "Welcome back."

She and her attendant bowed to him and then walked out of the repair room.

Two watched them leave. "They seem nice."

Doran did not talk or move.

"You know," Two said. "I don't know you. But… I know that I knew you. Does that make sense?"

Doran chuckled. "Some things have not changed. Luckily. Oh, that reminds me. I was told to ask you what you would like to be called."

"A name? Don't I already have one?"

"That has been an issue with you in the past. Think of this as a time to choose your own name."

"Well, I barely know anything as it is, I'm only five minutes old, after all. Why don't you tell me what she called me before?"

"Two. They named you Two."

He paused for a moment without moving. Only his eyes blinked on and off while he processed it.

"Are you serious? It's perfect."

Doran reached over and patted him on the back. "Well, Two, you will only have yourself to blame this time."

"See, it only makes sense, right? I mean, this is the second version of me, at least what I am aware of. 'Second' doesn't sound right. And Junior? No thank you."

Doran laughed.

"Plus, I don't want to hurt that little old lady's feelings. I don't quite remember, but it seems like she's my mom. Is that weird?"

"No, not weird at all. Many strange things have happened since we first met."

"Tell me." Two settled back further onto the wide platform he sat upon. "I'd like to know what I knew."

"The most important thing for you to know is that you have friends. Good friends. And they cannot wait to see you again."

"Where, here?"

"Someone will bring you there. It is close. But I have traveled far, and it took me a long time to get here. My power fades, and I must get home soon."

A chime rang in the distance.

"What is that?" Two said.

"They told me that you might have other visitors today, if that is all right with you."

"Guests? For me? That's great!"

Doran waved to an attendant at the far end of the room, and they left. Shortly, they returned with two people. Both wore elaborate belt systems that strapped upon their shoulders and back.

The younger girl nearly cried as she saw Two looking back at her. The older woman smiled and put her hand on the girl's shoulder.

"This is Raly and Kech," Doran said. "They are both in the Trades."

Two waved slightly at them but did not get up.

"It's okay," Raly said. "You don't have to remember us. We're just glad to see you again."

"What does a Trades person do?" Two asked.

"We travel," Kech said. "From one town to the next. Collecting artifacts, but mainly stories. Raly is just learning the art now, and I would like to mentor her here. That is, if you can help us out."

Raly smiled. "I have a Life Quest now. Mine is to master the knowledge of the High Ansels, and your home in Hinarum. And to share that. And make peace with everyone along the coastal cities from here to Metlar's Keep."

"That's a pretty big Quest," Two said.

Doran nodded to Raly. "She has seen what anger and vengeance can do to a soul. She is lucky to have earned that wisdom."

Raly smiled.

Two patted the stone floor next to him, motioning Raly to join him.

"I would be honored to speak with you. I am afraid I won't be able to fill any volumes, but I would be happy to help all I can."

"You always were a good helper," Raly said. She removed an empty book and sat down.

Doran stumbled as he tried to pull himself to his feet.

"What is it?" Two said. "Are you all right?"

Doran nodded and held onto a wall for support. "I am fine. But I've stayed here too long. I must leave earlier than I anticipated."

"Are you sure I can't go with you?" Two said.

"Intari said it would be best if you rested and allowed your system to acclimate. Raly will help you to remember as you wait. She has chronicled your part in our adventure."

"Ooh," Two said. "Am I a hero?"

"Indeed. And she will also remind you about other things that might help with your healing."

Raly nodded, clearly understanding what he asked for.

Two hesitated between following and listening to what was best for him, and chose the latter. Still, he stood and walked over to Doran's side. "I am lucky, like Intari said. I can't thank you enough. I don't know what for yet. But I know it has to be for something great. Right?"

Raly laughed. "Right!"

"Until the next time," Doran said.

Raly and Kech bid him farewell, and Two waved to him as he limped away to the doorway.

***

Familiar paths opened before Doran as he gazed upon the bay and the island that he'd called a forgetful home for longer than he could imagine. Which, he supposed, was not that long, since he had been resetting parts of his memory for quite a while now. Still, he longed for the cave, the grasses and mosses growing within, and the slow, steady passing of the sunlight across the stones. Those were a part of him that grew to his core.

The journey from the Blue Ice Mountains carrying Two had taken at least a month. And then the week or so waiting for Two to recover had felt like a lifetime, but this final stage home felt the longest. In the time he'd spent away, his closest friends had gone to their home. Would they feel differently about him now?

He felt older. Slower. Ready to rest.

He wondered if he should even stop at the High Ansels to see how they were doing. The bay would not be so difficult to pass in the late spring, perhaps. Waves still crashed upon the stones jutting up through the water like black towers, and he wondered how he would fare seeking passage.

But then a sweet song played in his mind. Bel's song. And he pictured her face in the sun, and his mind was made for him. He would stop at his friends' home before his own.

He walked through the night, and the silence of the stars filled him. The moon reeled overhead until it plummeted beyond the cliff where his friends awaited. The sun rose behind him as he approached the town, and a triumphant cry went up through the people there. Oen himself was tending the security system he'd helped to install, and he let Doran in.

"Doran! Word came to us from Hinarum that you were on your way! Welcome." Oen bowed and walked him through the town.

"We've done a lot to secure this place," Oen said. "Some say you can't even tell it was attacked a few short months ago. I've worked with Bruet though to construct a memorial to those lost in the attack."

He pointed to a large flat stone with names inscribed upon its surface. Doran read them all before heading into the center of the village. The people there cheered as he passed by.

"The savior! He is back!"

Children ran up and waved and tossed flower petals before him. Clar, the little farm girl they'd saved from the patarks, waved emphatically. But none of the children were Bel, or even Millar. Doran looked around for them.

"Don't worry," Oen said. "As soon as we heard you were coming, they prepared for you to go back to your home. For a time, if you wish. To rest a bit."

Doran increased his pace and led the way down the long path back to the water. Oen had to scramble along the path to keep up with him. They passed paths of cleared and tilled soil ready for farming.

"Slow down, they're not going anywhere." Oen had to stop and catch his breath before they reached the bottom, multiple times.

Doran walked through the low trees that acted like a gateway to the shore and saw them both a hundred feet away next to Raly's boat. Millar adjusted the sails on it and Bel skipped stones across the still water. A second later, Bel saw him and her little cheer went up. Millar stopped and hurriedly followed after Bel, who had already tore a path straight to the bot.

"My friends." Doran knelt and hugged Bel and then Millar.

"We've missed you, Doran!" Bel said. "You look really good." She placed her hands on the melted potion of his chest.

"You do too. And I missed you. More than you can know."

Bel shrugged. "I don't know, I can feel it myself. We've been preparing for you for a long time now. I bet you want to go to the island. Right?"

Doran felt the call to go there strongly now.

"I do. But I also want to stay with you."

"That's okay! Because we can go with you!"

Bel held his hand and led him across the sand.

"You know," Oen said. "You never told us about that final part you found. What was it? What did it do for you?"

Doran looked at him. "It was not a pair of power knuckles, if that is what you are asking for. Or any other weapon."

"That's too bad," Oen said. "So…?"

"It was a warning. For me. And I left it there so that others could be warned as well."

"You left it?" Oen shrugged. "Oh well. I guess you know what you're doing."

Doran did not respond but instead let Bel guide him to the boat. When they got there, she showed him the packs she had stowed for her and Millar.

"There's enough stuff for us so we can watch over you at your old home. You know, until you're better to come live up at the High Ansels. Or in Hinarum."

"You'll come stay with me?" Doran said.

"Yup," Bel said. "And practice our forms every day. And we can look for pretty rocks. If that's all right with you."

Millar smiled. "Is that all right with you?"

Doran gazed out upon the bay at the sun shining upon his towering island. A peace settled over him, and he felt better than he had for a long time. If he could smile, he would have.

"Let's go home."

The End.

Steve Davala is the author of other books including *Skywatch*, *Books are for Reading, Not Eating!*, and three books in *The Soulkind Series*. Steve lives in the Pacific Northwest and has been a middle and high school teacher since 2000, writing and carving when he can find the time.

Special thanks go out to those who helped me edit: Denny and Mo Robeson and Francesca Varela. And a very special thanks to my old friend Chris Walters who helped keep me focused on finishing this book while he wrote four of his own. Thanks for that motivation.